THE PROMISE KEEPER

NORMAN BRIDES SERIES

BY

LYNN WOOD

Hi Ian –
Thanks for your interest. I hope you enjoy the story –
Best,
L. W.

Follow Lynn on her Blog and website:
WritersBlockNot.com

Twitter.com/eternallynow

Cover design by Melissa Alvarez, BookCovers.Us
Cover photography ©Depositphotos.com/
luminastock/ Oleksminyaylo1/ msdnv1/ olly18/
exinocactus/ Gnilenkov

TITLES BY LYNN WOOD

Fiction:

Norman Brides Series:

The Keeper Trilogy:
Keeper of the Stone
Finders Keepers
The Promise Keeper

Coming Soon…
Mary Elle

ALSO BY L. M. WOOD

Awakening Series:
Awakening
Choose

The Firstborn Series:
Michael, Beloved of God, Prince of Heaven
Dancing with the Devil

Non-Fiction:
Lessons in Illumination
(…A Beginner's Guide to the Eternal Way)
Yoga Behind the Veil
(…A Journey of Self-Discovery)

...PROLOGUE

The old woman was aware of the slight trembling in her limbs as she waited in the ante-chamber for her audience with the new king. Though she was irritated with herself at the evidence of her very human weakness she quickly chastised herself for her annoyance. She was human after all, and fear was an inescapable human emotion. When the summons came she drew a calming breath and followed the armed guard who provided her escort through the entrance to the luxurious throne room with her head held high, but her attention focused inward. She heard her name echo across the high ceilings of the elegantly appointed room and approached the gold throne where the new king lounged carelessly with a glass of ale in one hand, while his other fondled the unfortunate young serving maid.

"Your Highness," she offered in a respectful tone. Though it pained her to do so, she knelt before him, and bowed her head low to the intricate mosaic floor, allowing herself a quick glimpse of the new monarch as she did so. She hid her disappointment at what she saw in the reverent manner expected of a lowly subject before her king, but within the privacy of her thoughts she sighed at the arrogance of men, who foolishly believed a sharp blade and a large army of followers could turn any man into a king. Perhaps in other, lesser kingdoms such was the way of things, but Calei's golden throne demanded more of those who would rest upon its highest seat. It had not taken more than a swift glance for her to conclude this was not the one who would put an end to the curse that had hung suspended over the small, but wealthy kingdom for as far back as anyone could remember. His thick features and the crude jests he exchanged with his loyal men who were scattered around the room ordering the harried servants about provided sufficient evidence of his lowly beginnings and coarse nature. No, she imagined this one's reign would be shorter than most. The throne of Calei did not suffer fools. With or without the assistance of the ancient curse, the new, self-proclaimed monarch's presence in this room was an affront that would not long be tolerated.

"Rise, witch, and do your duty. The ancient traditions must be observed." His coarse demand offered further proof her swift conclusions about the new king had not been unwarranted.

Mariel did not bother to dispute his assertion that she was a daughter of Wicca. She knew many regarded her as such and feared her because of it. Their fear was a double edged sword as far as Mariel was concerned. For the most part she was given a wide berth by those in power. The new kings had enough on their hands securing their precarious positions without upsetting the populace by interfering with their sacred traditions. Hence the reason for her summons today.

However, she comprehended all too well that men who wielded a sword to gain a throne were not shy about matters such as bloodshed, and had no real fear of ordinary citizens who were too frightened or too tired of war to elevate a sword to unseat them. She was aware each time she was summoned into this elegant chamber to perform the service she was called upon to perform today, that if the new monarch took exception to her words they would likely be her last.

"Get on with it, woman. I do not have all day to wait upon you."

Mariel bowed her head at his imperious command and carefully withdrew a crystal ball from the folds of her cloak. A hush fell over the room as the transparent globe was revealed in the uncertain light that abruptly settled over the room at its appearance. Her eyes met those of the bishop who stood on the king's right. Though the man of the cloth could not completely suppress the evidence of his disapproval when his eyes beheld the instrument of her talent, she was aware of the compassion in his when their glances locked for the briefest of moments. Religion and magic wove in equal measure through the hearts of the citizens of the small city kingdom. The church hierarchy in Rome had learned that painful lesson the hard way.

The prior bishop was a fervent defender of church teachings. Week after week he denounced the evils of superstition and magic from his place at the pulpit in the rich cathedral Caleinians had built to honor their Lord. Their generosity filled the church coffers with gold, the majority of such bounty being transported to Rome. The kingdom's generous support of the holy church accounted for the circumstances of the small parish warranting its own bishop.

Mariel could have informed the prior bishop he was grossly miscalculating in his attempt to steer the citizens away from their traditions, but he had never sought the benefit of her advice. The more the fervent bishop preached about the evils of magic, the less the faithful citizens contributed to the weekly collection plate. In the end, the decline in the people's generosity was enough to draw the attention of the bishop's superiors. It did not take long for those same superiors to recognize the prudence of reassigning the fervent bishop and leaving the local populace to its decidedly harmless traditions.

So it was the odd marriage between superstition and religion unique to Calei that brought the local witch and the bishop of the church together to provide both witness and legitimacy to the new king's rule. Aware of the growing impatience of the man who slouched carelessly in the elegant throne of his predecessors for her to commence with the reason for her summons, she gathered her power and raised the crystal over her head. Light from the setting sun streaming through the stained, crystal windows penetrated its depths, creating a prism effect that flashed around the room. For a moment, she was aware of the king's men lifting their arms to shield their eyes from the bright light, and then she turned her focus inward and allowed her awareness of her rich surroundings to fall away from her conscious thoughts as she gazed into the depths of the crystal.

"A new king has claimed the ancient throne of Calei and seeks his clue to overcoming the curse that lies over this house," she proclaimed loudly for the benefit of her audience.

Mariel was aware of the rustling in the crowd at her words, but did not allow it to distract her attention. She felt the change come over her, knew her woman's features altered subtly and her voice took on a deeper, almost masculine tenor, its impatience evidenced by its clipped tones in answer to her request.

"Must you harry us so frequently with your egotistical demands? The terms remain unchanged. When the daughter of the moon captures the heart of the sun the curse will be lifted and peace shall reign over these lands. Until then no blood of the blood of the reigning king shall ascend to the throne. So it is written. So it shall be."

...PROLOGUE

The inexperienced soldiers insulted and jostled each other as young men were wont to do. It was the changing of the guard and the end of a long and tedious shift of standing watch on the parapet walls of the massive stone castle and gazing out beyond the city gates and into the mountains as night wore away and the darkness gave way to the light of the unfolding splendor of a new dawn. Even the majestic view from atop the towers could not long hold a young man's attention, particularly when there was no evidence of a threat on the city kingdom they watched over, nor had there been for the length of their brief service in the king's guard. Calei's history had been a violent one, but the recent slumberous years of peace had lulled the watch guard into complacency. The novice soldiers kept watch over the gates as their older, battle-hardened compatriots basked in the unfamiliar gift of looking beyond the next few hours of what for the length of their youths had largely been a day to day life and death struggle for survival, to the gratifying prospect of a future in the prosperous land they shed their blood for.

The present king was a fair and honorable ruler. The widows and orphans of the many wars of the kingdom's past were sheltered and well-fed. With order restored and the dangerous paths over the mountains protected, a bustling trade between both neighboring and distant lands was filling to overflowing the kingdom's already rich treasury. When the king returned last year with a lovely young bride accompanying him, the citizens rejoiced to bear witness to his faith in the kingdom's future prosperity. The young queen was soon heavy with child and the citizens began planning children of their own. The king must surely believe the ancient curse on the ruling family had finally been broken; else he would not risk the long years of peace, or the life of the queen he appeared so fond of, let alone the child she carried, in his brazen defiance of the spell holding sway over his house.

The young captain of the guard, accompanied by a few of his friends and comrades, climbed the narrow steps from the soldiers' quarters beneath the main level of the keep on his way to the great hall to first break his fast before chasing after another, softer form of manly comfort. His thoughts were not occupied by the long strife-filled years of his homeland. At the moment his attention was focused on tripping his younger brother as he trailed behind him, a new, raw recruit to the order. The remainder of his concentration centered around the more compelling question of whether or not he carried enough coins with him to seek out the services of a particularly skilled lady of the night who plied her wares down a certain lane deep in the heart of the city where men who practiced the art of war could find ease for their manly lusts.

So when he heard the shouts coming from the level of the main hall, he assumed some of the other soldiers were amusing themselves at one of their comrade's expense. Not wanting to miss out on the fun, Amele and his friends hurried up the last few stairs and pushed open the door into one of the narrow hallways that led to the grand hall. The shouts grew louder, but now there was fresh desperation accompanying them, and another sound, an impossible one, greeted their astonished ears. They exchanged puzzled glances laced with the bitter evidence of unfamiliar fear on their young faces, then made their way cautiously towards the entrance.

Fortunately for the untried soldiers no one was aware of them standing there wide-eyed at the vision confronting them. The occupants of the hall couldn't spare a glance for the four young soldiers, more boys than men, who took in the bloody, chaotic scene with stunned disbelief. The sound of swords clashing drowned out their astonished gasps. Shaking off his instinctive horror, Amele backed away from the opening. He turned shocked brown eyes to his companions and whispered harshly, "The queen. We must protect her. They'll kill her."

Afterwards, Amele could never explain why it was to the queen's side he rushed rather than his king's. He was sometimes assigned to the guard rotation for the young queen so he was aware of her habit of retreating to the ancient chapel when she sought privacy for her prayers to the almighty, rather than taking advantage of the comforts of the magnificent cathedral built to serve the ruling family. So not wasting the time to ensure his friends were following, he set off back down the narrow stairs and hurried through the maze of tunnels and hallways beneath the keep and out a little-used passage that led to the older, rarely used parts of the king's home. All was quiet in the streets. The alarm had not yet been sounded. He turned to his younger brother and spoke urgently.

"Gabriel, go as fast as you can to the tower. Sound the alarm. Rouse the city's defenders. We will take the queen beyond the gates and into the mountains where she will be safe until the king puts down this outrage."

Amele watched until his brother's departing back disappeared from view and then with his remaining two companions, he stealthily crossed the courtyard to the entrance of the old chapel. He prayed he had guessed correctly and they would find the queen there, alone and in prayer, but when he pushed open the door to the sacred place tears stung his eyes. Apparently he was not the only one who was aware of the queen's habits. Blood stained the marble floor of the sanctuary, but thankfully it was not the young queen's. She stood over the bleeding soldier assigned to watch over her with a blade in her hand. It was a ceremonial knife, a dagger with a solid gold and jeweled hilt, small enough for a woman to handle. Her shock-glazed eyes met his and Amele approached cautiously, motioning for his companions to see to the defense of the entrance.

Amele knelt before his queen, more child than woman, who carried the king's blood within her womb. The unusual stone she wore around her neck was glowing blood red. "My queen, we must leave this place. You are in danger here. We will protect you until your husband vanquishes this blasphemy and it is safe for you to return."

He felt the force of her stunning blue eyes searching his, as if she could discern his trustworthiness from what she read there. Amele knew every moment counted. They would come for her soon. The only reason he guessed the traitors had not yet done so was because they assumed a single soldier would be enough to subdue a defenseless, pregnant woman. He had not missed the significance of the wounded guard's uniform, nor the fact he recognized his face. Today's events were not the act of an enemy storming the city's iron gates, but a deadlier, more insidious attack of treason from within, a traitor, no less, who would prey on an innocent young woman heavy with child. The wounded man moaned in his pain. Amele spared him a disgusted glance and noticed the queen did the same. Then Amele found his first smile since he had come upon the atrocity being committed in the great hall. The queen spit on the dying soldier, then without sparing him another glance, stepped over his prone, writhing body, still clutching the bloody dagger in her hand.

With fresh admiration in his eyes, Amele escorted her to the exit where the others kept watch. "Wait here," he commanded in a soft voice, and then he cautiously opened the door. The light of a new day streamed into the dimly lit chapel. Amele could see no sign of additional soldiers heading in their direction. With any luck the single soldier had been commanded to keep the queen secluded in the chapel until the leader of the traitorous group came for her. He understood enough about the game of war to know that until the king was dead and the city was under the traitor's control, the queen was a valuable pawn in this fresh battle for rule of the city. Once control had been asserted and the king's supporters defeated, Amele knew the queen would have then outlived her usefulness to the usurpers and she would be executed with or without great ceremony. More likely the latter, Amele reasoned, as it would not do to outrage the ordinary citizens of the city by such an act of cruelty against the young and popular queen. Formulating his plan, Amele stepped back into the chapel. He removed his cloak, turned it inside out to disguise the livery of the king's guard, and offered it the queen.

"Your Highness, we must get you out of the city. Paul

and Samuel will go ahead of us and gather supplies. They will meet us at my father's cabin in the mountains, but if things go ill in the city, we will not be able to remain there. We must pass over the mountains before they realize you are gone. Once we are through the passes we can lose ourselves in the ancient forests and you can rest."

Amele waited for her to object to his plan to take her away from the comforts of the city and into the surrounding mountains, still snow covered and with spring but a promise that whispered along the icy wind, particularly given the fact she was heavy with child. He knew from the growing excitement in the city her babe was due any day. He could not risk taking a mid-wife along. The queen must disappear into the vast wilderness surrounding Calei. If her husband survived and restored order to his kingdom, word would reach them. If not, they would have no choice but to put as much distance as possible between the queen and those that sought her death. She carried the blood and potential true heir of the throne of Calei. One day this atrocity would be avenged and the child queen along with the babe she carried would be restored to their rightful places.

He waited while Queen Alyssa donned his too-large cloak and hid her dark hair beneath its hood. He nodded approvingly and then watched his friends' departure, waiting to see if they garnered any attention. Above him the ancient bells rang out, proclaiming the threat to the city. "Good man, Gabriel," he whispered to himself, realizing his brother had successfully executed the task he assigned him. With the alert sounded, he knew they would need to hurry now as his remaining, silent companion had just become a more valuable hostage in the eyes of their enemies. He gripped her arm to escort her through the entrance, then releasing her momentarily, motioned for her to wait inside. He turned back and hurried down the aisle of the house of God to where the dying man lay grimacing in pain. As if sensing Amele's presence he opened his glazed, pain-filled eyes. The wariness within them widened to a terrified panic when Amele drew his sword and raised it high over his head. Holding the man's horrified glance Amele brought the sword down in a swift, sure stroke and severed the traitor's head from his body.

...PROLOGUE

Amele pushed his mount through the blinding snow, his destination, the lonely cottage near the peak of the tallest mountain looking down upon his former home. Though his eyes could not see the majestic city spread out in the valleys beneath him, his blood sensed he was close. He was a native son and the music and magic of Calei stirred his blood as no other place could, and told him he was home.

Only the city kingdom was no longer his home. It had been almost two decades since he gazed upon its beauty when he secreted his queen from those who sought her death. He could take comfort knowing the traitor who slit his childhood friend's throat in order to gain his kingdom had himself managed to retain the throne for only a few short months. Those loyal to the rightful king rose up against the traitor's forces and soundly defeated them. That had been the first time those loyal to the former king sent out messages far and wide in search of the queen. They're search proved futile. Not because word did not reach the small company where the queen hid with her loyal defenders and her infant daughter, but because she refused to return to her husband's lands. Queen Alyssa was not a native of Calei and did not feel the same pull to return her guards did.

Amele remembered the day she met his concerned glance over the head of her infant daughter who nursed at her breast. Rather than luxurious chambers that should be her right by her royal title, his queen's home was a damp cave carved out of the sharp, solid rock of the mountain. "I will never return to Calei, Amele. I am not its destiny, nor am I the one who will one day break the ancient curse on the ruling family."

"Yes, my queen," Amele heard the echo of his younger self's voice in his head.

"Why do you stay with me? I can see your heart longs for your homeland."

He was aghast at her question. "You are my home, my queen. Where you dwell, I will dwell. Where you journey, I will journey. When you lay down your life, mine will follow yours to the grave."

She'd shaken her head at his fierce declaration. "My husband's kingdom must be a special place to have bred such honor into its sons, but it was never mine. However, because of your loyalty and the service you have rendered me and my family I will bestow upon you this promise. Though my feet will never again walk across the tiled floors of the great hall of my husband's castle, blood of his blood will one day return with you to your homeland and reclaim what treachery stole. He will exact his rightful vengeance against those who fed on my husband's blood."

He hadn't believed her, not that blood of her blood would one day return to Calei to reclaim the throne, but that she would never return herself. Despite the pleas to come back and claim the throne that had reached them over the years where they wandered across the rich lands of

Europe, the queen remained staunch in her refusal. Amele understood her caution. Queen Alyssa feared for her daughter's life. She carried the blood of the true king. A challenger to the throne who was able to wed the king's daughter and return her to Calei would turn the people's hearts to their cause. Not only because of the royal blood that ran through her veins, but because of the fond memories the people held of her father. They'd known peace under his rule, the last meaningful peace his people could recall.

Amele was shaken from his musings by the light in the window of the retreat up ahead. He breathed a sigh of relief and thought he heard his own sigh echo in unison from his faithful mount. He reached out and patted his straining neck and urged him the final few yards to the promised welcome awaiting them. Amele's brother stood framed in the open doorway of their father's cabin. It was theirs now, he supposed, as his father had long since passed onto his eternal reward, another casualty of one of the many wars fought over the question of who would rule the rich wealth of their homeland. Amele saw to the comfort of his mount, then the two brothers embraced, before pulling back while each examined the other, seeking the telling evidence of the years since their last meeting. Amele nodded, pleased by what he saw.

Gabriel was the one who had sounded the alarm that pivotal morning, alerting the city to the act of treason being committed within its depths. Though he was no longer a young man, the light of justice still burned bright in his eyes. To Amele, it was clear his brother's heart was still set on their joint goal, to restore the rightful king to the inlaid jeweled throne of Calei. It had been too many years to rightfully recall the occasion of their last visit, but it was a full two decades since they parted at the borders a day's harsh ride from his father's cabin where they met briefly and learned the devastating news of the king's death. Gabriel had begged Amele to allow him to accompany them on their quest to protect the queen and lead her away from Calei and into the mountains, but as there was no other he could trust in the king's household and he needed eyes and ears at home to know when it was safe for him to bring the queen home, Amele had begged his brother to remain behind and keep watch.

His brother had waited twenty years to hear the news Amele braved a winter crossing through the mountains to deliver. So when they were settled beside the hearth, with a glass of ale in each of their work-calloused hands, and a pot of thick stew simmering above the fire, sending its hearty fragrance to chase away the chill of the cabin, Amele wasted no time in imparting his news. "The princess has born her husband a son." He saw the immediate hope at the news spring to his brother's eyes and felt compelled to temper it. "Remember brother, this child is not a son of Calei, but one of Saxony. He is the first born and will one day inherit his father's rich estates. He is not the one."

Disappointed, Gabriel nodded his acceptance of what must be, then responded with a smile, his hope obviously unwilling to be so easily tucked away again in the darkest reaches of his heart, "But the princess is young and her husband's lands and title will pass only to the first born. Mayhaps she will have other sons who will keep the queen's promise."

"From your lips, Brother, to the Almighty's ears,"

Amele had responded, taking a long pull of his ale. “Is that stew about ready to eat?”

….PROLOGUE

Two years later, Amele once again pushed his mount through the blinding snow. He knew it was safer for their cause for him to visit in the winter months when the watch was inattentive. Who but a madman would launch an attack on the well-guarded city in the depths of winter? Amele did not dispute their conclusion and admitted he sometimes wondered if he was indeed mad. His brother had once again prepared for his arrival with a roaring fire in the stone hearth to warm his limbs. Amele accepted gratefully Gabriel's offering of the warm stew and bread he borrowed from his own roof, and abused a goblet of wine before settling down into the chair opposite the hearth to deliver the news his brother and those aligned with their purpose eagerly awaited.

"The princess has given her husband a second son." He smiled as his brother jumped up out of his chair and performed a joyful little dance in front of the fire. Amele would not steal his brother's excitement away by delivering the caution his queen had given him with a teasing light in her bluer than blue eyes. 'He is not the one, Amele. Do not yet begin preparations for an immediate invasion.'

Twice more he made the same journey in the icy depths of winter. On his third visit he witnessed his brother's joy over the news of the birth of yet another rightful heir to the throne, and his report that the older two sons were healthy and active boys, but it was the final occasion he carried such news that would forever remain in Amele's memories. His brother's eyes were expectant as they sat down. "Well, brother, don't keep me in suspense."

"The princess was delivered of a healthy baby girl."

"Ah, well it was bound to happen. A blessing be upon her that she shares her grandmother's beauty. I suppose the queen is pleased with this birth to know the succession has been secured for the unusual inheritance from her own mother that she will bequeath to her daughter."

"Yes, she seemed quite pleased; especially when she informed me her daughter was also safely delivered of a healthy baby boy."

"What?!! Twins? Another heir to the throne?" His brother jumped up from his chair and pulled a reluctant Amele to his feet. Laughing, together they danced around the room in celebration. When their feet stopped shuffling they faced each other wearing wide grins.

"He's the one, Gabriel. He is the one who will fulfill the queen's promise," Amele confided in a near reverent voice.

His brother's expression took on a new seriousness. "The queen revealed this to you? She has seen this?"

Amele squeezed his brother's shoulders at the almost fearful resurrection of genuine hope revealed in Gabriel's gaze. "Yes. I have not shared with you on my previous visits the queen's caution at the birth of the princess' older sons that none of them would be the one to return. I feared it would mean we might be forced to await the birth of a new generation before we saw the king's rightful blood restored to the throne of our home. If such was the case, it is likely neither of us would have lived to see such a glorious day, but now I know the day of our redemption has arrived. The promise keeper is born."

"What is his name that I may include him in my petitions to the Almighty to keep watch over his young life, and that he may grow in strength and the wisdom needed to restore Calei to its days of grandeur?"

"Michel. The newborn king's name is Michel."

CHAPTER ONE

THE CITY KINGDOM OF CALEI, 1067

Elena stood in the doorway of the dimly lit chamber and watched her uncle sleep. His breathing seemed a little less labored this evening, his color not so pale, but there was no doubt the king was surrendering his life inch by painful inch. If he thought to escape the curse that plagued his predecessors by not siring a son to ascend to his throne, Elena did not consider the alternative of this slow death he suffered a more kindly fate than the one the ancient curse would have afforded him. Who knew? Perhaps the kings of Calei could not escape the archaic spell and her uncle's illness that was slowly eating away at his insides was the price he paid for attempting to strike a bargain with destiny.

With her uncle's every labored breath, Elena

felt the crush of her own inevitable fate closing in around her, reminiscent she thought of the stories of the young church in Rome where the faithful Christians were fed to the lions in the grand Coliseum for the entertainment of the mad emperor and his court.

She thought she could comprehend the terror they must have faced, knowing there was no escape from the violent, bloody death awaiting them beneath the clenched jaws and razor sharp teeth of the wild beasts. Though her own immediate future would likely not prove fatal, she did not think she dreaded it any less than the prospect of being torn apart by lions. At least the doomed Christians could console themselves with the thought that they were dying for their faith and the awful deed would be over in a matter of minutes. Elena faced the prospect of being consumed again and again, at least until the beast who would feed upon her young flesh was satisfied, or until he grew bored with her and sought other entertainment.

She could feel the baron's eyes on her from where he stood near her uncle's bedside, watching as closely as she did the king's tortuous breathing. But while Elena willed new strength into her uncle's frail frame and prayed for each shallow breath he drew, the man by his side sought the opposite outcome. Elena knew if he could stop the king's breath with the force of his will, her uncle would be dead by now.

Unable to bear the thought of what that day would mean to her, she turned silently from the door and slid into the hall. She was aware of the presence of the two guards who followed her down the torch-lit corridor to her own chambers. When she entered her rooms, one of the fierce soldiers more loyal to his baron than his king nodded and pulled the door shut behind her. She didn't have to peek into the hallway to know they stood watch outside her door, presumably to keep her safe from any threats lurking in the unsettled city, but Elena understood the real reason she was so closely watched in the latter days of her uncle's rule. Her prison might be a gilded one, but it was a prison all the same.

With the succession in doubt, the question of who would ascend to the throne upon her uncle's death had occupied the minds and hearts of Caleinians for long years. The uncertainty had assumed more urgency with the sudden onset of her uncle's illness. Elena was not the only one shocked by the king's abrupt decline from a man in the prime of his life, to the frail shadow of his former self who appeared to cling to his place in this physical world through the sheer strength of his will.

The majority of the kingdom's citizens blamed the curse for the king's imminent death. Elena was less inclined to do so. She suspected another more human cause, but she had no proof of her evil thoughts, and to give voice to them would likely serve no other purpose but to hasten her uncle's death and her own unwanted future.

She strode to the window and looked out on the majestic mountains surrounding the city. The moon was full and cast an almost ethereal glow to the snow-capped peaks even though by the count of days on the calendar the snow should be receding beneath the warmer, stronger sun of spring. The mountains provided a beautiful backdrop for the magnificent city kingdom they protected. *Spun from gold by a sorcerer's hand.* That was what the legends said about her uncle's kingdom and so it would seem to anyone looking down upon its magnificence from her vantage point.

Paved streets lined with grand homes and shops gave evidence of the wealth of the city's inhabitants. The stone sparkled in the light of the moon and little bits of gold appeared to be woven through the white stone, giving rise to the fanciful lore. As was the case with most legends, the truth was close enough to the whimsy attached to it that it had endured over the long count of years and had become part of the accepted history of Calei. There was gold embedded in the rock of the mountains the city both rested upon and was constructed from, but it was an onerous process to separate the precious metal from the ordinary stone, and the wealth of the city was abundant enough that few of its inhabitants considered the burdensome task worth the effort.

There was no shortage of gold in Calei, or of other precious metals. Gems were plentiful in the mines carved deep in the heart of the surrounding mountains. Calei was an enormously wealthy kingdom, but what most would naively assume was an unimpeachable blessing had proven a curse to its inhabitants. For where there existed great wealth all too often greater greed followed.

War was the price of the boon of Calei's wealth… unending, bloody, violent, ceaseless war. Caleinians craved peace the way other cultures craved gold. They longed for the day when they could trust with reasonable certainty that their young sons would grow to manhood and father sons of their own, rather than be cut down before they were given the opportunity to do so beneath the sharp sword and heavy hand of an enemy knight intent on claiming Calei's treasury. But if Calei was cursed, so too were those who sought to conquer her, because having entered the streets of the city kingdom with violent intent, by claiming the throne they purchased with the blood of its defenders, the enemy kings subjected themselves to the affliction of its native rulers. What they paid so dearly to possess would slip through their fingers in a single generation.

No son of a ruling king had ascended to the throne of Calei in uncounted generations. Most monarchs were able to hold onto the right to rule for short years before another sought to take his place. Those years were often spent in constant strife, defending their positions from the seemingly unending waves of enemies who sought to usurp them by force. Elena did not understand why anyone would aspire to the kingship when the price of doing so had proven so high. Was unlimited wealth worth the sacrifice of so many lives, even their own and the sons they fathered?

Though she was unable to comprehend the greed of men, she understood she too would be unable to escape the effects of the ruler's curse. Her uncle was a popular king and his passing would be genuinely grieved by the populace. How better for his successor to secure the people's loyalty than to marry his young niece? Such had been the plans of those aspiring to be her uncle's successor since she arrived as a little girl in the care of her uncle after her parents' death. Those designs had only grown more insistent as she'd grown into young womanhood and the king showed no signs of wedding and producing a legitimate heir. The competition for her hand was fierce especially because of the presumption her uncle would name as his legitimate heir the man who married her.

Knowing the day she dreaded would soon be upon her, Elena looked out with longing on the still night. Not unlike most maids she once dreamed of finding a true love and living happily-ever-after by his side. Perhaps somewhere beyond the mountains there was a knight who wore shiny armor about his muscular frame and one who would come to her rescue before she was sacrificed to the greed and lusts of the men anticipating her uncle's death.

Chiding herself for her refusal to give up her foolish girlhood dreams, Elena turned from the window and prepared for bed. She did not summon her maid, preferring the quiet and solitude of her evening ritual alone. When she'd exchanged her heavy winter gown for a thinner sleeping garment, she knelt beside her bed as she did each evening to offer a prayer for her uncle's recovery and for her parents' eternal souls.

Before she rose from her knees and slid beneath the thick quilt, she whispered another prayer, with her head bent in humble supplication, having no more expectation of her request being granted than the Christians who no doubt offered a similar prayer in anticipation of their deadly fates. She prayed God would save her from the beast. She prayed he would send her a savior to wrest her away from the grasp of Baron Raulf before it was too late.

CHAPTER TWO

Michel stretched out his arm to run a gentle hand along his mount's sleek neck. Arden tossed his head and danced restlessly beneath him. The two of them were still finding their way. Michel inherited the stallion when in a weak moment he accepted responsibility for the Salusian stone from his twin's trembling hands. The thin silver chain that bore the stone's weight fit more closely around his own throat than it had the more slender columns of either of his sisters'. He thought the ill-fit an apt representation of his lack of comfort with his family's ancient inheritance. Just as he and Arden were still finding their way, so too were he and the stone.

The Salusian king and the Salusian stone. Neither of the two bequests was meant to come to him. The stone had been in his mother's family for a thousand years. The inheritance was passed down through countless generations, mother to eldest daughter until it ended up in his unlikely, and in his mind, unworthy hands. Apparently there was a loophole in the line of succession for the stone. The gem was always to be worn by a woman, the next female descendant in line of the current keeper of the stone. The only exception being if the current keeper happened to have a male twin, as was the case with him and Melissa.

She had insisted he take the stone when they said their farewells outside the gates of her new Norman husband's estate in Normandy. Michel's puny attempt at refusing her request was swiftly over-ruled. Admittedly, he hadn't tried very hard in light of the tears glimmering in his twin's eyes, their sapphire depths identical to his own. Michel always had a weakness for a woman's tears. When those tears were threatening to fall from the eyes of the other half of his heart, his defenses crumbled completely. What was it about a strong woman's tears that brought a man to his knees?

Seemingly irritated by his long delay his mount shifted beneath him. With a slight smile curving his lips at the stallion's impatience and Arden's willingness to share that impatience with his rider, Michel gave the signal to break camp and urged his mount forward. The Salusian stone and the Salusian king. Arden was the other half of his unusual inheritance. The Salusian king went with the keeper of the stone, regardless of either the former or new keeper's inclination. Not that Michel objected to having Arden's services, but he knew what a wrench it was for Melissa to be forced to part with him. So he'd left his own mount, a blinding white Salusian mare, with his sister in exchange for her loss of Arden.

Despite the mystical nature of his mother's

heritage, there was enough of his Saxon father's rational blood running through his veins that made Michel uncomfortable with the notion of wearing a legendary amulet around his neck. He dismissed as myths the stories he heard about the stone's power when he was a boy sitting around the fire at night in the summer camps of his grandmother's people. Certainly he placed no reliance on the stone's ability to assist him in his current quest. An unusual jewel did not win kingdoms. No, he fully expected to be forced to claim his inheritance from his mother's father in the old fashioned way, through his skill with a sword and the loyalty of the highly trained army that rode at his back.

Of course, even if they were successful in defeating the armies of the usurpers, there was still the little matter of an ancient curse to be dealt with. Surprisingly that particular whimsy was not passed down through his grandmother's blood. While the Salusian stone was reputed to possess mysterious powers that could prove dangerous in the wrong hands, there was no curse attached to it when held in the hands of its legitimate keeper. He reached up to slip a finger beneath the thin chain around his neck and pull it away from his skin as it was wont to close around his throat in the rocking motion of even Arden's fluid gait. Just a reminder he thought, that the stone was no more comfortable resting against his hard masculine chest after being nestled between the soft flesh of a woman's breasts, than he was having it there. Of course the easiest solution was to simply remove the chain from around his neck and stow the stone in the leather pouch he carried on his belt, but he accepted he would continue to wrestle with the will of the stone the way he was destined to do with his new mount. Melissa demanded his promise to wear the stone around his neck. He'd never broken a promise to his twin and he didn't intend to start now, regardless of the stone's inclination in the matter.

"The advance scouts report the king is near death."

Michel turned to meet the intent gaze of the man at his side. He noted the mixture of both compassion and anticipation riding in the chocolate brown eyes of his companion. Over the course of Michel's young life, Amele had played the parts of stand-in grandfather, mentor, teacher, trainer and historian. He was one of the very few who rode among them who remembered that black night when Michel's grandfather was murdered by a trusted friend intent on claiming the kingship. As a young soldier Amele escorted Michel's very pregnant grandmother through the chaotic streets, passed the city gates, and over the high mountain passes to the relative safety of the sparsely populated lands beyond.

His grandmother gave birth to Michel's mother just short days later. Fearing the pursuit of the new king's soldiers intent on killing the king's heir before she could become a threat to their claim on the throne, Amele led the young queen and her infant daughter ever west and away from his troubled homeland. Surprisingly, Michel's grandmother did not share Amele's regret over the loss of her husband's kingdom.

Queen Alyssa had been a child-bride of the king. His grandfather had surprised everyone when he returned from a trip south with a new bride. His grandmother's charm and beauty soon won over the hearts of the populace and the mystical stone she wore around her neck endeared her to the superstitious souls of the people. Michel knew his grandmother had been approached on numerous occasions by emissaries of one delegation or another in the hopes of persuading her to return to Calei. When all such efforts failed, it was his father who was approached with the promise of the throne for one of his sons. The duke had no interest in his father-in-law's kingdom, even less in subjecting one of his sons to the constant strife that Calei was forever wrapped in, but his constant refusals did not stop the emissaries from returning, always with the same request.

When the duke declined to send one of his sons back to Calei, the messengers turned their attention to his daughters, Michel's sisters. There had been promises of vast wealth in exchange for the right to marry one of the true king's granddaughters. The duke would merely have had to agree to what would have amounted to the sale of one of his daughters in order to receive such wealth. Michel's lips curved in a reminiscent smile at the memory of his father's vehement response. The messengers had not returned to Heaven's Crest to pester the duke again. Still, Michel was pleased his sisters were now beyond the reach of such efforts. With their marriages to powerful Norman lords he no longer had to worry about that threat to their futures. He grinned at the prospect of his brother-in-laws' reactions to a stranger's suggestion they give up their wives in exchange for even the most extravagant promises of wealth.

Michel was aware of Amele's silent presence at his side and his patient expectation of a response to his announcement that the current king was near death. With an inward sigh, he pulled himself away from his inner musings to nod his acknowledgement of the news. The truth was Michel was surprised to learn the king still lived. He was a very sick man months ago when the two first met.

"The timing serves our purpose." Amele added when Michel failed to respond to his earlier comment.

With a slight shrug, Michel broke his moody silence. "Perhaps."

He knew Amele wondered what Michel would decide to do about the proposal the current king had lain at his feet that night in the humble cottage of his loyal retainer. Michel was certain the bitter cold of winter in the mountains and the damp and icy passage beneath the paved streets of his city had cost the king precious days off of his already, soon-to-be shortened life. Regretfully Michel had been unable to grant him the promise the king sought from him, but he did vow to protect his young niece. With the king near death, Michel comprehended the girl was in a precarious position, alone in her uncle's household with the wolves all but growling at her door. He was moved to pity by the thought of her plight, if only because it reminded him so forcefully of his sisters' precarious position in his father's household during the course of the Norman invasion. War was no place for a woman, even less so for a young girl caught in its relentless grip.

If her uncle died before they reached the city, there would be little Michel could do to keep his promise to the dying king. So though weariness from another long day spent in the saddle tore at his will and echoed through the men who rode behind him, he pushed on. The moon was bright enough to guide them on their way. Another few hours and they would make camp for the night and be up again when the new light of dawn appeared to lead them on. Michel understood that for young Elena, every moment was precious.

Though he did not confide his purpose for why he drove them so hard, none of the men following him grumbled at his hurry. They were anxious to see the land the majority had heard about only from their elder companions…a city spun from gold. His grandfather's kingdom may as well have been conjured from the depths of a fairytale such were the legends surrounding it. He could all but see the dreams of unlimited riches dancing through the heads of even his most battle-hardened soldiers.

Michel's own motivations were of a more banal nature, though some would claim his constituted the greater romantic quest. In his mind his intent was simple. He was returning to right a wrong done to one of his own and to keep a promise his grandmother made to the man at his side. He had no real interest in the fate of Calei or in becoming its next king. It was vengeance that drove him. Though the traitor who murdered his grandfather was long dead, the city kingdom had its own debt to pay to his family. He intended to see to it that it was paid in full.

Long hours later they camped for what was left of the night and Michel's lips echoed the relieved sighs of his men as he dismounted and surrendered Arden to the competent care of his squire. To stretch his legs, he strode through the line of trees surrounding their camp and stared off into the distance trying to catch a glimpse of the city kingdom whose throne was his by right of birth. No such view was afforded him as there were still higher peaks yet for them to ascend that blocked his view, so instead he allowed his thoughts to dwell on the memories of his extraordinary meeting with the dying king. Amele and his younger brother, Gabriel, a life-long citizen of Calei and an admirer of the current king's rule, were conduits of the unusual gathering.

Michel uncomfortably recalled the near reverence in Amele's younger brother's voice when the two were introduced. The older man had knelt before him when Michel extended his hand in greeting, and with tears in his eyes and in a voice of near awe declared, "My king. I praise God that I have lived to see you in the flesh." Michel had been uncertain how to respond to the other man's hushed declaration so he had urged him in a gentle voice to rise and gripped his hand. Still Michel had feared a trap when Gabriel confided the reason for his visit, but Amele had persuaded him to agree to the unusual circumstances. Once Michel met the current king, he understood why.

Michel guessed King Barnabas was close in age to his own father though from his pale skin and thin frame anyone seeing him would be excused for concluding he was a much older man. He'd been robust, a man in his prime just months earlier, before he was struck down by a mysterious illness half the population of his kingdom attributed to the mysterious curse on the ruling family. Amele and Gabriel believed treason the more likely cause of the monarch's sudden decline. Poison in the king's cup, they reasoned, though there was no proof of their suspicions. Michel thought it just as likely the king could have been afflicted by some as yet unnamed illness. Such events occurred in other places as everyday occurrences. Only in Calei did a sudden ailment automatically become the work of curses and/or treason.

On the occasion of their meeting, the king had rested on a chaise in his retainer's small cottage in the mountains. He sweated profusely but Michel took note his fair eyes were still sharp when they beheld him. Michel did not kneel before him, and he was somewhat surprised when the older man took no offense at his obvious slight. In fact the king seemed to find his reluctance to do so both admirable and somewhat impudent. His lips smiled in amused understanding, even as his eyes grimaced with pain.

"So, you are Nathaniel's grandson. You have the look of him about you, but it is your grandmother's eyes I see watching me, wondering why I requested this meeting."

Shocked at the other man's courteous greeting, Michel had asked, "You knew my grandfather?"

The king sighed wearily. "Knew would be too strong a word. He was my king when I was a boy. Like all Caleinians I loved him. I was on the streets hoping to catch a glimpse of the new queen when he returned with his young bride, and like every other impressionable boy, I fell immediately in love at my first view of her. Queen Alyssa is still well, I trust?"

Michel was having difficulty controlling his reaction to the stunning revelation the current king had been an admirer of his grandfather, and was still loyal to his memory. He referred to his grandmother as Queen Alyssa. What was this meeting all about? Did he intend to simply hand over his kingdom into Michel's somewhat reluctant hands? He became aware the king was waiting for his response to his question about his grandmother's health and he nodded absently. "Yes, my grandmother is well, thank you."

"News has reached us of the Norman duke's invasion of Saxony. I pray your family is safe."

"Thank you. The last I heard all was well, but the trail of news is uncertain in these troubled times."

"Yes, and there is no bottom to the well of the treachery of men."

"Indeed."

Silence fell between the two men, and the king motioned for Michel to sit in the chair placed near where he lounged. Wearily the ill man leaned his head back against the chaise and closed his eyes for a moment. "You are no doubt wondering why I requested this introduction."

"Yes."

King Barnabas nodded and turned his direct

gaze in Michel's direction. "I am dying, young prince, and my kingdom will soon be in need of a new king."

"I imagine there is no shortage of applicants for the position," Michel replied wryly.

Laughter shook the king's frail frame. "No, that is true, but none are acceptable to me."

"And I am?"

"Your grandfather's blood runs through your veins. He was my king. The usurpers who followed his reign were not worthy of the title. We waited…those loyal to your grandfather. I waited for the queen to return and claim the throne, at least until an heir with the true king's blood could ascend to his responsibilities. I was one of challengers to the throne to send emissaries to your grandmother, but they returned each time with the same answer. Queen Alyssa would not return, nor would she allow her daughter to do so. Even after I became king I sent word to your father, hoping to persuade him to send us one of his sons to assume the kingship. He refused, but still I held out hope. I deliberately refrained from marrying and took care to father no bastard sons so that none would contest your family's rightful place."

Michel said the first words that came to his mind, humbled by the loyalty and humility of this gentle king, who he imagined assumed the throne to prevent another evil usurper from doing so. "I did not have the privilege of knowing him as you did, but my grandfather must have been a great man to have instilled such loyalty and honor in his followers."

The king's eyes were closed and Michel thought his attention was turned inward to memories of his younger days when he replied, "Yes, I imagine he was, but I was not in a position to know him any better than you. I was still a child when he was lost to us, but I do know he was a great king and the land prospered under his rule. I have done my humble best to lead the people and to restore peace and prosperity to our city, but I have been unable to unite the disparate factions among the nobles. That, I think is left for you to do, my prince."

When Michel remained silent the older man opened his pain-filled eyes and turned to regard him with his piercing gaze. His lips curved slightly in a smile of understanding. "I think you are no more anxious to claim the kingship than I was."

"You speak the truth." Michel reluctantly agreed.

A wider smile stretched the older man's lips. "A reluctant king is more of a blessing on the land than one who is so eager to grasp the reins of power he will let nothing and no one stand in his way to the throne, not even at the loss of his own honor."

"I was not born here, nor have I ever walked the streets of your kingdom," Michel offered by way of explanation.

"No, but once you do, you will never again be free. I believe it only fair to caution you that once you enter the city, your spirit will find its true home in Calei and the people's hearts will awaken at the return of their true king. Can you not feel the anticipation in the air? The people's spirits sing to them that their long vigil is almost over. The time approaches when the true king will return and cleanse our city and our lands of the stain of blood upon them. He will root out the deceivers and I and my just predecessors will know peace in our long sleep that the kingdom we ruled and loved will once again prosper in his hands."

The king's fervent declaration seemed to exhaust him. As he leaned back against the chaise Michel knelt by his side and grasped the other man's failing grip with his own strong hand. Uncertain how to respond to the king's spirited proclamation, he cautioned quietly, "Your Highness, I fear you have become a willing victim to the mystical nature of your kingdom."

His frail shoulders shook at Michel's gentle admonition and he turned to regard Michel with amused eyes. "And I think, my young heir, you speak dismissively of what you have no personal experience of."

"True enough," Michel acknowledged, for a moment an answering amusement reflected in his glance.

"And yet you mock my own superstitious nature?"

"It was not my intent to mock you, Your Highness, only to caution you. I am not the fulfillment of some ancient curse. The truth is I have only recently learned of its existence."

The king's glance held Michel's, filled with both understanding and speculation and then he issued a caution of his own, "Because you have never known of it does not in any way change its course, or your part in its resolution."

"I think, Your Highness, your illness has made you fanciful."

"No doubt, but I believe, young prince, it is you who deludes yourself. You still believe you can turn from the promise your grandmother made on your behalf, but I think your reluctance to accept who and what you are will in the end not alter your destiny."

"There is no such thing as destiny. A man's future is what he makes of it."

"Yes, I once believed as you do, and certainly there is no disputing a man's choices set his course, but I have come to accept fate has its own hand to play and it is not easily thwarted, despite a man's intent to the contrary."

"Perhaps." Michel reluctantly conceded and felt a shiver of his own destiny press down upon him. Hadn't he sensed the inevitability of his return to his grandfather's kingdom in a way none of his brothers did? Hadn't the tales Amele shared with him about his former home stirred his blood? There was no doubt but that he'd been caught up in the romance of the stories he heard. What young boy could resist tales about a city spun from gold, perched high upon the highest peak of a majestic mountain? Of wars fought over the question of who would be its king, and then being told that he and his brothers were the rightful heirs to its rich throne. Was it destiny that led him to take this course or his own determination to avenge his grandfather's bloody death?

How was any man to answer such a question? He shook off his unsettling musings and turned back to the king. "Even if you speak the truth, I am certain, Your Highness, you did not request this meeting to debate the course of fate in the making of a man's life."

"No, though I have enjoyed our conversation immensely. You do not address me as if I am an imbecile whose illness has robbed him of his wits."

"I see no evidence of a decline in your wits, Your Highness. Those who presume as much, will, I think, learn too late of the foolishness of their mistake."

"Let us hope you speak the truth. Which leads us to the reason I requested this introduction." The king struggled to sit up straighter against the back of the divan and Michel hurried to assist him.

Nodding his gratitude, King Barnabas faced

him with steely resolve. Michel thought it only the other man's fierce, unbending will that was keeping him alive. "You have two sisters, I believe."

At the mention of his sisters, Michel's protective instincts went on full alert. Certainly, the man did not think to use his sisters as some sort of bargaining chip in whatever his plan was to induce Michel's cooperation. "Yes, but they will not return to Calei."

Nodding, the king proclaimed the obvious. "You seek to protect them."

"Of course. They are my sisters."

"No doubt a precious treasure to you and your family."

Confused by the winding trail of their conversation, Michel merely nodded his agreement.

"I too have a precious treasure to protect. My niece, Elena. Though I never fathered children, I cannot imagine a daughter of my own blood could be dearer to me."

"You are concerned for her fate when your illness…" Michel allowed his voice to trail off rather than baldly announce the unpleasant truth.

"When my illness takes its inevitable course," Barnabas inserted starkly. "Yes, my enemies will seek to use my Elena for their own ends."

"She remains with you in Calei?"

"Yes."

"Why do you not send her away?"

"To whom shall I send her? I have no family. Nor does she. Her mother was my sister. She and her husband died in an accident in the mountains when Elena was but a young girl. Calei is the only home she has any memory of."

"Surely there is someone you can trust who would be willing to take her in."

"Of course, but of what use is their willingness to do so against the ones who would rule after I am gone? They will use my beloved Elena to gain the people's acceptance."

Michel did not doubt the king's conclusion, but he was still trying to figure out why the king summoned him to his side at this late hour. "I am not certain what you believe I can do to assist you."

"You can marry her."

"What?!!!" Michel made no effort to disguise his shock at the king's suggestion. "No, that is quite impossible. I have no intention of marrying. At least not anytime in the immediate future."

"I realize it is a great deal to ask, but the arrangement is not without benefit to you. The people love her." When Michel would have interrupted, the king silenced him with a weak sweep of his hand. "Though I recognize you do not need to marry my Elena to gain the people's acceptance they will regard you all the more favorably for seeing to her protection."

"I am willing to see to your niece's protection, Your Highness, but I will not promise you I will marry her to ensure it."

The king nodded as if he had expected no more from his guest and then motioned to his servant to bring him a scroll resting on the wooden table that appeared to have been pushed to the side of the small room in order to make space for their gathering. The servant hurried to see to the king's request. Barnabas accepted the rolled scroll from his servant's hand and then placed it in Michel's reluctant grasp.

"This scroll has my seal upon it. There are witnesses among the populace of the city who will attest to its authenticity. This parchment makes you my legitimate heir." When Michel would have returned the rolled scroll to his hand, the king hurried to add, "Not that you need my blessing to vouch for your right to assume the throne of Calei, but again it will ease your way. Not all will welcome your return. You will have a fight on your hands."

At Michel's acknowledging nod, the dying king added, "But when war is done, the more difficult struggle for peace must begin. A throne can be taken by force of arms, but a people's hearts and loyalties cannot be won with a sword, no matter how skillfully it is wielded. I think you are not a fool to dismiss so valuable a weapon."

Michel regarded the scroll in his hands, though he did not unfold it to see if it indeed contained what the king claimed. "You did not need me here to give me this. Before I accept it I would know the price attached to it."

"And you will honor that price even after I am dead?"

"Yes, if I agree to it, I will honor it."

"I ask that you see to my Elena's protection."

"I have already sworn to do so without this added inducement."

The king's lips curved at Michel's blunt reminder. "And I ask that you do not wed another until you have at least met my Elena."

"It is no hardship on my part to agree to your request as I've already informed you I am in no hurry to marry. Is it your presumption that once I meet your niece I will be so overwhelmed by her feminine charms I will agree to wed her?"

"Not my presumption, but my hope at least. The parchment gives my consent for the marriage of my niece to you and no other. It also places Elena under your guardianship at my death."

"Would it make any difference if I assured you I am not a man easily charmed by feminine beauty? My sisters are the most beautiful women I have ever seen. Your niece would have to be a paragon indeed in order to tempt me."

"She is that, young prince, but I will content myself with your pledge to see to my Elena's protection and to assume guardianship over her when I pass from this world. And to answer your earlier question, yes, it was necessary for me to meet you first so I could ascertain for myself that you are a man of honor and worthy of the trust I place in you."

"It is you who honors me, Your Highness, by entrusting to me your greatest treasure."

"Yes, that is true, but I think King Nathaniel's grandson is worthy of my trust."

CHAPTER THREE

Elena knelt by her uncle's bed and held his hand, praying his labored breathing would not stop this night. Baron Raulf had been in earlier, no doubt debating the count of days or hours he must continue to bide his patience before he became king. For both of them knew the current king could not hang on much longer. Though she refused to meet the baron's glance, she was aware of the way his eyes swept over her, as if disrobing her with his glance.

Elena understood it was not only the throne of Calei he was anticipating claiming. There was possessiveness in his increasingly bold gazes in her direction she found unsettling, as if she already belonged to him and would soon share his bed. Elena tried to comfort herself with the notion there would likely be many contenders to the throne, but she reluctantly acknowledged it was a false hope she consoled herself with. Baron Raulf's men filled the great hall at meals. His soldiers escorted her whenever she left the castle, even to attend mass, and stood watch outside her door at night.

Bitter tears stung her eyes at the thought of his

hands caressing her virgin flesh. She would rather die than submit to the intimacies he would force upon her. She suspected knowing of her reluctance would only make consummation of the deed more appealing to him. Raulf was a man who enjoyed another's fear. He no doubt amused himself with visions of her cowering before him, begging him for mercy.

If she thought her maidenly pleas would gain her a reprieve from his lust she would not restrain her lips. For what was foolish pride when measured against the rape of her person? But of course in the eyes of the law and the church there would be no rape. The baron would wait to satisfy his lust for her until after their marriage vows were exchanged and then her reluctance would be meaningless. He could force himself upon her for the entertainment of his cheering soldiers on the floor of the great hall and none would contest his right to do so. A wife had no right to deny her husband.

Sometimes when she was alone in her bed at night her desperation drove her to contemplate taking her own life. Though suicide was a mortal sin, and she would condemn herself to suffer the fires of hell for all eternity if she chose such a cowardly escape from her difficulties, she did not immediately dismiss the idea. Elena firmly believed there were fates worse than death, but she wasn't certain she could equate being raped by the baron with an eternity spent being consumed by the flames of hell. Maybe she would have a fortuitous accident that would result in her quick death. She supposed it would have to be a true accident and not a contrived one. God would not be fooled by subterfuge.

While she waited for an unlikely accident to claim her life, she considered other ways out of her worrisome future as the baron's wife. She could leave Calei. It was true she was closely watched, but it could be done, either when she was in the kitchens consulting with the cooks for the meals, or on her way to morning mass. Her guards were not all that attentive. They understood as well as she did how limited her options for escape were. Where could she go after all? She could not take refuge in one of the homes in the city, even if its residents were sympathetic to her plight. She had a feeling the baron's vengeance would be swift and brutal against anyone who thought to stand in his way. She would not put any of her uncle's faithful subjects in such a perilous position.

Even if she thought to lose herself in the mountains surrounding the city, her refuge would soon turn into her tomb in the winter snows still covering the peaks. Her education had not prepared her to survive alone in the wild. She didn't have the slightest notion how to wield a blade or bow in her own defense. Lost in the wilderness she would likely soon become a meal of one of the wild animals who wandered the vast empty spaces in the surrounding mountains where men did not dwell and travelled only in well-armed parties. If given the choice, she thought she would sooner become a meal of some vicious swine rather than the baron.

She wondered if the church would judge a flight into the mountains a form of suicide on her part. She didn't think so. There was always the chance she could be taken in by a kind traveler or humble citizen who lived beyond the limits of Calei. There must be someone in the world who would be willing to provide her with a safe refuge. She was not afraid to work for her keep, though her useful skills were somewhat limited. She could direct the staff of a large kitchen, but she had no idea how to cook a meal herself. She had never made her own bed or washed the linens. She didn't sew her own clothes. Somehow she didn't think her ability to paint pleasing pictures would be a highly prized skill in the eyes of those who lived beyond the confines of the luxurious keep.

Such was the hopelessness of her plight that she prayed for the opportunity to put just such a bold plan into action. She no longer had any real hope of her uncle's recovery though she still prayed for a miracle. She knew her beloved Uncle Barnabas was dying, but if he could just hold on a little while longer until the spring thaw was more certain, she might have a chance. So she added a prayer that she would have the courage to take it if and when the opportunity presented itself. As if sensing her dark thoughts, her uncle turned his head in her direction.

"Elena." She squeezed his hand and bent close to his lips so he wouldn't strain himself to be heard.

"I'm here, Uncle Barnabas. Is there something you need? Cool water perhaps?"

"No, child," he whispered and then added with an effort, his hand squeezing hers with surprising strength. "I want you to know you won't be alone. I have made arrangements for your care after I am gone."

"Don't speak such, Uncle Barnabas. You will recover soon."

A resigned smile curved his lips at her attempt at deception. "The true king will return. He has promised to protect you."

"Thank you, Uncle. I will rest easier now."

He nodded, and giving her hand another, gentler squeeze, he dropped back to sleep. Elena dipped a fresh cloth in the cool water by her uncle's bedside and wiped his sweat-covered brow and face with it. For a moment she felt true hope rise within her breast when he informed her he had made arrangements for her care, but her relief quickly turned to dread at the thought he would most likely place her under Raulf's control at his death. Was the baron not her uncle's closest friend and confidant?

Her uncle referred to the true king. If only that

were true. She would willingly take her chances on the mercy of a stranger rather than rely on the foolish hope the baron possessed any. Regretfully she accepted her uncle's illness was making him delusional. She waited until his restlessness stilled and knew he had fallen into a deep sleep, and then rose on stiff legs to seek her room for the night. Her uncle's faithful servant and friend met her concerned glance from where he sat across the room. "Go take your rest, milady, I will sit with my lord overnight."

"Thank you, Joseph. I know he draws great comfort from your presence."

She was aware of Raulf's men following her down the long, silent hall to her room. They held open the door; one of them entered ahead of her to make certain no unpleasant surprises awaited her there, and then bowing he retreated from the room. He gestured for her to enter and then pulled the door shut behind him. As exhausted as she was Elena did not immediately seek the escape of sleep. Instead she wandered over to gaze out on the view where the moon hung suspended above the surrounding mountains. In the reflected light of the glowing moon they brought visions of heaven to mind.

She always assumed she would live out her life in her uncle's kingdom. Calei was the only home she could recall. She had only the vaguest recollections of her parents and her former home. Now she knew she would soon set out to carve a new life for herself in whatever lands lay beyond the mountains, or she would die in the attempt. She would let fate decide whether it would be the former or the latter. Her decision made, a peace settled over her spirit, and she turned away from her uncertain future to rest in her soft bed, knowing such comforts would soon become a part of her past.

CHAPTER FOUR

Elena thought she must be dreaming, or perhaps she was trapped inside a nightmare, she swiftly corrected herself as her middle was slammed against a hard saddle and her head bounced against the side of what she would swear was a galloping horse. When she tried to move her hands to right herself, she realized they were bound together. She had no memory of being taken from her room. They must have drugged her while she slept, she concluded bitterly. She winced as she was once again slapped against the saddle with an audible thump. Her kidnappers must not have tied her very securely, she realized, as with each tortuous stride of her racing mount she felt the binding holding her in place loosen a bit more. She reasoned at any moment she would fly off the back of the galloping horse and land very painfully on the hard ground.

Despite her rage at the indignity of being stuffed into some kind of sack and being tied face down on a galloping horse, unlikely hope stirred within her heart. Her kidnappers had unknowingly done her a great service by aiding her plans for escape. Now if she could only get away from them, she could put her plans in motion. This certainly wasn't the way she envisioned leaving the city. The truth was even if she could separate herself from the evil men who took her, she would be alone in the mountains without food or drink.

Shaking off her dire fears, she forced herself to concentrate on the bright side of her predicament. She was on her way to her new life and every powerful stride of her mount's charging gait took her farther away from the fate she prayed constantly over the past weeks and months of her uncle's illness that she would be able to avoid.

Her burgeoning joy was short-lived as with the next stride, her racing mount broke his rhythmic stride and leapt across some barrier in its path, causing Elena to bounce hard against his back when he regained his footing, and then fly off into the air. Moments later she endured a painful impact, and then rolled down a steep incline, over stones and tree branches before coming up hard against the wide trunk of a mature tree bringing her uncomfortable flight to an ignominious halt.

"Ouch," she whispered behind the cloth that gagged her mouth, laying there stunned for a moment in the darkness of her burlap prison. Then the pain hit her, followed swiftly by panic. She did not do well in closed spaces and she began to struggle in earnest against the ties binding her wrists. She released a relieved sigh when she regained the use of her hands, then proceeded to reach up through the hole in the top of the bag in a frantic attempt to free herself.

True panic set in when she realized the rope binding the sack closed was much thicker and secured a lot tighter than the restraint on her hands. She knew it would be more helpful for her to remain calm, but she couldn't seem to stop her breaths from coming more and more quickly between her parted lips until she recognized she was in danger of losing consciousness.

"Stop wriggling and I will free you."

The insistent command issued in an impatient, and somewhat amused male voice, froze her in place. Tears stung her eyes. How could they have found her so quickly? She hadn't heard any indication of their approach down the steep incline. Probably because she was so busy with her frantic attempt to escape from her cloth prison.

In an instant, the stranger cut through the rope and freed her. A deep breath calmed her panicked struggle for air, and then she turned a fearful glance in the direction of her rescuer, praying she would not recognize him as one of Raulf's men. The stranger's booted feet were not reminiscent of the heavy boots the soldiers of Calei wore. Nor were the leather breeches that clung to his muscular legs. Hope growing in her breast, Elena slowly ran her gaze up the stranger's long, lithe form, passed his broad chest to his young and handsome face, until she finally met the amusement in his stunning blue eyes. Her lips curved in a relieved smile. He was not one of Raulf's men. She was certain of that. In fact, she was quite certain she'd never seen him before in her life. Despite her youth and inexperience, she instinctively grasped that no woman could ever forget the stranger's face or his incredible eyes.

Michel was having his own struggles recovering from his astonishment at the turn his morning scouting ride had taken. He drew in a sharp breath at the hesitant expression in the feminine eyes raised to his. They belonged to the unexpected bounty that rolled down the hill and literally landed at his feet. At first he assumed the squirming sack contained the stolen prey of some unlucky poacher. When he drew closer to investigate, he heard the furious, oddly smothered muttering of its feminine captive and quickly moved to free her.

When she burst free of her confinement his initial impression was that of a young girl with a tangled mass of dark, sable-colored hair streaming down her back. Then she raised her frightened, soft brown eyes to his and sat at his feet regarding him with dawning, impossible hope filling her gaze, as if he was some god sent to rescue her from the evil pursuing her, and he recognized immediately his plans for the day were completely overset.

Cursing himself for his inability to walk away

from the situation he frowned down upon this latest source of distraction to his carefully thought out plans, none of which he was quite certain, included a doe-eyed innocent looking to him to rescue her from whoever tied her up in a burlap sack.

That the child was in need of rescuing was increasingly clear. She was clad in nothing but a thin sleeping gown. Seeing her shiver in the cold air of a new dawn, Michel quickly removed his rich, fur-lined cloak to wrap her in it and then assisted her to her feet. He noted her ankles were bound together and he swiftly bent to free them, and then released her mouth from the gag meant to ensure her silence.

"Thank you."

He nodded in response to the girl's shy offering of gratitude even as he wondered what in the name of all that was holy he was going to do with her. "You're safe now. I won't hurt you."

"Who are you? I can see you are not one of Baron's Raulf's minions."

By the cultured, educated tones of her voice, and the rather arrogant way she referred to the offending baron, Michel concluded she was no servant. Another uncomfortable conclusion followed fast on the heels of the first. The girl might be young, but from the way the fullness of her feminine breasts pressed against the thin material of her night gown, visible beneath the opening where his cloak rested around her shoulders, he realized she was no child.

The situation was growing more complicated by the moment. With a single, discerning glance, he took in her refined features, the rather haughty tilt of her chin, and the directness of her gaze and decided she was likely a daughter of one of the city's noble families. How in the world she managed to get herself tied up in a sack on the back of a galloping horse was probably not an answer he really wished her to share with him.

No it would be better for the success of his plans to extricate himself from the maid's misfortune at the earliest opportunity, before she discovered any more about him, and about the army of men waiting to attack her home hidden in the woods atop the mountain. But before he made a decision about how to go about extricating himself he needed to know what exactly, or who more likely, he was up against. "Who is Baron Raulf?"

Her eyes widened in astonished wonder at his query. "You do not know Baron Raulf? You must be a stranger to the city then."

"Yes, we have only just arrived. We are visitors to your fair kingdom," he replied, nodding to where Amele observed their exchange from a few feet away.

"I suggest you turn around then," she immediately instructed him, after nodding politely in Amele's direction, then added in a hopeful voice, "And if it would not be too much trouble, perhaps you would take me with you."

"And why would we do that?" Surprisingly, Michel found himself not indisposed to prolonging their conversation. He justified the obvious sign of weakness on his part by reminding himself that the long days and nights he'd spent in the company of his men these past months made him more susceptible than usual to her shy femininity and soft voice.

"Because you would be rescuing me from a fate worse than death."

Michel's lips curved at her dramatic announcement and he queried curiously, "Might I assume Baron Raulf is somehow involved in this dreadful fate you speak of?"

"Yes, he intends to marry me."

Michel turned in the direction of his silent, equally amused, companion. "Ah, Amele we have captured a runaway bride."

"I am not a bride and I have no intention of becoming one."

Michel grinned outright at the maid's assured declaration, thinking how often he'd been the recipient of the same dramatic vow uttered from between his twin's lips. In the end Melissa had been unable to avoid her Norman husband, despite her not inconsiderable efforts to do so. "Well, you appear a bit young to wed. Perhaps you can convince your father to change his mind about this betrothal to Baron Raulf."

"My father is dead and there is no betrothal.

He kidnapped me and thought to…"

"Thought to?" Michel couldn't resist his teasing when words failed the maid and a fierce blush stained her cheeks. He immediately regretted his banter because the girl's blush only deepened and she bowed her head in shame.

When she continued it was in a hushed voice he had to strain to hear, "He was going to force me…you know…then I would have no choice but to marry him. But I wouldn't have…even if he…" she couldn't bring herself to utter the foul word.

"Even if he raped you?" Michel supplied for her, his jaw clenching at the foul picture the girl drew for him. Despite the evidence her appealing, feminine curves presented to the contrary it was obvious the maid was still a child and certainly much too young to know about such obscenities let alone be forced to confront her very real fear of falling victim to them.

She nodded, her soft eyes filling with unshed tears. "Yes. I won't marry him. I'm not going back. I'm never going back."

"Is there someone you can stay with who would protect you from this Baron Raulf?" He asked, concerned enough at the fate she outlined to bestir himself on her behalf.

"No," she admitted forlornly, and then raised a hopeful, expectant glance to his face. "Do you know anyone I can stay with?"

Michel evaded her question with one of his own. "If your father is dead, who do you live with?"

"My uncle."

"Surely he would not force you to marry the baron against your wishes."

"No, but he won't be able to stop the baron from taking what he wants after he's dead."

"Your uncle is dying, too?"

"Too?"

"You said your father was dead," he reminded her.

She nodded. "My parents died when I was a little girl. I was sent to live with my uncle."

"The uncle who is dying?"

"Yes, he's the only uncle I have."

Michel suppressed the urge to smile at the girl's desolate confession. "What about your uncle's wife?"

She shook her head and Michel was forced to conclude either her uncle didn't have a wife, or she would not be able to provide assistance to defend the girl against the baron's foul intentions. "Another family member perhaps?"

"I don't have any other family. When Uncle Barnabas dies I will be quite alone in the world."

"Uncle Barnabas?" Michel echoed stunned. He should have seen this coming, he realized. Then, as if in a belated warning, Michel felt a prickle of unease slither up his spine as he recalled the dying king's request of him. *'All I ask is that you not wed another until you have at least met my Elena.'* Well the deed was done, Michel concluded bitterly. He had met Barnabas' beloved Elena.

Michel was no believer in coincidences, but since he very much doubted Barnabas would put his niece in deadly danger on the off chance Michel might be around to rescue her; he was forced to conclude that fate elected to involve itself in his affairs and had taken matters into its own unpredictable hands. His mind still boggled at the consequences of the king's niece literally dropping out of the sky to land at his feet. Michel was distracted away from his musings by Elena's impudent response to his earlier question.

"Yes, my uncle is the king. Don't you know anything?"

Despite his unease at becoming further entangled in the untenable situation, Michel couldn't help but be amused by her autocratic tone. "Apparently not. So let me guess. Your name is Elena?"

"Yes. How did you know my name? Who are you?"

"My name is Michel and this is Amele. The king lives?"

"Yes, as of last night when I retired to my rooms, but I can no longer be certain. He is very ill. I think he will not live much longer. I suppose the baron grew tired of waiting for him to die. He must have instructed his men to kidnap me from my chamber while I slept. They drugged me and tied me in that dreadful sack."

The sound of approaching horses interrupted their discussion, this time coming from the opposite direction of their initial pass. It didn't take any great powers of reasoning to deduct the girl's abductors must have realized they lost their captive and were returning to look for her.

Elena turned tearful, terrified eyes in Michel's direction. "You won't let them take me, will you?"

Her fear was his undoing. Both cursing the restlessness that drove him out of the camp to scout the surrounding area that morning, and the dying king's premonition he would be unable to turn his back on his defenseless niece, Michel reached out and grabbed his soon-to-be ward's small hand and began pulling her behind him to where the horses waited at a break in the trees.

A brilliant smile bloomed on his companion's lovely young face when Michel led her to where Arden grazed. She stood quite willingly in his grasp as he lifted her up and settled her on Arden's back, then mounted behind her, wrapping one arm loosely around her slender form to keep her from falling. The fact she did not pester him with questions as to where he was taking her forced him to acknowledge Elena concluded accompanying a stranger to an unknown destination was preferable to the one she feared Raulf would lead her to.

The realization brought home to Michel just how much Elena feared the mysterious Baron

Raulf. Michel decided he would have to do something about the baron. He could not have one of his nobleman kidnapping young ladies from their beds. His mood lightened in anticipation of doing so. The coming war for control of Calei would no doubt provide him with ample opportunity to carve the traitorous baron's heart from his chest.

Though Elena maintained her wary silence, he could feel her tension in the way she held herself stiffly in the saddle in front of him, as if not entirely certain the direction he would take would be away from the men who sought her. It wasn't until he turned Arden in the opposite direction, back towards the cover of the trees, that he heard Elena's relieved sigh and felt her relax against him. As Arden's swift and sure gait increased the distance between them and her would-be pursuers, Elena turned into his arms, wrapped her own around his waist and rested her head against his chest in a gesture of innocent faith he found unnerving. Within moments, she was sound asleep.

Sighing with annoyance at the way his body was reacting to having her softness cuddled close against him, and reminding himself the maid was little more than the child he had at first assumed she was, he adjusted his cloak more closely around her back to protect her from the cold, and then directed Arden back to the camp where his men awaited their return.

Dawn was giving way to early morning when they rode into camp. Barnabas' precious treasure slept blissfully in the warmth of Michel's arms until the sudden halt to the rocking motion of Arden's even steps woke her. Elena could not suppress her gasp of surprise when she took in the number of men and horses in their midst. Their tents covered half the mountain. Michel raised an inquiring brow when she stared up at him with wide, curious eyes, but she only shook her head in response, obviously concluding it was best for her chances to remain among them if she refrained from giving voice to the questions he could see swirling in her gaze.

His squire hurried to take charge of Arden, and Michel waited while Amele dismounted, then helped Elena to find her feet. Michel dropped down beside her and motioned for one of his men to join them. "Take care of our guest. I imagine she would appreciate breakfast." Elena raised fearful eyes to his when she realized he meant to leave her. "It's all right. You're safe here. No one will hurt you."

Nodding uncertainly, she allowed the soldier to lead her away from his side, but Michel noticed she kept glancing back over her shoulder in his direction as if to assure herself he wasn't going to disappear on her. Sensing her anxiety, Michel sent an encouraging nod in her direction, and then he and Amele set off together across the camp towards his tent.

While the two men waited for the others to join them Michel enjoyed the food prepared for his return. The leaders from Calei still loyal to the blood of the true king, as well as Michel's own commanders, soon gathered in the tent, filling the confined space with excited, masculine voices. Michel waited in silence, allowing their comments and exchanges to roll over him as he ate.

Between them, they debated the unexpected bounty of having the king's niece in their midst and what use her presence could best be put to in order to further their aims. After he took the measure of each man's stance on the subject, he effectively called a halt to their fleeting proposals about Elena's use to them with his blunt pronouncement.

"We're sending her back to her uncle."

"But, my prince, the maid could prove a valuable bargaining chip for our cause," one of the Caleinians pointed out.

"A child is not a bargaining chip," he rebuked sharply.

The man accepted Michel's reprimand without affront, but that did not stop him from pointing out the obvious. "As you command, my prince, but even if we do send the child back there is no way for us to prevent the culprit from simply spiriting her off a second time. If the king's guard has been penetrated there is no guarantee Lady Elena will be safe in the palace."

Michel nodded, aware the man spoke the truth,

but he was reluctant to deprive the gentle king of his niece's presence in what would likely prove his final hours. He was still puzzling over how to ensure the maid's safety when the opening of the tent was suddenly thrust aside and the topic of their discussion stood framed in the center of it.

His lips curved in an amused smile at her disheveled appearance, still wrapped in his overly large cloak, and with her tangled hair trailing behind her. There was an indignant expression on her face as her gaze hurriedly searched the tent for his presence. Her indignation didn't lessen any when their glances met, but Michel sensed her relief at seeing him again.

An astonished silence fell over the gathering as everyone turned to see the identity of the intruder who would dare to interrupt their conference without invitation. Michel's glance met Elena's suddenly uncertain one, but he couldn't help but be impressed by the way she stood her ground beneath so much disapproving, male scrutiny. "You're not sending me back to the city."

Michel suppressed his amusement at her command and raised his brows in response to her fierce declaration. "We're not?"

Elena's lovely face flooded with color at his mild reply and she quickly dropped her gaze from the challenge in his, becoming belatedly aware of their interested audience. Her response to his challenge was offered in an embarrassed voice in the direction of her feet. Michel missed her muttered response. "I'm sorry, what did you say?"

A fresh blush stained her cheeks when she raised her glance to his. "I said I'm not a child."

He let his eyes roam over her as if testing the truth of her assertion. He was more comfortable with his need to protect her when he could safely tuck her away into the category of a child in need of rescuing. But reminded of her uncle's wish that he marry his precious Elena, Michel reluctantly acknowledged there was more to her effect on him than the uncomplicated excuse he previously thought to employ that his honor demanded he keep his vow to her dying uncle to protect his niece.

He was drawn to her, Michel conceded, the way a man is attracted to a woman's beauty. Certainly she didn't lack a woman's feminine charms. He had not been unmindful of the fullness of her breasts when she slept in his arms or of her enticing womanly fragrance that clung to her even after a hard ride in a filthy sack tied to the back of a horse.

Such an attraction was an inconvenience he could ill afford at this stage of his plans. What was he supposed to do? Attack the city with the king's niece riding to war at his side as one of their company? He could hardly leave her behind in the wilderness to fend for herself and he was loath to assign a guard to remain with her. The majority of the men who rode beneath his banner had waited their entire lives to take back their homeland. He would not deprive them of their moment. No. It would be best for all concerned if he could find a family in Calei willing to take the maid in and keep her safe until the question of the kingship was resolved. Once peace had been restored, he could assume his role of guardian of the girl and let her grow up a little before becoming some other man's wife.

Satisfied with his reasoning Michel turned his attention in the direction of their uninvited guest and sought to inform her of his decision in regards to her immediate future. He noticed the way Elena was blushing beneath his intent regard and realized without the least bit of enthusiasm on his part that the budding attraction between them was not purely one-sided. Things were getting more complicated by the moment. He silently cursed the dying king even as he responded to the challenge in his niece's intent gaze. "As you wish," he replied in a somewhat belated manner to her claim she was not a child, and then indicated with a nod towards the opening in the tent she should leave him and his men alone to continue their important discussion.

Ignoring his silent command, Elena instead peered curiously around the tent and at its occupants. Michel concluded from her surprised gasp that she recognized some of the men gathered there. She turned back to him and demanded imperiously. "Who are you?"

At the directness of her challenge, beneath the heavy weight of masculine outrage filling the tent, Michel was reminded once again of his twin. Smiling at the memory, but unwilling to satisfy her curiosity, Michel replied, "I am not in league with your kidnappers, and that is all that need concern you at the moment."

"They called you 'my prince'."

When her rescuer simply shrugged in response to her pointed reminder, Elena was forced to come to her own conclusions about his identity. Her first impression that he was a stranger simply passing through the mountain trails on his way to another, undisclosed destination was obviously incorrect. One did not travel with an army trailing after him for a simple trespass through the mountains.

She examined the faces of each of the men regarding her silently and with more than a hint of umbrage at her disruption of their important conference. Many of the men she recognized to be members of ancient Caleinian families, some of them nobleman in their own right. Yet none challenged the royal greeting this stranger was given. She also noted that though he was the youngest among them, they appeared to accept without question the stranger's authority over them. Comprehension was slow to dawn, but when it did, she almost tripped over her own astonishment. She turned accusing eyes in Michel's direction and exclaimed in an awed voice. "You're one of them."

"One of them?" Michel echoed innocently.

"One of the grandsons. My uncle explained that he was not the true king and how he sent emissaries to your family in Europe seeking the return of one of the true heirs to the throne. You're one of them. You're one of the grandsons, aren't you? Why do you not enter the city? My uncle would be overjoyed and so relieved to welcome you."

"It is not that easy," Michel replied, evasively, to Elena's way of thinking.

"Why not?"

"Your uncle is no longer in control of the city."

Puzzled by his conclusion, Elena contended, "That's ridiculous. He is the king."

"Whose niece was kidnapped from her own bed, in his home, and while under his guard," Michel spelled out for her. While Elena was still puzzling through the repercussions of his statement, he added pointedly, "If we enter the city now, they will kill your uncle."

"They will kill him regardless," Elena's voice broke on her bitter retort.

"Yes," Michel agreed, holding her tearful glance, "but I would rather not have his death on my hands."

"Please don't send me back. You know what they will to do to me."

Sensing, despite her desperate pleading, he

was still undecided as to the matter of her fate, Elena hurried across the distance separating them and flung herself on her knees at his feet. She clasped his hands in her own smaller ones and lifted tear-filled eyes to his. “Please don’t send me back. I beg of you. I will not be in your way here. I can be useful. Put me to work. I do not know how to hunt or cook, but your men could teach me. I can fetch clean water from the stream and help tend the horses.”

Michel stared down into her dusk colored eyes and knew he was lost. He met Amele’s amused if resigned glance over the maid’s head, before bending down to assist Elena to her feet. “You may stay.”

She let go of his hands and raised them to her face to cover her mouth. He watched the relief flood her eyes and could only wonder at her terror of the past months, knowing her uncle would soon die and leave her completely at the mercy of the wolves that fought for the throne.

“You may have this tent. Do not leave the camp without an escort.” She nodded, as if unable to trust herself to speak the gratitude he saw shining in her eyes. Michel cuffed her chin in an affectionate gesture as if she was one of his sisters and turned and motioned to the others that they would continue discussing their plans elsewhere.

Michel was the last to file out of his now former tent. He glanced back in time to see Elena fall to her knees, her relief at her narrow escape obviously overcoming her ability to remain upright. He watched her succumb to the deep sobs that wracked her slender frame, her back to the entrance to the tent, no doubt assuming she was safely alone to indulge in her emotional display. When he would have returned to comfort her, Amele's hand on his arm stopped him and drew him away from the entrance.

"You have done enough, my prince. Leave the maid to her tears. She would be embarrassed by your pity."

Michel reluctantly nodded his agreement and allowed himself to be led away from the sounds of the weeping girl.

They resumed their discussion about the dilemma of what to do with their young guest in another tent hastily prepared for their use.

One of the Caleinian noblemen gave his opinion of Elena's circumstances in scathing tones. "She must have been kidnapped in her sleep from the castle. I do not hesitate to lay the dastardly deed at Baron Raulf's door. It is obvious he means to force the lady into a hasty marriage to ensure he will ascend to the throne upon the death of the king."

"But why force matters? The king is near death, is he not?" Michel countered.

"Yes, or so it is rumored in the city. But there are others besides Raulf who will contend for the throne. If Lady Elena preferred one of the other challengers as her husband it would present a big obstacle to Raulf's plans for a seamless coup."

"The girl is too young to wed." Michel was adamant in his conviction. Why he doubted Elena was even his sister Rhiann's age, and she was barely six and ten when she was forced to wed the new lord of their father's estates.

"Under normal circumstances that is true, but the circumstances are hardly normal, and the child is close enough to maturity that there is every expectation she will wed the future king, sooner rather than later."

"As long as the king lives, she cannot be legally wed without his consent," Michel persisted.

"True enough, but once the deed is done and the marriage consummated who is going to contest its legality?"

Michel shoved a frustrated hand through his shoulder length hair. "So what do you suggest we do with her?"

CHAPTER FIVE

A week following their guest's arrival Michel rose before dawn and sought the privacy of a nearby stream to bathe. He was not eager to rise at such an hour, particularly when he would spend the remainder of the day cooling his heels while he waited word of the king's death. It was not his original plan to skulk around the outskirts of his grandfather's kingdom in such a ridiculous manner. He had assumed he and his army of skilled soldiers would storm down on the city's unsuspecting defenders as soon as they were within reach of the city, but all of his half-formulated plans changed when he met King Barnabas.

His honor now prevented him from taking his birthright from the man who had watched over it in his stead in the guise of his faithful steward. No, he would not have the king's final hours disturbed by the heinous cries of war and worry over his people's welfare.

As he passed through the entrance of his tent, Michel noted most of his men still slept around the now slumbering fires. He nodded in the direction of the guards posted nearby, and followed the path towards the stream from which he and his companions and horses drew their fresh water each day. His men were not obliged to rise at such an early hour because they did not share in Michel's burden.

Since Elena's arrival at their camp, Michel had acquired a second shadow from the moment of his rising until he sought the privacy of his tent in the late evening hours. The maid followed him around wherever he went. Even when he was out of her sight, she seemed to have a sixth sense as to his movements. She sat nearby as silent as the shadow she brought to mind when he trained with his men. When he rode off towards the city to take the measure of its defenses, she followed in his wake, her watchful eyes always on his face. Such was her devotion to him it had become a source of amusement to his men. Even Amele wondered at his patience with the king's young niece.

For his part, Michel took her silent presence in stride. From the time he was a boy, he was used to having his twin trailing after him, pestering him with questions or giving him the benefit of one of her outrageous opinions. He found Elena's silent company a pleasant contrast to Melissa's constant boasts and competitive nature, but he drew the line at having her tagging along when he bathed. Amele jokingly suggested he allow her to accompany him on one of his early morning excursions. Their young guest would likely be so shocked by the view afforded her she would scurry back to her solitary tent and think twice before pestering him again. Michel had laughed at Amele's cajolery but merely shook his head denying his helpful suggestion and continued with his very early morning trips to the stream.

Upon reaching the water, Michel shed his clothes and stepped into the icy stream, accepting the resulting discomfort as just one more test of his will. He ducked his head beneath the surface and scrubbed his shoulder length hair and bearded face. He ran his fingers across it and decided he would not be sorry to rid himself of the thick growth of facial hair, but for now he would leave it unshaven. He had more pressing matters on his mind than the scruffiness of his beard.

He dipped his head again and then irritated to find the thin silver chain he wore around his neck tangled in his hair, he pulled on the chain to free it. The stone seemed intent on making its presence known to him at every possible moment. Michel wasn't certain how he could forget it, as he'd been forced to free both his hair and his beard from the chain's restraint innumerable times since becoming the stone's reluctant guardian.

A muttered curse escaped his lips as the thin silver strand only entwined itself more fully in his wet hair the more he attempted to free it. Fresh annoyance lent added strength to his impatient yank on the restraining chain. His frustration quickly dissolved into stunned horror as Michel watched the source of his irritation fly high into the air and land with a loud plop in the rushing stream a dozen yards or more from where he stood shivering in the icy water.

Michel cursed louder at this latest disaster and set off in desperate pursuit of the stone he'd moments earlier been doing his best to free himself from. It wasn't a particular fondness for the ancient amulet that sent him racing down the stream. It was the realization his twin would cut off his own male jewels with the dagger he made a gift to her of if he lost her precious inheritance. He didn't even want to conjure his grandmother's reaction when he revealed to her he had managed to lose an heirloom of her house that had been in her family for over a thousand years.

In the shadows beneath the thick branches lining the path to the stream, Elena watched with wide eyes as her rescuer set off with a resounding splash after the strange, blue stone he wore around his neck. Her lips twitched as she witnessed his mad dash down the stream in a race against the swift current carrying his prize away faster than he could keep up with. A giggle emerged at the memory of his panicked expression when the stone had flown high into the air and then entered the water. She wondered if the stone was a keepsake given him by a lady admirer. If so, she was glad of its loss.

Her eyes went dreamy as she indulged in her pleasant fantasies. If Prince Michel was to be the new king, then he was supposed to marry her, not whoever made a gift to him of the stone. She found the prospect much more to her liking than that of becoming Baron's Raulf's reluctant bride. She'd made a point to keep an eye on her future husband so he didn't disappear as suddenly and unexpectedly as he entered her life. If he decided he didn't care to be king, and who could really blame him given the curse accompanying such a life, she was determined on one thing. Prince Michel saved her when he rescued her from her kidnappers. Her life belonged to him now. She was never going back to the city, at least not without him.

Elena turned away from her hiding place and set off in the direction of the camp. Prince Michel might not know it yet, but his former life was slipping away as surely as the odd stone he wore on a woman's slender chain around his neck. Whoever had given him the token was part of his past and no longer had any place in his present. No, as far as Elena was concerned, she was the young prince's present…and his future.

She blushed at the memory of what that future might hold for her. She had never seen a naked man before and she barely managed to swallow her surprised gasp where she hid in the thick growth of trees along the river bank when the prince removed his clothes and the new sun streaked over his naked form as he slid into the icy water. His unscarred, bronze skin stretched tight across his broad shoulders and framed the thick rope of muscles in his arms and chest. His thighs and legs were equally muscular and even his backside was the same bronze color as the rest of him.

Her face had heated up to a fiery blush, and her breath caught in her throat when he shifted his position and stepped sideways into the rushing stream. For a brief moment she caught sight of his stirring manhood resting between his thighs. She was not so innocent she was unaware of how a man mated with a woman. The prospect of such a joining filled her with terror when she thought of Baron Raulf thrusting his manhood into her untried flesh, but she could not summon any of her previous horror at the thought of sharing such intimacies with Prince Michel. No, far from fear, she felt a strange thrill of anticipation coursing through her, leaving her breathless when she dreamt about the young prince's rough hands on her.

CHAPTER SIX

After long hours spent searching for his sister's lost inheritance, Michel returned to camp wet, bedraggled and in a foul mood. He'd chased the damn stone a mile down the stream before he admitted it was gone, likely forever. His mind boggled at the thought of its loss. He was not a particularly superstitious man but the loss of the Salusian stone at this critical juncture of his long quest could hardly be taken as a fortuitous sign by even the most optimistic of souls. He passed by his men standing around the morning fires and couldn't blame them for their amusement they hastily hid at his condition.

Amele left him to his temper long enough for Michel to change into dry clothes and then begged entrance to his tent with a tray of food to break his fast. Michel had instructed the older man to leave such menial tasks to his young squire, but Amele simply ignored his numerous requests and continued to serve him as if he was already sitting on his homeland's ancient throne.

Michel gratefully accepted the tray from his hands then motioned for Amele to sit and join him on the cushions in the center of the tent while he ate. Michel didn't volunteer the information that he'd lost the stone, understanding Amele would feel its loss almost as much as he did, but for different reasons. While Michel's regret centered on the prospect of having to confide his carelessness to his sister and grandmother, Amele was fully convinced of the legends surrounding the stone's mysterious power. He could not comprehend why his grandmother's fierce protector could be persuaded by such foolishness, but he was soon forced to admit his own foreboding over the heirloom's loss was not completely without merit.

"The king is dead," Amele announced into the silence.

"What? Are you certain?" Even though he'd been expecting the news for several days now, Michel was shocked by his friend's blunt announcement.

"Yes, the bells tolled at dawn and his colors have been removed from the castle's parapets."

"Your countrymen don't waste any time, do they?" Michel remarked drily.

"Our countrymen," Amele corrected sharply.

Michel's quick grin flashed, and then he sighed at the thought of Elena's grief at the news of her uncle's death. He regretted the illness that struck down King Barnabas in his prime and decided they would allow the city its grief before setting their plans in motion.

"We will wait until after the king has been laid

to rest before proceeding with our plans," Michel announced and then at Amele's surprised, admiring nod of agreement, Michel added, "Where's Elena?"

"Still in her tent, I believe."

"Has she been told?"

"No. I thought you would like to be the one to inform her of her uncle's death."

"It is not a duty I relish, but yes, I think the news should come from me."

Since she was never far from his side it took Michel only a few moments to locate Elena, where she sat waiting for him near the entrance to his tent. She looked up surprised when he stopped in front of her.

"Come walk with me," he invited and assisted her to her feet.

Fear immediately entered her eyes at his unusual demand. She gripped his hand in an effort to get him to slow down and looked up at him wide-eyed. "Is something wrong? Are you going to send me back?"

Michel slowed his pace and stared down at her upturned face. "No, I'm not going to send you back. You may stop asking me if that is my intent whenever I seek you out."

"Then why did you want me to walk with you? And you never seek me out," she tacked on, disputing his assertion.

He waited to reply to her query until they passed through the shadow of the surrounding trees in order to provide her a measure of privacy for her grief at the news he was to deliver. He stopped just inside the tree line and turned to face her, his hands reaching out to grip her shoulders, "I'm sorry Elena, but your uncle died last night."

Puzzled by her lack of reaction, Michel wondered if perhaps she hadn't heard him. The maid had an annoying habit of day-dreaming in his presence so he was often forced to repeat his remarks to her. He was loath to be forced to repeat the news he'd just delivered, however. "Elena?"

"Yes?" she whispered.

"Did you hear what I said?"

"Uncle Barnabas is dead," she repeated dutifully.

"Yes."

"What will happen to me now?" she asked dazed, unaware seemingly of the tears streaming down her cheeks.

Sighing at her obvious distress, Michel pulled her into the comfort of his arms. She burrowed close against his chest and wrapped her slender arms around his waist and gave into the sobs that shook her slight frame. Long minutes later, after the storm had passed he continued to stroke her silky hair in a gesture of comfort and reassurance while she rested her cheek against his chest and drew deep, broken breaths, with the occasional hiccup thrown in.

"Will I be allowed to offer my farewell to my

uncle?" she asked softly.

"Yes, I will arrange for you to attend the funeral," he promised her.

"Will you come with me?" she asked, still avoiding meeting his glance by keeping her cheek resting against his chest.

"Yes."

Her voice dipped lower until it was only a hushed whisper that escaped her lips when she asked him fearfully, "Are you going to let him keep me?"

Michel was forced to bend his head in order to hear her. "No, I'm not going to let the baron keep you. Your uncle placed you in my care upon his death. You are my responsibility now. I won't let anyone hurt you."

She lifted her head to meet his glance, her eyes probing his to discern the truth of his words, and whether or not she could rely on his promise. "If you leave here, will you take me with you?"

"You would leave your home?" he asked surprised.

"Yes, you are my home now. I do not wish to stay where you are not."

Michel was stunned by Elena's solemn declaration. She was too young of course to know of what she spoke. She was still a child whose only family had just died leaving her completely alone in the world. It was perfectly natural for her to want to cling to him. She'd grown accustomed to him in the time they'd spent together but when her grief passed he was quite certain she would think differently about things. He had no home. He'd spent his life traveling from one place to another, his restless spirit never finding ease in any single place. Whether Calei would prove anymore of a home to him than his Saxon father's magnificent estate he could not be certain.

"My life is not a gentle one, Elena, nor one you would find to your liking." He thought it only fair to warn her. He knew she was attracted to him and that she considered herself half-betrothed to him. The fact he rescued her from the grip of evil men and had kept her safe and warm and well-fed in the interim no doubt clouded her innocent feelings towards him. She was too young to distinguish her feelings of gratitude from those of the love a woman feels for a man. Surely there was a nobleman's son in Calei she would find an acceptable husband when the time came. Until then he would continue to keep her safe from the Raulfs of the world. At the very least, he owed her uncle that much.

"I am not a child," As if sensing the direction of his thoughts, Elena repeated her earlier fierce declaration. Drawn from his distracted musings, Michel's lips curved in an amused smile.

"As you wish," he echoed his own answer from their earlier exchange, and his grin widened at Elena's obvious frustration at his mocking dismissal of her claim. As much to silence the budding argument he could see brewing in her expressive eyes as to appease her, he bent his head to lightly brush his lips across hers. When she made no move to evade him, but simply stood close within the circle of his arms, her lovely face upraised and her serious glance clinging to his, Michel contrarily elected to accept the challenge she threw at him. His hold tightened around her and he folded her soft womanly form closer against his chest, dipping his head to breath in her feminine scent until his senses were swimming in it.

Cursing himself for his stupidity in starting something he was in no position to finish, he rebuked his body's ready response to the maid's alluring femininity. This was hardly the time for him to allow his masculine lust to direct his course. For a moment his will tried to force his passion into compliance, but for once his body was successfully resisting his will's restraint. The maid declared she was not a child.

Perhaps it was time to put her claim to the test. He had done his best to ignore the brewing attraction between them. He had acted the part of an honorable guardian around his young ward, but how was he supposed to continue to ignore Elena when she followed him around twenty four hours a day, with those serious eyes of hers following his every move, and regarding him as if he was the center of her young life?

Michel took his time, giving Elena every opportunity to back away from the consequences of the gauntlet she threw at his feet. When he bent his head to claim her lips in a kiss far different than the innocent exchange they previously shared, she didn't back away, though he was quite certain she read his intent in his eyes. If anything, she leaned closer into his embrace until her soft breasts were pressed against him, arousing his manly passions to an even greater degree as he was uncomfortably reminded of his long abstinence.

The maid he held was the innocent. He was the experienced one, but afterwards when he thought back on their first taste of shared passion, he would swear he had been the one who was seduced by her alluring femininity and not the other way around. It should have been Elena's thoughts that swam with the heady promise of newly ignited desire. It should have been Elena who lost all sense of where they stood just inside the line of trees shielding them from the curious eyes of his men.

But it was he who stumbled beneath her intoxicating mixture of innocence and allure. He who grew so disoriented by the taste of her, by the eagerness with which she offered herself to him, that he temporarily lost the will to maintain a safe distance between curiosity and true passion. For a moment, Michel allowed himself to surrender to the lust she roused in him.

He ravaged her soft lips, taking what she so willingly tendered, unaware in her innocence of the jeopardy she courted. Unable to resist such rich offering after long months of fasting, Michel drew her ever closer against his hard frame until he knew she must be aware of his straining manhood perched at the entrance of her woman's heat, with only a few layers of thin cloth and his quickly faltering control shielding her virginity from him.

Finally, after being forced to wage a fierce battle to regain his control, Michel drew back, framing Elena's flushed face with his hands. Slowly she lifted heavy lids over glazed, languorous eyes. "Don't stop," she whispered, turning her face in his hands until her lips brushed his calloused palm, and her tongue trailed over his hard flesh.

He should set her apart from him, Michel reasoned, even as his body urged him on, advocating for him to take what the maid was so innocently offering him. His mind pushed back against his body's urging. He could not allow his thoughts to become clouded by passion. He had a war to fight, a throne to win. How had the very near child he held managed to do to him what no other woman before her ever had…to lure him to the brink of temptation, to turn his back on his hard-won control over his passions? And she a young innocent with no comprehension of the danger she courted.

As if sensing the silent conflict raging within him, Elena took matters into her own hands. She brushed aside the constraint of his hands on her face that held her apart from him and wrapped her slender arms around his neck, drawing him back down to her, parting her lips as theirs met to trace his bottom lip with her tongue as he taught her. When he drew in a sharp breath at her boldness, her tongue slipped inside his mouth, to taste, to tantalize, to duel with his, and he was lost. Michel tugged Elena's clinging form deeper into the forest, all the while his lips clung to hers, their tongues dueling, mating, until on a sigh of surrender, she leaned her head back and let him simply take whatever he sought from her.

He knew he should be mindful of her innocence. He should draw back, set his young ward away from his embrace, but he was a man who'd been constantly surrounded by her femininity in almost every waking moment since he freed her from that ridiculous sack. She'd followed him around with those dusky, doe's eyes always on him, wondering, curious, needy, eager for his attention, desperate for his strength to shield from the evils besetting her. He thought he was immune to her constant, silent presence, but at night his dreams betrayed him. More than once he'd woken in his tent fully aroused, with her name on his lips, and the memory of her eyes on him, the invitation he read in hers not solely a product of dreams fueled by manly fantasies.

She'd seduced him in her innocence until she somehow managed to take up residence in his heart without him even being aware of his defenses being penetrated. Discovering he was not as immune to her feminine appeal as he previously convinced himself he was, did not sit well with him. He was angry enough by the ease with which she ingratiated herself into his life, without any encouragement on his part, to take his frustration out on her now.

So against his rational urging to the contrary, he allowed himself to feast on her young flesh, intent on sating himself, resolved to satisfy his curiosity and then free himself from her shimmering magic she wove so skillfully around him. His lips trailed over her soft skin, across her closed eyes, along the line of her fragile jaw, down the long column of her throat, tasting, arousing, both the seducer and the seduced. When his hand reached up to cup her soft breast through her thin gown, he gloried in the telling moan that escaped her parted lips. His thumb brushed across Elena's erect nipple and she moaned again, staring up at him with heavy, dazed eyes.

"Show me, teach me to please you," she begged him, and Michel was forced to close his eyes against the promise he read in hers, lest the temptation become too much for him to withstand. Elena's eagerness to please him, to be with him, only drew him deeper within the circle of her bewitching innocence.

Feeling his control slipping through his mind's slackening grip and into his aching loins, Michel gathered himself with an effort and removed his hand from the temptation of her softness.

"No," she protested tearfully, and when she would have reached for his hand to replace it on her aching breast, he captured it within his gentle grasp and raised it to his lips.

"This is not the time for us to give reign to the attraction between us. Your uncle is dead. I will not take advantage of your very near grief and your maidenly innocence. When you give yourself to me, Elena, it will not be with the pain of loss and the fear of being alone clouding your thoughts and influencing your surrender."

"My thoughts are not clouded," she denied, and then at the challenge in his gaze steadily holding hers, she added in a burst of honesty, "at least not by grief or fear. But I can see your attention is once again far from me and these precious moments between us. When I give myself to you, Michel, it will not be with the weight of your responsibilities distracting you from our coming together as a man and woman."

He nodded, his eyes filled with new admiration as they acknowledged the answering challenge in her words and her direct gaze maintaining contact with his. He could see the evidence of how much her little burst of bravado cost her. Such was the fierceness of her blush, her pale cheeks appeared as if she'd spent too much time beneath a summer sun, but still he was impressed when she didn't lower her gaze from his even as he stroked his knuckles across the smooth, flaming color.

Sighing with reluctance, Michel set her away from him and waited impatiently, clamping down on the urge to draw her back into his suddenly bereft arms, while she clumsily steadied herself and set her gown and hair to rights. When he would have led her back to the camp, Elena tugged on his hand and he raised an enquiring brow in her direction.

"With your permission, lord, I would like a few minutes to be alone with my grief. I would sit by the river bank for a while and offer my prayers for God's blessing on my uncle that he may be granted peace and eternal rest, and speedy passage through his sojourn in purgatory so that he may enter into the promise of heaven." Sensing his uncertainty at the thought of leaving her alone, Elena added, "You may send a guard to keep an eye on me. I will not wander off. I will stay right there beneath the shadow of the tree with that large branch reaching over the river." She pointed to a spot not far away and Michel reluctantly nodded his permission.

He bent his head to brush his lips across hers and admonished her sternly. "I expect you to keep your word not to wander off and I will indeed send a guard, or perhaps two, to keep an eye on you."

She smiled at his gentle kiss and wonderingly lifted the fingertips of one hand to her lips as if she could capture his caress and keep it there.

Where the woman emerged just moments ago, the child was back in her place, her soft gaze clinging to his as if he was the embodiment of all her innocent, maidenly dreams. As he watched her walk away, Michel could feel himself being pulled inexorably deeper beneath the spell of Elena's bewitching purity, then shaking his head to clear his thoughts, he chided himself for his foolish thoughts. It had indeed been too long since he'd indulged in the company of a woman if he was suddenly finding himself bemused by a doe-eyed innocent who seemed to believe he hung the moon in the night sky.

CHAPTER SEVEN

Elena did a lot of sighing as she sat on the damp ground watching the swift current of the spring stream hurrying by. She wondered what its hurry was. Would its crisp, clear water not end up at the same destination regardless of whether it raced towards its journey's end or traveled at a more sedate pace? Did the same hold true for human beings? Had her life's course already been laid out in front of her and she had only to place her feet on the path and follow along? Was Prince Michel her destiny or only a young girl's daydream? And how was someone of her limited life experience to know the difference?

It was at times like these when she most missed her mother. Though her memories of her mother were but a hazy recollection of soft arms, a gentle manner and a lovely countenance, encased in those memories was the certainty that she had been loved. Uncle Barnabas did his best to replace both of her parents in her young life, but there was no denying he'd been woefully inadequate as a substitute for a mother's love. Elena felt certain if her mother was still alive, or even if her Uncle Barnabas had married and she had grown up with a woman's influence in her life, she would not now be so ignorant about the chaotic feelings Prince Michel roused in her.

At the reminder of her uncle, she tried to offer a sincere prayer for his eternal soul, but her thoughts were swirling inside her head and she couldn't concentrate on her petitions. Feeling guilty at her lack of focus, she promised herself and her uncle's gentle spirit, she would pray for him again when she was feeling more settled. She did not chastise herself too harshly, however, as even one of the lord's most devoted followers could not be expected to keep her thoughts straight in light of her first experience with a man's passion.

Those same feelings even now intruded on her thoughts and made her catch her breath as she relived those priceless moments of being held against Michel's strong chest and the feel of his lips pressed against hers. She'd been shocked when his head dipped to claim her lips and she realized he was going to kiss her. Somehow she'd known even as she tried to conceal her astonishment at his intention, that he was not going to kiss her the way a brother kissed a younger sister or perhaps a young, and somewhat irritating cousin, but as a man kissed a woman he desired.

Here, she remembered thinking, was her opportunity to prove to Michel she was not the child he thought of her as. The problem with her proposed plan was that she'd never before been kissed by a man so she had no notion as to how to go about disputing his infuriating opinion. Still she wasn't about to pass up the opportunity fate had granted her.

She remembered the challenge in his expression when she didn't pull away from the circle of his embrace as it slowly tightened around her. She guessed he expected her to flee in terror at the sight of the masculine desire she could read in his intent gaze. Or to be so shocked by his boldness she would scurry away back to the safety of camp.

Men could be surprisingly stupid at times, Elena concluded. Despite her youth and lack of feminine role models she played mistress for her uncle's household long enough to reach her just conclusion. Hadn't she spent the past weeks since their initial, unorthodox introduction attempting to gain Michel's attention? Hadn't she been bound and determined that he look at her as a woman and not the child he persisted in referring to her as whenever her presence among his followers came up in conversation?

So it was with a feeling of heady relief when she saw the challenge in his eyes and realized he meant to test her claim that she was no longer a child, but a woman worthy of his consideration as such. Elena sighed again, her lips curving in a dreamy smile as she remembered the sensation of Michel's lips crushing hers. She grinned, recalling how she was forced to disguise her shock when his tongue slid along her bottom lip seeking entrance to her mouth. Her lips had parted on a breathless gasp, and then his tongue swept inside to engage hers. After that her recollections weren't so clear. She could only recall the avalanche of feelings that swamped her when Michel pulled her closer against him, and then filled his large hand with the softness of her breast. Even now her breath caught in her throat at the way his thumb teased her erect nipple until she thought she could no longer stand on her own and realized it was only his strong arm around her keeping her upright.

She'd felt his male hardness nestled against the soft flesh of her belly and understood what it signified. Elena's lips curved in a satisfied, reminiscent smile because even in her innocence she understood Prince Michel was not thinking of her as a child when he held her close against his hardness. His breathing had grown harsh and uneven as his lips trailed across the delicate skin of her throat.

Dreams of what her future would hold if she became his wife and the intimacies they would share replaced her terror of what she once believed her future would hold. All of a sudden the future appeared bright and full of promise. She supposed she should give her maker his due. Hadn't she prayed for God to send her a knight to rescue her from Baron Raulf's evil clutches?

Smiling, she sent up a heartfelt prayer to her

heavenly father, and then suddenly recalling her desire for a few moments privacy to pray for her uncle's eternal soul, she hung her head in contrite shame and offered a fervent petition for her uncle's gentle spirit.

After but a few moments of quiet prayer and reflection, however, her thoughts were back to swirling around inside her head in a chaotic manner and she was unable to concentrate further on her petitions. Her lips curled upward in a foolish smile and her hands drew playful designs in the sandy earth where she rested near the stream. Her fingers brushed across something hard and sharp, and distracted from her pleasant day-dreams, she let her gaze drop downward to see what her busy hands had unearthed. Her eyes widened in surprise at the sight greeting her, and her lips formed an astonished, "Oh!"

The familiar stone was caked with mud and sand, and the silver clasp that kept it tethered to the thin silver chain around its owner's neck was no longer polished and shining, but she reluctantly acknowledged what she had uncovered. The gem no longer glowed blue in the early morning light as it did when it rested against Michel's flesh, but there was little doubt in Elena's mind she'd found the treasure he so frantically pursued against the current after he lost it while bathing that morning. For a brief, guilt-inducing moment Elena considered leaving the stone where she found it. Given their recent exchange, she was reluctant to remind Michel of the lady who had likely made a gift to him of the strange jewel.

Recalling his stricken expression at its loss, Elena knew it would not be right for her to deprive him of a keepsake Michel so obviously valued. So with studied reluctance, she carefully dug the stone out from its resting place and lifted it onto her lap so she could examine the odd amulet more closely. It wasn't the work of a particularly skilled artisan, she thought, eyeing its sharp edges and uneven lines. Even as she lifted it from her lap to examine it more closely, the gem slipped from her grasp and rolled down the bank towards the stream.

Gasping in surprise, Elena stretched out her arm and closed her fist around the stone just as it would have fallen back into the rushing water. Silently rebuking herself for her carelessness, she scooted herself back several feet away from the river's edge with the jeweled stone clasped firmly in her closed fist, only belatedly becoming aware of a burning sensation in her hand, as if the treasure she held resented her interference in its course. Muttering beneath her breath she quickly dropped the stone into her lap and shook her hand to ease the stinging pain.

Her brows drawn together in confusion she examined the palm of her hand that held the stone. There were red marks on her skin mirroring the shape of the stone. Confused by the evidence she could not make sense of, she carefully used her skirts to cradle Michel's lost treasure while she crawled back to the stream to dunk her hand in the cold water to ease her discomfort.

When she pulled her hand back out of the stream she was relieved to find the pain had left her but the odd imprint remained. More careful now, she scooted back away from the edge, wrapped the stone in a handful of her skirt and stowed it in her pocket, only to have it slide through a previously undiscovered hole, fall to the ground and bounce along, seemingly of its own accord, back in the direction of the stream.

Astonishment froze her steps for a brief moment before she set off in pursuit of what she now concluded must be a magic stone. No wonder Michel was so devastated by its loss. She managed to catch up with the fleeing treasure before it was once more lost beneath the rushing current, but not before she slid from the slippery bank and fell head first into the icy water. Muttering over her own clumsiness and the stone's seeming intent to escape her grasp; she once more wrapped the recalcitrant treasure in a length of her skirt and awkwardly climbed out of the stream. She wasn't taking any chances on stowing it away again, so shivering with cold, and using her free hand to drag the wet tail of her long hair away from her face, she set off along the trail in the direction of the camp.

While she squished along in her wet, borrowed boots, she prayed fervently there would be no one around to witness her embarrassment when she returned to camp. Of course, her prayers went unanswered. The two guards Michel assigned to watch over her, upon hearing her surprised scream at finding herself in the icy water were already hurrying along the path to her rescue. Seeing her bedraggled and obviously unharmed condition, one of the men did his best to suppress his amused grin while at the same time removing his dry cloak and offering it to her.

Elena muttered her less than gracious gratitude for his consideration, then expressed a second, more heartfelt thanks when she enfolded her shivering form in its warmth. Fortunately her guards didn't compound her embarrassment by asking her what had happened or pestering her with questions about whether or not she was all right. As if sensing her discomfort at her own clumsiness they thankfully escorted her in silence so she could wallow in it in peace.

She was thankful Michel was not around to witness her return to camp. She did not doubt he would have enjoyed the sight of the ridiculous spectacle she made in her muddy, damp gown and tangled, wet hair, trailed by two guards who she suspected were grinning like fools behind her back. After their passionate exchange she did not wish to give him any reason to revert to thinking of her as a troublesome child in need of constant looking after. At the entrance to her tent she returned the soldier's damp cloak to him and avoided meeting his amused expression as she once more expressed her gratitude for coming to her rescue.

Once inside, she immediately stripped out of her wet gown and set about drying herself the best she could. It soon became apparent the only way she was going to get the mud out of her hair was to brave the icy stream. Since she had no intention of making a return trip to the source of her embarrassment before the following day, she contented herself with washing the mud away from her skin and face with a cloth and the pitcher of fresh water Michel's squire kept her supplied with.

She hid in her tent for the remainder of the day, feeling ridiculous and not a little bit sorry for herself, which only contributed to her feelings of shame and stupidity when she remembered her uncle's passing just hours earlier. Pitiful tears stung her eyes and she sank to the ground in the middle of her tent with her arms wrapped around her legs, wishing more than ever for the company of another woman to share her complaints and her sorrow with.

She hadn't moved from her place in the center of the tent when an hour later, Michel's squire called out to her from outside the closed opening of the tent, seeking entrance. She brushed the traces of self-pitying tears from her eyes, and swiftly gaining her feet, granted him permission to enter.

When he did so, it was with a wide smile on his face that puzzled her. The prince's squire had never been particularly friendly towards her and he had made it clear without being insolent he resented having to see to her needs and considered the duty beneath him. His smile widening at her confusion, he stepped aside from the entrance. Holding the cloth back he motioned for the two men trailing him to enter.

Elena gasped with stunned pleasure at the sight of the copper tub the men carried between them and then burst into astonished sobs at the trail of soldiers following their comrades, each carrying a bucket of steaming water to fill the tub with. She was too overcome to properly thank them for their consideration. Where in the world had the tub come from? Surely an army did not travel with such conveniences.

"With Prince Michel's compliments," the young squire informed her with a gallant bow, then seeing she was beyond a reasonable response, turned to follow the grinning soldiers from the tent with a wide smile curving his own lips.

Elena was too delighted with the prospect of a real bath to regret too much the realization that Michel must have witnessed her humiliation after all. As she stripped out of her clothes for a second time in the middle of the day, she decided a little embarrassment was not too high a price to pay for the precious gift she'd been given. She let out a little moan of pleasure when she stepped into the steaming water and then dipped her head beneath it to scrub her hair free of the dried mud from the stream and luxuriated in the warm water until it grew as cold as the surrounding air.

CHAPTER EIGHT

Michel had been deep in conversation with Amele and the messenger who just returned from the city with information about the king's funeral arrangements when he spotted Elena emerging from the shadow of the trees and hurry in the direction of her tent. His lips curved at the realization she somehow managed to fall into the stream and was doing her best to pretend she hadn't. The two soldiers trailing her were obviously vastly amused by her condition and Michel found his own lips curving in response. It was hard to reconcile her bedraggled state with the passionate woman he'd held in his embrace not so many minutes earlier.

Shaking his head, he recognized Elena had a disconcerting habit of shifting back and forth between the child he vowed to her uncle he would protect and the desirable, beautiful woman who was only just beginning to emerge from the innocence of childhood. He was a bit disgusted with himself when he was forced to acknowledge he was drawn to her on both levels. Watching her return, he was surprised when her eyes didn't scan the camp in search of him as was her usual habit.

Perhaps she was embarrassed by the intimacies

they shared. If a few kisses were all it took to relieve him of her clinging presence, he decided he should have availed himself of the strategy sooner and saved himself the inconvenience of waking up before dawn for an unpleasant appointment with the icy stream.

As he watched her pass through the opening of her tent, he hoped it was embarrassment only and not fear that kept her from his side. He would not wish to be equated in her mind with Baron Raulf. After all, young, innocent maids were wont to dramatize every little thing and turn them around in their silly heads until they became the victims of fire-breathing dragons or randy knights who took advantage of their innocence to steal a few kisses.

"So we are agreed, Prince Michel?"

At the sound of his name, Michel drew his attention away from the source of his annoying distraction and back to the matter at hand. "Agreed on what?"

Michel was aware of Amele's quickly suppressed smile at his inattention, but his old friend refrained from commenting on it and simply repeated the conclusions they reached while his focus was occupied elsewhere.

"King Barnabas will lie in state so the citizens of the city will have an opportunity to pay their respects. You mentioned Lady Elena wished to bid her uncle a final farewell," Amele reminded him of their earlier exchange before Elena's appearance drew his attention away from their conversation.

"Yes. I believe it's time for us to make our presence felt," Michel remarked. At Amele's speculative look, Michel added with a grin, "In the most peaceful and respectful manner, of course. What better way to accomplish both objectives than by accompanying Lady Elena on her visit to the castle to pay her respects, and at the same time bidding my own farewell to my friend, Barnabas?"

"You intend to escort Lady Elena personally?" Amele asked.

"Yes. I am now her legal guardian. She is my responsibility," Michel reminded him.

Baron Gallagher interjected, "Are you in a position to prove your guardianship over Lady Elena?"

"If necessary," Michel acknowledged, "but I would prefer to delay such a display until after the king has been laid to rest."

The older man's lips curved in a satisfied smirk. "The king appointed you guardian over his niece?"

At Michel's confirming nod, amused laughter erupted from between the other man's grinning lips. "Please, my prince, you must promise me I may be present when you reveal this news to Raulf."

Michel nodded, "Then you had better accompany us into the city. I am not certain how much control we will be able to exercise over the timing of events once it becomes clear I have no intention of allowing Elena to remain in the city after she pays her respects to her uncle."

The other man bowed his appreciation. "It will be my very great pleasure to accompany you, my prince."

The following morning as they prepared to leave on their errand to the city, a keen sense of anticipation hovered over the camp. It was accompanied by a sense of genuine relief that the long days and nights spent in anticipation of the order to take the city were coming to a close. The fact that their long deferment in the mountains might come to an abrupt end that very morning was on every soldier's mind. The commanders were on full alert and had the men under their command ready to invade Calei at the first sign of a threat to their cause.

Not everyone was in agreement that the future king should enter the city as a member of such a small company. What if one of their enemies discovered Michel's true identity? The other contenders to the throne were not so foolish as to think they could challenge for the people's affections over the potential return of a true heir to the throne. In such an event, seeing the new king riding in such a small and seemingly ill-defended party might provide a source of temptation too tempting for them to refuse. Michel was aware

Amele shared in their doubts, but when Michel made his wishes known, his counselor merely nodded his acceptance and made the necessary preparations.

Elena rode between Michel and Amele. Gabriel, as the captain of the king's guard, was already at the castle standing watch over the now defenseless body of his dead king. In addition to Baron Timothy, three other noblemen along with their retainers accompanied them. In all, they were a group of twelve who approached the honor guards at the city gates. From where he rode at her side, Michel looked down upon his silent companion.

"Are you certain you wish to do this?"

Elena raised an uncertain glance to his. Her eyes appeared huge and hesitant in her pale face, but her response, when it came, reflected her determination to see her decision through. "Yes. My Uncle Barnabas is the only father I can remember. I will not let them keep me away."

Michel nodded, and reminded her sternly, "If things become complicated, you are to go with Gabriel. He will secret you away from the castle and see to your safety."

Her intent gaze probed his, and for a moment Michel thought she might protest his order, and then apparently thinking better of her inclination to do so, she nodded her reluctant agreement. A moment later she reached out her hand to clasp his arm and leaned closer towards him, asking softly in a voice only he could hear, "You promise you will not leave me behind?"

"I promise," he assured her solemnly and reached up to squeeze her hand where it rested on his arm. Reassured, Elena reclaimed her hand and left him to his thoughts.

Michel wasn't sure what to expect in the way of a reception from the guards manning the gates to his grandfather's kingdom. He was reminded of his predecessor's fanciful prediction that once Michel passed through them his heart would forever belong to Calei. Michel could still summon a smile for the dying king's whimsy but it was with a sense of a man facing his destiny that he pulled on Arden's reins at the challenge issued by the head of the guard manning the gates.

"My lords. Lady Elena. Welcome to our fair city. I am certain you have heard of our near grief. A period of mourning has been called so that our citizens might have the opportunity to pay their respects to King Barnabas' memory. No weapons are allowed to pass these gates while the king's body lies in state."

It had been agreed among them that Timothy would speak for their company as he was well-known in the city and was not considered one of the many contenders for the now vacant throne. "We are unarmed, my friend. As you can see we escort Lady Elena so she may pay her respects to her uncle's memory."

"You may pass," the guard announced with all

due formality given the solemn occasion.

Michel looked around with expectant curiosity as they passed through the gates. If there was surprise at their appearance it was directed in Elena's direction not his. No doubt the guards and the citizens they passed were startled to find Elena outside of the city gates at the time of her uncle's passing. He could feel her tension escalating beside him with each step they drew closer to the huge keep that dominated the skyline. She gripped her mount's reins as if they were a life-line. In an instinctive protective gesture, Michel moved Arden closer to her side, silently assuring her that she would not be forced to face the beast alone. He nodded reassuringly when she raised her pale face to his.

Michel's first impression of his new kingdom was a not unfavorable one. For all of its violent history, it was obvious Calei remained a wealthy kingdom. Michel had been in enough capital cities to know to look beyond the well-kept streets and store fronts, the fine ladies dressed luxuriantly, with their coiffed hair and jeweled necks. No, the true judge of a city's prosperity was to be found in how the lowliest among the inhabitants lived.

As they rode along the paved streets, Michel could see no sign of beggars or orphans forced to rely on the generosity of strangers for their daily fare. None of the children he saw were dressed in tattered rags, or in desperate need of a bath or a firm parental hand. Unless such unpleasant sights had been swept from the streets so as not to detract from the somberness of the occasion.

Closer now, Michel could see the intricate details decorating the façade of the castle. The distinctly, mostly light stone appeared to have flecks of gold embedded in it that caught the bright sunlight and reflected it back into the sky like a mirror. Scenes had been painted on the stone surrounding the entrance depicting, he assumed, various important moments in Calei's long history. Seeing them Michel felt a whisper of a memory sweep across his soul, accompanied by a cold shiver up his spine. Chiding himself for his foolishness, he immediately suppressed the shiver and rationalized away his fanciful thoughts. He'd never been in the city, had never seen the keep, nor did he participate in any of the dramatic scenes depicted on its thick walls.

"Raulf's men." Timothy passed along the information in a pointed tone, indicating the men who lined the steps leading into the main entrance of the keep.

Michel nodded but offered no verbal response. He understood from the prominent position of the baron's men that while the question of the royal succession had officially been set aside in order for the citizens of Calei to mourn their lost king, for all intents and purposes Baron Raulf had taken control of the keep and presumably, the affairs of state. Though there was a long line of mourners in front of them waiting for their turn to view the departed king, seeing Elena in their company, they gave way before them. Michel was aware of their hushed whispers and their curiosity at seeing Elena in the company of strangers.

Michel dismounted and passed Arden's reins to one of the stable boys who hurried forward to take charge of their horses. He turned to assist Elena to the ground, and noticed how pale her complexion had gone in the space of the distance they travelled from entering the city to where they stood preparing to ascend the gleaming marble steps of the castle. She raised haunted eyes to his and he gave her slim waist an encouraging squeeze before releasing her. When he would have turned to climb the stairs with her in his wake, she reached out to grip his arm. He paused and turned back in her direction, and the eyes she raised to his face held his in a glance of barely suppressed panic.

"You remember your promise?" She asked tearfully, her nails digging into his arm revealing the extent of her fear.

He reached over and covered her hand with his. "Yes, I remember my promise both to you and your uncle. I will not leave you behind, nor will I allow anyone to hurt you." Michel was aware of the start of surprise among some of their company at his revelation that he'd been in contact with the former king. He had not shared with his supporters Barnabas' request to be introduced to him. “Trust me, Elena. Raulf will not risk a challenge to his authority on a day set aside to honor your uncle’s memory. It will only lessen his stance in front of the other noblemen and the common populace.” The assurance with which he spoke seemed to calm her fears and she allowed her hand to fall from his arm.

A hushed silence stilled even the quiet whispers that could be heard among the mourners as they entered the great hall. Michel took in the crowd arrayed there, noticed the majority were ordinary citizens with tears in their eyes as they paid their last respects to the popular king. Surrounding the casket were representatives from the noble families of Calei. Michel could see the speculation in the glances they cast in their direction, noting their noble compatriots in their company and the fact that Elena made up one of their number.

Michel, followed by Elena, and with the others filing in behind them took their place in line. The silent mourners in front of them stepped back from the king’s casket to give Elena a private opportunity to pay her final respects to her uncle. Michel and the others waited while she knelt beside the casket and raised her uncle’s cool hand to her cheek and then kissed it gently before returning it to its resting place. She bowed her head in silent prayer then regained her feet and proceeded silently towards where Gabriel stood quietly speaking with his brother.

In her wake, Michel approached the casket of the dead king and looked down with fondness and regret at the still face he'd seen only once in life, glad to observe it was no longer wracked with the pain it had born in his final days.

"Farewell, Barnabas, my friend. May you rest in peace with your royal predecessors. Give my greeting and my love to my grandfather, and may you both guide my steps along this path destiny has seemingly laid out for me to follow." After his whispered farewell, Michel bent his head and offered a silent prayer, then joined the others where they had gathered near where Elena stood silently flanked by Gabriel and Amele. He raised an inquiring brow in Elena's direction, silently asking if she was ready to leave. At her assenting nod, he took her arm, and with a silent gesture towards the others to follow, began to make their way to the exit.

"Wait." The loud command echoed harshly in contrast to the respectful hush that hung over the hall. Michel felt Elena stiffen at his side and needed no further confirmation of his guess as to the identity of the man who hailed them. Turning to confront Elena's beast, Michel's eyes swept over him, taking his opponent's measure in a swift, discerning glance. The maid's description was a bit harsh in Michel's opinion. Baron Raulf was a man after all, and not one he thought the ladies would find particularly unpleasing to look upon. His features were not gentle, but nor were they scarred. Dark eyes stared out of a thin patrician face, but Michel recognized the impressive breadth of his shoulders was not due solely to the cut and padding of his luxurious cloak.

But for all of the baron's noble bearing, Michel noted his powerful hands were clenched in tight fists at his side. Michel suspected one of those hands would even now be reaching for his sword if the circumstances did not forbid such an unpardonable breach of manners. No, not a beast, Michel felt confident in concluding, but certainly a man who would not look kindly upon another man challenging his authority over a woman, nor his claim for a kingship.

"Yes?" Michel responded to the other's command.

"Who are you?"

Michel took in Raulf's haughty glare and the disapproval and askance at the way Michel's hand rested possessively on Elena's arm. He felt the slight shiver of fear that passed through her and he gently squeezed her arm in a gesture of reassurance before replying in a courteous voice. "We are friends who have come to pay our respects to the king."

"Elena, who are these men?"

Elena's eyes sought his, seeking permission to respond to Raulf's arrogant inquiry. Michel nodded his assent and allowed his lips to curve upward slightly at Raulf's bristling outrage at her gesture.

"Surely, Baron, you know Barons Timothy, Paul and Gallagher and their men."

The baron regarded her as if he conversed with a slow-witted child and made a sweeping motion with his hand. Michel was forced to bite down on his lip to suppress a grin at Elena's silent outrage at the baron's dismissive gesture and condescending tone when he replied, "I am aware of the identity of those you speak and they are welcome here, but I think it is not a time to bring strangers among us to disturb our grief."

Elena ignored Michel's warning squeeze on her arm and replied boldly. "These strangers you speak of saved me from malicious kidnappers and have provided for my protection when I was unsure who I might trust."

Michel observed the ripples of shock across the faces of those gathered in the room at Elena's claim of her abduction and was aware of the surreptitious glances that were being cast around the hall as each of the various contenders to the throne wondered who had dared such a bold step.

Recovering quickly from Elena's disclosure, Raulf rebuked her, "You should have come to me."

At Michel's silent warning, Elena clenched her lips closed to stifle the sarcastic laugh he could feel threatening to erupt at the baron's obscene suggestion, and obediently offered in its place, "There was no opportunity to do so. I was kidnapped from my bed and taken from the city. Were it not for these men, I shudder to think what may have happened to me. Given the great service they have rendered me, I no longer consider them strangers. They have been my saviors."

Michel had to give the other man credit. He barely paused for breath before responding in a tone one might judge almost friendly in its courtesy, "Then we of course owe them a debt of gratitude for their intervention. But the risk has now passed and it is time for you to return to the safety of the palace."

"I think not, Baron," Elena did not hesitate to refute Raulf's suggestion. "Until the question of my uncle's successor has been resolved, I have no plans to return to the keep."

One autocratic brow arched over the baron's piercing glance but it was in a condescending tone of almost gentle regret that he responded to Elena's challenge. "Forgive me, my dear, but you have no choice other than to obey me. With your uncle's death, I am now your legal guardian and responsible for your welfare. You will return to your chambers in the keep immediately."

Michel witnessed the color drain from Elena's face at Raulf's claim. Her arm he still held clasped in his shook noticeably, but Michel couldn't help but admire the way she stood her ground in the face of the baron's assured proclamation. "You lie. My uncle would never appoint you my guardian."

Amusement lit Raulf's expression now at her spirited challenge. "And why not? I was his closest friend and most trusted advisor. Who else would Barnabas appoint to see to your welfare?"

Elena raised desperate eyes to Michel's face. He met them, willing her to remain calm with a slight pressure on her arm. He cast a mild glance in the direction of the man who no longer appeared amused by the way Elena looked to Michel to rescue her and the way she was now clinging frantically to his hand. "Do you have proof of your claim, baron?"

"I do not answer to you, boy." Raulf's calm demeanor slipped a little in his outrage at Michel's query.

Keeping his tone mild, as much because it served to further enrage his opponent as because a display of his own temper would not serve his purpose, Michel asked innocently, "But surely you answer to the friends of the king gathered here. They must be aware of the king's great affection for his niece. Do they not act as her guardians in the king's stead?"

"The stranger speaks the truth." A voice called out from among the previously silent, but deeply interested witnesses to their exchange. "Do you have proof, Baron Raulf that King Barnabas appointed you Lady Elena's guardian?"

Raulf swung his enraged glance on his new target. With obvious effort he forced himself to reply calmly to the other man's challenge, while at the same time his expression promised a day of reckoning for his insult. "Barnabas spoke the words with his dying breath. His thoughts were ever on his beloved Elena's future."

"So there were no witnesses to the king's proclamation?" Michel prompted in a voice of feigned innocence, then added as Raulf's glance swung back to duel with his, "Was there no one else in the room at the moment of the king's passing?"

"No. We were alone."

"Convenient for you," Michel commented and knew he only gave voice to the implication the others were unwilling to.

"He wished to speak with his closest friend in his final moments." It was obvious Raulf did not care for being put in a position of having to explain his actions.

"You say the king's main concern was for his niece?"

"Of course." Though Raulf clearly felt on firmer ground with this line of query, he was obviously restraining his impatience with an effort.

"And the king had been ill for some time?"

"What business the answer to your question is to you, a stranger amongst us, who seeks no doubt to profit from our grief and that of Lady Elena's innocence, I cannot fathom."

Michel bowed his head, aware of the scrutiny

Raulf's comment was now rendering him. "Lady Elena tells me the king had been ill for some time. It seems to me if she was his most pressing concern, he would have made more formal provision for his beloved niece's future."

He could see his argument struck home among the witnesses to their exchange and Raulf was once again forced to defend his claim. "Barnabas was hopeful he would recover. It was not until the very end he was forced to accept the truth."

"Forced by you, Baron?"

Raulf took a threatening step forward. "Be careful of your tongue, boy. I do not care for your implication."

"I imagine the king did not care for it either."

"Get out! You have no rights here." Raulf's hand instinctively reached for his sword and Michel guessed he would have issued a challenge to settle the matter between them then and there had not his hand come up empty.

Eyeing his frustration, Michel proffered a rather mocking bow in Raulf's direction. "As to my rights, Baron, that is a matter to be decided upon another, more appropriate occasion." Michel then turned his attention to his silent companion. "Lady Elena, have you completed your farewells?"

He smiled at the expression on her upturned face. She was regarding him with shining eyes, her relief evident, and a stunned astonishment of his defense of her reflected in their dusky depths, as if she did not expect him to champion her, as though she had expected he would simply hand her over to the beast. “Yes, my lord, I am quite ready to leave with you.” Her voice was clear and rang out around the hall.

Michel sent another mocking bow in Raulf’s direction and did not bother to attempt to temper the great satisfaction he took in leaving him seething in his wake. He gave Elena’s hand a quick squeeze where it still rested in his and was aware of the amused sparkle in Amele’s glance when they passed by his side, though his old friend maintained an appropriately reserved expression when they turned away from the gathering and strode confidently from the king’s hall. Michel had little doubt their passage through the gates of his new kingdom would give rise to significantly greater interest than had their arrival. He also suspected there would be a few hastily assigned spies to follow in their wake.

Elena paused on the steps to greet some acquaintances who hailed her to offer their condolences. Michel could see by her reception Barnabas had not exaggerated the citizen’s affection for his young niece. She kept her exchanges brief and quiet, and then as if unwilling to keep him waiting any longer, she allowed Michel to assist her onto her mount and sat staring down at him with an expression that implied he was the beginning and end of her entire world. A light blush stained her lovely face and Michel witnessed a riot of conflicting emotions chase themselves across her expressive features… relief, gratitude, admiration, and a new deeper emotion he was hesitant to put a name to.

Wary of it, he quickly inserted into the silence between them, "I believe you would be safe now if you chose to remain within the city. I imagine you are not accustomed to sleeping on a rough pallet on the cold ground."

Elena did not hesitate to deny his suggestion she remain behind. "At least I find the comfort of slumber on my rough pallet and do not lie awake dreading what is to come when night falls."

He nodded, and then turning to retrieve the reins of his own mount, gained Arden's back in a single, graceful movement and as one, their company turned and rode down the streets, aware of the whispers that followed them as they did.

CHAPTER NINE

Finalizing the details of their plans took on greater urgency after their confrontation with Raulf and his supporters. Michel comprehended Raulf would not rest idly with the knowledge his ascension to the throne and his rights to Elena would not be accomplished without a challenge from a source he had been previously unaware of, and consequently unable to prepare for. The baron would not have missed the significance of the presence of Barons Timothy, Paul and Gallagher among their company and would have concluded that some of the noble families would not support his claim for kingship and had aligned themselves with a stranger to Calei.

Michel comprehended Raulf was not the only one of his future subjects speculating as to his identity. He imagined everyone present in the hall today had their own theories, but that the majority would rightly conclude he must be one of King Nathaniel's grandsons. Why else would three of the kingdom's noblemen be in his company?

The other impetus for pushing forward with their plans was the increasing restlessness of his men. After long months and years in training to be so close to their goal and be forced to wait around shirking in the mountains would only lead to trouble and dissent among them. They were primed for a fight. Michel did not want his men to waste their deadly skills on each other.

Still he hesitated to give the order to attack the city. Was he some enemy marauder that sought to steal Calei's rich throne? Was he not the rightful king? Did a just man attack his own people?

"Perhaps it is time you revealed your presence to the people, my prince," Amele spoke into the silence that had fallen among those gathered to debate their next move, interrupting Michel's inner debate.

Baron Paul agreed. "There is already a great deal of speculation among the citizens as to your identity. There were a few present in the great hall this morning who remember your grandparents. The majority of the servants at the keep have outlived their kings. The news of a stranger who was not afraid to openly challenge Raulf's authority and whose striking blue eyes bring to mind Queen Alyssa's own must be even now spreading like wildfire through the city. The people will not be slow to conclude rightfully that one of the true heirs to the throne has at long last returned to Calei to restore the royal line."

Persuaded, Michel nodded, "Then let us not keep the people in suspense any longer to have their speculations confirmed. Send word to the noble families that the time has come to settle the question of who will rule Calei in the wake of

Barnabas' passing. We will assemble in the great hall of the castle tomorrow at noon. Raulf will not appreciate our taking over the king's home for our purposes, but nor will he prevent the nobles from gathering to discuss the very matter he wants resolved as quickly as anyone. Prepare the men. Though we all hope for a peaceful transition of power, my heart tells me there will be blood shed before the matter of the succession is settled."

"If you seek my opinion, my prince, your heart speaks truly. It will not matter to Raulf how just is your claim to your grandfather's throne. The baron already considers himself king and will not surrender either the kingship of Calei or the Lady Elena without a fight." It was Gabriel who spoke out and the others quickly added their assenting voices to his.

Michel replied, "If it is my blood Raulf seeks, I am in the mood to accommodate him. It is only the blood of the innocent I am reluctant to shed and I have a feeling the baron is no innocent."

"What will you do about Lady Elena in the interim?" Paul asked.

Michel turned to Timothy. "I cannot leave her here in the forest. Will your family take her in and see to her protection until the matter of the kingship is resolved one way or the other?"

"I should be honored to render you this service, my prince, as I previously assured my friend, Barnabas," Timothy replied with a slight bow, and then added with a knowing smile curving his lips and laughter lurking in his expression, "but I think the lady will resist any plan that takes her from your side."

Amused concurrence with Timothy's conclusion was echoed in the laughter of those surrounding him. Michel greeted their amusement at his expense with a resigned shrug and an answering smile, "Undoubtedly, but I can hardly wield a sword with the maid seated on the saddle in front of me." Fresh laughter erupted at the picture he painted, and he added on a sigh, "I will speak with Elena and attempt to convince her I am not abandoning her to a fate worse than death." When his companions' amusement died down, his voice took on a new seriousness when he turned in Amele's direction, "If things go ill for me, my friend, you will act as the maid's guardian in my stead. If she wishes to leave Calei, take her to my grandmother. I have a feeling the two will discover they have much in common."

Amele held his glance for long moments as if seeking some sign of a purpose Michel had not shared with the others, then apparently satisfied by what he read in Michel's expression, nodded his assent. "As you command, my prince."

"We will leave in the morning with enough show of force that the baron will think twice about challenging us before the meeting has been called. As we planned, the remaining men will surround the city and engage only upon my order, if and when, a peaceful transition of power eludes us."

Elena sought the privacy of her tent as soon as they returned to the camp after paying her final respects to her Uncle Barnabas. She hadn't realized the true extent of the terror she'd lived under these last long months of her uncle's illness until she was forced to confront Raulf face to face. When he made his bold announcement that her uncle had left her in his care, her heart had lodged in her throat. Along with her heart was a solid knot of horror that had made it impossible for her to draw a breath.

She stood now in the center of her tent staring down at her hands clasped together in front of her, unable to do anything to still their uncontrollable trembling. Her thoughts were busy reminding her of the narrowness of her escape. If she hadn't been kidnapped from her bed… if Prince Michel had not been her savior that fateful morning, she would even now be dreading the prospect of marriage to Raulf and all that such a commitment implied.

For a moment, while their company gathered in the castle hall, surrounded by the heads of the noble families of Calei, she feared, despite his repeated promises to the contrary, that her rescuer would abandon her to the baron's mercy. The recollection of that awful moment settled harshly on her unsteady shoulders. She thought she must be suffering from some sort of delayed reaction to the reprieve she was granted.

Her hands were shaking so badly her entire being was trembling. She tried to raise one of them to her face to brush the stinging tears from her eyes and found herself unable to do so. Instead she wrapped her arms around her stomach as much to still their trembling as in an instinctive gesture of protection and the next moment found herself doubled over in her effort to stifle the deep, rending sobs that threatened to overcome her.

That was how Michel came upon her, almost on her knees struggling to reconcile a mixture of dazed fear that her reprieve from Raulf's grip would be short-lived and a desperate hope that it was real, that she would be granted lasting freedom from the jaws of the beast who readied himself to feed on her tender flesh. The sound of her name pierced her dazed thoughts and she swung around at the echo of her savior's familiar voice coming from the entrance of her tent.

Their glances met. She saw him take in her pitiful state and immediately his incredible eyes filled with understanding and compassion. Ashamed of her weakness, yet unable to prevent herself from acting on it, she closed the distance between them on trembling legs and flung herself against his chest. His strong arms closed around her and drew her close against his heart until she abandoned her shaky attempts to regain control of her unsteady limbs and simply clung to his strength. Here was safety. Here was warmth.

Here was everything she'd dreamt of in the blackest nights of her despair.

Her sobs flooded his chest. She was so occupied with her tears, she was barely aware of Michel half-tugging, half-carrying her back to the center of the tent.

"I'm sorry, I'm sorry." She whispered her broken apologies against the side of his neck, her lips brushing his ear.

Michel was not immune to her softness pressed up against him, but he understood what she needed now was his comfort and reassurance, not his lust. "Did I mistake your wishes then? Did you prefer to remain in the city?" He teased and was relieved when Elena let out a little, soggy laugh against his chest.

She raised her damp glance to his and shook her head, thinking to explain her piteous condition. "No, it's just I didn't realize how frightened I was of what would have happened to me if you hadn't saved me. Before you came I had concocted all of these foolish, half-formed plans to escape Raulf's reach by fleeing the city and seeking out a hiding place in the mountains. When I was kidnapped, even though I was terrified, part of me was grateful to my abductors for making it easy for me to leave the city. When I fell off the back of the horse, I was convinced that if I could only escape my bonds and avoid being captured again by my kidnappers, I would have a chance." Shaking her head at her own foolishness, she tacked on with a self-deprecating smile, "As if it was a simple matter for me to survive alone and find shelter in the mountains even though I possess no useful knowledge or skills pertaining to such things."

"You planned to leave the safety of the city?" Michel echoed stunned by his young ward's confession. All he could think about was the disastrous consequences of his twin's flight away from their ancestral home in advance of the Norman invasion of Saxony, and Melissa had been very well-trained in the skills required to survive on her own in the wild. Michel's heart clenched when he thought of Elena at the hands of the madman who very nearly killed his twin. The young innocent he held in his arms would have been no less than a lamb led to slaughter beneath his vicious assault. "Have you any comprehension of what you risked if you were able to execute such a ridiculous plan?"

Elena was oddly comforted by Michel's blatant disapproval. Willing to acknowledge the foolishness of her desperate plan to escape Raulf's reach, she braved Michel's blazing blue eyes and responded in a soft voice, "I am certain you are correct and I had no real understanding of the risks I would have confronted outside the city's gates. I thought it likely I would die trying to escape, but death was preferable to the alternative awaiting me at Raulf's hands. My greater fear was that the holy church would consider my flight into the mountains an act of suicide and I would be condemned to hell for all eternity because I passed from this life with the stain of a mortal sin on my soul."

Michel couldn't get past his astonishment at the realization of the true depths of Elena's innocence. He hadn't realized such purity still existed in this world. At the same time he was trying to recover from the casual way she spoke of her own death. Didn't she comprehend that there were worse fates than freezing to death in the mountains?

"Elena..." he decided it was his duty to set her straight, but his voice trailed off when she simply stared at him with a knowing expression in her soft brown eyes that belied his conclusion of her naivety.

"I know what you're thinking, but you are a man and therefore could never truly comprehend what it is like to be alone and defenseless in the world and at the mercy of someone like the baron."

Michel swallowed his instinctive denial when he realized she spoke the truth. How could he truly enter into her feelings about the bleak future she faced subject to Raulf's power? What did he know of being truly defenseless against an opponent of far greater strength? For a man, for a soldier, death, or being so gravely injured as to render him useless, were the most feared outcomes on the battlefield. For a woman, particularly a young innocent like Elena who could not even raise a sword in her own defense, there were greater fears to be confronted than death.

Hadn't Melissa tried to make him understand the very same point? He'd thought his twin was simply overdramatizing things, the way she was wont to do, but seeing the remembered terror in Elena's eyes he acknowledged he'd never fully understood the reasons prompting Melissa's desperate gamble to elude capture by the invading Norman army. Yet this young maid entered into his twin's feelings as he, the one closest to her, had been unable to. Despite his revelation Michel recognized it would not serve his current purpose to agree with Elena's point.

"Elena, you are not to worry about such things. I want your word you will never do anything so foolish as to attempt to flee into the mountains on your own."

She evaded giving him her promise by pointing out, "Your grandmother escaped into the mountains. She knew what the king's enemies would do to her. She recognized her only hope to save her life and that of the child she carried was to take her chances in the wilderness."

In a gesture of pure male frustration, Michel thrust a swift hand through his hair and immediately pointed out the flaw in her logic, "My grandmother did not flee into the mountains alone. Amele and a company of soldiers accompanied her. In time, others joined them. She was never alone."

Elena nodded in acknowledgement of his point, but just when Michel felt the hard knot of tension begin to dissolve in his chest, she added obstinately, "But I would wager if there was no one to accompany her she would have fled into the mountains alone in order to protect the child she carried...your mother."

Michel was willing to bet his grandmother would have done exactly that but didn't think such an admission would gain him the promise he sought. "You are no longer faced with the prospect of being forced to flee on your own. Baron Timothy's family will see to your care until..." Michel swore softly and let his voice trail off at the stunned expression that came over her face. He hadn't meant to deliver the news of the arrangements he'd made for her protection while he was occupied fighting for a kingship quite so casually. When Elena tried to pull away from his restraining embrace, he shifted his grip to her arms as much to shake some sense into her, as to prevent her flight.

"Elena, listen to me." She was frantically fighting his restraint and staring up at him as if he'd just pronounced her death sentence. When she kicked him in the shins in an attempt to free herself, he drew her close against him and wrapped one leg around both of hers and held her slapping hands in one of his own larger ones. She continued to struggle against his constraint but without effect until finally accepting she had no hope of prevailing against his greater strength she resorted to a woman's weapon. Tears filled her eyes and streamed down her white face, even as she continued to shake her head in denial and mewling sounds escaped between her clenched lips.

"Elena," She shook her head against his gentle call. He thought if she had the use of her hands they would be covering her ears to block out the sound of his voice. "Elena, I have not forgotten my promise to your uncle to see to your protection and stand as your guardian, but I cannot allow you to accompany me into a battle for control of the city."

At his reasonable explanation she stopped struggling and lifted her crushed eyes to his face. "I don't understand. Why would there be a battle for control of the city? You are the rightful heir to the kingship."

His lips curved at her naïve presumption his right to ascend the throne would be enough to convince Raulf and the other contenders to simply relinquish their plans, likely years in the making, to follow in her uncle's stead. "Not everyone will be swayed by my right of ascension."

"You speak of Raulf," she concluded bitterly.

"Not only Raulf, but yes, he is likely to be the most obvious threat."

"Why can't I stay here?"

Michel smiled at her whispered cajolery. "What kind of guardian would I be if I did not make proper provision for your safety? Do you have a particular objection to Baron Timothy? Do you fear for your safety while under the care of his family?"

For a moment, he could see she considered lying and telling him she did fear being placed under Baron Timothy's care, but then she quickly reasoned out that even if he believed her lie, he would only find another family to take her in. Eventually she sighed defeated and leaned her head against his chest. "No."

Michel realized what the admission cost her, and was surprised when she surrendered their contest so easily. If he had been attempting to convince his twin of the justness of his position, Melissa would still be threatening him with her dagger and claiming she was as skilled as any soldier in the ways of combat so there was no reason she shouldn't accompany him into battle. In fact, she would be highly insulted by his plan to leave her behind. He did not intend to risk sharing any of his twin's outrageous opinions with his young ward, however. He certainly did not wish to plant the idea in her head that she could learn to wield a weapon and ride by his side into armed conflict. The picture of the gentle maid he held doing exactly that was enough to coax a grin to his lips.

"Why are you smiling? Are you so happy then

at the thought of being rid of me?" Elena asked in a desolate voice, catching sight of his amusement when she lifted her head from his chest at his extended silence.

Michel's grin widened and he bent to brush his lips across hers. "No."

Seemingly resigned to her fate, she asked, "How long do I have to stay with Baron Timothy's family?"

"Until the throne is secure," he promised her.

"And then I can come back to live in the castle?"

"Yes."

"Will you live there too?"

Michel kept his inward sigh at her question to himself. The living arrangements had obvious pitfalls, not the least of which, he could hardly continue to allow a young, unmarried, and unrelated maid to live under his roof indefinitely, but he thought now was not the time to bring up any additional complications. One hurdle at a time. "Yes, I will live there."

"All right."

His eyes lit with amusement at her reluctant agreement, as if the maid believed she actually had a say in the matter.

"Michel?"

"Yes?" he lowered his voice to match her hesitant whisper.

"May I call you Michel?"

Hadn't she just done so? His grin widened.

"Yes."

"Will you promise me you won't die and leave me alone again?"

Michel wasn't certain how to respond to her ridiculous request, but understanding the fear prompting it, he didn't think this was the time to mention he'd made provisions for her future in the event of just such a contingency. Instead, he reached up to brush a stray silken strand away from her face, watched her face flood with telling color at his gentle touch, and seeing it, understanding what prompted its cause, dropped his gaze to her parted lips. He suddenly realized that this was likely the only opportunity they would have to exchange a private farewell. If things did not proceed as planned on the morrow, it was likely he would never see her again. Though he was reasonably confident of the success of his plans, he imagined Raulf and the others were equally confident of their own strategies they had in place in anticipation of the coming confrontation.

"Elena," he began in a serious tone, but she immediately stopped the flow of half-formed words from his lips when she raised her fingertips to them.

"Don't," she pleaded in a suddenly agonized whisper.

"Don't what?"

"Don't say goodbye. I cannot bear it. Are you certain I cannot accompany you? I am a very good rider. I will promise to stay out of your way."

Michel kissed the fingers pressed against his lips and shook his head in a gesture of gentle denial. "You know that is impossible."

"It's not fair," she complained softly, burrowing closer against his chest.

He tightened his arms around her softness and curious, asked, "What's not fair?"

"That you get to determine your own fate and I must remain safely tucked behind and wait for someone to come to me and deliver the news of my future."

His lips curved and he nodded, acknowledging her point. "I suppose you are right, it is not fair, but I would not be able to concentrate on winning this battle for our futures if I had to concern myself with your safety while I was in the midst of it."

He'd said, 'our futures', Elena realized breathlessly. As if they were one and the same. "You didn't promise me," she reminded him, suddenly realizing his earlier oversight.

"What did I fail to promise you?"

"You didn't promise me you wouldn't die and leave me alone."

She made no effort to disguise her desperate longing in the glance she raised to his and when Michel's strong arms tightened around her, drawing her closer, she gloried in the feel of his masculine strength and leaned against him as he lowered his mouth to claim hers. He didn't coax her lips apart to allow him access, his tongue demanded and she gave, moaning softly in the back of her throat as the now familiar feelings swamped her. Familiar, yet not familiar. There was a new urgency in his kiss that had not been present before.

When his hand cupped the fullness of her breast, she whimpered against his lips and her head fell back to grant his lips uninhibited freedom to trail along her chin, down her throat, impatiently pushing aside the offending barrier of her gown and then dampening her chemise as his mouth closed over her breast through the thin material.

Elena never wanted the glorious feelings coursing through her to stop. She thought to tell him so, to demand he never let her go, never stop touching her in this intimate way, but she couldn't catch her breath long enough for the words to form on her lips.

"Elena, love, we must stop." Michel's mouth blazed a trail across her heated flesh to whisper in her ear.

"No." The single word of denial was all her scattered thoughts could summon in argument against his intent, and she felt his lips curve upward in a smile against the sensitive lobe of her ear. As if conceding the justness of her position, for a moment he allowed his lips to tease her flesh as he drew a deep breath against the side of her throat, then, with obvious reluctance, moved both hands to rest on her shoulders and set her away from him.

Michel stared down into the passion-glazed eyes she raised to his and wondered at his own recklessness. She was his ward. King Barnabas had placed his young niece in his care, and though it had been his predecessor's wish he marry Elena, Michel had made no such commitment in his heart or in his mind to the maid. He had no right to awaken the passion for him he read in her innocent gaze if he did not intend to satisfy it. Since the only way he could rightfully do so was to marry her, he wondered at his insistence in seeking her out. For he did not fool himself into believing it was only Elena's determination not to be parted from him that accounted for the attraction between them. She affected him as no woman ever had. Whether it was her youth or innocence, or her desperate need for a champion that tugged at his will, he did not know, he only knew he was beginning to regard her with a possessiveness that went beyond that of a guardian for his ward. It should have worried him. She was disrupting all of his carefully prepared plans for the future, none of which included marriage to a maid barely old enough to enter into such a sacred covenant, and one who regarded him with all the love in her pure heart shining from the depths of her eyes as they beheld him.

He realized he could barely recall all of his carefully prepared designs from his previous life and he was once again reminded of his predecessor's warning, "Once you enter the city your heart will find its true home and you will never be free again." Michel had dismissed Barnabas' prediction as a fanciful longing on the dying king's part for his successor to love his kingdom as he did, but no longer could he pretend there was no truth in it. Less and less did his thoughts dwell on a future beyond the rich and fertile lands of Calei. The restlessness that had haunted his spirit and led him to pursue a wanderer's life, the only one of his brother's so afflicted, no longer drove him as relentlessly as it once did.

His visions of the woman who would one day capture and hold sway over his heart the way his mother had bewitched his very rational, very straight-laced Saxon father were no longer fuzzy images of a lady who was at once a combination of his twin's stunning beauty and bold spirit, and that of his younger sister's deep and gentle femininity, but now, inexplicably, all of those half-formed dreams seemed more and more to be coalescing into the lovely features of the young maid who was regarding him now with fresh anxiety in her serious glance.

He should be furious at the inevitability of it all, the way fate seemed intent on leading him along on a path of its own choosing. He'd always been fiercely independent, disregarding the shackles of expectation and conformity with the same ferocity a determined bachelor avoided the bonds of matrimony. Yet here he stood with the claws of his destiny closing in around him, and the proverbial sword of Damocles hovering over his head and he felt no driving urge to evade the bonds of expectation he sensed from every angle binding his future to that of his grandfather's kingdom.

He nodded in silent acknowledgment of Barnabas' cunning, remembering his own careless dismissal of the king's request that he at least commit to no other until he had met his niece. Now his memories of every other woman of his admittedly wide experience were slowly fading from his thoughts to be replaced by the pure virtue of the young innocent he was so reluctant to loose from his arms.

"Michel?" Elena whispered hesitantly at his long silence.

"Yes?" It amused him to hear the anxiety in her voice whenever she addressed him, as if she was afraid he was about to disappear into thin air.

"Have I displeased you?"

He could also admit Elena's innocent eagerness to please him stroked his masculine ego in a way no other woman's bold compliments had ever done. "No, Elena, you have not displeased me, but I have no right to take advantage of your innocence and my position as your guardian to force such intimacies upon you."

She appeared both stunned and offended by his choice of words, but it was the very real anger he read in her glance that both surprised and intrigued him at the same time. She pushed away from his embrace and boldly faced him, "I am not the child you insist on seeing me as, nor am I some spineless twit without a mind of her own. I was willing to face my own death rather than allow Raulf to force his attentions on me and you insult me most grievously by implying that I would accede to yours by the simple virtue of my uncle having appointed you my guardian."

He was so pleased by her show of spirit, Michel grinned into the furious gaze she was blistering him with. Elena stamped one foot in frustration at his obvious amusement and Michel only just managed to dodge the clenched fist she aimed at his grinning face. He laughed outright at her show of temper and clamped his hands over her arms. Entertained by her efforts to squirm away from his embrace, he drew her closer, showing her without words his superior strength and his intent to have his way.

When she stopped straining against him, but contented herself with expressing her outrage at his manhandling of her with the seething glance she regarded him with, he merely bent his head to brush his lips across hers and admonished her to be mindful of Baron Timothy's instructions before abruptly releasing her and striding through the entrance of the tent with a wide smile curving his lips. He was beginning to think Elena had more in common with his twin than he previously realized; a thought that both pleased and alarmed him in equal measure.

CHAPTER TEN

Elena barely caught a glimpse of Michel the following morning as she was awakened shortly after dawn and hurried from the camp under an escort of Baron Timothy's men. There was an air of anticipation riding along the chill air as they passed the soldiers hastily consuming their morning meal and preparing themselves for the day ahead. Most of the soldiers sported wide smiles on their usually stoic and intimidating faces, as if a highly anticipated treat was about to be bestowed upon them. Elena was unable to reconcile their excitement and high spirits with what she knew the day might hold. Michel had warned her he could not take her along with him into what might very well prove to be a battle for control of the city. She supposed her fear of such an eventuality was what was responsible for the soldiers' high moods.

As she rode from the camp, she cast a last glance over the gathered forces, wishing for just a single glimpse of the man who'd been a stranger to her short weeks ago, but who now held her heart and her every hope for the future in his grasp. She was denied her wish and was forced to content herself with sending up a silent prayer to her maker to watch over Michel and his men when they rode off to a potential war against Raulf's followers. Once again she silently bemoaned the fate of women which required her to point her mount in the direction of safety rather than in the direction of the place she most wished to be…at the side of the man she loved.

Michel refused the armor Amele urged on him. "We are riding to a conference, not a war, my friend. If we arrive arrayed for battle, then we would only precipitate its advent."

"No doubt, my king, but the failure to array ourselves for war is unlikely to prevent us from ending up in the middle of one. In such an event, the armor will provide you better protection against an enemy sword than the justness of your position."

Michel grinned in response to his friend's ironic observation and merely waved his squire from the tent. "Ah, my friend, I cannot imagine what enemy you speak of. Surely all of the noble families of Calei wish only for the rightful king to ascend to the throne of their homeland."

Amele rolled his eyes at his continued obstinacy as Timothy entered the tent in the wake of Michel's squire. "If only that were true, my king, I would not blanch at the sight of you riding with your person so exposed into the lion's den."

But Michel merely laughed off his

companions' concern. "Assemble the men. I will speak to them before we ride off to meet our common destinies."

"As you wish, my king," Timothy bowed in Michel's direction and retreated from the tent to see his command carried out.

"Do you trust him?" Michel asked.

"Timothy?" Amele echoed astonished.

"Yes."

Amele considered and admitted cautiously, "I do not know him well enough to make such a judgment. Gabriel trusts him and insists he is loyal to our cause. Frankly, I was relying on your easy acceptance of him to guide my own. Why? Does your heart trouble you in regards to Timothy's fidelity?"

Michel shook his head. "No, but I sometimes wonder why it does not trouble me more. As you stated, neither of us know him well enough to have placed such trust in him and though I don't dispute Gabriel's greater familiarity with the baron and his aims, I do marvel at the ease with which he has insinuated himself among us."

"You entrusted Lady Elena's care to him," Amele reminded him.

"Yes and my heart tells me she will be safe with him. He is old enough to be her father and I think counted Barnabas a true friend. I believe he can be trusted to do his best by her."

"But not by you?" Amele countered stunned. He was obviously growing increasingly uneasy at the direction of their conversation. Baron Timothy was in their deepest confidence and was familiar with every detail of their strategy to claim the kingship for Michel.

"Do not fear, my friend. All will be well, but I think Baron Raulf is not the only contender we will be forced to defeat before Calei will be ours."

"Of that I have no doubt," Amele agreed, not without bitterness.

So it was clothed only in a fresh linen shirt and close-fitting breeches, with his sword riding low on his hip and a rich, violet, fur-lined cloak depicting his noble status with the royal family's crest emblazoned in gold upon his breast, that Michel faced his mail-clad army, more than four decades in the making. The sun speared through the low hanging clouds, its rays striking the bright armor the soldiers wore and reflecting it back into the sky where its light was muffled by the clouds, preventing the guards on the parapet walls of the castle from seeing the evidence of their deadly intent.

Each of his soldiers wore a cloak similar to his, proclaiming their loyalty to their cause. They were lined up in three long columns in accordance with their assignments that day, and assembled in rows of six across at the head of each column, their mounts restless beneath them. It was an impressive sight, worthy of a king, and Michel felt a fire ignite in his breast at the knowledge this long awaited day was finally upon him, and upon them all.

His squire held Arden's lead in his hand, the boy's excitement and apprehension etched across his young face in equal measure. Michel gave him a reassuring smile, took the lead from his outstretched hand and gained Arden's back in one fluid motion. A king for a king. The fanciful thought whispered through his mind and Arden shook out his mane, as if in agreement with his silent conclusion. Turning Arden to face his men, Michel signaled for silence and a hush immediately fell over the soldiers as they trained their eyes on him.

"Today is the day we have trained all of our lives for." A large cheer rose from the ranks. Michel raised his voice to carry over the din of a thousand voices. "Today we remove the stain of dishonor and the blood of traitors from the throne of our homeland." The men yelled even louder. "Today is the day we take back what is ours!!!"

Fury erupted over the mountains as with one voice the soldiers roared their purpose and clapped their swords against their shields, the din loud enough to shake the still sleeping foundations of the city. When the noise quieted, Michel added in a voice of deadly intent, "Our long vigil is at an end. The time for reaping our destiny is finally upon us. Let us make the most of it."

The columns of soldiers fell silent as each man

accepted the weight their young king laid upon them. They moved in silence through the mountain passes and met with no resistance from the seemingly non-existent outer defenses responsible for guarding Calei from marauders. Apparently those in temporary charge of seeing to the city's defense had concluded the greater threat to the peace would come from within its heart, rather than prey upon them from outside the city's intricate gates.

When the passes diverged, the three columns of mounted men diverged as well according to their respective purposes. Two columns would flank the city and hold their positions until the order was given to attack. Though it was his sincere hope that the transition of power would be accomplished peacefully, Michel was prepared to re-take his grandfather's throne by force if necessary. The third column, with Michel at its head, included Barons Timothy and Paul as well as the core of their most experienced forces. Amele rode at Michel's right as they passed through the gates, unchallenged by the astonished guards who could do no more than present their swords in a show of loyalty to the colors of the royal family that had never been so openly displayed in the course of their young lives.

As the noon hour approached and they took the main road through the center of the city towards the keep, Caleinians came out of their shops and their houses to view the spectacle of an army of mounted men bearing the royal colors and to see for themselves the handsome, young man who led them. Rather than cower in fear at the threat of impending war about to break apart the tenuous peace that still held sway over the grieving and anxious inhabitants, they cheered loudly the promise of the return of the true king hinted at by the livery of his men. Michel exchanged a surprised if somewhat amused glance with Amele at the warmth of the reception afforded them, thinking to himself an invading army had never been so fondly welcomed by the city it was intent on conquering.

Amele remarked over the cheers of the gathering crowd, "Did not King Barnabas predict the people's hearts would awaken at the return of their true king?"

Michel acknowledged his point with a somewhat self-mocking nod and Amele was seemingly unable to resist the urge to remind him, "I believe at the time you accused your predecessor of succumbing to the mystical nature of his kingdom."

Michel refused to rise to his friend's teasing, merely shaking his head and grinning in response. Then as the castle's imposing entrance came into view, both men turned their attention to the more serious matters awaiting them. It was decided that only eight of their company would attend the gathering. Along with Michel and Amele, were Barons Timothy, Paul and Nicholas, all heads of noble Caleinian families, accompanied by their commanders.

The discordant conversations echoing among those already assembled for the meeting to decide Barnabas' successor fell silent at their entrance and all turned the focus of their attention in their direction as soon as they entered. Michel took in the expressions of the men gathered in the grand hall, most of whose attention was focused squarely on him, the majority of which did not bother to hide their curiosity and/or disdain at the presumption of a stranger, dressed in the colors of the royal family, to insinuate himself amongst them at a meeting called for the exclusive attendance of Caleinian nobility to decide who would be king.

Michel knew they were aware of the speculation surrounding his identity, but he was in no hurry to confirm those speculations just yet. In his mind, and in the minds of his supporters, there was still some uncertainty as to the alliances of the remaining contenders for the throne and he wished to discover as much as possible before revealing himself. He was not surprised, however, when Raulf appointed himself the spokesman for the gathering he had not called and hailed their company in an arrogant voice.

"Barons Timothy, Paul and Nicholas you are welcome amongst us but as I have previously made clear this is not the time to have a stranger in our midst while we decide the important matters confronting the noble families of Calei and the future of this kingdom."

It was Paul who responded to Raulf's challenge. "We have brought no stranger to this gathering. This man is of Caleinian descent and he has proven his noble status to me and my companions."

A slight murmuring spread through the crowd, but for the moment Raulf's focus turned to the omission of one of their company, rather than Michel's inclusion among them. "Where is Lady Elena? Why did she not accompany you? We only entrusted her care to this stranger on your word he was worthy of our trust."

Timothy offered in response, "Lady Elena is under the care of my family until the matters under consideration here today have been decided."

Raulf nodded his reluctant approval. "You reassure me of your judgment, my friend. I had not thought you so careless as to allow the king's niece to be under the supervision of our noble guest." The title he afforded Michel was done with a good deal of mockery.

"It was the guest you refer to who asked me to see to the lady's protection," Timothy replied, his own voice laced with amused mockery.

"And what right does this stranger have to make any requests in regards to Lady Elena?" With a respectful nod in his direction, Timothy deferred to Michel the answer Raulf's challenge.

When Michel was certain the attention of the entire gathering was focused on him, he announced into the silence, "I am the lady's guardian and therefore the only one with the right to make any requests or arrangements in regards to her future."

Michel was not surprised by the astonished reactions to his assertion, nor when Raulf immediately challenged it. "Ha! Your noble stranger certainly does not lack a vivid imagination. And do you possess any proof to substantiate your ridiculous claim, boy?"

"But of course, no reasonable man would make such a claim without sufficient proof to substantiate it," Michel responded, referring rather mockingly to Raulf's attempt to do just that at their previous confrontation.

"Well then, for the benefit of the king's loyal friends who must all concern themselves with his niece's welfare and act as her guardians in his stead, please produce this proof you speak of," Raulf challenged, his voice indicating he had no doubt whatever proof Michel might produce would be easily dismissed as a fabrication.

Michel turned to Amele who removed the scroll he had hidden beneath his cloak. He indicated with a gesture for Gabriel to approach from his position near the entrance to retrieve it from his outstretched hand. No one questioned Gabriel's role in the proceedings. Even with the king's death, he remained captain of the soldier's assigned to see to the security of the throne. Any of the men among the gathering who held aspirations to ascend to the kingship would need his support and the loyalty of the men under his command in order to solidify their position as the new king.

So the gathering waited in silence as Gabriel crossed the hall and with a guarded, unrevealing expression and a slight but respectful bow in Michel's direction, accepted the scroll from his brother's outstretched hand. He turned to face the gathering and asked its representatives.

"Shall I read its contents?"

"Yes, please entertain us with its claims," Raulf commanded imperiously

A hush fell over the crown as Gabriel unrolled the scroll.

"I, King Barnabas, being of sound mind and aware of my deteriorating physical condition leave these instructions with my trusted friend and emissary to speak in my voice in regards to my wishes and intentions for both my beloved niece, Elena, and as to the heir I would appoint to rule after me as if I was present at the gathering this document has no doubt been produced at to decide these very matters."

A deeper hush fell over the room as Gabriel read the opening words of the document he held reverently in his grasp. It seemed to those assembled that it was almost as if he spoke with the voice of the dead king himself hailing his former subjects from the grave.

"Please continue, Captain, I am certain we are all desirous of hearing our friend Barnabas's wishes in these matters."

Michel turned in the direction of the new voice who called into the silence. The man met his frank examination with one of his own, and then nodded an equally forthright acknowledgement of Michel's interest.

"In the matter of my heir: I have made no secret for the duration of my kingship that it has always been my wish that a true heir to the kingship could be persuaded to return to Calei to ascend to the throne. Had I been able to accomplish my wish during my life, I would have gladly abdicated my throne in his favor. Alas, such a joyous day has eluded me in life, but I am hopeful it will not elude me in death. I therefore appoint as my heir, not of course that he needs such an appointment from me, as the throne of Calei belongs to him by right of birth, Prince Michel, King Nathaniel and Queen Alyssa's grandson, and the son of their daughter."

When Gabriel hesitated, the voice of the man who pressed him to continue with his duty of reading the scroll, spoke into the silence, his voice both understanding and amused at the king's naïve pronouncement of his heir. "Yes, well, we were all well aware of King Barnabas' wish and all of ours naturally, to have the blood of the royal family restored to the throne, but I imagine the king's wish will remain as elusive in death as it was in life." There were a few sympathetic and equally amused chuckles at the man's wry comment among the gathering, and then he gestured for Gabriel to continue.

"As to the matter of my niece Elena," At this a tense silence fell over the gathering, all of the men's earlier amusement absent. *"I give both my permission and my blessing for the marriage of my niece to the heir I have appointed and to no other."* The tension was momentarily interrupted by another course of amused chuckles and then Gabriel continued in a loud voice so as to be heard over the disruption, as if he was now in a hurry to read the rest of the document. *"That being the case, and with a full understanding that a marriage cannot be arranged without the consent of both parties, I appoint as guardian of my niece's person and her estate, Prince Michel, the grandson of King Nathaniel and Queen Alyssa."*

A stunned silence came over the assembled crowd, all amusement at the former king's foolish, but romantic nature forgotten as they each remembered the stranger's claim to be Lady Elena's guardian. If he had spoken the truth, Michel knew the others were even now concluding he could be none other than the grandson of the last true king, and the only one among them with the undisputed right to ascend to the throne of Calei.

Raulf was the first to recover from his surprise and give loud voice to his outrage, "You dare to call this ridiculous fabrication proof of your claim? Not only giving you guardianship over Lady Elena, and the king's permission to marry you and no other? But now you add to your previous audacity by claiming to be King Nathaniel's long-lost grandson? To repeat your own charge, stranger, that is very convenient for you, is it not?"

This time Michel could feel the other contenders aligned as one behind Raulf's accusation. He waited to respond to it until silence had once more fallen over the room. "Ah, but in the case of the proof I offer you, King Barnabas took the precaution of ensuring there were witnesses to see to it that his wishes concerning his niece and his throne were carried out."

Another rustling among the gathering. This time the men turned to eye their neighbors, wondering if they were one of the witnesses to which he referred.

"And who are these witnesses you speak of?' Raulf demanded in a voice that proclaimed he would dismiss without a second's hesitation all but the most unassailable of those he produced.

Michel turned his attention in Gabriel's direction. "I believe the good captain here is aware of the identity of those the king trusted to bear witness for him beyond the grave. I do not know the names of the chosen ones, and have only King Barnabas' assurance that they exist at all."

All eyes turned back to Gabriel with avid interest. It was obvious to Michel that if the captain of the king's guard denied his claim of witnesses to the scroll, or Barnabas had failed to see to the matter as he indicated he would, his position among them would be considerably weakened.

Gabriel faced Raulf and the others proudly, and for the first time used Michel's rightful title in their presence, "Yes, Prince Michel speaks the truth. I know the identities of those who were called to witness the king's seal on the scroll, the contents of which I have just disclosed to each of you, just as I was the one who arranged the meeting, at the king's request, between the two men."

Stunned silence greeted Gabriel's announcement that the king had met the stranger the captain of his own guard now referred to as Prince Michel. The silence was quickly filled with muffled whispers until Raulf's furious demand effectively silenced them. "Then send for these witnesses you speak of, Captain. I would hear their testimony with my own ears."

"As you wish, Baron," Gabriel replied with a bow, but made no move to hurry off to see his errand carried through.

Then Baron Timothy stepped forward and his voice proclaimed into the awkward breech, "I am one of the witnesses you seek. It was King Barnabas' last request of me that I provide such witness if the authenticity of the scroll was called into question. I do so now in honor of my pledge to my good friend and king."

"As do I," Baron Paul called out and also stepped forward to stand at Gabriel's side. "King Barnabas made the same request of me, and in honor of my pledge I too can attest to the authenticity of the scroll and its contents the captain holds in his possession."

Baron Raulf swung from one to the other of his equals, his eyes threatening what his lips could not express with so many witnesses present.

"I too, was one of the witnesses of whom the captain speaks." A young man in priestly robes stepped forward and Michel assumed he was the king's confessor.

One of the older noblemen, who had not spoken up to this point in the proceedings turned to the priest. "Bishop Maren you will vouch for the authenticity of this scroll?"

"Yes, though I was not present at the meeting the captain speaks of, King Barnabas requested that I provide witness to the scroll's authenticity, and also to his intent to name King Nathaniel's grandson his legitimate heir and his niece's guardian upon his death."

The older man nodded, silenced Raulf's budding outrage with an impatient gesture, and then turned back to direct his next comment to

Gabriel. "Thank you, Captain, for your loyal service to your king. I think there can be no remaining question as to King Barnabas' intent to name King Nathaniel's grandson his heir and the guardian of Lady Elena. In point of fact, it would not be necessary for him to name the grandson of the last true king his rightful heir as the throne would belong to him by right of birth. However, I am concerned that after so much time and given the king's failing state near the end of his life that he may have been deceived by a stranger thinking to take advantage of his greatest hope and gain the hearts of Caleinians and the throne itself under false pretenses. What proof do we have this man you refer to as Prince Michel is actually the grandson of King Nathaniel? After all, the king has been dead for over forty years. There has been no word in all that time from Queen Alyssa, and all of our attempts in the intervening years at persuading one of the true heirs to the throne to return have proven unsuccessful. Why are we to believe that one of them has suddenly changed his mind? It all seems rather too convenient to be believed."

"Exactly my point, Baron," Raulf heartily agreed.

Gabriel nodded, "If I may, Baron?"

"Please, if you are able to shed additional light on this matter, Captain, I am certain we would all be happy to consider your testimony."

Gabriel turned to face Michel from where he

stood in the center of the circle of men debating Calei's future. Though the older man did not kneel before him, as Michel could see was his inclination, he bowed most profoundly, and then turned back to the waiting company. A profound silence fell over the gathering as he drew a deep breath, released it in an audible sigh and then began his testimony. "I was there that black night when King Nathaniel was murdered." A rustling at his shocking disclosure passed through the assemblage, and if anything, the silence deepened and filled with expectation as they gave him their full attention. "I was a raw recruit, still in training, and assigned to my older brother's command so he could keep an eye on me. Those of you who remember that evil day will also recall it was a time of peace in our city. There was little threat of an attack by our enemies, so the younger and more inexperienced soldiers were given the watch on the wall. We had just completed our assigned watch and were climbing the stairs to the great hall to find some food to fill our stomachs before seeking our beds."

"When we entered the hall we couldn't believe our eyes. There was blood and swords and men fighting for their lives. At my young age I had never seen a man gutted with a sword. Seeing the combatants all attired in familiar livery was too confusing for my young eyes to put a name to what was happening, but my older brother guessed immediately that there was a traitor in our midst and that they would try to harm the queen. If you recall Queen Alyssa was heavy with child and was expected to give birth any day. My brother led us away from the fighting, back down the steps and through the tunnels that run beneath the keep. He sent me to sound the alarm to raise the city's defenders while he and the others looked for the queen. He instructed me to meet him at our father's cabin in the mountains after I completed my task and that he would bring the queen there so we could protect her until the king could put down the insurrection."

"Our plan was to return Queen Alyssa to her husband's care when word reached us that the city was secured. Of course all of us know such word never reached us. Instead, we heard the blackest news, that King Nathaniel had been murdered by his closest friend and confidant. We were young, but we understood enough of such things to know Queen Alyssa would not be allowed to live long enough to deliver a child that carried the blood of the rightful king. So we escorted her through the mountains until we reached the very edge of our lands and there I parted ways with my brother."

"I begged him to allow me to accompany him, that it was my sworn duty to protect the queen and the child she carried, but my brother urged me to stay. Those who accompanied the queen would need to know when the threat to her life was put down and it was safe for Queen Alyssa and her child to return to their rightful place in Calei.

Though my heart urged me otherwise, I remained behind while the others hurried our queen away from her home, away from her husband's kingdom, because evil men sought her death, and we did not know who was aligned with the traitors or who it was safe for us to trust."

When he fell silent, another man, old enough to remember that evil day, spoke into the hushed silence. "You do your family honor by the great service you rendered our king and our people upon the occasion of that black night, Captain, but is there anyone who can take up the story from where you parted with your brother and attest to the truth of this man's claim to be a grandson of King Nathaniel and Queen Alyssa?"

Gabriel nodded solemnly. "My brother, Amele, has remained by the queen's side all of these long years."

"Then where is he? Can you summon him to Calei to provide testimony as to the truth of this stranger's claim?"

"It is not necessary to summon him, Baron. He is among us even as we speak." Gabriel turned and exchanged a fierce glance with Amele before raising his arm and pointing in his direction. "There is my brother, Amele, who has never forsaken the oath he took to protect the royal house of Calei."

Stunned faces turned to regard the man who stood at the side of the stranger. Amele stepped forward, bowing slightly to the gathering and faced the baron who raised the question. "I can indeed pick up the story where my brother, Gabriel's ended, and provide testimony of this man's identity," he proclaimed, indicating a silent Michel with his hand.

"Then do so," the older baron, who had first requested proof of his claim, urged impatiently.

Amele stood silent for a moment as if gathering his thoughts and then began the account of his long years in exile. "As my brother, Gabriel, told you we escorted Queen Alyssa into the mountains and within a few days she gave birth to her daughter. The queen suffered her labor without attendants, and without benefit of a midwife gave birth in a cold, damp cave carved from the rock of the mountains. Neither I nor the men who accompanied us were of much help to our king's young widow, for we were men and what do men know of such things? Still in all the years of our exile Queen Alyssa never voiced a word of complaint about the loss of her husband's kingdom and the luxuries that were hers by right. Her only concern was for her daughter."

"You spoke the truth, Baron, when you stated there had been no word from Queen Alyssa in the intervening years. She feared for her daughter's safety and refused to even consider returning to Calei, knowing that evil men sought not only her own death, but the death of her child. She urged me to return to my homeland because she knew my heart and my thoughts were ever on its gilded streets, but I could not return while my queen lived if she refused to do so. Seeing my grief at the loss of my home, she made me a promise. She vowed that one day blood of her husband's blood would return to Calei and restore the blood of the rightful king to the throne of Calei. I was forced to content myself with her promise as I could see she would not return herself, nor would she allow her daughter to do so. In the intervening years we pushed ever west over the mountains and into Europe, never calling a single place home, but living a wanderer's life, capturing and training wild horses and selling them off at need to provide for the little luxuries and supplies we required from time to time."

"Over time our forces grew as those loyal to King Nathaniel's memory heard word of us and sent us men, sometimes boys, from their households to join our purpose to protect the bloodline of the true king. Throughout the many years we remained exiled from our homes we trained and we remembered our homeland, and we passed on the stories of its heritage to those who followed us and to those who joined us, so that we would never be distracted from our true purpose. When the princess married a Saxon duke, our queen wept joyful tears, not only at the sight of her daughter's happiness, but because she knew the princess was safe at last from the designs of evil men who would use her for their own ends. When the princess gave birth to her first son, it was my joyful task to deliver the news to my brother Gabriel, and those who remained loyal to our cause here in Calei that a new heir had been born and the king's blood lived on in his grandson."

"It was unfortunately also my duty to caution him that the princess' first son would inherit the rich estates of his Saxon father and would likely not return to Calei, where he would be a stranger, to ascend to his grandfather's throne. Three times more I traversed the mountain passes in the depths of winter to deliver the news of additional sons the princess bore her husband, but I refrained from spoiling my brother's joy by sharing the queen's vision. With the births of each of the older sons, Queen Alyssa tempered my happiness by sharing with me that none of her daughter's older sons would be the one to return to Calei and keep the queen's promise to her humble servant to restore the blood of the true king to the throne. But when the princess gave her husband twins, a boy and a girl, and our queen shared the joyous news with me, she revealed her vision to me. I will never forget that morning or her words when she proclaimed, 'He is the one, Amele. He is the one who will return to Calei and restore the blood of the true king to the throne.' From the first time I held him in my arms as a babe, he has been my king. While he lives, I will kneel before no other, nor call another man king."

When he finished speaking Amele turned

away from the awed, astonished crowd and removed his sword from the belt at his side. Kneeling before Michel, he offered the blade hilt first. "Your Highness, my sword and my life are yours to command."

Before Michel could bend to assist his closest friend to his feet, Gabriel stepped forward and knelt at his brother's side. "My sword and my life are yours to command, my king."

The rest of the king's guard followed their captain's lead and as one knelt and bowed their heads in Michel's direction, offering their pledge of loyalty to defend his life at the sacrifice of their own.

The gathering followed suit. All knelt before the new king and offered Michel their pledge of loyalty. All but one. Baron Raulf screamed his outrage, as he grabbed at the kneeling barons, urging them to rise. "Get up. Get up. You kneel before this stranger? These outsiders? What do they know of Calei? What do they have to do with it? Get up. I tell you. It is blasphemy!"

Raulf was panting with exertion and his face was flushed with furious outrage. With a gesture, Michel signaled for his new subjects to rise and observed in a calm voice. "Surely it is the bishop's place to instruct the church's faithful followers as to what constitutes an act of blasphemy."

Raulf turned an accusing eye in the bishop's direction as did the entire assemblage. It was a calculated risk Michel took, but one he felt confident in. The young bishop turned and nodded in Michel's direction. "It is not blasphemy for the loyal subjects of a king to give him the respect he is due. Did not our lord himself instruct his faithful followers to render unto to Caesar what is Caesar's and unto God what is God's?"

"This man is neither Caesar nor God, but an imposter who seeks to steal the throne from a true Caleinian." Raulf was so incensed, he drew his sword. Gabriel immediately stepped in front of Michel and drew his own as did Amele and the entire member of the king's guard represented in the hall.

"Stand down my friends," Michel commanded them softly. "Let us put an end to this dissension here and now." Reluctantly the guard lowered their swords. Michel stepped through their protective line. "You challenge my right to ascend to the throne of my grandfather?"

"Yes. I challenge you in the name of all loyal to the honor of Calei. You are a usurper, a stranger among us who seeks to rob us of our rich treasury and return to the land of your birth with the wealth purchased on the backs of ordinary Caleinians."

Michel's lips curved in a derisive smile. He doubted Raulf had ever given a moment's thought to the burdens of true Caleinians. "How do you propose we settle your challenge?"

Raulf met his mild gaze with an almost rabid one of his own. "The way such things have been settled from the beginning of time. I will fight you here and now."

"Here and now?" Michel echoed mildly. "You and me?"

"Yes, unless you are afraid to face me. It is better for the people to learn now that their new king is a coward."

His insult had Gabriel stepping forward to stand next to Michel, his sword ready to retaliate on his king's behalf. Michel placed a restraining hand on his arm and turned back to Raulf. "And if you lose?"

"I will not lose, boy," His disdain evident, Raulf nearly spat his answer into the space separating the two men.

Satisfaction surged through Michel at Raulf's words. So he was to fight for his birthright after all. "Well then, let us not waste any more time debating the matter." He turned and passed his cloak to Amele, who cautioned him with a single glance. Ignoring it, Michel nodded his impatient acknowledgment. He was restless for a fight. It did not sit well with him his long years of training would be for naught. Though Raulf was not the man who murdered his grandfather, Michel had no issue with making do with the obnoxious baron as a substitute.

"Be careful my young prince. His mouth and temper may lead you to conclude otherwise, but

he is skilled with a blade and thinks to take in a moment of violence what he was unable to win by treachery."

"Who are you?" Michel silently wondered of the warning voice in his head, even as the rest of him continued preparing for the coming confrontation.

An answering chuckle whispered through his thoughts, *"Let us just say that I am a friend of the family."*

Shaking off the strange, imaginary encounter, Michel turned his attention to his challenger. The incensed baron was a large man, and there was strength in his broad shoulders and in the hand that gripped his heavy broadsword. Michel preferred a lighter blade, but he comprehended that if Raulf was able to connect with even a sweeping blow from the thick, finely honed sword, the wound it inflicted would likely prove fatal. A large circle formed around the two contenders and Michel stepped boldly into it. Raulf brandished his heavy weapon while eyeing Michel's own with derisive laughter.

"A boy's blade for a boy challenger. Let us put an end to this idiocy now."

Michel sidestepped the older man's first reckless charge, and used his blade to nick his opponent's sword arm as Raulf brought his blade down in a broad sweep to where Michel no longer stood. "First blood to me, I think," he remarked in a coolly amused voice.

In fresh rage Raulf swung around, "When you lay dying, your blood staining the floor of the hall you will never rule over, may your last thoughts be of me sitting on the throne you thought to steal, presiding over the citizens that will never call you king and with the woman you desire serving my pleasure."

Michel was too canny a fighter to be drawn in by the other man's insults, but he could be grateful to his opponent for reminding him what was at stake. At the other man's reference to Elena, Michel's blood froze and his expression took on a new seriousness as he responded in kind to the challenge the other issued, "When you lay dying with your blood staining *my* floor, still dreaming of the throne you sought to steal and the woman who preferred death rather than subject herself to your vile lust, may your last memory be of the rightful king standing over you with his sword at your throat and his curse sending you to hell."

Raulf charged again at Michel's dark promise and Michel skillfully deflected the killing blow to his chest before deftly spinning around and sliding his blade down the other's sword arm. The wound was not deep but it bled profusely, and Michel knew it would make it more difficult for his opponent to keep a firm grip on his blade. Again Raulf used a wide-sweeping motion in attempt to inflict a single fatal wound that would demonstrate his superiority in combat and impress their observers with the ease with which he dismissed the insignificant challenge Michel presented, to both the throne of Calei, and to his fighting skills.

When that failed, Raulf seemed to gain control over his rage and the two combatants settled into the serious matter of a battle to the death. For both men understood only one of them would survive the deadly contest being waged between them. There would be no compromise, no reconciliation. Before the end of this day one of them would stand before their maker giving an account of his life and the gifts He bestowed upon him. The other would still have his remaining days or years on earth to prepare himself for such an eventuality.

For long minutes the only sounds that could be heard in the hall were grunts of exertion from both combatants, gasps of pain when a blow landed, and their heavy breathing as the contest took its toll on their reserves. To those watching, the two seemed surprisingly evenly matched. Raulf's advantage of greater bulk and years of experience were equalized by the young prince's speed and agility. For all his youth it was obvious to those watching the young contender to the throne was no stranger to hand-to-hand engagement, and as the fight drew longer than anyone expected, it became clear that Raulf's greater bulk and his luxurious life-style were proving to be a disadvantage.

Michel had spent his entire life training for this chance, recognizing only now how much harder Amele had pushed him than he had his older brothers, how many more trials he faced and the great odds his mentor deliberately stacked against him time after time. In his youth, Michel had cursed the unfairness of it all and supposed Amele favored his older brothers over him. Only now did he understand his friend's true gift. Today was the first time he had heard of his grandmother's prophecy that he would be the one to return to challenge for his grandfather's throne. There was no need for Michel to continue to be burdened by the guilt of being the sole surviving male member of his family. Seemingly it had been his fate to face this challenge and to rise above it.

He understood the contest with Raulf was only the initial challenge he would face to take his place as his grandfather's successor, and it was proving more difficult than he expected, but he called now on the reserves of strength and endurance he'd built over the years of a warrior's singular focus to train and to better his skills. He comprehended Raulf had not been awarded a similar gift. He'd had estates to see to, alliances to make, a young and popular king to dispense with and his lovely young niece to kidnap in order to force himself upon. The ice in Michel's veins melted quickly beneath his outrage at the sins of this man. Maybe God was the only rightful judge of a man's offenses against His holy will, but Michel had been given the opportunity this day to stand in His place and execute His wrathful judgment in the name of the innocent. He wasn't about to waste it.

Michel was aware of the slowing of the other man's steps and the way his sword slipped in his bloody hand. He sensed the lessening of his opponent's focus as his assumption of the quick triumph he expected over his youthful and presumably inexperienced adversary began to slip away beneath the fierceness of the struggle he was engaged in. Michel risked his chance before Raulf could regroup and re-focus his concentration. He parried a half-hearted thrust of his opponent, and then drove in swiftly before Raulf could recover. Michel buried his sword up to the hilt through the other man's broad chest. While blood blossomed on his opponent's tunic and stunned shock, followed quickly by hideous pain bloomed across his harsh features, Michel notched his blade upward widening and deepening the damage before Raulf could lower his sword and dispatch his blade, or worse, sever his arm. Michel managed to free his sword only moments before Raulf attempted to fulfill his bloody expectation and Michel couldn't help but be impressed by the ease with which the man dismissed an injury that would have brought a lesser opponent to his knees.

A deeper silence hung over their audience,

laced now with the expectation of seeing Raulf succumb to his wounds, and a new admiration for the young prince who appeared on the brink of claiming the throne out from under Raulf's long reach. Still the two men engaged each other. Michel did not lessen his focus, even when victory appeared assured. He'd been trained too well to lower his sword or slow his attack until his opponent had dropped his sword and was completely defenseless. So he continued to press his advantage, the silence between the two men broken only by the clash of metal upon metal and Raulf's crude insults thrown in his direction and the painful gasps he was unable to completely suppress when Michel's quicker blade pierced his flesh. For his part, after inflicting the wound to the baron's chest, Michel allowed his challenger to exhaust himself chasing his quicker feet around the circle and allowed the loss of blood and his enemy's fierce rage to do its own damage. Finally Raulf stood, breathing heavily and lowered his sword, eyeing Michel with an intense hatred that dared him to take advantage of the opportunity he was affording him.

Michel would not allow himself to be drawn in by the other's ploy. Raulf was wounded yes and likely mortally so, if the wound to his chest was not soon tended to, but Michel was quite certain he retained enough strength to deal him a killing blow if he followed the other's example and allowed his emotions to take precedence over his warrior's training.

"Afraid, boy?" Raulf taunted and then held his arms out to his sides. "Finish it if you dare."

Michel stood a safe distance away, enjoying the show and wondering if the man was truly the fool he appeared to be, or if he really believed Michel would allow himself to be goaded into closing the distance between them. "I do not need to finish it. If your wounds are not soon tended you will bleed to death, baron. If you wish to live, I suggest you concede your challenge and kneel before me and offer your pledge of loyalty to the true king."

Michel's amused comment wiped the mocking smile from the baron's lips, as Michel knew it would. Holding his sword in both hands Raulf charged again, like a bull, swinging his blade wildly, and with such fierce intent, the spectators to the contest backed away several steps to avoid becoming collateral damage of the struggle they observed. Michel stood his ground until the last possible moment, and then stepped left while at the same time slipping his sword beneath the baron's upraised arms and burying it deeply in the baron's chest. The heavy broadsword dropped to the tiled floor and Raulf crumbled to his knees, his eyes still spewing hatred and his lips still cursing Michel and his ancestry.

Michel pushed the fallen man onto his back with his boot and held his sword to the baron's throat. "Do you concede?"

An evil curse passed through Raulf's grimacing lips. Michel applied pressure to the point of the blade and drew blood.

"You poisoned your king. You kidnapped Lady Elena."

Bleeding in his arms and legs, his blood soaking the tile from the mortal wound in his chest, his enemy still swore up at him. He swiped at Michel's arm holding the sword to his throat, his booted foot on his chest, and earned only more cuts on his hands for his trouble.

He cursed again and Michel pushed harder on the point of the blade. "Why?"

The dying man spit at him. "I don't answer to you, boy. Nor will I ever bend my knee to you."

Michel arched an imperious brow over his stunning blue gaze. "That is hardly necessary as you are flat on your back with my boot on your chest. You could hardly be in a more submissive posture than you are now."

Raulf further diminished his waning strength in an attempt to buck Michel's boot from his chest. Michel remained firmly planted.

"He denied my petition for the girl and refused to name me his heir. I who kept the peace. I, who kept the mountain passes open so trade could resume in Calei. He said it was his hope that the true king's heirs would one day return. The true king? Barnabas ruled this land for twenty years. What did your grandfather last? A few insignificant years? Who even remembers now?

His rule was irrelevant. It's ridiculous any true Caleinian would kneel before you."

Astonished gasps echoed around the room at his confession and Raulf recognized whatever chance he had of gaining the loyalty of the other noblemen was lost to him now. "A curse on all of you. Enjoy your time as king, boy. Do you plan to live as a monk under your own roof the way your predecessor did? My death does not abolish the curse awaiting you and your sons. Enjoy your whore for the time granted you. We will meet again in hell."

His outrage was cut short when Michel increased the pressure on the sword in his hand effectively silencing the baron's dying curse. He withdrew his blade and wiped the other man's blood from it with Raulf's own cloak.

"Well done, my young protégé'. I believe your sister underestimates you."

The voice was back. Michel wished there was time to engage the strange apparition in conversation, but there were more pressing matters demanding his attention at the moment.

"Does anyone else wish to challenge my right to rule?" He demanded as he stepped away from the dead man and allowed his gaze to sweep the room.

"No, Your Highness."

"No, Your Highness."

Michel's inquiry was met with quick denials from the other barons and then a shout was heard from the back of the room. "Long live, King Michel!"

"Hear! Hear!"

"Hear! Hear! Long live King Michel!"

Michel's eyes met Amele's admiring glance across the distance separating them. His lips curved at the glimmer of tears in his friend's eyes, tears belied by the sound of his deep voice echoing his loud agreement with the proclamation.

As the noise diminished one after another of the assembled noblemen approached Michel to both introduce themselves and offer their services to ease in the transition of power. Gabriel ordered two of his men to remove Raulf's bloodied corpse from the room, and turned to cross the room and throw open the wide double doors at the end of the hall. A loud cheer greeted his action and Michel found himself half led and half carried by the celebratory crowd in the direction of the room revealed behind them. They paused on the threshold to give Michel a chance to take in the significance of the room he was being led into.

If the great hall was the gathering place for ordinary assemblages the throne room was the one used for state occasions. Michel immediately understood its purpose was to impress and awe anyone who approached the magnificent throne to plead for favor in front of it. The very magnitude of the spacious room diminished any supplicant who presented himself before it. Seeing it, Michel was both humbled and somewhat amused by his ancestors' obvious ploy to terrorize those who would seek their favor.

With some reluctance Michel allowed himself to be led to the base of the inlaid throne, liberally decorated with gold, and then stood, still hesitating to ascend the wide platform as he came face to face confronting his seeming inevitable destiny. His boisterous escort, sensing his hesitancy, and as if only just becoming sensitive to the enormity of the occasion in the young prince's life, stepped back and allowed the new king his moment. An expectant silence hung over the room and Michel sensed it wasn't only from his audience. It was as if the room itself had curious eyes and was waiting to see the quality of the man who would ascend the platform and fill the empty seat there. The longer he waited the heavier the silence lay across the room.

Michel felt as if his feet were weighted to the ground. He instructed his legs to move to gain the platform and take his place in the throne of his forefathers, but they remained rooted to the floor. He suddenly recalled the curse he dismissed so casually, his grandfather's murder by his close friend, and his immediate predecessor's mysterious illness. Was it the curse that led the king's friends and confidants to madness, urging them to abandon their honor to gain the throne, or was it ordinary human greed? Would Amele begin plotting his death the moment he sat in the imposing seat? The absurdity of his musing was enough to bring a chuckle to his lips and free his weighted feet. He stepped up onto the platform, his motion instantly relieving the growing tension in the room. Then with a theatrical bow, Michel seated himself in the royal throne, bringing a rousing cheer of approval from the gathering.

Thus began Michel's informal coronation. The boisterous celebration went on long into the evening hours with both ale and food flowing freely. Word was sent to their men waiting in the mountain for the signal to attack the city that the transfer of power had been accomplished peacefully. After their initial disappointment at being deprived of the excuse to exercise their soldier's skills, the men of war joined with the ordinary populace, the shop keepers, the traders, the guides, the bankers, young and old. All gathered for an impromptu celebration in the streets to rejoice in the return of the true king.

As night fell one of the barons stood on a bench and loudly called for the gathering's attention. "All hail, King Michel!" He yelled and the revelers gladly responded with loud cheers. The man repeated his call over the din of hundreds of voices, and the assemblage yelled even louder in response. Then into the competing shouts, one of the attendees suggested they send for the witch to give the new king his clue in overcoming the curse on the royal family.

After Michel nodded his somewhat confused

assent to the latter suggestion to find the witch and bring her before him, he signaled for Amele to join him, and beneath the expectant curiosity awaiting the witch's arrival, the two men separated themselves to indulge in a moment's private conversation.

"The witch?" Michel inquired mildly.

Amele's lips twitched and one shoulder rose in a resigned shrug. "Yes, well, there may have been a few details I omitted when I explained about the curse on the royal family."

"How many such omissions constitute a few, I wonder?"

At Amele's somewhat guilty expression, Michel asked with a resigned sigh. "What's this about a clue?"

Amele shrugged. "I have never witnessed the actual occasion, but I am told when a new king is crowned, the current head of the…coven, for lack of a better word, is summoned to provide the new monarch with his clue to unravelling the ancient curse."

"You're being uncharacteristically evasive, my friend."

"Not intentionally. The truth is the entire process has always been cloaked in mystery. Those present upon such occasions are often reluctant to speak of what they have seen or heard."

Michel eyed the boisterous gathering and remarked wryly, "Well at least that is one tradition that appears as though it will come to an end tonight. We certainly do not lack for witnesses to assist me in unravelling the clue that I presume is about to be bestowed upon me."

"That is true," Amele commented with an optimistic nod.

CHAPTER ELEVEN

Michel wasn't certain what he expected the local witch to look like, but he supposed in the back of his mind he carried a picture from the fairy tales of his youth of an old hag with a crooked nose, covered in a dark cloak and with a fierce expression meant to frighten foolish children away before they fell victim to her spell. Therefore he was surprised, pleasantly he supposed, when the steward of his clue to assist him in unravelling the ancient curse that beset his blood turned out to be a young maid of about Elena's age and with the same hesitancy in her gaze when she regarded him he often observed in his ward's eyes.

The maid looked about her curiously as Gabriel led her toward where Michel awaited her approach near the throne. The rest of the witnesses of the occasion quickly gathered around to see the spectacle few, if any, had ever been privileged to observe for themselves.

"The maid, Rowena," Gabriel announced and the girl hurriedly knelt before Michel, bowing her head.

"Your Highness," her voice was an awed

whisper, but Michel noted both the surprise and curiosity in her glance when she regarded him. He thought perhaps she expected to be brought before Raulf this evening and Michel couldn't be certain if she was pleasantly surprised or disappointed by the change in the order of things, or if she held no opinion on the matter at all.

"You may rise, Rowena." As the maid did so, he added courteously, "Forgive us for interrupting your evening, but I am told you have a task to perform for the benefit of your new king."

"Yes, Your Highness," the girl replied blushing at his address, but made no move to get on with the imparting of the rumored clue.

"You may proceed," Michel added in a slightly amused voice causing the maid's face to flood with embarrassed color. Feeling guilty at his gentle mockery, Michel added in a soft voice, "You are among friends, Rowena. There is no need for the anxiety I can see in your eyes."

Michel's reassurance went a long way to dispelling the fear he'd witnessed in the girl's expression, but it was still with more than a hint of worry that she lifted her clear green gaze to his. "Thank you, Your Highness. Forgive me. 'Tis the truth I am a little nervous. I have never been called upon to perform this task. My grandmother tended to the duty for the former king, but she is ill and bade me come in her stead."

"I see. I must conclude then that your grandmother knew what she was about in sending you to us. It may comfort you to know this is my first time as well to be present at these proceedings, so we may learn together what is expected of us."

The girl released an audible sigh and her lips settled into a relieved smile. Despite his reassurance to Rowena, he was not all that certain her grandmother knew what she was about to send this child in her stead. Since he was quite certain there would be no shortage of Caleinians who doubted his fitness to rule given his youth, he was willing to give the girl a chance to prove herself up to the weighty task before her.

He watched while she took a step back and removed a crystal ball from the folds of her cloak. From the way she clutched it carefully in both of her hands he assumed it was heavier than it appeared. After taking a moment to compose herself she raised her arms above her hand and proclaimed into the sudden silence suspended over the previously boisterous crowd of witnesses, "A new king has ascended to the ancient throne of Calei. He seeks the clue to overcoming the curse that holds sway over the royal family."

Despite himself, Michel was fascinated by the subtle changes in the girl's voice and mannerisms as she petitioned some invisible force to respond to her request. A rustling passed through the crowd when the young girl's features coalesced into a more masculine appearance and her voice dropped several octaves when she next spoke.

"Ah, so you are Nathaniel's grandson. Michel, is it not? The promised one. We have followed your progress for some time with great interest. You have the look of him, but the eyes are your grandmother's. I imagine she will not be pleased when you confess you have managed to misplace the treasure of her house your sister entrusted to you." The voice speaking through the maid's lips laughed as if amused by Michel's carelessness, then regaining control of himself, he added, "Do not be concerned my young monarch, the stone is in trustworthy hands."

Michel's interest was caught despite his intention to remain objective in the face of what he considered just one more little odd tradition surrounding his grandfather's kingdom. He had yet to confide in Amele or anyone else that he had managed to lose the Salusian stone, so he was stunned whoever spoke through the girl knew of its loss. He took comfort from his assurance that his sister's inheritance was safe and in good hands.

"We had great hope when King Nathaniel returned with his young bride that he would be the one to break the curse, but unfortunately he never fully comprehended what he held within his grasp. Ah, forgive me, I spoke hastily. That was unfair I think. Your grandfather's life was cut short by the designs of evil men. Perhaps had he lived longer this burden would not now fall upon you, my young king."

When the maid fell quiet, Michel asked into the silence, "Who are you?"

Amusement lit the girl's unseeing eyes and a light chuckle escaped through her stiff lips. *"The answer to your query is beyond your ability to comprehend in your current, and quite limited, physical state."* He paused as if in anticipation of Michel's affronted response, and then when none was forthcoming, added in a voice of near respect, *"You are not quick to take offense. That is good. In answer to your question, I will only say we are the arbiters of such matters and it is for us to ensure justice is served and the terms met before your family is freed from this burden."*

"Justice? You name it justice to murder the sons of my sires?"

A haughty brow lifted above one of the girl's young, but cannily knowing eyes, *"You speak of what you do not know, my young king. Are you aware of why this curse was laid upon this house? Do you have knowledge of the atrocities that were committed by your ancestors who shed innocent blood that must be atoned for before the curse can be broken?"*

Michel was stunned and dully chastised by the mention of the atrocities his unusual companion referred to. "Your words are true. I stand corrected. I do not know of what you speak, and would gladly offer recompense for the evils of my ancestors' past deeds, but how am I to do so if I do not know of the sins committed by this house or against whom, so that I might repay my family's debt?"

"You give me hope, my young king. You are more than your predecessors, even your grandfather. I think you have your grandmother's blood to thank for that. You are not quick to dismiss that which you cannot see with your eyes and do battle against with your sword."

"Can you not speak more plainly? How am I to undo this spell on the basis of insinuations and misty references to the past?"

"A clue I am permitted to offer you, as I have each of your long line of unsuccessful predecessors."

"Then I gladly accept what assistance you are allowed to proffer."

"The clue remains unchanged in the long march of time across the bloody past of your fair kingdom. When the daughter of the moon captures the heart of the sun the curse will be lifted. So it is written, so it will be. You must begin your search in the past, but you will find your answers in the present. Do not be too quick to dismiss what I have already revealed to you. I must leave you now, my young king. I have stayed too long already and this vessel is immature and untried. To remain any longer might cause irreparable damage to my courteous host. Good eve, young Michel and good fortune."

With that the girl's features returned to their previous innocence and she collapsed to the tiled floor in a dead faint. Michel rushed to attend to the fallen maid. He knelt beside her still form and lifted her head, signaling a servant for a glass of water. Her eyes fluttered open, but remained confused and unseeing until they locked on his. "Your Highness," she whispered blushing, and then struggled into a seated position.

"Take a moment," Michel instructed her and removed the cool water from the tray the curious servant held and offered it to Rowena.

She blushed profusely as their fingertips brushed against each other when she accepted the cup from his hands. Michel pretended not to notice her discomfort. She took a dainty sip then asked anxiously, her eyes clinging to his over the rim of the cup, "Were you pleased with my service, Your Highness? 'Tis the truth I cannot remember anything I told you, but my grandmother warned me it would be such."

"Quite pleased, maid Rowena. You may inform your grandmother you executed your office with both grace and poise. When you have recovered sufficiently the captain will see to it that one of his own men escorts you back to the care and supervision of your grandmother. I trust you will convey my wishes to her for a speedy recovery."

"Thank you, Your Highness. You are exceedingly kind."

"Not at all," Michel replied smoothly, "It is I who stand in your debt for the service you rendered my house this evening."

Michel left the maid in Gabriel's competent care, then stood and joined Amele where he was engaged in quiet conversation with Timothy. "I suppose it is too much to expect that either you or Gabriel know the meaning behind our, ah…visitor's reference to either the heart of the sun or the daughter of the moon."

Amele shook his head. "Regrettably not, but I must tell you I found the entire performance quite entertaining and somewhat disturbing if the truth be told. I was not present the night King Nathaniel received his clue from the girl's grandmother as my father was still alive, but we discussed it at length over the years."

Michel recognized Amele pointedly refrained from mentioning the voice's reference to the loss of the Salusian stone. Sighing, Michel, admitted reluctantly, "The chain broke while I was bathing in the river one morning. I chased it nearly a mile through the current but finally abandoned my search. Whoever it was speaking through the girl did not learn of its loss from me."

Amele nodded, as if Michel's admission came as no great surprise to him. Michel concluded his good friend had already learned of the stone's loss likely because there was very little he missed, and the two men were constantly in each other's company. He no doubt noticed Michel no longer constantly tugged on the restraint of the too-close fit of the chain around his neck as had been his habit since the evening he took possession of the Salusian stone at Melissa's insistence.

Michel released a deep sigh and remarked, "At least he indicated the stone was not completely lost and now resides in trustworthy hands. It's odd he would remark upon the stone. It is not a keepsake of my grandfather's house, but was only introduced to Calei when he brought my grandmother here as his bride. Why should the stone's loss have any bearing on the resolution of the curse that besets my blood?"

"I wish I possessed the answers to your questions, my king, but despite my long years in your grandmother's company, I remain but a simple soldier in the service of my king. I fear I will be of little use to you in unravelling this mystery of the curse."

"So you can think of nothing that might point me to the daughter of the moon or the heart of the sun? Are there any ancient writings that might mention one or the other? Surely there must be a record somewhere about my predecessors' attempts to solve this riddle. At the very least, it would be nice not to be condemned to simply repeating the failures of my ancestors."

"You raise an interesting point. I will speak to Gabriel about where the kings kept the papers and records that were passed to them from their predecessors. As the captain of the guard, he must surely know of such matters. I think it might be worth a discussion with Bishop Maren as well.

He is young, yes, and this too would have been his first experience with the events we all witnessed this evening, but the church is often called upon to act as the guardian of ancient truths. It would not be unreasonable to assume the church has its own records in regards to the history of Calei."

"That is a very perceptive comment, my friend. You discover what Gabriel knows, and I will seek out the bishop and find out if there are any records in the church's possession that go back beyond where the memories of the living can reach."

CHAPTER TWELVE

The celebration in honor of Michel's ascension to the throne of his grandfather seemed to go on endlessly before Michel finally excused himself and sought the comfort of his chambers. It was not surprising his ale-dampened thoughts dwelt on the comfort to be found in gentler companionship than he'd shared for the majority of his first day as king. A vision of Elena's feminine beauty swam before his eyes and he instantly banished it. Accepting such comfort from a young, nobly born virgin was accompanied by a high price he was not yet certain he was willing to pay. He wasn't even certain he was in a positon to offer just recompense for such comfort. Not that there was any shortage of opportunities for him to enjoy the kind of casual feminine companionship his body yearned for in the hours before dawn broke on the second day of his kingship. His new friends and subjects were not only willing to provide him such entertainment but they seemed anxious to render him the service of arranging for a feminine companion for the remainder of the night.

Under other circumstances Michel would not have been reluctant to accept such a service. He realized part of his unwillingness to do so stemmed from the thought of Elena's devastation when she heard the rumors of how the new king spent his first night as king, and with whom. Though such activities would normally not come to the ears of an innocent young maid, he comprehended it would be all but impossible to keep Elena from learning of such intimate details of his life when they would be sharing the same roof for the foreseeable future. There was always someone eager to gossip about such matters and he doubted the wagging tongues would be overly careful about Elena's feelings on the subject.

But it was not only the thought of her disappointment in him that fueled his current celibate state. The fact was his manly passions had recently centered around a single subject. Elena. It came as a shock to him to discover he missed his shadow and her wide serious gaze fixed upon him. His musings engaged his attention until he was at the door to his chambers. He bid his accompanying guards a good night and then passed through the double doors into his large, elegantly appointed chambers.

His lips curved in amusement at the contrast between the luxurious bed in the accompanying room and the damp pallet he'd rested on for the past several months. The bed was large enough to accommodate any number of female companions if he was so inclined. He thought it might take a harem of women to fill the bed and wondered if any of his ancestors had availed themselves of just such an opportunity. He crossed the intricately inlaid floor into the adjoining chamber and crossed to the window to throw open the coverings allowing the cool night air to enter. Though most men would likely consider the warm chamber and the fire that burned in the hearth inviting, Michel spent the past several months in the elements and rather than find comfort in the warmth, he found it oppressive.

As he stripped out of his clothes and prepared for bed, he realized this chamber was very likely the same room his grandfather was murdered in. Murdered by a close friend. He wondered if his grandfather had awakened in time to see his attacker, or had the cowardly traitor who ended his life simply slit the sleeping king's throat? Not exactly a restful mystery to contemplate as he sank down on the thick mattress, but he was exhausted enough from the events of the day and the pressures of the previous months leading up to it that he fell into a dreamless sleep almost before he was fully stretched out upon the luxurious bed.

Despite his exhaustion, Michel's sleep was restless and burdened with violent, conflicting dreams where both a dead, bloodied Raulf played a starring role opposite the maid Rowena and the strange voice that spoke through her. In his dream state he engaged in earnest conversation with the voice and walked by the side of the young witch as the voice escorted him through scenes from the bloody past of the kingdom he now ruled. Bells could be heard in the distance, just as Gabriel described sounding the bells to alert Calei's defenders on that pivotal night when his grandfather was murdered and his grandmother was forced to flee for her life into the wilderness. In the course of his dreams, the ringing bells tolled loudly and often as Michel wandered through his country's misty past, a testament to the constant strife that assailed Calei over its long history.

Despite Michel's fervent urging, his misty escort seemed disinclined to reveal the secret behind the inception of the ancient curse laid against his family's blood. Michel stirred restively on the bed as the clanging of the bells became more insistent, distracting his attention away from his bodiless companion who shared his dreams.

An odd pounding sound now accompanied the ringing bells and even as Michel turned to demand an explanation from his misty escort, the significance of the noise assaulting his overtaxed senses suddenly forced its way through his foggy brain. He shot up in bed and was already on his feet getting dressed and reaching for his sword when Amele thrust the door open. The grave expression on the older man's face told Michel everything he needed to know.

"The city is under attack. Fortunately, despite the celebratory mood prevailing throughout the streets, the guards in the watchtowers remained vigilant enough to spot the enemy swarming down the mountain passes. They sounded the alarm and the gatekeepers managed to shut the gates before the enemy forces were able to enter the city. Our men are engaged even now in a fierce struggle to defend the gates. If the gates fall we will soon find ourselves under siege."

"Gather the commanders who are not actively engaging the enemy. How many of the nobles remain within the city?" Michel demanded as they left his chambers and strode quickly in the direction of the great hall. He could hear distant shouting and the echoes of frightened screams giving evidence to the chaos in the city. In the distance were the unmistakable sounds of men and horses engaged in armed combat.

He could find irony in the realization his unspoken dissatisfaction with the largely peaceful transition of power and the resulting wasted years of training for his men was about to be challenged. His premonition he would face a fight for his grandfather's throne would come true after all. There were already a number of men gathered in the hall and they looked up expectantly at their entrance.

"Gabriel, along with several companies of our most experienced soldiers are engaging the enemy in front of the gates, always our most vulnerable point of defense. If they fail to force the enemy away from the gates and the attackers enter the city, we will not be able to protect everyone.

Likely we will have a slaughter on our hands."

Michel turned to address two of his own commanders who accompanied him to Calei. "Melos, Amister take your men and reinforce the defenses at the gate. My guess is whoever planned this heard of King Barnabas' passing and thought to take advantage of the uncertainty of the transition to a new ruler. It is very possible they are unaware of our arrival or the fact that we brought with us an additional thousand fighting men, who are itching for just such a confrontation."

"Yes, my king, I do not doubt your words. The enemy is in for a very great surprise and we are just the men to give it to them," Melos replied grinning. Then with respectful bows in Michel's direction, the two men hurried off to gather their men, their light-hearted expressions giving evidence of their great anticipation at the thought of the battle ahead as if they had just been handed an unexpected boon.

When the nobles were gathered around him, Michel prepared to give his instructions for the defense of the city. At the same time, a single soldier rushed into the hall and hurried to where Michel stood in the center of the gathering. The soldier's tunic was covered with blood and grime, but he appeared uninjured. He quickly knelt before Michel and rose at his command. "Your Highness, forgive my boldness, but Captain Gabriel sent me to report to you the news he has gathered of our enemy."

"Then please do so," Michel commanded, motioning a hovering servant to bring the man water and food.

"Captain Gabriel states there are three waves of attack. Forgive me Your Highness, but he indicated I should tell you the enemy's strategy appears similar to the attack you planned to execute on the city."

"What is your name soldier?"

"Hunter, Your Highness."

"Take a moment to refresh yourself, Hunter, and then return to your captain with the order to hold the passes for an hour's time, and then sound the retreat."

"Retreat, Your Highness?" the veteran soldier appeared aghast at the idea.

"Yes, my friend," Michel responded. "It will take us an hour to align our soldiers behind their rear flank. When you retreat, we will swarm down from the hills behind them."

"And they will be caught in our vise and be crushed between us."

"Exactly."

The soldier's eyes gleamed with excitement and he bowed before Michel then gratefully accepted the tray the servant held out to him. He quickly swallowed the fresh water and meal the servant provided and then hurried from the hall to deliver his welcome message to his captain.

"Amele, you and I will reinforce our soldiers at

the gate. Barons Timothy and Paul, you and your men take the east passes, Barons James and Donnell, your men will lead the attack from the west. Wait for the bells to sound to signal all is in readiness, and then force the enemy down against the walls. We will prepare a suitable welcome for them."

"But King Michel, surely it would be safer for you to lead one of the forces down the passes. The fighting will be fiercest along the wall. We have only just regained our true king. I am loath for you to take such a risk. Allow me and my men to reinforce the soldiers at the gates and you and your men to accompany Baron Paul along the east passes."

Michel shook his head, denying Timothy's request, even while he smiled over the evidence of the older man's concern. "Thank you, my friend, but the defense of our homes is a king's worry therefore it is a king's duty. Let us not waste this opportunity provided us to send a message to our enemies that if they think to come and steal our treasure they will pay a high price indeed for their foolishness."

A rousing cheer sounded from the gathered men and as one, they turned to see Michel's commands carried out.

For the defenders at the gates, their reinforcement arrived not a moment too soon. Michel immediately grasped the enemy's strategy, as it so closely mirrored his own. If the gates fell and the enemy was able to enter the city, chaos would erupt among the residents, hindering their own soldiers' ability to protect them. He could see from the maturity and the skill with which they wielded their weapons that the enemy's leaders had sent their most experienced men to breach the gates. He suspected some of the enemy's forces were being held in reserve until the gates were opened, and the city's defenders were in retreat. At that critical moment, another wave of enemy forces would overwhelm the depleted defenders in both force and spirit.

Concluding his reasoning was just Michel wasted no further time contemplating the enemy's strategy or his own planned response. There came a time when strategy took a second place to a man's willingness to stand in the face of an enemy assault and defend himself and all he held dear with the strength of his sword and his will. Michel rose in Arden's stirrups and let out a fierce battle cry that was echoed in brutal unison by the soldiers riding behind him and forged his way into the center of where the enemy's assault was at its most savage, hoping with their fresh reinforcements they could hold the gates for the hour it would take for the others to gain their places in the mountains.

Within moments of engaging the enemy, the clash of swords, the screams of dying men and the grunts of the combatants engaged in a life and death struggle for survival occupied all of his senses. Michel put every thought from his mind except that of his sword and his skill in wielding it. Rivers of blood, more blood than he had ever seen in a single place, even in his clashes with the northern enemy of his Saxon king, stained the white stones surrounding the artful gates announcing the entrance to the wealthy city. He wondered idly even as shifted in his saddle to defend the back of one of his men against an enemy sword, how those responsible for such menial tasks would ever manage to remove the deep red stain from the previously gleaming entrance.

The smell of death assaulted his senses and pervaded the air of the new dawn being birthed over the east mountains. Accompanying the unmistakable scent, he thought he detected the echo of a subtle whisper drifting through the ranks of fighting men, inciting their hatred of the enemy and prodding them to take greater risks, to shed even more blood. For a moment, Michel felt the familiar whisper resonate with some dark, deeply buried part of him before he quickly dismissed the notion. He'd spent the past day engulfed in the mysticism of his new kingdom, but this was not the time to allow himself to fall victim to it unless he wanted to join the dead and dying on the ground at his feet.

Arden shifted his weight, alerting his attention to the deadly threat from his right. Michel turned in instinctive response and raised his shield to deflect the blow aimed to split his head open. At the same instant he swung his sword with all of his considerable strength in a downward sweep that cut through the helmet of his attacker and sank deep into the bone and softer flesh it protected. He didn't waste time watching the man slide off his horse and crumple to the ground, already dead before his blood joined the river of his comrades' as another enemy soldier boldly took his fallen comrade's place, his sword brandished in a confident swagger and bloodlust in his eyes.

The enemy soldier's confidence was dealt a crushing blow when Michel parried the thrust of his heavy blade. Too late the man realized he faced an opponent whose skill with a blade exceeded his own. He was still raising his shield to deflect the blow even as Michel's sword found purchase in the man's soft middle. He died in the company of his fallen comrades, his astonishment frozen into a wide-eyed death mask as he lay unseeing, staring up at the lightening early morning sky.

As the battle raged on, Michel lost count of the number of men he'd slain and pushed to the back of his mind his grief at the number of friends and comrades who fell beside him. Despite their own lives sacrificed in this contest, he knew that greater still were the number of enemy soldiers littering the ground around him, but as soon as one of their attackers fell it seemed as if two rushed to take his place. Michel began to doubt his initial conclusion this assault was launched in order to take advantage of the confusion surrounding the succession of the kingship. The fierceness of the battle and the numbers engaged against them, as well as the staggering losses the enemy was willing to sustain, made him think whoever was behind this had another end in mind.

They weren't just after carrying off gold and wealth a quick raid would afford them. He thought whoever was behind this assault was after Calei itself. Why settle for what they could claim in a single night's raid, when if they could defeat the city's defenders they could take advantage of the inner turmoil they concluded would result from the competition for the throne and claim not only the rule and wealth of the city but the rich treasure to be found in the surrounding mines?

He understood his faceless enemy's strategy…to crush…to annihilate the defenders of the city so they could not rise against them and their rule. Michel realized if he and his men had not arrived to reinforce the city's defenders, that is exactly what would have happened. The thousand men who rode with him evened their numbers. Without them, the city's brave defenders would have been overcome.

Rage filled him. He understood such was the ways of men and the evil of their hearts. Hadn't Barnabas told him there was no bottom to the well of evil in men's hearts? But the viciousness of the merciless assault they defended against struck him as the Norman invasion of Saxony failed to do and stirred in him a stake in the outcome he'd never truly felt before. All of a sudden the contest they waged was personal. He took the assault against his grandfather's homeland personally. He suddenly realized Calei was no longer simply his grandfather's home. It was his. These men who fought by his side were his. He'd be damned if he'd lose his destiny before he'd spent a single night as its ruler.

With fresh resolve he cleaved a bloody trail with his sword through the line of enemy soldiers. The clash of his blade rang out swift and sure causing the enemy to fall back before his righteous fury. As if in response to his new ferocity, the long awaited signal for their remaining forces to attack sounded menacingly in the misty air of the unfolding dawn. The majestic bells sounded in the air followed swiftly by the horns and shouts of their fellow Caleinians swarming down upon the enemy from the surrounding peaks.

Dismayed, the enemy forces were now forced to do battle on two fronts, defending both their front and rear flanks from attack. The city's tired, disheartened defenders emboldened by new men to fight by their sides and by the sight of their new king, careless of his own safety in his fury to defend their beloved homeland, wielded their swords with renewed vigor and might.

With the enemy cinched between them, it was only a matter of time before the Caleinian forces came together through the breech they cleaved in the ranks of the enemy lines. Still there was no break in the opposing soldiers' discipline, no hint that they were on the brink of being crushed between the city's defenders. They held their ground, drawing together in tight circles until the attackers became the defenders, like islands in a stormy sea threatened by a fierce storm. Michel was impressed by their courage even though on another level he could bemoan the useless waste of lives. With no pleas for mercy from their enemy, the Caleinians began cutting down the remaining enemy forces in a precise businesslike manner that was almost artistic in its display of savagery.

The victors all wore wide smiles as the last of the enemy's forces finally took off for the hills. Michel motioned for his eager soldiers not to pursue them. "They won't be back and their retreat will perform a valuable service for those they sought to conquer and deliver our response to whoever sent them."

"Be careful my young king, not all of your enemies reside outside the boundaries of your fair kingdom."

He was back. Michel could be amused now by the mysterious voice's dire warning, thinking he would really have to be careful about succumbing to the mystical nature of his new kingdom.

Another voice sounded in his ear, this one was also familiar but was spoken through the lips of a living man, though the chill his warning sent up Michel's spine was more ominous than the amusement he felt at his imaginary companion's warning.

"You've had a busy first day, Your Highness and an effective one, soundly defeating both your strongest challengers from within and without Calei's boundaries. Ironically, I find myself deeply in your debt. Allow me to repay you in a manner befitting your royal status."

Too late, Michel realized he would pay a deadly price for his recklessness and the excessive assurance only a man in his prime possessed of his own immortality. Only now in the split second before the assassin's blade penetrated his yielding flesh did he comprehend how cunningly he'd been separated from his own men until he was surrounded solely by those of another contender for Calei's ancient throne.

Too late he acknowledged his own foolishness in not only trusting in the pledges of loyalty from the men who, before he killed Raulf, had their own designs on his grandfather's throne, but in dismissing the warning of the mysterious voice echoing in his own head. Had not the betrayal of close friends that led to the deaths of both his grandfather and his immediate predecessor been enough to put him on his guard?

As if in an alternate world, one that proceeded

with excruciating slowness, he felt the point of the sharp dagger pierce his back and carve upward, and knew his reign was destined to be a short one. His cry of astonished protest at the ghastly pain assaulting him was smothered by a gloved hand so no sound emerged. His strength deserted him with shocking swiftness and his knees crumbled, as his sword slipped from his grasp. He was prevented from sliding to the damp, blood-soaked ground by the strong arms of his assailant coming around him to hold him upright. As he lost consciousness, he thought he heard an echo of his own silent cry coming from the lips of his murderer.

CHAPTER THIRTEEN

Elena sat huddled along with the female members of Baron Timothy's family in the tunnels beneath the family's estate. Servants and the younger male members of the household retainers waited anxiously for word of the battle raging above ground at the entrance to the city. Elena waited on the damp stone somewhat removed from the others, leaning back against the wall with her arms wrapped around her knees.

The air in the underground tunnels was dank and musty, but Elena barely noticed her uncomfortable surroundings. Her breaths came in short, terrified gasps, and not only because of the attack on the city. Though the majority of her uncle's years as king had been peaceful ones, this was not the first time she'd been sent to safety underground while she prayed fervently that Calei's defenders would emerge victorious over their enemies. Never before though had she been so overwhelmed with her worry.

Earlier in the day she'd been overcome too, but then it was with joy when the news reached her of Raulf's death and that Michel had been accepted by the heads of the remaining noble families as the new king of Calei. She spent the day in a dazed state of happy dreams and grand plans, alternately feeling laughter bubble up inside of her, a reaction she attributed to her dazed relief that Raulf would never be able to reach her again, and wiping tears from her eyes. She did not even mind when Michel did not immediately ride out to Baron Timothy's estate to bring her back to take up residence with him in the castle. She understood, better likely than the new king himself, of the constant demands his new responsibilities would thrust upon him.

When the sounds of the battle being waged above them fell silent, a deeper hush settled over their dark retreat, as all awaited the news of their futures. It seemed to Elena as if long hours passed before Amele stood framed in the doorway, his skin and cloak streaked with blood and sweat and grime, his grave expression confirming her worst fears. She would have sworn her heart stopped beating in her chest when her eyes met those of the older man's. She was unaware her head was shaking silently back and forth in agonized denial, as Michel's close friend approached where she sat.

"No." The hushed denial escaped her lips as the older man, his weathered face etched in deep lines, regarded her out of dark, grief-stricken eyes, squatted in front of her.

"Lady Elena…"

Elena closed her eyes against the scalding tears

that forced themselves through her clenched lids and reached up to cover her ears in a futile gesture meant to prevent her from hearing the words she knew he was about to deliver. The cruelty of having her newly resurrected hope snatched away from her fleeting grasp was too much for her fragile heart to contemplate. She buried her head in her knees and prayed she was in the grip of some hideous nightmare.

"Lady Elena, you must accompany me now."

She heard the words spoken in his deep, now familiar voice, but merely burrowed her head deeper between her knees and clenched her hands more tightly against her ears.

"Lady Elena, the king would want you to return to the castle." When she only ignored his quiet plea, he spoke the words that for a moment resurrected her dead hope and made her heart begin beating again. "Lady Elena, the king is gravely injured."

"Injured?" Elena parroted blankly, lifting her head from her knees so she could read the confirmation she sought in his eyes.

Both his expression and confirming nod were solemn and Elena recognized, though he was giving her the truth that Michel still lived when he came in search of her, Amele held no real hope of finding him alive when he returned with her to his friend and his king's side. It was obvious the older man did not expect his young king to recover from the grave injury he spoke of. Fresh tears stinging behind her lids, she nodded silently and allowed him to assist her to her feet.

Neither spoke to the astonished, silent witnesses of their exchange when Amele grasped her hand and led her back the way he had come. When they approached the men who awaited them outside in the cool, early morning light, their expressions all mirrored the same disbelieving grief echoed in Amele's eyes.

Elena allowed herself to be assisted to the saddle and waited numb while Amele mounted behind her. His strong grip around her waist secured her in the saddle, so with nothing else to do with her icy hands she slipped them into the pockets of her cloak. Inside, the fingers of her right hand came up against something hard and cold. The stone! She'd forgotten all about it, first in the excitement of the earlier joyous news she received, and then in the dread of night. The stone heated in her hand. She'd meant to return it to Michel before he left the previous morning for his meeting with the noblemen to claim his rightful place as the new king, but she never had the chance. Would the stone have protected him against the wound that even now threatened to take his life? Maybe it wasn't too late. Maybe the stone really was magic.

With irrepressible hope burgeoning in her breast, Elena clasped the stone in her clenched fist. She was not taking any chances it would attempt to escape her grasp again. To her surprise, the stone made no effort to do so, as if it too was in a hurry to be reunited with its rightful owner, and had reasoned out that accompanying her was the fastest way for it to achieve its objective. The distance to the castle was accomplished quickly as the crowds of shocked, grieving citizens hurried out of their way when they became aware of their approach.

Their small company came to a halt in front of the castle steps and Elena offered no protest when Amele helped her dismount then gripped her hand and pulled her through the throng clogging the entrance as ordinary Caleinians awaited word with tears glimmering in their eyes and staining their cheeks, on the fate of their new, young king. The inside of the keep was no less crowded, but the soldiers gathered there, still in their blood-soaked cloaks and tunics stepped back to allow them to pass, the silence among so many strangely overwhelming in its oppressive weight.

Elena thought she was prepared for the sight of Michel stretched out, helpless, his skin deathly pale, his breath barely discernible, a bloody bandage wrapped tightly around his naked chest to stem the flow of blood. Hadn't she tended her uncle for long months in this same room, watched him lying in this same bed, his life slowly draining away? But though she loved him as a father, her uncle was not her beloved. If she needed proof of the depths of her feelings for the man who rescued her from another man's lustful intent, it was evident in the blow she absorbed to see Michel in the same, helpless condition as her uncle, only he appeared in a greater hurry to depart this burdensome life. Had Amele's strong arm not reached out to steady her, she would have fallen to her knees at the sight. Gathering herself, and making no effort to stem the flow of tears on her cheeks, she stepped away from Amele's firm grip and hurried across the distance between the door and the large bed on trembling legs.

There she allowed her strength to desert her and she sank to her knees at his side, her hand reaching out to smooth her beloved's long dark hair, matted with blood and sweat away from his pale face. She reached into the pocket of her cloak and retrieved the stone from it. She glanced down at the odd jewel and was surprised when for a brief moment it seemed to gleam with a shining, white light, but when she blinked and lifted the odd gem to her face for closer inspection, the illusion vanished. Elena grasped Michel's limp hand at his side and pressed the stone into his palm, then closed his fingers around it, holding the stone captive in his closed fist as the unconscious man was unable to perform this service for himself.

Then she closed her eyes, rested her head against the strength of his still arm, and holding his hand in hers, she prayed to her heavenly father not to take her last hope, and the man she suspected would be her only true love, from her side.

CHAPTER FOURTEEN

Some part of Michel's weary mind and pain-wracked body comprehended he was in the unrelenting grip of his nightmares, but though his body slept there was no lessening of his weariness or his pain. He couldn't recall what brought him to this place, nor did he understand clearly where it was he lingered. Violent memories intruded on his thoughts of war and blood, of dying men and dismembered limbs strewn about like so much refuse on the blood soaked earth. If he possessed the strength he would have covered his ears to drown out the sounds of the ghastly, agonized cries of the wounded and dying, lying unattended, staring up at the pitiless sun just beginning to traverse its daily path across the heavens, while their comrades contested above where they lay for their own lives.

Other less strident sounds whispered across his consciousness....voices...feminine voices, and just as he didn't possess the strength to block out the screams of the dying, neither did he possess enough to cling to the gentle strains of the familiar feminine voices. He thought he heard the echo of his twin's beloved voice among the whispers, "…then when you pray for death I will refuse you the comfort of its release…"

"Melissa…" The name formed on his lips and escaped in a hushed whisper between them. Michel had no way of knowing of the pain his twin's name inflicted on the soft companion who knelt beside his bed, her hand closed around his.

Other voices muscled their way into his chaotic dreams. Some demanding, others caring, some amused even, but they were all united in the expectations they heaped on his back. He had a part to play in their destiny and they had every reasonable anticipation of him fulfilling his debt for their faith in him. Beneath the clamor of their voices, was another whisper, this one barely discernible to his dazed spirit. It was soft and gentle and he somehow recognized it belonged to the small hand joined with his own.

"Elena…"

This time a soft cry echoed at his whispered recognition and the hand covering his closed more tightly around his fist. He thought he heard his name on her lips, and then he felt her rest her head against his chest and was aware of her tears cleaning the stain of violence from his skin and his battered spirit. He reached up his other arm to stroke, to offer comfort, and to thread his fingers through the silky hair teasing his naked skin where the long strands lay across his bare chest.

Content, he sighed heavily and fell into a deep, restful sleep.

A new, yet vaguely familiar voice woke him from his restful sleep, but this voice was accompanied by a misty form standing at the end of his bed, regarding Michel with a considering, speculative look in his eyes.

"Who are you?" Michel wasn't certain if he voiced the words aloud or not, but the stranger did not seem to have any trouble understanding him.

"Ah, you are awake at last. I was beginning to think I would be forced to return to your sister with unpleasant news."

The voice struck a familiar chord but in his dazed state, Michel could not remember when or where he had encountered the stranger. When the answer continued to elude him, he asked, "My sister sent you?"

"She requested I accompany you on your return to your grandfather's kingdom, as she could not."

Michel sighed, not certain he wanted to know how it was the stranger's path had crossed that of his reckless twin's. "You speak of Melissa."

"Yes, I am not acquainted with your younger sister, Lady Rhiann. Though our destinies have intersected upon occasion, for the most part they were rather distant exchanges."

"You are more intimately acquainted with my twin, then?"

"I am not certain I would refer to our

acquaintance as intimate, but yes, we have known each other many years." There was amused self-mockery in the stranger's voice and in his manner that Michel found difficult to comprehend in his current weakened state.

"Then how is it we have never met?"

"That is easy enough to understand, my young king. You were not present at any of my previous encounters with your twin, except the first one when your sister went over the falls in a boat she could not control."

Michel shook his head, protesting, "That was years ago, when we were children."

"Yes, I remember the occasion quite well and your lovely twin's determination to keep up with you." The stranger laughed, apparently enjoying his recollection of the day he referred to. "She was most upset at the thought of being left behind, so she pushed the last remaining boat from the side of the river bank and barely managed to catch a hold of it and climb in and seat herself before her little vessel was swept away by the current. Unfortunately, she didn't bother to retrieve an oar to guide her way when she set off in her reckless pursuit."

His lips widened into an amused grin as he lifted one shoulder in a philosophical shrug, "Not that she could have wielded the instrument at her young age. She was much too excited about the prospect of showing all of you that she could keep up with the warriors and deserved as much as you did to be trained as one, regardless of the great inconvenience, in her mind, of having been born a girl."

Michel had no difficulty recalling the events the stranger referred to. Even in the innocence of youth he had understood Melissa was going to die when her boat was catapulted over the falls by the rushing current. "I remember that day, but I don't recall your presence there."

"No, of course not. You were in no danger that day. It was Melissa who went over the falls."

Even after a dozen years or more, Michel could still taste the raw terror on his tongue at the memory of Melissa barreling towards him, but it was the look on Amele's face that morning that he would never forget. As if their guardian had known Melissa was going to die in the next few moments and there was nothing he would be able to do to prevent it.

Michel had always assumed it was merely random providence that intervened on his twin's behalf that day. For the first time he questioned his conclusion as another memory from that fateful day intruded. When they found Melissa asleep beside the rushing water after a long and desolate search convinced at best they would recover only her lifeless body from the water to carry back to their parents for burial, Melissa was adamant a stranger had rescued her from the river and sat with her on the bank and kept her warm while she waited for Amele and the warriors to find her. Amele tried to convince her she was imagining the stranger she spoke of. Michel always assumed Amele must be correct.

"You're the stranger she spoke of. The one whose name she forgot to ask. You fished her out of the water," Michel's awed voice sounded almost like an accusation in the silence between them.

The stranger nodded his affirmation of Michel's conclusion. "Yes, it was not supposed to end the way it did. Your reckless twin should have died that morning, but sometimes, very rarely, I am moved to pity when my labors lead me to the very young and the very brave. Your sister was both. Besides, she was so reckless with her life, I didn't think I would have long to wait before she joined me."

Again the stranger's self-mocking amusement surfaced when he added with a wry smile, "Admittedly, given your sister's lack of regard for her own life, there have been numerous additional occasions when our paths have intersected, but I have always restrained myself from taking her despite the great temptation to do so. Melissa considers me a friend. There are so few who do, it would pain me to betray her trust and take her without her permission."

Michel knew he must be dreaming, because the thoughts drifting through his glazed mind and coalescing into a single, untenable conclusion must surely be the product of a deranged mind.

"Who are you?" His demand escaped his lips in a hushed whisper, and then when the stranger remained silent, he added in an even quieter voice, "Are you Satan?"

The stranger laughed with genuine amusement, and relieved beyond measure, Michel swallowed his sense of dread at the thought of Melissa's seemingly close acquaintance with the lord of the underworld. His unease was immediately resurrected when his companion explained, "No, no, I am not Satan, but certainly our sometimes similar purposes often lead to my being mistaken for him. No, when the occasion warrants it, I merely inform the living that their deaths are upon them. It is the purpose of the lord of darkness to claim the souls of the damned."

Michel could no longer discern if he was caught in the throes of a dream or contesting with the clinging tentacles of a nightmare, but he was certain this exchange was the most bizarre conversation he'd ever engaged in. "You make it sound as though he is rendering the world a valuable service," Michel remarked.

"But of course," his misty companion quickly agreed. "The Almighty does not allow the filth of evil souls to stain the perfection of heaven."

"So they are sent to hell," Michel confirmed, fascinated despite himself.

The stranger shrugged. "Sometimes there is no avoiding that unpleasant destination, at least for those souls who have proven particularly resistant to corrective teaching. Nothing like the fires of hell to pry open a closed mind."

Despite their unholy topic, Michel's shoulders shook with laughter. "No doubt."

"Ah, it is only the truly just who find such truths amusing. I think your sister is not as unique as I have always assumed. You do not fear death, my young king?"

Michel sighed heavily at the reminder of Melissa. "While I do not court it with the same zealous disregard as my twin, no, I don't particularly fear it. Is not death simply a birth into a new life?"

The stranger nodded, the expression in his dark eyes mirroring his surprise. "Your grandmother taught you well."

"Yes," Michel acknowledged. A not uncomfortable silence fell between them. Michel took the opportunity to go over in his thoughts all that he had learned, no longer certain he was dreaming. Perhaps he was caught somewhere between the experience of life and death. As if his body was not quite certain which side of the mysterious veil separating the two it would next awaken on.

His lips curved upward at his fanciful conclusion, then realizing the unique opportunity presented him by his companion's presence, and willing to set his disbelief side for the moment, he regarded his companion with a speculative gleam in his eyes, "You know things that mortal men do not."

"Yes," the arbiter of death acknowledged smiling, as if he'd been waiting for Michel to make this very leap.

Michel continued eagerly, "Your memory extends far back beyond the reach of mortal lives."

"Further, my young friend, than you can begin to comprehend."

Satisfied, Michel leaned back against the pillows supporting him and got to the point, unsure how long his opportunity would extend, "Ah, then you are aware of the origin of the curse that besets this house."

His companion's laughter filled the space between them. As Michel had no idea what he found so amusing, he merely waited for his companion to gain control over his amusement and rejoin the conversation. Finally, his laughter subsided and he stood regarding Michel with a wide grin. "You know who I am, the advantages against the living I can offer you, and yet all you seek from me is the answer to an archaic riddle?"

Michel shook his head, denying his conclusion, "Not the answer, because I do not believe in cheating fate. If my blood has a debt to repay I would rather see it settled than attempt to evade its course and therefore pass it along to future generations. I am anxious to do so, but I do not know where to begin to seek the answer to a curse that was laid beyond the memory of all living Caleinians."

"Beyond the memory of the living, certainly, but not the memory of the dead."

"Yes," Michel acknowledged with a hopeful smile, "That is where I was sort of hoping you might be able to assist me."

When his companion merely remained silent regarding him with a considering look, Michel added with what he hoped was a winning smile, "You being a friend of the family and all."

Another amused chuckle emerged at Michel's daring, but this time it was accompanied by a regretful sigh. "I will consider your appeal, my young king, but for now, as it does not appear you will be requiring my services any time soon, I shall be on my way. I have enjoyed our interlude, but my work calls for my attention and will not wait."

"Thank you," Michel replied his appreciation no less sincere for all he was almost entirely convinced the interlude the stranger referred to was a product of whatever illness beset him and its effects on his imagination.

"For what do you offer me your gratitude?"

Michel was quiet for a moment, before replying seriously, "For giving me all of these years I have enjoyed with me sister, and for watching over her when I could not." At the others acknowledging nod, Michel added, his mind finally recalling why the stranger's voice seemed familiar to him, "And for your warning about Raulf. I realize now you also tried to warn me after the conclusion of the battle when I let down my guard thinking our victory was assured, but I arrogantly dismissed your caution and have paid dearly for my foolishness."

"Graciously spoken, my young king, but you will live to see a new dawn. See to it that you do not waste it." With this final word of advice, his fascinating companion disappeared as suddenly as he emerged. Moments later, Michel woke to searing pain in his back and chest and the sight of Amele's familiar face bending over him, his dark eyes reflecting his concern. When their eyes met, Amele's lips split in a wide, relieved smile, "Ah, you are finally awake. Thank the good Lord. I was not looking forward to carrying the news of your death back to your sisters and grandmother."

Michel grimaced against the pain and struggled to sit up in bed, but allowed himself to succumb to Amele's gentle pressure to keep him in his prone position. "What happened?" he demanded in a raspy voice, even as a fresh stab of pain ripped through him.

"Baron James was in league with Raulf. He was no doubt quite pleased when you conveniently removed the baron from his path to the throne. Suddenly you were the only one standing in his way to becoming king. I imagine he found the temptation too great to resist when he realized you stood by his side, surrounded by his men and separated from your own. He seemingly decided to take advantage of the opportunity afforded him and acted on it, thinking in the confusion he could blame the enemy and claim he had been unable to save you."

Michel nodded, remembering the older man among the nobles gathered in the hall the day he called them together to decide the question of the kingship. He was stunned by his own naivety for accepting without question that the remaining nobles were loyal to him simply because they knelt at his feet and offered him their pledges of loyalty. "Where is he?"

"He is dead." Amele announced the traitor's fate with obvious satisfaction. At Michel's enquiring brow, the older man added, "No, my king, not by my hand, though I would have gladly rendered you and Calei this service. No, his own commander was the first to put his sword through him the moment he turned on you. Each of his men took a turn running their blades through him. The baron made a grave miscalculation when he assumed his men would follow him in his treachery. They are loyal to you now and were appalled at their baron's act of treason." Michel nodded, gritting his teeth against his pain, but quickly shook his head in response to Amele's offer of the cup he held which Michel assumed contained an opiate to help alleviate it. "And the baron's family? I seem to recall a young son."

"Yes, the baron's older sons were killed some time ago in defensive raids on the mountain passes, and one in an accident while inspecting the mines. The baron's youngest son, Colin, waits outside these chambers. He was posted on the walls during the fight, and by all accounts fought bravely in Calei's defense. He is as appalled as his father's men were by his father's act of treason and fell behind the procession carrying you back to the castle, stunned tears on his cheeks when it was revealed to him his father was the one responsible for your injury. I believe his prayers for your recovery are exceeded in sincerity only by those of your young ward," Amele tacked on, his head gesturing to the corner of the room.

Michel turned his head in the direction Amele indicated and saw Elena sitting there regarding him anxiously with tear-filled eyes. "Elena," he called out softly and with a soft anguished cry, she jumped up from where she sat huddled in the corner and rushed to his side, throwing herself on her knees and burying her face against his bandaged chest. Michel suppressed the cry of protest that wanted to escape his lips at the evidence of her enthusiasm, and then as her hot burning tears dampened his skin, he reached up a gentle hand and threaded his fingers through her hair and trailed his hand down her back in a soothing gesture.

"You are safe now, Elena. There is no need for this display," he reassured her awkwardly. Despite having two sisters Michel never knew how to respond to a woman's excessive displays of emotion.

As if sensing his discomfort with her tears, Elena made an effort to collect her composure. She lifted her head from his chest and stared down solemnly into his eyes, as if to assure herself he was truly out of danger and was not going to die on her in the next moment and leave her alone again in the world.

Despite his struggle with his pain Michel found himself very much aware of her softness cuddled close against his naked flesh and the way her innocent doe's eyes clung anxiously to his. Incredibly and damned inconveniently, he thought given the circumstances, he felt his manhood stirring. He clamped down on his rising lust with an effort and suppressed the urge to both push away the source of his temptation and gather her close and give into it at the same time.

He was prevented from the latter by Amele's lingering presence in the room, though he'd very courteously distanced himself from the bed and stood with his back facing them, staring silently out the window into the night. He was prevented from acting on his former inclination by Elena's fearful expression and the knowledge that she was too innocent to reason out why he felt the need to put some distance between them. She would see such a move as a personal rejection of her, no matter the necessity warranting it for him to gain a safe distance from her alluring softness so he would be afforded the opportunity to draw in a breath without being filled with and surrounded by her heady feminine scent, a light, alluring fragrance that even now had his thoughts turning fuzzy in his head.

The soft and tender glide of her fingers across his bare chest was not helping him to regain control. In other circumstances he might have found his current predicament wildly amusing, but in his current pained condition he could only treat them as one more trying test of his discipline and his ability to control his manly passions.

He'd waged such battles before, he reminded himself. A man who would rule an ancient kingdom could not himself be ruled by his own lusts. So from a very young age, he'd set out to conquer his own. Lust not only for a woman's soft flesh, but for power, for wealth, for comfort, for luxury, for freedom from burdensome labor and the test of an enemy's blade that could lead to the end of his mortal life. For the most part, he'd been successful in overcoming the trials he set for himself. He was actually quite astonished the most severe test of his will should come in the form of an innocent young maid who regarded him with a look in her soft brown eyes that made him feel as if he could one day become the man she already presumed he was.

The pace of his breathing increased with his struggles not to taste the softness of her lips, to refresh his memory of the pleasure he took in her warm response to his every overture of manly passion. Sweat beaded on his forehead and his glance dropped to her lips, then lower to where her soft breasts lay crushed against his chest. In her prone position the top of her gown lay loosely across the fullness it was designed to conceal, giving him a tempting glimpse of her womanly curves. He felt more than heard her quick indrawn breath at his close perusal and with an effort he lifted his glance from the promise of the pleasure awaiting him to return to her face.

His eyes roamed over her delicate features, taking in her lovely countenance. Everything about her was soft and yielding against his hardness. Her tender flesh was made to entice a man to surrender to its beckoning allure. He'd been resisting it since he first pulled her out of that absurd sack. His life had been in turmoil when they met and was no less endangered now.

It would be grossly unfair of him to take advantage of her innocent faith in him, to let her become more deeply involved with a man who was incapable of promising her the secure future she so desperately sought and needed from the man she pledged her heart to, but in moments like these it was easy to forget his scrupulous sense of honor. It was easy to forget she was younger even than his younger sister, Rhiann, and to simply give in to the temptation to take what she was so obviously willing to offer him.

So it was with a sense of inevitability he increased the pressure on the hand holding her head cupped in his to bring her closer to him. She didn't resist his inducement, but let herself be drawn closer to him, her intent gaze, tears stilling swimming in their mysterious depths, clinging to his as their lips met and for one brief moment, Michel gave into the urge to take, to challenge her innocence and to reveal to her, perhaps unfairly, the depths of his longing for her. His hand at the back of her head prevented her escape even if she had been so inclined, but as if she too had grown weary of the skittish dance they had been engaged in since the fateful morning of their first meeting, she made no attempt to elude his grasp.

If he was intent on giving her a glimpse of the fullness of his passion for her, she appeared equally determined to take advantage of the very limited opportunities they had to be alone together. As though recognizing such opportunities would become even more precious when he rose from his bed to resume his duties as king, she apparently wanted him to know, wanted him to fully, mind-numbingly be aware of what she not only could, but what she was more than willing to offer him in return. Her lips parted eagerly beneath his and invited him inside her warmth to grant him respite and soothing shelter from the enemies that beset him from all sides.

Here was a woman he could trust with his honor and his life and who, despite her youth and her sheltered upbringing, and even despite her terror of the unknown and of the likely evils awaiting her beyond the safety of her uncle's kingdom had planned to risk all to escape another man's unwanted embrace. Yet to him, she was willing to surrender all, to share all of her warmth and love and shyness and gentle kindness. For a man who'd spent his life assuming such gifts would be beyond his reach, the genuineness and simplicity of her offering was a heady temptation Michel was finding more and more difficult to resist.

Though she might lack the sophistication of his previous lovers and the knowledge of how to serve a man's passions, her eager innocent response to his demands aroused him as no other had. Closing his eyes in an effort to gain control of himself, he drew his lips from hers to slide them over her face, amazed anew at the softness of her skin, and whispered in her ear, "Elena, love, we cannot. You must return to your rooms while I still possess enough discipline to allow you to leave my side, and I must see to setting my kingdom to rights."

He felt the resigned sigh that passed through her, and opened his eyes to see the smile claim her lips before she allowed her lips to glide along his face to caress the sensitive skin along his ears when she whispered in reply, "I am not certain I still possess the discipline to allow you to banish me from your side."

With a grin at her quick wit, he lifted his head to meet her challenging glance, but kept his voice soft when he responded. "I'm not banishing you from the keep, only from my chambers so I might concentrate on my responsibilities."

She pouted, making her dissatisfaction with his very reasonable dictate well-known to him. His grin widened and despite the lingering pain in his back, his amusement at her very feminine tactic brightened his mood. Just to see her reaction, he lifted his hand to pat her head as he would a child's and admonished in a voice of that of an adult with a recalcitrant tot, "Be a good girl now, and do as you're told."

Though she was aware of his ploy, she couldn't quite suppress her outrage at his dismissal. He saw the temptation to take her revenge flit across her lovely features, then at the reminder of his weakened condition, he watched her abandon her evil thoughts. In the next moment she seemed to remember the brevity of their time together and her expression shadowed and she regarded him with pleading, anxious eyes.

"Will I see you again?"

Even though her pitiful question was a foolish one given they would be sharing the same roof, he understood her fear, because it so closely mirrored his own. When would he have the opportunity to hold her like this again? And even now, they weren't truly alone.

It was Amele's silent presence across the room that had allowed him to retain control over his raging lusts with her softness curled so closely across his chest. And it was his presence now that brought him back to a sense of his duties to Calei. A king's time was not his own and he could no longer spend his life as he had in the past, focused only on his own will and his own pursuits.

So he didn't try to dismiss Elena's question as he once might have, with a joking rejoinder about the two of them being unable to avoid each other's company now that they would be sharing a home. There was no denying their previous unstructured relationship was a thing of the past and could not be resurrected even with a vow of marriage exchanged between them. He no longer played the romantic part of the lost prince on a quest to claim his grandfather's throne. Now he sat upon that throne and the romance of it, while perhaps not completely lost to them, was about to be buried beneath the weight of the difficulties confronting him as the new king of Calei. "Yes, you will see me again, Elena, but there is much for me to see to and I cannot yet grasp my way through to the end of it."

She nodded her reluctant acceptance of what must be, and Michel was impressed by her quick understanding of the difficulties he did not enumerate for her. She neither demanded promises he was in no position to offer, nor did she appear to have any expectation that he would put the needs of his kingdom and its people aside to focus on his own desires. As she was one of those desires, and for the foreseeable future her destiny was bound to his, she would not have been without the right to protest his dictate or to seek his reassurances of the place she would occupy in his life, if not in the immediate future at least at some definitive point in the not too distant one.

Instead she neither protested his command nor demanded his promise, only slid away from him to rather awkwardly regain her feet and stare down at him with a sad, but resigned expression, a slight crease between her eyes, marring her flawless features. He immediately felt the loss of her warmth against him and it required a very real effort on his part not to tug on the small hand that still rested in his and bring her back to lean close against his chest.

For the first time he became aware that something hard lay between their two hands and he released hers to lift the contents of his closed fist to his eyes for closer inspection. He was too stunned by the sight greeting his examination to immediately process its portent. His eyes remained frozen on the stone and he reached out his other hand to turn it around and around to assure himself it was indeed his sister's lost treasure. As soon as he held it within his hands the dark, black stone came to life and took on the color of a deep, midnight blue.

"You needn't be concerned...the stone is in trustworthy hands..." The words of the voice who spoke through the maid Rowena's lips seemed to belong to another life, or to herald from

a long-lost dream. Yet had not only a single day passed since he was given his clue to assist him in solving the mysterious curse that beset his blood?

"How?" His astonished will was only able to force the single word through his lips.

Elena blushed guiltily and admitted softly, "I found it by the river. I remembered seeing you wearing it."

His brows creased together and he asked confused, "But you did not return it when you found it?"

Her color deepened and she shook her head. He waited in silence for her to continue, and reached down to regain possession of her hand as it appeared she might try to escape his question by fleeing from his side. He could see his query distressed her, but he was too curious to hear her answer to refrain from pressing her. Finally, in a voice so quiet he had to strain to hear her even across the slight distance separating them, she confessed, "I could see how you valued the stone and assumed it was a keepsake from a woman you treasured."

His lips twitched at her guilty admission. "You were jealous."

Her head was bowed and her shoulders slumped in abject desolation, but she didn't deny his conclusion. "Yes."

Curious, Michel asked, "Then why did you retrieve the stone? Why return it to me?"

Still avoiding meeting his probing glance, she

replied, "You treasured it. I meant to return it to you before you entered the city for your conference with the nobles, but I didn't see you that morning. When you were injured, I thought maybe it could help you." While he was still trying to understand why she believed a stone could help him with his wound, she added in an even softer voice, "The stone is magic, isn't it?"

Michel was too astonished by her question to keep his voice down, "Magic?" He echoed, chuckling. "What made you conclude the stone is magic?"

Elena finally braved meeting his eyes. "It turns blue in your possession. And it kept trying to get away from me. That was how I fell into the river that day. Then when Amele came to inform me you had been wounded in the battle with our enemies, I remembered I still had the stone. When it realized Amele was taking me to you, it seemed happy and no longer tried to escape from my hand. Then when I knelt by your side, for a moment it seemed to turn a blinding white in my hands before turning back to its usual dark appearance."

"Escape from your hand?" Michel was careful to disguise his amusement at Elena's fantastic account. Apparently he was not the only victim of Calei's superstitious nature.

"Yes, it kept trying to get away from me. It even burned my hand when I held it."

"What do you mean it burned your hand?"

Elena held her palm out for his inspection. The scar of the stone's imprint could still be seen embedded in her soft flesh. Seeing it, Michel's eyes knotted together. He'd never heard of the stone having any reaction when it was held by someone who was not in line to become its keeper. Certainly he'd never heard of it inflicting a painful burn on another. Maybe he'd been too quick to dismiss the legends surrounding the stone he'd listened avidly to around the fires of his grandmother's camp when he was a boy. Pushing the matter of this fresh mystery aside, he slid his thumb across Elena's scar in a soothing gesture, and then reluctantly released the hand he held.

"Thank you for returning the stone and for keeping it safe for me. You are right when you concluded it was a keepsake from a woman I treasure." At Elena's resigned nod and the glimmer of fresh tears in her eyes, he added gently, "Her name is Melissa. She is my twin sister."

Elena's head shot up. Her tears forgotten, she asked anxiously, "Your twin?"

Smiling, Michel nodded. "Yes. The stone is an heirloom of my mother's family. It passes through the eldest daughter of the house. She entrusted its care to me when I informed her I was returning to Calei as a reminder of the bond we share and to wish me good luck in my quest."

"Oh, then I'm very glad I restored your sister's treasure to you," Elena admitted naively.

Michel's lips kicked up. "So am I. Thank you."

Nodding in acknowledgment of his expression of gratitude, and with obvious reluctance, Elena allowed her hand to slide from his, then turned away from him and silently crossed the distance to the door. Without turning back, she just as silently left the room.

CHAPTER FIFTEEN

Amele waited for the sound of the door closing behind Elena before turning around to face the bed. "Bring the baron's son to me," Michel ordered in a harsh voice.

With a raised brow, but no comment, Amele nodded and approached the door. A moment later he stood aside while a young man about Michel's age, still cloaked in his soldier's garb, his face and garments stained with dirt and blood hesitantly preceded him into the room. The soldier kept his eyes downcast and Michel could read only defeat in his stance. "Come here," Michel commanded and waited while the youngest son of the man who attempted to kill him shuffled across the room towards him.

When he reached Michel's bedside he knelt beside the bed, his eyes still downcast, and his voice barely a whisper when he addressed him, "Your Highness."

"Rise." Michel waited for him to do so and then noticing the soldier still refused to look at him, asked, "What is your name?"

"Colin, Your Highness."

Michel sighed impatiently. "Look at me when you speak to me, Colin." When the boy raised his glance to his, Michel saw the stark fear revealed there and was moved to pity. He wondered how he would feel if their situations were reversed, if it had been his father who dishonored not only himself but his family by abandoning his pledge of fealty and had run a sword through the man he'd sworn to serve. "My commander tells me you fought bravely in defense of Calei." The words were out before he knew what he was going to say.

The boy's head shot up to probe Michel's eyes as if searching for the lie in them. Despite the closeness in their ages, Michel could see the young man had yet to cross the line separating boyhood and manhood. If he survived and prospered after his father's heinous deed, Michel had no doubt he would have crossed the dividing line between the two. The journey would not prove a gentle one. The first step was to face the challenge ahead.

"My father tried to kill you." The words sounded as if he had to force them between clenched teeth, but Michel was impressed the traitor's son did not try to hide behind them or obscure the damning fact.

"You are not your father," Michel reminded him.

Tears stung the boy's eyes and he fell to his

knees. "Your Highness, I know there's nothing I can do to make reparations for my father's treachery, I only ask that whatever punishment you decree you exact it from me alone and not my mother and sisters."

"And what punishment do you deem fitting for such an act of treason?"

The boy's face lost all color at Michel's quiet question. "There is no way to equal the scales, to undo what my father did. My life itself could not do so, but I offer it, Your Highness. I only ask that you allow my mother and sisters a home in your kingdom. Not, of course, my father's estate, but a cottage perhaps and a small retainer so they are not forced to leave Calei."

"You willingly offer to exchange your life for theirs?"

"Yes, Your Highness."

Michel could see what his fierce vow cost the boy, but he didn't back away from it, nor take it back. "Tell me, Colin, how does depriving Calei of one of its loyal defenders make reparation for your father's treason?"

"Your Highness?" There was confusion in Colin's hesitant question. Confusion, and the dawn of improbable hope.

"If you wish to make reparation for your father's sin, you may serve my interests more effectively alive than dead."

His eyes widening, Colin exclaimed fiercely, "Send me to the mines, Your Highness. I will do the work of ten men to repay my family's debt to you."

Michel leaned his head back against the pillows and briefly closed his eyes while his will struggled against his body's pain. Annoyed at his own weakness, he replied sighing, "I would prefer, I think, that you train as a member of the king's guard."

"The king's guard, Your Highness?" Colin was so astonished by his suggestion; the boy could only echo it in a hushed whisper.

"Yes, you will report to the captain of the guard in the morning. Return to your mother and sisters and assure them they may remain in their home for as long as you serve me well. Your family's ability to continue doing so now rests upon your shoulders. See that you do not let them down."

"Yes, Your Highness. Thank you, Sire. I will train diligently and study hard."

When the door closed on Colin's fervent pledge, Michel felt Amele's considering glance upon him. "Whenever I am convinced I know what you will do, you manage to surprise me. That was well done of you, my king. Though not everyone will understand, nor agree with your considerable act of mercy towards the boy and the baron's widow and daughters."

"The boy fought bravely, did he not?"

"Yes, by all accounts."

"You believe he knew what his father

planned?"

"No. Frankly I'm not certain it was planned. The baron saw an opportunity and he acted upon it. Foolishly, rashly, definitely. He took a calculated risk and lost."

"That is one way to think of it," Despite his pain, Michel lips twitched at his mentor's cold assessment of the traitor's heinous deed.

"Yes, and now that you are safe and I know you will recover, I am not displeased with the way things worked out. Two strong challengers to your rule are now dead. It is unlikely we would have rooted out Baron James' true plans quickly, nor once his treachery was discovered could you have treated him as mercifully as you did his son. He would have been too dangerous an adversary. But his own men sent him to hell, without you needing to act, or set his punishment which may have garnered sympathy for the baron's memory."

"Instead, you act mercifully on behalf of the son and widow and daughters of the man who attempted to murder you. The threat of his treachery has been removed and its result has been to solidify your position as king. Did not King Barnabas say he'd spent twenty years trying to unite the nobles behind the crown? Yet, in a single night, you have accomplished what he was never able to."

"There are members of every noble family waiting in the hall outside this chamber, all united in their concern for their new king. In the same twenty four hours, you have sent a message to our enemies that if they think to attack Calei they will pay a high price for their daring. I think you have not only removed the two strongest challengers to your rule from within Calei, but you have also struck a heavy blow against the strongest challenge to your rule from outside Calei's borders. All in all, you have enjoyed remarkable success on your first day on the throne."

Michel's shoulders shook with laughter. "Yes, thank you for pointing out the advantages of having a sword run through my back and chest. I should no doubt be grateful to the baron for his service."

Amele's amused glance met his. "Let us not get carried away," he commented drily, then added, stroking a gentle hand across Michel's damp brow. "Rest now, my king. I will stand watch. Tomorrow is a new day and you will need all your strength to confront it."

CHAPTER SIXTEEN

Amele's prediction proved prophetic. Michel was happy his youth and excellent physical health sped along his recovery from his near mortal wound, because there was no denying he needed to call on all of his remaining strength to address the demands of his new position. Even after he rose from his bed, he tired easily and the pain of his wound lingered. He often found himself fingering the Salusian stone that once more lay against his flesh on the thin silver chain that had been repaired with the broken clasp reinforced by one of the Caleinian artisans. He and the stone appeared to have come to a truce of sorts. The tight fit of the chain around his neck no longer annoyed him as it once did and he discovered he found the stone's warmth and weight a surprising comfort to him in his trials. Of which he found there were a surprising number.

Before ascending to his birthright Michel had no clear notion of the demands on a king's time. Being his father's youngest son and with no expectation of inheriting his vast estates, Michel had not concerned himself with the myriad of details it took to keep his father's lands running smoothly. He wished now he'd been more attentive to his father's attempts to teach him land management and felt the stirrings of real regret at their largely distant relationship while the duke lived. Accompanying his regret was a very near grief that he would not be given the opportunity to repent of his sometimes careless indifference towards the man who gave him life.

He had been too busy to properly mourn his parents' and brothers' deaths, and too concerned with the prospect of his sisters' fates at the hands of the invading Norman army, to fully comprehend the loss of his family, but more and more his thoughts dwelt on those who'd come before him and who accompanied him into this life, and he couldn't help but wonder at the futility of it all.

What was the point of striving for justice when a man's friends could so easily put aside their own honor and slit his throat for the promise of gold and power? What was the point of ascending to a throne when a man was denied the comfort of a wife and sons to give meaning to his days and provide soft comfort to his nights? Michel was not certain he completely believed an ancient bane was the cause of so much of the death attributed to it, but he could not argue that the citizens' of Calei's perception was that the curse was real. Whether it was a curse or those who merely sought to take advantage of its usefulness as a handy excuse for the evil of men's deeds, it hardly mattered to its victims if the end result was the same.

Amele had reported back to him that Gabriel knew no more than he did in regards to the curse's origins. Gabriel also reported that Barnabas had been understandably frustrated, despite perusing the castle's extensive library, and his predecessors personal papers, by the lack of information regarding either the origin of the curse or the references to the daughter of the moon and the heart of the sun contained within the clue he was given to solve it.

The spirit who spoke through the voice of the maid Rowena had apparently not lied when he stated the clue had remained unchanged through the long march of years. The same clue was recorded in every king's personal journal that remained in the keep's possession:

'When the daughter of the moon captures the heart of the sun the curse will be lifted.'

Was the daughter of the moon a living woman then? It seemed unlikely, as even if the words of the curse had at some point referred to a living woman, she would be long dead by now. Perhaps a female descendant of hers would satisfy the terms of the curse. Even if he were able to make such a connection to a family who still had connections to Calei, a rather fantastic leap to be sure, what in the name of all that was holy did the heart of the sun refer to? Was this imaginary woman, assuming she existed at all, then supposed to fly like a bird to the sky and carve out a piece of the sun? The premise was ridiculous, and damned frustrating when so much relied on its resolution.

Even with so much of his future seemingly tangled up in the fantastic whims of an ancient curse; it was some weeks before he was able to carve out time to seek out the young bishop to ask him if the church maintained any records in regards to it. In the interim he had been swamped with the many duties and responsibilities of simply running the day to day affairs of his kingdom. While his ascension to the throne was a very recent one, Barnabas' long illness and his inability to address issues as they arose meant that there was a backlog of numerous petty and some not so petty decisions that only the king could affirmatively act on.

The most important of these was ensuring the future security of the city and its citizens. His own men were a welcome addition to the existing forces, but Michel commanded each of the noble families to send a company of men on a rotating basis so that everyone who most benefitted from Calei's wealth also played a part in seeing to its defense. This seemingly simple request entailed several meetings with the heads of the noble families to work through the number of men to be assigned to the guard of the city and the mountain passes, the length of time the soldiers would serve the throne, who would be responsible for their training, and whether or not they would report to their own commanders or be assimilated into the king's men for the length of their service.

Of immediate concern and of almost equal importance to the security of their own boundaries was to ensure the safety of the trade routes over the mountains. Calei was some distance from the great cities of Paris or Rome and if it were not for the rich gems and gold to be found in the surrounding mountains, there would be no reason for merchants and tradesmen to make Calei a stop on their regular trading routes. It was inconvenient enough for travelers and tradesmen alike to travel the lengthy, sometimes, depending on the weather, uncomfortable distance to conduct business with Calei, if that travel was accompanied by worries over being attacked in the mountains by murderous thieves, the source of Calei's wealth and consequently its very existence would be threatened.

In addition to security matters, Michel was forced to concern himself with housing the additional men and their horses who accompanied him to Calei. There was plenty of land at his disposal, and willing hands to do the work, but setting an overseer in charge, making certain the wages were paid to all who served the king and the keep, meeting with the heads of the mining operations, meting out justice when called upon to do so, and just dealing with the seemingly unending demands for his time and attention left him very little time for his personal concerns, even if one of those concerns involved a curse that plagued the royal bloodline.

He had even been expected to host a reception at the castle for the nobles and their wives, along with the other important citizens of his new rule so that the ladies of his new kingdom would have an opportunity to meet the new king and take his measure. He was extremely grateful and more than willing to place the planning of the event in Elena's surprisingly competent hands. He hoped to catch the bishop that evening and set a time on the morrow for their meeting.

In the meantime, he reluctantly accepted that he was going to be late as the host for his own reception, as some problem arose in regards to the new stables being constructed that required his input with the end result being that he was delayed in returning to the keep until his guests were already beginning to arrive.

Michel took the back stairs two at a time in his haste to reach his chambers and change into more fitting attire for the occasion and to avoid running into his arriving guests in his current, somewhat disheveled state. He found a steaming bath awaiting him in his chambers and he silently blessed his ward's anticipation of his need of one. Stripping out of his shirt and breeches, he stepped appreciatively into the steaming tub and allowed himself the luxury of leaning back and closing his eyes for a moment, while the hot water eased the lingering pain from his wound in his aching chest.

The injury was healing, but he acknowledged it would trouble him less if he rested more and gave his insides time to properly heal. Easier said than done, he sighed to himself, particularly when one was a king over a land that had been run by proxy for the past several months. Welcome scents reached him from the feast awaiting him and his guests in the grand hall, and he thought he detected the strains of musicians playing a soft, pleasing melody for the comfort of his guests. He really would have to find time this evening to take Elena aside and express his very real appreciation for her efforts.

He'd seen very little of his ward since she returned to the keep to take up residence under his roof. The few occasions when their paths crossed, there had been no time to exchange more than a perfunctory greeting as he was usually either on his way out of the keep after breaking his fast in the morning, or returning to change for an evening obligation elsewhere. By the time he sought the privacy of his chambers late at night, he assumed Elena was already asleep in her own rooms.

He missed her and he regretted the new distance between them, even acknowledging there was very little that could be done about it unless he was prepared to marry the maid. Even if they were already man and wife, he imagined the past weeks would have been very little different in regards to their personal time together, except at night and the early mornings in the privacy of his chambers. Soaking in the warmth of the water, he let his thoughts wander to fantasies of exactly how their time would be spent in the privacy of his chambers. He realized he missed her anxious glances and gentle smiles, and her very real concern about his recovery, but he missed most the feel of her soft lips opening beneath his, the silken texture of her skin, and the way she fit herself close within the circle of his embrace, eagerly molding her lithe, young body against his so there was no separation between them.

Not surprising given the direction of his thoughts, he felt his manhood stir. He'd gone long months without the comfort of a woman beneath him. While such a sacrifice was necessary when he was preparing to take back his birthright, now that the kingship was his, the same constraints no longer prevented him from seeking the release to be found in a woman's soft embrace.

He admitted it was not the constraints of his duties that kept him in his celibate state, it was his unwillingness to hurt Elena, knowing her tender feelings for him, and that she wouldn't understand that a man did not require warm feelings for his companion to find a much needed physical release in her arms.

Aware of the time passing as he lingered with his bath, Michel used the nearby cloth to swiftly wipe away the day's sweat and grime and rose from his seated position and stepped out of the tub. He needed to make a decision soon about what he was going to do about Elena. Not only could she not remain indefinitely in a bachelor's household without a proper chaperone in residence, he had no intention of continuing to live a monkish existence in his own home.

It was not surprising that when he was dressed in his fine evening clothes and presented himself at the top of the stairs leading down into the grand hall, with the members of his guard flanking him, that the first person his eyes sought in the crowd beneath him who stopped to bow and curtsey at the sight of him was Elena. He was somewhat overwhelmed by the sight of his subjects arrayed in all of their finery. Jeweled ladies in their grand gowns accompanied by their equally impressive husbands filled the great hall with a glittering array of finery. Descending the stairs his eyes passed over their bent heads in search of Elena. He'd nearly reached the bottom step before he caught sight of her.

When he gestured for the assemblage to rise, their eyes met across the throng standing between them. If he had been taken aback by the sight of his subjects in their evening finery, the vision Elena presented in the cream colored gown, with gold stitching around the not exactly modest neckline and around the cuffs of her sleeves set his heart galloping in his chest. Her hair was swept up off her back and arranged in a braided crown that framed her face, accenting her delicate features and the slender column of her throat. Any remaining question in his mind as to whether it was a child and not a beautiful, desirable woman he stood silently regarding was answered by the swell of her full breasts peeking out above the scooped neckline of her gown. A large pearl rested between them and glimmered subtly in the light from the candle-lit chandeliers overhead, its beauty no more striking than the maid who displayed it.

Michel's earlier fantasies returned with a vengeance and he was forced to exercise considerable control not to stroll across the room, sweep the maid up in his arms and return to his bedchamber to act on them. The knowledge Elena would raise no objection to his alternative plan for the evening only made the test of his discipline that much more challenging. Finally, recalling their surroundings and the hundreds of guests gathered, their eyes on him, waiting for him to speak, he nodded in Elena's direction then approached Timothy with a request to be introduced to his lovely wife.

Elena felt her cheeks heat up in a full blush at the memory of Michel's close perusal. She drew some small satisfaction at the astonished look on his face when their eyes met across the room. She was glad to have the opportunity for him to see her in something other than the borrowed, ill-fitting gowns she'd worn in the mountain camp after he rescued her from the villains who kidnapped her. But her own surprise at seeing him standing so proud, so fit, his eyes scanning the crowd of his loyal subjects had been no less than his at seeing her, and only made her feel more uncertain of her place in his life. Was he not the epitome of every young maid's dreams? As king, he could have his choice of any woman in his kingdom. Why should he settle for one he regarded as much a tedious child as he did a woman full-grown?

"Elena, dear." A rather amused voice repeated near her ear and Elena started and turned to find Lady Madeline, Baron Gallagher's wife, by her side, apparently anticipating a response to the comment she no doubt directed at her, but which Elena had not heard because she'd been too wrapped up in her daydreams surrounding the new king.

"Forgive me, Lady Madeline, my thoughts were elsewhere," she quickly apologized to the older woman.

"Yes, dear, so I noticed. Not that I blame you. If I were twenty years younger, I am certain my thoughts would also be directed elsewhere whenever our dashing, young king was within my line of sight."

Elena blushed profusely at the older woman's inference, but was too embarrassed at her directness to know how to respond.

Madeline reached out to give her hand a comforting squeeze. "Forgive me, child, I did not mean to cause you discomfort. 'Tis the truth I would worry more about you if you did not notice what a fine young man our new king is. I understand from my husband it was King Barnabas' dying wish that the two of you wed."

Elena knew there was nothing she could do about her flaming cheeks, but she was more interested in making certain she understood Lady Madeline's inference correctly. "I'm sorry, perhaps I misunderstood you?"

"I sincerely doubt that, my dear. Surely you knew Barnabas loved you like his very own daughter. He made it very clear in the scroll he left appointing King Michel your guardian that he granted his consent for you to wed Queen Alyssa's grandson, Michel, and no other."

Elena lifted trembling hands to her cheeks. "I had no idea my uncle left such instructions. I suppose that is why everyone seems to assume that we will be wed."

"No doubt, my dear, but I think the circumstance of our new king allowing you to remain in his household without the benefit of a proper chaperone leads people to conclude he has every intention of marrying you after an appropriate time has elapsed for you to mourn your uncle's loss."

"I see," Elena replied in a hushed voice. "Admittedly I hadn't considered that. I have always lived in the keep. I am certain it is merely a kindness on King Michel's part not to have removed me from the only home I have any memory of. Where would I go, after all? Uncle Barnabas was my only family."

"Yes, well, though you are too young perhaps to be fully aware of the consequences to your reputation by continuing to live under the roof of our bachelor king, rest assured the king is not unaware of his responsibilities towards you. Knowing my husband's regard for him, and now having met him myself, I am completely confident he will not be remiss in fulfilling those responsibilities."

"I see," Elena echoed hollowly. "Thank you for explaining. You are quite right. I had no idea people would assume I was the king's mistress simply because we both had our quarters in the keep. Especially considering the fact that I have barely seen him since he recovered from his wounds and assumed his duties as king."

"Don't be foolish, Elena. No one assumes any such thing. Our new king is a man of honor. Look how he treated Baron James' son and family after the man attempted to murder him. A lesser king would have forced them to forfeit their lands and exiled them from his kingdom at the very least. Certainly no one would have challenged his right to do so under the circumstances. Frankly we were all shocked by his generosity towards the baron's family and the personal interest he has displayed towards young Colin. Such a man, so mindful of his honor, will not be slow to protect an innocent young maid's, particularly the niece of our former king."

"Yes, of course, thank you for your reassurance. Would you excuse me? I have to consult with the cooks in regards to dinner." Elena forced the words through her stiff lips, all of her joy in the evening's entertainment forgotten. At her companion's assent and gracious offer of assistance, Elena summoned the words to politely decline her overture and then turned away, blindly seeking the means to escape the now oppressive gathering.

She needed to be alone for a few moments to regain her composure and to absorb what she'd just learned. Her uncle left instructions with Michel that he wished him to not only act as her guardian, but to marry her, as well. To make matters worse, her uncle's dying wish was apparently well known among the citizens of Calei, at least among the noblemen.

Michel's kindness to her by granting her request of him to be allowed to return to the keep and live there with him had all but forced him, in the eyes of the nobles, to marry her or surrender his honor in their eyes. No wonder he'd been avoiding her. She needed to leave. He saved her life. She would not repay him by forcing him into a marriage he did not want, to a woman he regarded as a child.

"Elena?" She swung around at the sound of her name, convinced she must be imagining it was Michel who hailed her. When she saw him striding towards her, his long legs swallowing up the distance between them, her own feet were suddenly frozen to the floor.

"Elena?" he repeated, when she just stood there staring up at him, with what must surely be a silly, dazed expression on her face.

She quickly sank into a deep curtsey before him. She heard his amused chuckle at her respectful gesture and then he reached down to assist her to her feet. "I think we have progressed beyond such formalities when we are alone."

Her tongue felt as though it was stuck to the roof of her mouth and she quickly dropped her stricken gaze before his searching one.

"Elena is something wrong?" he prodded at her continued silence.

Gathering her scattered wits, Elena drew in a calming breath and braved meeting his probing glance. "No, no of course not. I was just heading to the kitchens to make certain all is in readiness for dinner. I believe the majority of the guests have arrived. We should be able to sit down to dine soon."

A puzzled frown entered his glance and he replied, "Elena, I am certain the housekeeper will make sure our guests do not starve. I would not detract from your pleasure in the evening by having you run yourself ragged over such matters. Not, that I don't realize it is because of your efforts the evening has gone off so spectacularly. I hadn't realized you acted as your uncle's hostess before he fell ill."

"Yes." Elena couldn't think of anything more sparkling to contribute to the conversation beyond her single word response.

Again his confusion was evident in the blue eyes that met hers. At her continued silence Michel pulled her deeper into the dimly hallway and away from the speculative glances that watched them from the crowded hall.

"Tell me what's wrong. Did someone say something to upset you?" He took her cold hands in both of his and squeezed them gently.

Elena recognized the genuine concern that prompted his question. There was no avoiding their circumstances. She was no more prepared to survive in the wilderness than she had been when she concocted her half-formed plans to flee being forced to marry Raulf. "May I ask you a question?"

"Of course," he confirmed, even as his eyes probed hers for a hint of what she wanted to know from him.

"Did my uncle ask you to marry me?"

Whatever he thought she was about to question him about, the query she just directed at him was obviously not it. He released one of her hands to thrust one of his own through his shoulder length hair and sputtered uncertainly, “Elena…”

She swallowed the lump of suppressed tears lodged in her throat. “No, never mind, I can already see the answer in your uncertainty of how to respond. Forgive me for approaching such a delicate matter with you when you have other matters on your mind. I only hope you will not…Please do not feel as though you must…” Elena abandoned her attempt to get the words out.

She drew a shattered, embarrassed breath and offered feebly, “I have to go. I am not able to have this discussion with you now and then return to *your* guests as if nothing is amiss. It was foolish of me to broach the topic now. I suppose you are right. I am not quite grown up all the way yet where I can pretend all is well between us when clearly it is not. Please excuse me, Your Highness.” She didn’t wait for him to respond to her tearful plea. Instead she slipped her hand from his unresisting grasp and fled down the hall.

Elena stopped in an empty alcove to gather herself. She pressed trembling hands to her hot cheeks and brushed ready tears from her eyes with an impatient gesture. Then drawing in several bracing breaths, admonished herself not to act any more like the child Michel already believed her to be and continued on her way to the kitchens.

She supposed she shouldn’t be surprised Michel believed such matters as the details involved in presiding over his first official reception as king could be left in the hands of a servant who had no personal acquaintance with the guests in attendance. Even in her own limited experience, she had already learned that most men assumed their households ran themselves and seemed to think such things as warm food, fresh ale and clean linens appeared at their ready hands as if by magic.

After confirming the details with the housekeeper and the cooks, Elena made her way back to the grand hall. She had acted as her uncle's hostess on enough occasions to comprehend what was expected of her. At the entrance she pasted a bright smile on her face, nodded in response to a summons by Lady Margaret, Baron Paul's wife, and set off across the hall, some sixth sense alerting her to the fact Michel's eyes followed her progress across the distance.

Elena managed to avoid the king's company for the remainder of the evening. It was not difficult. Michel was constantly surrounded by his new subjects seeking to gain his attention. For her part, she nimbly evaded allowing herself to be cornered into any additional conversations in regards to the new king's intentions towards her. There were broad hints in her direction about the gathering no doubt being called together again soon to celebrate her marriage to King Michel but Elena pretended to be oblivious to their implication and only managed to excuse herself from one well-meaning matron only to be cornered by another.

It was with a feeling of intense relief when later in the evening she slipped away from the gathering without making her formal excuses to the king. As the evening progressed, the married knights and nobles had sought their own homes in the company of their wives and the king's company had taken on a younger, overwhelmingly male flavor. She deduced correctly her presence among them would only serve to dampen their rising, ale-enhanced spirits.

Entering her rooms she rubbed her temples to ease the pounding headache she struggled with for the majority of the evening. Lissel, her maid, waited to help her remove her gown and prepare for bed. For a moment, Elena considered sending her away. She was quite capable of undressing herself and pulling a sleeping gown over her head, but she could see Lissel' s glance was alight in anticipation of the opportunity to discuss the events of the evening and Elena could not bring herself to squelch the girl's enthusiasm with a careless dismissal.

"Lady Elena, I swear you must have been the most beautiful lady in the room. Do you think the king noticed? But of course, he must have...the two of you being so close and all. It's so romantic the way he rescued you from those black-hearted kidnappers and kept you with him in the mountains."

Elena suppressed the agonized groan that rose to her lips. Did even the servants assume she was Michel's mistress? No wonder Michel regarded her as if she was still a child. She certainly retained the naivety of one. She listened with half an ear to Lissel's chatter as the girl undid the ties to her gown and carefully lifted the heavy material over her head.

They were about the same age, Elena concluded, but Lissel was apparently far more possessed of worldly knowledge than she was. At least enough to have assumed Elena and Michel's relationship was far more intimate than that of simply a guardian and his ward.

Elena again felt the absence of her mother in her life. Wasn't it a mother's place to make her daughter aware of such matters about the intimacies between a man and a woman, and the assumptions others would be bound to jump to in regards to a king sharing his home with his young, unwed ward? A proper chaperone? What did that mean exactly? There were dozens of servants living within the walls of the keep, not to mention the soldiers' quarters down below. How many chaperones were required to ensure her virginity remained safe from the king's manly passions? Was the man not guarded twenty four hours of every day? How was he supposed to conduct such liaisons without the knowledge of his guard?

Not that Michel had shown any sign of

wishing to conduct a liaison with her since her return to the keep. Now that she understood the way things stood between them, and the expectations he was laboring under in regards to his intentions to his predecessor's niece, she didn't blame him for avoiding her company.

She was only just beginning to comprehend it didn't matter if Michel had acted honorably towards her or not, since everyone apparently already believed they were lovers, or had been when she remained under his protection in the mountains. Elena very much feared those assumptions, despite their inaccuracy, would prove enough to force Michel to wed her.

She sighed heavily and moved to take the brush from Lissel's hand where she was brushing the intricate braids from her hair with long strokes. "Is everything all right, milady?"

Elena summoned a reassuring smile. "Yes, Lissel. I suppose the excitement of the evening was too much for me. I have a slight headache. I believe we will finish dealing with my hair in the morning. Thank you for waiting up for me."

Lissel blushed with pleasure. "Oh, yes, of course, Lady Elena. I am so blessed to have been chosen to serve you. There's nothing else I can get for you? Perhaps a tonic from the kitchens for your headache?"

Elena shook her head and rose from her perch on the stool. "No, that is very kind of you. A good night's sleep is all I require. You should seek your own bed as well. It has been a late night for both of us."

Elena breathed a relieved sigh when the door finally closed behind Lissel's retreating back, and then she crossed the room to stare out the window as she debated her future course. She was reminded of a similar night not so very long ago when she stood at this same window plotting her escape from Raulf. Such a foolish plan was denied her now, even if she could find the courage to execute it. Michel would simply find her and bring her back. Hadn't she confided in him her half-formed plot to flee into the mountains to escape Raulf?

She supposed she could seek out Bishop Maren and inform him she wished to become a bride of the church. She immediately abandoned the notion when she acknowledged that even if the bishop could be convinced she had suddenly become aware of a calling to enter religious life, she doubted very much Michel could be convinced of such a bald-faced lie. As her guardian he would simply order her back to the keep and to abandon her foolish notion of becoming a nun.

She found it ironic that she stood before this very same window trying to plot her escape from having another marriage forced upon her. She would have gladly accepted death as a replacement for Raulf as a husband. Now, though she longed to be the woman who would share

Michel's life and his bed, she did not think her heart could accept knowing the life she most longed for had been forced upon the man she loved. She would rather spend the rest of her years alone and miserable than to make Michel miserable by being compelled to accept her as his wife against his inclination.

At the insistence of her pounding temples, she finally abandoned her watch by the window and sought her bed. Sliding between the fresh sheets, she fell quickly into a deep slumber. As if prompted by the turmoil of her waking thoughts, her dreams were troubled.

Raulf's bloodied corpse awaited her at the cathedral altar where Bishop Maren in his priestly vestments stood waiting to bind them in the sacrament of holy matrimony. Elena tried to run away from her fate. In her dreams she cried out for Michel to rescue her, but Raulf's amused laughter filled the cathedral, blocking out the sound of her desperate pleas. When she refused to draw any closer, his skeletal hand reached out to grasp her arm and draw her to his side.

Elena moaned in her sleep. Where was Michel? Why didn't he come to rescue her? Would he just leave her to become a victim of Raulf's evil lust? "No, no, please…"

Suddenly Elena became aware of something pressed into her palm. She looked down to discover it was the strange stone she found buried in the mud by the river. Clutching it close against her chest she peered down into its depths and saw a strange flicker echo deep within. Her lips curved in an astonished smile and she used her dainty handkerchief to wipe the mud away. Her new treasure appeared to appreciate her careful attention because the light returned, stronger this time, and delighted, Elena's lips curved in a wide grin.

"Maybe it was truly a magic stone," Elena thought to herself. 'Perhaps it was the kind of magic that could grant wishes,' she tacked on hopefully. As if in response, the stone began to glow beneath her hands. "Oh, aren't you beautiful," she exclaimed softly as the light spread from the stone's center until it reached its outer borders. "Will you save me from Raulf?"

In answer to her hushed plea Elena was suddenly swept away from the cathedral smiling happily when Raulf roared his outrage at her fresh escape. Grinning, Elena flew ever higher away from her dead suitor and laughed with true joy when the stone carried her through the very peak of the cupola and out into the warm night.

It was like dancing through the stars, she decided amazed. A full moon watched her as she glided by with the shining stone in her hand, and seemed to wink in her direction, as if they shared a secret. Laughing Elena waved in his fat, happy direction as she flew past, then the stone led her higher still until there were thousands upon thousands of stars surrounding her. The stone she held in her hand now gleamed as brightly as if it was one of them. She thought to leave the stone here with its brothers. One of them should get to go home, she reasoned, as though even in her dreams she realized it was impossible for her to do so.

Her parents were dead. She was being sent far away to live with her uncle. Now her uncle was dead too. Everyone she loved was gone, except Michel, and he didn't want her. In her misery she fell from the stars and landed back in her bed in the keep, no longing grasping the stone in her hand. It must have stayed behind with the other stars. She was glad at least one of them found their way back home. She didn't have a home anymore. Where would she go? What would she do? Who would take care of her? Tears filled her eyes and she sobbed as if her heart was broken.

"Why do you weep, daughter?"

At the sound of her mother's voice, Elena only wept louder. It had been so long since she'd heard her voice, or felt the gentle glide of her hand through her hair. She turned her cheek against it and breathed in her mother's familiar scent. "Mother? Why did you leave me? Why does everyone I love have to leave me? I'm so tired of being alone."

"I'm sorry, Elena. I did not wish to leave you, but sometimes we don't get what we wish."

Despite her youth, Elena had already learned that unwelcome lesson the hard way. "I know. I wish you had taken me with you."

Her mother's gentle laughter echoed in her thoughts. "I think it is not for me you weep, daughter. At least not tonight."

"No," Elena reluctantly admitted.

"What has upset you so?"

"I don't know how to make him love me," Elena confessed in a soft whisper.

Her mother didn't laugh. She only continued stroking her hair in a soothing gesture. "You cannot force him to love you, Elena. You can only offer your own without a price attached to it."

"What will happen to me if he decides he doesn't want me?"

"You will find your way, daughter, I promise. I left you too soon. There's so much I never had the chance to tell you…to explain."

Puzzled, Elena asked, "Explain what?"

But her mother didn't answer. Elena felt her drift away and even in sleep, she felt the fresh loss as keenly as she did the first.

CHAPTER SEVENTEEN

Michel planned to seek Elena out in the morning before he began his day and finish the conversation they started the previous evening. He didn't like the memory of her devastated expression when he had been unable to respond to her direct question about whether or not Barnabas had asked him to marry her. He could hardly dispute the truth of her assertion since he was fairly certain there had been no shortage of those present at the reception the prior evening to share with her the contents of the scroll Barnabas left upon his death appointing Michel his niece's guardian.

But as was the case with so many of his finely laid plans since he ascended to his grandfather's throne, the morning did not follow the carefully constructed path he laid out for it. Before he had a chance to track Elena down, he was called away from the keep to address a problem that had come up at one of the mines. He returned to the castle early in the evening with just enough time to change into fresh clothes and keep his appointment with Bishop Maren. Though the bishop had indicated he would be happy to present himself at the keep at the king's convenience, Michel preferred to meet with him at the bishop's residence in an effort to avoid prying ears at the keep overhearing their conversation.

The young bishop answered his own door to Michel. "Your Highness, please come in. You honor me with your presence."

Michel waved off the other man's formal greeting and responded frankly, "If you wouldn't mind, I would prefer you call me Michel when we are alone."

An answering smile tilted up the corners of the other man's lips, "As you wish, Michel," He hesitated over the familiar form of address, and then added, "If you will address me as John." At Michel's raised brow, the young bishop added quickly, "When we are alone of course."

Michel nodded, then followed the bishop into a room he assumed the priest used as his private office.

"May I offer you refreshments, Your...forgive me, Michel?"

"I wouldn't say no to a goblet of cool ale," Michel replied frankly bringing an understanding smile to the other man's expression.

"Of course." His host gave his instructions to his hovering servant and waited by the open door, until the servant returned with a tray of light refreshments, including the requested ale, then the bishop closed the door and set the tray on his writing desk. John poured the ale into two goblets and passing one to Michel offered, "Long life, my king. Before we begin I hope you will not mind if I express my joy at your speedy recovery from what many of us feared would prove fatal injury? I know for a certainty my joy is reflective of the majority of the citizens of Calei."

"Only the majority?" Michel echoed with a smile, raising his glass and drinking deeply of its contents.

The bishop laughed and retook his seat. "I imagine you have suffered through a few very busy weeks since you returned home. I trust your wound is fully healed?"

Michel shrugged off the other man's concern. "Well enough, but it was not to discuss my health that I requested this meeting." At the other's gesture he should continue, Michel added, "I wished to speak with you privately about a few matters."

"Of course, I am at your service…Michel."

Michel paused for a moment to gather his thoughts. "Two concerns actually. I was wondering what you know of the history of the curse upon the royal family, but before we begin, may I ask you a personal question?"

"Of course."

"You seem very young to have risen to such an exalted position within the hierarchy of the church."

Unoffended, the bishop laughed. “I might say the same of you, Your Highness.”

Michel nodded, acknowledging the other man’s point, then countered, “But my title is bestowed upon me by right of birth. I do not believe the church operates in the same manner as a monarchy.”

“True, but there are times I wonder,” John admitted with a rueful smile. “You cannot guess as to why a native Caleinian has been assigned to this office?”

Michel considered the bishop’s question. “I imagine an outsider would be uncomfortable with the mysticism that seems to permeate the entire population, not all of which I think the church is completely comfortable with.”

“True, and very perceptive of you.”

“Then why elevate a bishop at all?”

“Have you perhaps had an opportunity to inspect the cathedral your subjects built to honor our Lord?”

Michel admitted somewhat guiltily, “Regrettably not. I have been extremely busy getting my house in order since my arrival.”

“No doubt, my king. Might I be so bold as to suggest the Almighty is an incomparable ally?”

Michel let out a rueful laugh. “Duly noted, but what significance would a visit to the cathedral have on the answer to my question?”

“Had you visited the cathedral, my king, you would no doubt notice the fine materials and liberal use of gold in its construction. In fact, I believe no expense was spared, nor any grudged, by the generous citizens of Calei in providing a fitting home for the worship of our Lord."

"Ah, of course. Calei is a wealthy parish."

"Wealthy and historically generous to the church's mission," John confirmed.

Michel was not certain if the other man was issuing a challenge to his new king or not, but as he had no issue with his predecessors' generosity to the church, he did not feel any need to make an issue of it now. "Rest assured, Your Excellency, as king I applaud Calei's generous support of the church and have no intention of instituting any changes as to the throne's previous support of the church's mission."

"You reassure me, Your Highness. I will certainly include your generous words in my next report to my supervisors in Rome. They will no doubt be relieved to receive them and to send their own best wishes for your successful reign."

Curious, Michel inquired, "Were all the contenders to the throne avid supporters of the church's presence in Calei?" Somehow Michel had difficulty of conceiving Raulf kneeling in humble supplication before anyone, even the creator of the universe.

His companion shrugged, and with an amused sparkle in his eyes, admitted, "But of course, my king. You remarked earlier on the people's mystical natures. Do you believe they would long tolerate a king who despised God and those tasked with performing his mission on earth?"

Michel realized somewhat belatedly he would do well to present himself at Mass at the earliest opportunity. He thought the bishop had just given him a hint, without overtly giving his new king unasked for advice, as to how to endear himself to the hearts of his own people. "Thank you for your insight. It is obvious the church's superiors knew well what they were about in appointing you to the office you occupy. I would be happy to include a token of my gratitude for their foresight and a personal note expanding on my appreciation in your next report to your supervisors in Rome."

"You are too generous, my king. But I believe you had other matters demanding your attention that you wished to discuss with me this evening, specifically the history of the curse on the royal family?"

At Michel's confirming nod, he added, "I can certainly understand your interest given the very personal nature of the consequences to you and your heirs, but unfortunately I fear there is little I can do to assist you. Yours was the first… ah… 'clue' I was privileged to witness."

"Mine as well," Michel acknowledged, grinning over the bishop's obvious discomfort with the topic of their conversation. "What did you think, Father? Forgive me…John."

The bishop's eyes lit with an answering smile and he countered, "As a priest or as a Caleinian?"

"Both, I believe."

The bishop nodded and began, "As a priest I am well versed in the kinds of events that defy logical explanation." At Michel's raised brow, he added with a smile, "We call them miracles."

"And what does the church call them when the events are not of a benevolent nature?" Michel challenged.

"There is no shortage of church teachings on the subject of Satan and his minions, but I am certain you comprehend the church's reluctance to attribute a particular evil to Lucifer's handiwork."

Michel nodded his understanding, "Or no doubt there would be plenty of men willing to take advantage of such a convenient excuse to exact a personal vengeance."

"Yes," the bishop sighed resigned, "When all too often men do not require the urging of the devil to commit their monstrous atrocities against one another."

"I do not disagree. What is your opinion in regards to the curse under discussion?" Michel asked curiously.

His companion hesitated before admitting quietly, "As I said, yours was the first such occurrence I witnessed personally. King Barnabas was already king when I was appointed bishop here, but I cannot deny I was much affected by the maid Rowena's, ah…I hesitate to use the word performance, because I do not believe that what we witnessed that evening was an act on her part. The voice that came from the girl… I don't believe it would be possible for her to change her voice and her appearance that dramatically without some type of intervention beyond the understanding of this world."

"You believe she was possessed?"

"No. The act of possession implies the taking over of another soul's physical form without his or her consent. In this case, the maid allowed herself to be used as a vehicle to facilitate such communication with, well, whatever the source of such communication was."

Michel nodded. "All right, we are in agreement that the maid's performance was not feigned. Let us move for a moment beyond the church's teachings on the matter. What then is your opinion of the curse as a native Caleinian?"

This time there was no hesitation on the other man's part. "Whether concocted by evil men or from a more elusive source, the curse is real and its effects have been well-documented in Caleinian history."

"Well-documented, how?" Michel leaned forward in his chair. This was what he had come here for.

The bishop regarded him with a speculative look in his eyes. "Have you not researched your own family's history?"

"How would I do that?" Michel enquired.

"I would imagine there is no shortage of official records at the keep. The church keeps its own." At Michel inquiring expression, he added, "I am certain you are aware the church is often called upon to act as a guardian of such documents. While there is little official documentation in the church's records in reference to the curse, there still exist old family bibles and a scrupulous documentation of the royal bloodlines."

Michel felt his excitement rising. "Where are these records?"

"In the cathedral library. I would be happy to share them with you or give them to you, if that is your wish. They are, after all, a history of your family, and whatever records are in the church's possession more rightfully belong to you."

"Thank you, John, but I believe I would prefer the church retain its guardianship over the old records of my house. I would however like to spend some time familiarizing myself with what they contain and to see if there are any references to the curse on the royal family."

"Perhaps I can save you some time. I imagine you are particularly interested in discovering if there is any reference in the records the church maintains as to the daughter of the moon and/or the heart of the sun."

"Yes," Michel held his breath in anticipation or the other man's response.

"Regretfully not." At Michel's obvious disappointment, the other man added, "As a native Caleinian I have a vested interest in seeing to the end of the curse. When I was first appointed to my current position, I spent several months researching all of the references I could find in the church's records to the royal family and the curse, but regrettably I found nothing helpful or I would have certainly shared my findings with King Barnabas."

Michel nodded, not surprised the solution to the riddle would not so easily present itself. It made sense that Barnabas and the prior kings had already followed his same line of reasoning.

The two men lapsed into a companionable silence, and then the bishop commented, "You mentioned there was another matter you wished to discuss with me?"

Sighing, Michel pulled his thoughts away from his family's checkered history and back into the present. "Yes."

At the bishop's inquiring brow, Michel added reluctantly, "Elena."

"Yes of course. What is it you wished to discuss with me in regards to Lady Elena?"

Michel hesitated then commented, "An unmarried maid cannot continue to live indefinitely under my roof."

His companion nodded, "Agreed. May I speak frankly?"

"Please."

"Then, Michel, I would tell you that there is every expectation in the city that Lady Elena will not remain unmarried for long."

"There is the expectation that I will marry her."

Even though his words were not voiced as a question but as a statement of fact the bishop offered his confirmation, "Yes."

Michel nodded. "I am in somewhat of an awkward position."

His companion's lips twitched at Michel's admission, "You speak perhaps of the lady's warm feelings for you?" Michel raised his brow at the bishop's obvious amusement at his expense. "Forgive me, Your Highness, but it is very apparent to anyone who has seen Lady Elena in your company that she regards you as the beginning and end of her very existence."

"She's very young," Michel excused, feeling his cheeks flush at the bishop's extravagant description.

"Yes, and you have been no less than a heroic figure in her young eyes."

"Be that as it may," Michel began with a rueful sigh, "Elena is still very young, perhaps too young to truly know her feelings in such matters. She has been through an ordeal. She was kidnapped from her bed and recently lost her uncle, the only father she has any memory of, after a long and protracted illness. It is not all that surprising she would develop a crush on the man who rescued her."

The bishop shook his head, denying Michel's explanation, "I think, Your Highness, you are over complicating the matter. Lady Elena's feelings for you are not those of a young girl's crush, but of a woman in love."

"Even if what you say is true, would it not be wrong of me to marry her and subject her to the very well-documented curse that besets the royal bloodlines?"

"I see your point and honor you for it, but I think in this case, it would be a far greater cruelty to spurn the lady's love and leave her wondering at the cause of your disinterest in her."

After a long moment, Michel nodded and gained his feet. "You've given me a great deal to consider. I thank you for your honesty."

"It has been my pleasure, Michel, both as your bishop and your subject. I am relieved to see the kingship of my homeland in such competent and caring hands."

Michel nodded and held out his hand. The bishop clasped it and released it and the two men turned towards the exit. "Will you want to see the records housed in the cathedral library before you leave?"

"No, not right now anyway. If you've already researched them, I think my time would be better served seeking out the maid Rowena, or preferably, her grandmother, if she is sufficiently recovered to receive my visit. Perhaps she will be able to shed some additional light on this mystery."

"I don't disagree," the bishop concurred, "And

if you don't mind my forwardness, Your Highness, I would be very interested to hear what you learn."

Grinning at the other man's eager curiosity, Michel nodded. "I will see to it you are among the first to know what, if anything, I am able to discover."

CHAPTER EIGHTEEN

Michel wasn't certain what to expect when the following afternoon he sought an interview with the local witch, but it certainly wasn't to find her neat cottage, indistinguishable from any of its neighbors on a quiet street with spring flowers framing a pretty, well-kept entrance. He smilingly shook off his guard's approach in the direction of the door to announce his arrival to the inhabitants, thinking the veteran soldier appeared very ill-at-ease at the prospect of knocking on a witch's door. It said much about his own experiences lately that Michel could summon no similar unease at the prospect of seeking advice from the local witch.

Smiling at the thought, Michel stepped forward and rapped sharply on the door. A few moments later Rowena appeared in the doorway.

"Your Highness?!" Recovering quickly from her astonishment, she curtseyed before him.

"Maid Rowena, forgive my unannounced visit. I stopped by to inquire if your grandmother was recovered from her recent illness, and if so, I hoped she was up to answering a few questions."

"Please come in," Rowena offered, and stepping back added hesitantly, her color high in her cheeks, "My grandmother is much better. I am certain she would be honored to answer your questions, Your Highness."

Michel followed Rowena through the small home and then back out of doors to the garden in the rear where he glimpsed an older woman, who he assumed must be Rowena's grandmother, tending neat rows of newly emerging fragile seedlings.

"Mesme, King Michel has honored us with a visit," Rowena announced.

The older woman rose and turned in their direction, her eyes immediately and frankly meeting Michel's curious blue gaze across the width of the small patch of yard. A noticeable silence descended between them as they each took the other's measure. Michel noted out of the corner of his eye Rowena stood a few steps away wringing her hands together in a nervous gesture.

Finally his host executed a minimal curtsey; a generous man might attribute to her advanced age, and with a sparkle in her eyes nodded in his direction. "Your Highness. Welcome to our humble home. How may I serve you?"

"Thank you for your gracious welcome. May I assume you've recovered fully from your recent illness?"

A slight shrug as the older woman approached

where he waited with her granddaughter. "There are some afflictions one never fully recovers from," she replied philosophically and then added, "I can see your own injury still plagues you. Come inside and let me give you something to ease your pain."

Michel stepped aside to allow the two women to precede him back into the small cottage. "That is very kind of you, but sometimes I wonder if the pain of the wound lingers because I have not yet learned completely the consequences of my own foolishness in trusting the pledge of a false friend."

The older woman's discerning glance probed his. "That is a painful lesson indeed for one so young to learn, and one I think a soul never fully recovers from, but there is no need for you to carry the burden of your injury along with your regret at not foreseeing it. Come sit. Allow me to offer you this service in return for your gentle welcome of my granddaughter the night I sent her to the keep in my stead."

Michel took the proffered stool in front the table set up near the hearth, but protested, "It is I who am indebted to this house and not the other way around."

"You give me hope, my king," she replied somewhat mysteriously then busied herself in the kitchen taking herbs and such from the various array of jars on one of the shelves attached to the wall near the hearth. Rowena lit a fire and set a metal kettle to boiling above it, to which her grandmother added the herbs she retrieved. Immediately a pungent but not unpleasant fragrance filled the room. It reminded Michel of the newly tilled earth on a summer day, with the manure from the animals used to sweeten the soil and prepare it for the seeds that would be planted there. "This must simmer for several minutes. In the meantime, tell me, my king, how I may serve you."

Michel indicated his hostess should join him at her table and she did so, motioning with a silent gesture for Rowena to leave them alone. "I imagine you have already deduced why I am here. I seek information on the curse that besets the king's blood."

"Yes, you are correct, I had concluded as much, which is why I sent Rowena away. She is young yet and I try to protect her from the weight of the burden that will one day fall upon her at my passing from this world, though I was unable to do so the evening you ascended to the throne."

"Forgive me. It was not my intent to burden her. I was not aware of that particular tradition prior to its being thrust upon my unsuspecting shoulders."

His companion laughed with true amusement. "No doubt it came as something of a surprise to you."

Michel thrust a hand through his hair and admitted wryly, "That is understating the case somewhat."

"Perhaps those who convinced you to return to Calei and claim your grandfather's throne were unwilling to present too grave a picture of the challenges you would be forced to contend with upon your arrival. Though by all accounts, my young king, you have dispensed with the most pressing trials with remarkable ease, courage and grace."

"Thank you. I fully expected to contend with the living in order to claim my birthright. In fact, I spent my entire life preparing for just such an opportunity, I am afraid my skill with a blade and as a leader and trainer of men are useless weapons in a struggle against an ancient curse, the origin of which appears to have passed beyond the reach of the memories of the living."

"Yes, a sharp blade, no matter how skillfully wielded is not the proper response to every challenge. I am afraid I cannot help you with the origin of the curse, as my own blood has ever acted only as the messengers of the clue you received the evening you ascended to your birthright."

"Blood of your blood has always served as the vessels through which the clue is offered to each new king?" Michel asked curiously.

His hostess shrugged one frail shoulder, "It is not as though the new kings have much choice in the matter. There are so few of us left who remember and still practice the ancient ways."

"Is there nothing more you can tell me?" Michel urged. He got the impression the older woman knew more than she was willing to admit to.

"What did the elder say to you?"

"The elder?"

"Our name for those who utilize our services in the manner Rowena demonstrated the evening the clue was given to you."

Michel nodded and repeated everything he could remember from the night in question.

His hostess listened intently and leaned back from the table, apparently in intense concentration, her focus on Michel's face never wavering. "You were given more than your predecessors, my king, whether you know it or not. The elders, I think, were hopeful your grandfather would bring about a resolution of the curse, but alas, we both know how that hope ended."

Michel's glance narrowed. "Yes, the elder indicated as much, but then he said something about my grandfather not knowing what he held in his grasp."

"You didn't mention that earlier. When did he say that? What exactly was he referring to?"

Michel thought back to the interview with the mysterious voice, trying to recall the exact words of their exchange. "His comment followed his mention of my grandfather returning to Calei with my grandmother. Something to the effect of him returning with his young bride and about how Nathaniel never understood what he held in his grasp…that is as close as I remember."

"He mentioned your grandmother specifically? I am certain you are aware your grandfather was married before and fathered two sons."

"Yes, both of whom were killed before he married my grandmother."

"Yes, but the mention of returning with his young bride must refer to Queen Alyssa. Your grandfather's first wife was a native of Calei."

Michel fell silent, his hand idly fingering the Salusian stone around his neck as was his habit lately.

"The amulet you wear. There is something vaguely familiar about it."

Michel dropped his hand away from the stone. "You probably remember seeing it around my grandmother's neck. The stone is a family heirloom of her line. It is known now as the Salusian stone and passes through the eldest daughter of my grandmother's blood."

"Yet it is in your possession?"

Michel nodded. "As a temporary steward only. The stone belongs to my twin sister, Melissa. She urged me to wear it when I returned to Calei. I am afraid there is a fair amount of superstition attached to it. The stone is rumored to possess mysterious powers, though I have seen no evidence of such. It's funny though, I believe the elder mentioned something about the stone that night."

"Indeed? Your earlier account made no mention of the stone."

Michel's lips kicked up at the older woman's impatience with his omission. "I only just recalled his interest in it. Frankly at that point I had lost the stone and was somewhat worried about confessing my sin to my sister and grandmother, as you will recall the stone is only temporarily in my possession. But the elder told me not to concern myself about its loss and that the stone had found its way into trustworthy hands."

"And whose hands did the elder deem trustworthy?"

"Lady Elena's," Michel supplied.

"Lady Elena restored your family heirloom to you?"

"Yes, I lost it in a stream in the mountains while bathing. It must have become embedded in the mud on the bank. Elena unearthed it and returned it to me the night I was wounded."

"A deadly wound, many feared, my king."

"Yes, but fortunately it proved otherwise."

"And still you doubt the powers of the stone?"

Michel laughed at his companion's implication. "You believe the stone had a hand in my recovery?"

The older woman shrugged. "It is obvious, Your Highness, that you do not, but I would not be too quick to dismiss the stone's place in unravelling your destiny. Did not the elder refer to it? Did you assume his remark about the stone and your grandmother's arrival were merely idle chatter on his part? Or the comment he made about your treasure being in trustworthy hands? Trust me, Your Highness; the elders do not make idle comments. He was giving you further clues to the riddle you seek to undo, but you dismissed them as unimportant. If you would discover what you need to know, dwell carefully on what you were told…on everything you were told that night. Write it down. Ascertain with the other witnesses that you have not forgotten even the smallest detail. My heart tells me you are close, closer perhaps than any of your predecessors have been over the long march of years. I think you must seek first the daughter of the moon. She will lead you to the heart of the sun."

Michel felt the mysterious force of her words settle around him. Once again he suspected his hostess knew more than she was willing to share with him, but even so, she'd given him a great deal to consider. "I will take your advice to write down and consider everything I was told that night. Thank you for your kind assistance." When Michel would have risen from his stool, she quickly waved him back down to his seat and jumped nimbly to her feet. She hurried over to the stove and stirred the mixture she was brewing with a wooden spoon, before lifting the spoon from the kettle and sampling a small amount with her finger.

"Your tonic is ready, Your Highness. Allow me to perform this small service for you, as I was able to provide so little assistance in response to your questions." She reached for a cup from a shelf near the hearth and poured a healthy portion of the mixture from the kettle into it.

Michel accepted the cup from her outstretched hand with ill-disguised hesitancy, bringing an amused smile to the lips of his hostess. "Drink it, my king, and be free of the pain that still troubles you. Calei needs you fit and strong and unburdened by the past."

Michel thought her benediction a rather unusual one, and fully aware the old witch could very well mean to poison him with her concoction, he lifted the cup, tipped it in her direction in a not unkind salute, and then swallowed its contents all the while observing her watchful, probing glance as he did so. He tried to hide his grimace at its less than pleasant after-taste.

"The bitterness of the brew is necessary to seek out and remove the lingering darkness still cleaving to your injury. The wound will heal quickly now and trouble you no more."

Michel was not certain he believed his companion's promise, but still he rose and bowed his respectful appreciation for her care of him. "Thank you. You have been a most gracious hostess. I will leave you now to return to your own affairs, but I will remember your advice and heed it. I hope if any additional questions come to mind I may return here and seek out the benefit of your wisdom."

His hostess smiled benignly upon him. "You have been blessed with a golden tongue and a charming manner. It is no wonder a young and innocent maid like Lady Elena has fallen victim to it. You will give her my fond regards, I trust? And my condolences on the loss of her uncle?"

Michel nodded, thinking how the older woman had very shrewdly snuck in her two pence about his responsibilities to his young ward.

CHAPTER NINETEEN

Amele waited for his return on the street near the entrance to the cottage and fell into step beside him as they made their way back to the keep. "Did you learn anything useful?"

"Perhaps. I'm not entirely certain," Michel replied honestly, then asked, "Did my grandmother ever speak to you of my grandfather?"

"In regards to the curse?"

"Not necessarily. Did she ever speak to you about how they met?"

"How they met?" Amele parroted.

"Yes. Did you never wonder after my grandfather was widowed, and his sons from his first wife were killed, why he travelled to a distant land and returned with a bride young enough to be his daughter rather than choosing a second wife from among the available maidens here in Calei?"

Amele took a moment to consider the question. "No, frankly I did not. I was a young man at the time, a raw recruit to the guard. I do not believe it would have occurred to me to question my king's decisions, let alone speculate as to his reasons for choosing his new bride."

"I realize that, but over the years you spent together in my grandmother's company, the topic never came up?"

"No." At Michel's surprised expression in response to his honesty, Amele added with mystified look of his own, "It surprises you that your grandmother never discussed her marriage to your grandfather with me?"

At Michel's resigned nod, acknowledging his point, Amele added curiously, "Why are you all of a sudden interested in your grandparent's marriage?"

"Rowena's grandmother raised the question."

Amele seemed to consider the matter and then speculated, "I imagine King Nathaniel felt it was his responsibility to remarry and sire an heir to the throne. As to his reasons for choosing his bride from a distant land, it may very well be that the noble families of Calei were somewhat reluctant to subject a daughter of theirs to the vagaries of the curse that the majority of its citizens believed were responsible for the deaths of King Nathaniel's sons and very possibly, his first wife."

"The citizens attributed the death of my grandfather's first wife to the curse?"

"I was a young man at the time, but I remember the heavy pall that hung over the city when the queen died so soon after the loss of their sons." Amele added curiously, "Do you believe your grandfather's reasons for marrying your grandmother had something to do with the curse?'

"I am no longer certain what I believe. Rowena's grandmother was very mysterious about the whole thing."

"You've made me curious as well, but surely if your grandmother was aware of anything that would help you solve this mystery she would have told you."

"What if she was unaware of my grandfather's reasons for pursuing her? She was little more than a child when they were wed was she not?"

"Yes, I think perhaps you are right. She didn't know, and perhaps never found out, but even if that was your grandfather's motivation for marrying your grandmother, he was apparently mistaken in his presumption."

"Why do you say that?"

"He was murdered in his sleep."

Michel nodded, then protested, "But his child survived, as did her children."

"But they were forced to flee Calei."

"True."

The two men settled into a considering silence when they were joined by the members of Michel's personal guard to provide the king with an escort back to the keep. Michel noticed young Colin made up one of their number and he hid his smile at the boy's awed expression when he nodded in his direction.

They proceeded silently through the relatively

quiet early evening streets of the city. Michel's thoughts turned away from his focus on the curse besetting him and to another pressing matter, his dilemma over what to do about Elena. He'd yet to gain a private moment with her to continue the conversation she ended so abruptly the evening of the reception. He thought his failure to do so could be attributed to his suspicion that Elena was avoiding him, as much as it was his demanding schedule as king.

He planned to speak with her this evening before she retired to her rooms. Unfortunately he still had no idea what he was going to say to her. There was no denying the fact that her uncle was wishful of a marriage between them. Despite her warm feelings for him, he imagined being wed solely to protect her reputation and to satisfy her uncle's request of his successor was not likely to fulfill the romantic dreams of marriage a young maid like Elena no doubt cherished in her tender heart.

He was not certain how to spare her gentle feelings without lying outright as to the depth of his own for her. He suspected that even if he were able to overcome his reluctance to enter into such a sacred commitment with that lie between them, Elena would, despite her innocence, see through his attempt to deceive her. It would be easier on both of them if the circumstances forcing his hand to settle things sooner rather than later between them allowed for more time for Elena to grow up a little. He thought he would find it easier to broach the coming discussion with her if her tender heart did not prevent him from doing so with a frankness of manner she would no doubt be offended by.

Regardless of the constraints of their circumstances, he admitted that while he was not in love with her, he did not like this new distance between them, nor was he comfortable at the recollection of her devastated expression the other night when she asked him if her uncle had attempted to arrange a marriage between them. There could be no question that it was time for them to come to an understanding about their futures. The entire city was speculating as to his intentions in regards to his ward. It wasn't fair to leave Elena to bear the brunt of the gossip.

As they drew nearer to the keep, Michel realized with some annoyance that his ward had anticipated he would attempt to corner her this evening for their long delayed discussion, and she had managed to head off his efforts to do so before he could put his plan into action. From where he approached the well-lit entrance to the castle, he could see Elena's slender figure outlined in the window of her room he suspected she sought to escape his reach. He sensed she remained unaware of his perusal of her from below because she stood with her arms wrapped around her middle staring off into the horizon. Her expression was pensive, as if she was contemplating weighty matters too burdensome for a maid of her young years to have to bear.

Coming to a sudden decision, he turned to the men that followed in his wake and summoned one to his side, "Colin?"

Apparently astonished at being addressed directly by his king, the young man stuttered over his reply, "Yes, Your Highness?"

"Fetch me a rope," Michel commanded.

"A rope, Your Highness?" Michel watched the young soldier's eyes dart to his companions and then back again.

"Yes, a rope. Make certain it is strong enough to bear my weight, and long enough to reach yonder window from the ground." Michel enlarged on his order, then pointed in the direction of the keep where Elena still stood in her window, unaware her solitary sanctuary was about to be violated by her guardian and king.

Colin's line of vision followed Michel's outstretched arm. A wide grin split his lips at seeing the object of Michel's attention. "Yes, Your Highness. Right away, sire."

Colin took off at a run toward one of the sheds that housed the keep's supplies. Michel met the quickly concealed grins of the remaining members of his escort and then turned to meet Amele's speculative expression.

"Have you any advice to offer your king, my friend?"

Amele shook his head and smiling, replied,

"You are asking the wrong man, my king. I have remained a bachelor all of my years in your family's service. Perhaps you should direct your query in young Joseph's direction. I understand he has quite a reputation with the ladies."

"Is that so?" Michel turned his focus towards the young soldier Amele jokingly indicated with a nod of his head.

His companions barely bothered to suppress their amusement at their friend's discomfort. The young soldier with the now obviously reddened face was saved from further embarrassment by Colin's hurried return, his breathing labored by his quick pace and the heavy rope he carried in his arms.

"Here you are, Your Highness. I wasn't certain if you also wished me to obtain a grappling hook so I retrieved one and attached it to the end of the rope, just in case."

"Good man, you have anticipated everything. If you will excuse me, I have a young maiden to woo."

He spun around to grin at the sound of the male chuckles directed at his retreating back and with a mock salute turned back and made his way purposefully towards the window where his future bride still stood staring out into the night.

"Elena," he called up to her from where he stopped beneath her window.

"Michel, is that you?" She leaned out of the window and over the ledge to stare down at the shadows from where his voice hailed her.

"Yes, it's me. Step away from the window," he commanded and began winding the rope in preparation for throwing it the distance separating them.

"What? Michel what you doing?" She demanded, then swiftly recalling who she was addressing, added in embarrassed voice, "Forgive me, Your Highness."

"Elena, step away from the window." He ignored her apology for her familiarity in addressing him by his given name, and repeated his earlier demand.

He grinned at her mystified and disgruntled expression before she disappeared from his line of sight as she retreated from the window, then swung the rope with the iron hook on one end in a wide arc. It landed with a satisfying clank, and then it slid scraping along the wall until it found purchase in the iron supports near the window ledge. Michel tested his weight on the dangling rope and began scaling the keep's thick wall even as Elena reappeared in the window and looked down.

Their eyes met across the narrowing distance between them, his smiling, hers regarding him with wide-eyed astonishment. Loud male voices from the soldiers manning the walls and from the crowd gathering near the entrance to the keep could be heard cheering their new king on his romantic ascent to his lady's chambers.

"Michel, what in the world do you think you are about?" Elena's hushed question was only loud enough to reach his ears, as Michel reached where she stood in the opening, swung one leg over the ledge and climbed into the room to the echo of even louder cheers from their avidly interested audience.

Michel waved in the direction of his faithful soldiers and then gained Elena's limp hand and led her away from the window. He definitely did not need an audience for this next part.

Elena was too stunned to resist his gentle tug on her hand and she followed him unresisting back into the confines of her bedroom. The sight of the bed, too close for his suspect control around his young ward, had Michel changing directions to the bench set in front of the hearth on the other side of the room.

"Michel…Your Highness…" she tried again before words appeared to fail her.

"We're alone now, so I believe we agreed it would be Michel," he inserted gently, refusing to release her small hand she was trying unsuccessfully to free from his grasp.

"You can't be here," she protested stunned, "People will think…"

Michel debated how to respond to her … and immediately decided it would be best not to leave her any choice in the matter of how their relationship was going to proceed from this moment on. "Elena, you're going to marry me."

Tears immediately filled her eyes and her attempt to free her hand from his grip became laced with desperation. "No," she whispered, shaking her head in denial.

"Yes," he countered, his certainty increasing the more she attempted to deny him.

"No, Michel, you can't. You do not wish to marry me. You feel you have no choice, because of my Uncle Barnabas' request of you."

Michel captured her other hand and using his additional leverage forced her to face him. "It is true your uncle asked me to marry you." Elena dipped her head in resigned defeat before he added seriously, "But I denied his request."

"You denied his request?" Elena parroted, her head lifting swiftly so her eyes could probe his for the truth. "I don't understand."

"It is very simple, Elena. I denied your uncle's request to marry you. I did, however, agree to do all in my power to protect you from his enemies and to act as your guardian upon his death."

She shook her head in confusion. "I don't understand. If you denied my uncle's request, then why do you think to marry me?"

His lips curved in a gentle smile as he spelled out how things were going to be between them in the future. "I am the king. I do not think to marry you. I will marry you."

"I don't understand."

Taking advantage of her obvious confusion, Michel pulled on the hands he held in his and tumbled her into his arms. He let go of her hands and framed her lovely face between his own. "I've missed you, Elena," he confessed.

Tears glimmered in her soft eyes, but she didn't draw back when he bent and kissed her. She stopped struggling beneath him and he let his arms slide around her softness when she burrowed closer into his embrace. She pulled away long enough to lift her head and search his eyes for some sign of deceit on his part. "You truly denied my uncle's request to marry me?"

"Yes, love. I was not willing to make such a serious commitment despite your uncle's assurances that doing so would help me achieve my goal of becoming king." At her puzzled look, he added, "Because the citizens of Calei all adore you."

Her cheeks colored up in a full blush. "That's ridiculous! Uncle Barnabas could not possibly have thought to sway you with such a foolish argument," she protested, then sighing, cuddled back close in his arms, her hands trapped against his chest. "I've missed you too," she added in a soft whisper, her face heating up at her honest confession.

At the feel of her softness close against his chest, he heaved a resigned sigh and with his hands on her shoulders, he reluctantly set her away from him. "Soon, Elena. You are going to have to marry me soon. I'm tired of fighting both of us and being forced to always play the part of a gentleman around you…a very frustrated gentleman, I might add."

She colored prettily at his bold pronouncement, then Michel brushed his lips across hers, and very aware of their interested audience waiting to see if he would reappear in the window, he stood and said, "I must leave you now, as much as doing so will only lead to another painful, sleepless night. I've waited this long to claim my bride, I have no intention of allowing my men to speculate as to whether or not my discipline failed me tonight."

"They already think that," Elena replied, not completely swallowing the taste of bitterness the thought left in her mouth. If everyone already believed they were lovers there was really no need for Michel to continue to act so honorably towards her.

"No, love, they do not. Those whose opinions matter know that I would not act so dishonorably towards you and betray the trust Barnabas placed in me when he appointed me your guardian. But before I leave, I want to be certain there are no further misunderstandings between us. I will give you a fortnight to make whatever arrangements you deem necessary before you become my wife. Bishop Maren will marry us on the fourteenth eve from tonight. Do we understand each other?"

At Elena's wide-eyed nod, Michel released his hold on her shoulders and then crossed the room in the direction of the window. When he threw one leg over the ledge and reached for the rope he used to scale the wall, Elena gasped and hurried after him.

"What you are doing? Wouldn't it be safer for you to leave by the door?"

He grinned back up at her from where he was already descending along the rope to the echo of the loud cheers of the even larger crowd gathered in the courtyard staring up at his lady's window. "Safer, but not nearly as much fun," he replied with a grin. Then he blew his future bride a kiss in a dramatic fashion to the cheers of his men and reaching the end of his rope, jumped the remaining few feet to the ground where Amele and his escort for the evening awaited him.

He met Amele's amused glance and said, "Congratulate me, my friend; I am soon to be wed to the lovely Lady Elena."

CHAPTER TWENTY

Elena decided the fortnight she was allotted was not nearly enough time for the thousand and one arrangements Michel so casually tossed in her direction the night of their official betrothal. An ordinary wedding required a masterly amount of intricate planning. A royal wedding, the first in more than half a century in Calei, when King Nathaniel married his first wife, required almost an act of divine intervention for things to go off as planned while at the same time making it appear as though no great effort was mustered to achieve it. Between the planning for the additional guests the keep would need to house for the event, ensuring there was enough food to feed the equivalent of an army of people at the wedding feast, not to mention seeing to the details of her gown and making certain there was sufficient quantities of freshly brewed ale to quench the thirsts of their guests, Elena was near exhaustion by the time her actual wedding day arose.

Despite the demands of the event, she could not be sorry about the aura of celebration that hung over the city. It was in such sharp contrast to the grief of the previous long weeks and months since her uncle had fallen ill. Everywhere she went she was greeted with smiling congratulations and comments expressing the people's pride and pleasure in their new king. It was clear to Elena at least, that Michel had not needed to marry her in order to gain the people's affections. He'd accomplished that on his own long before the highly anticipated announcement of their official betrothal.

While she was able to take in stride her fellow Caleinians best wishes for a happy future, she was uncertain how to deflect the well-meaning matrons' offers to instruct her as to the more intimate side of her wifely duties. Her cheeks flamed just at the memory of some of those conversations, which invariably began with one of the fine ladies drawing her aside and whispering in her ear,

'Elena dear, we really must talk. I know you must be nervous about what the king will expect from you in your bridal chambers after the ceremony, but it would not do to for you to approach such intimacies completely unprepared lest you offend the king…'

Somehow Elena had escaped Lady Madeline's intent to instruct her, only to be cornered the following afternoon by Lady Emily,

'Elena dear, do you have a moment? I really must speak to you. I know you have no mother to instruct you else I would never consider broaching such a delicate topic with you. It is completely natural for a young virgin to approach her wedding night with some small degree of trepidation, but it really would not due for you to give into your terror. The king might be offended by a bout of hysteria from his bride on his wedding night…"

As she stood at the entrance to the cathedral and waited silently for her attendants to make the final adjustments to her gown, the sound of all of the helpful, feminine, invariably older voices, echoed through her head.

'Elena dear, I am loath to intrude on your privacy, but with no mother to instruct you, I consider it my duty to offer my instruction in your duties as a wife to the king…such a virile young king at that. I'm certain you must be aware dear, the king will have certain expectations of you…of an intimate, *physical* nature…'

'Elena dear, my advice to you is to indulge in a few goblets of ale at the wedding feast. No one will remark on it. Of course it wouldn't do for you to become drunk. Such ill-advised behavior would be a disaster of no small making…'

'Elena dear…'

'Elena dear…'

'Elena dear…'

"Elena, my dear, are you ready?"

"What?" she answered with a start.

Baron Timothy smiled gently down into her

pale face and reached for her hand to place it on his arm. At the lingering confusion he read in her expression, he gave her hand a fatherly squeeze and said, "It's time, Elena dear. You do wish to marry the king do you not? I realize it's a little late to be asking you your inclination in the matter, but I was one of your uncle's closest friends. I feel it is my duty to stand in his stead. He would not want you to wed King Michel only because he wished it. You do understand he only sought to protect you."

The baron's kindly manner was enough for Elena to gather her composure. "Thank you, Baron, for your concern and for standing in for both my uncle and my father this night. Please do not concern yourself. I am quite content with Uncle Barnabas' choice of a husband for me."

The older man nodded, and Elena was touched by the relief that spread over his face at her words. "I admit I believed that was the case. You have always seemed quite fond of our new king, but fondness alone should not make you feel compelled to make this commitment if you are not ready to do so. I realize now I should have spoken up sooner, but if you should wish to consider the matter of your future more fully, you are always a welcome guest in my home."

Touched beyond words, Elena reached up on tiptoe and placed a gentle kiss on the older man's cheek. "Thank you, Baron. You cannot know what a comfort your words are to me, but I have no need to consider further my decision to marry the king. I am not merely fond of him, as I am certain is obvious to all. I am in love with him. To marry him is a dream come true for me. I would imagine every young lady in Calei feels the same," she tacked on ruefully.

"Perhaps my dear, but it is you the king has chosen to be his wife. All of the other young ladies will have to make do with your leavings."

Elena giggled at the older man's teasing. Giving her hand a final squeeze, he added, "Shall we go? I imagine your groom is growing anxious over his bride's delay in coming to him."

Smiling, Elena nodded and the two of them took their place at the head of the long aisle. Elena's hand shook noticeably where it rested on Baron Timothy's arm as he escorted her down the long aisle of the ornately appointed cathedral where Michel awaited her with Bishop Maren in front of the candlelit altar. She knew it was typical for the bride to be the center of attention at her own wedding. Though she knew she looked her best in the jeweled and pearl gown in the purest white signifying her bridal virginity, in her mind, it was Michel who would receive her vote for the most beautiful member of the bridal party. He awaited her in a crisp white shirt, with the royal crest embroidered in gold threads over his heart and tight fitting black breeches that accented his muscular thighs. His black, shoulder length hair was tied back away from his face, but it was the look in his bluer than blue eyes as he watched her approach that quickened her breath and left her mesmerized and unable to draw her gaze from his.

She decided it was safe as they reached the front of the church and Baron Timothy placed her cold hand in Michel's warm one, to stop fighting her attraction to this man. He was, after all, about to become her husband. An unreasonable fear suddenly gripped her when Michel gave her hand a gentle squeeze and they turned to climb the marble stair leading to the altar where the young bishop awaited them. For a moment she was convinced she must be dreaming.

How could this be happening? How could her most dearly held dream actually be coming true? Everyone she loved left her. She'd been deathly afraid that Michel would leave her too when she saw him lying in his bed, so deathly pale, after a betrayer ran his blade through his back and chest. Then she thought she would lose him to the weight of the expectations surrounding them and to the demands of the kingship. But here she was about to become his wife. Here he was staring down at her as they turned to repeat their vows to each other binding their futures for the length of their remaining lives. He looked like he was pleased to claim her for his wife, even though he could have his pick of any of the fair maidens of Calei.

Ironically, it was Michel whose voice rang with certainty when he recited his vows before

God to honor and protect her until the day death parted them. Despite her certainty this was the man she would love to the grave and beyond, her voice was barely audible in the hushed silence of the holy church when she repeated her own vows. When the bishop spoke the final blessing and asked if Michel would seal their vows with a kiss for his bride, Elena lifted anxious, surprised eyes to her new husband's face.

Without turning his glance away from her face, he responded to the bishop's query with an easy, amused assurance. "I've waited long enough to do so, Your Excellency."

Elena felt her cheeks heat up at the bishop's amused chuckle, but her eyes never strayed from Michel's intense blue gaze as he bent his head towards hers and his warm, probing mouth covered her own. Loud cheers erupted from their guests at the kiss exchanged by the newlywed couple, but Elena was too dazed to pay any attention to the noise. Her complete attention was absorbed in the feel of Michel's lips on hers, his strong hands sliding along her sides and around her back and pulling her close into his embrace. When her lips parted beneath his insistent pressure, he drew back with obvious reluctance and his lips trailed along her skin to whisper in her ear, "I will definitely no longer be thinking of you as a child in another hour or two."

He grinned at Elena's embarrassed blush, and then turned her in his arms to meet their waiting guests.

The evening passed in a confusion of dazed wonder for Elena. She was separated from Michel's grasp almost from the moment they entered the keep. One of her new husband's boisterous subjects placed a full glass of ale in his hands then proceeded to toast him, along with his bride, his kingship, his future progeny, his royal ancestors, and any other excuse they could dream up to lift their full glasses with great enthusiasm. At the same time, Elena was drawn aside from the male ritual by the ladies in attendance and given subtle and not so subtle hints about how to please her young and virile groom on this most important of nights. The effect of which meant Elena spent the majority of her wedding feast with flaming cheeks and feeling increasingly insecure as the evening progressed of her ability to please her husband on their wedding night.

By the time Baron Timothy's wife, Lady Suzanne, and two other high ranking nobles' wives, led her away from the festivities to prepare the bride and the bridal chamber for the groom's arrival, Elena was sick with anxiety and fighting tears at the knowing looks the women exchanged between them. A warm bath awaited her and Elena blanched at the thought of disrobing and then bathing in front of the three older women who were virtual strangers to her. She knew they meant well, but their helpful little suggestions were only making Elena more nervous about the night ahead.

Elena was ready to escape her chamber the same way Michel had arrived in it the night he informed her she was going to marry him in a desperate attempt to get away from the well-meaning matrons surrounding her and helping her into the elegant but nearly transparent sleeping gown in preparation for her wedding night. She even approached the window and glanced down to see if the rope Michel used to ascend to her window was still available for her use, before she remembered she was not in her old chambers, but in the king's.

"Come away from the window, Elena dear. You'll catch a chill."

At the sound of Lady Suzanne's gentle admonition, Elena schooled her expression and turned around to face the three women who were huddled together near the bed, their silence now almost deafening in comparison to the previous wealth of advice they offered her, as if their nerves too were wilting beneath the enormity of the occasion.

"We'll leave you now, dear. I don't imagine you will have long to wait before the king joins you."

"Thank you for your assistance, ladies." She almost added she would try not to disappoint them, then realized how ridiculous that would sound given the circumstances, and bit her tongue while the three women regarded her sympathetically and then filed silently out of the room.

As soon as she was alone, Elena sank to her knees with her arms wrapped around her stomach and struggled mightily not to lose the contents of her stomach. She couldn't go through with this. What was she thinking? She would simply explain her feelings to Michel. Surely he would understand. Didn't he still regard her as a child?

At the sound of the door opening, Elena jumped up off of her knees and urgently chided herself to calm her fears. It didn't matter how young she was, or if she was raised without the benefit of a mother's advice. She would still be forced to face this moment and her virgin's fears alone...well not alone, she added silently, swallowing the terrified lump in her throat as Michel entered the suddenly too-warm chamber and turned to slide the lock into place, before turning back around to face her.

Elena tried silence her panting breaths that were audible in the heavy silence of the room. Michel's intent blue gaze slid over her where she stood outlined by the moonlight filtering through the open window, his eyes darkening with intense male passion. Elena belatedly realized the moonlight framing her would make the transparent gown she wore appear even more transparent.

She swallowed again and attempted to keep the

trembling in her hands from spreading through the rest of her in the chill breeze she suddenly became aware of where she still stood on frozen legs near the opening.

Michel finally broke the silence from where he stood leaning negligently against the door, a slight smile curving his lips. "If I promise not to pounce on you, will you come away from the window before you freeze to death?"

Elena shook her head, denying his too-reasonable request, with terrified tears shimmering in her eyes.

For a moment, Michel almost grinned at her panicked expression, but he managed to control the inclination in time before taking a few, measured steps into the room, his eyes never leaving his terrified bride's face. Her own glance remained glued to his every move, as if she would leap from the open window to escape his manly passion if he pressed her. He had every intention of doing so, but didn't think admitting as much to his bride was going to soothe her jittery nerves any.

He stopped half-way across the distance separating them and saw Elena release a relieved sigh when he halted his approach. "Your turn," he commented in a feigned casual voice.

Confusion came over his bride's face. "I don't understand."

"I met you half-way. It's your turn to meet me the rest of the way."

Elena eyed him warily and took a cautious step in his direction. When he merely raised his brows in askance of her tiny advance, she took another wary step towards where he waited for his reluctant bride. If he hadn't waited so long to claim his bride, or been so long without the comfort of a woman, he might be able to appreciate the humor of his situation. As it was, he could feel the sweat beading across his forehead from the strain of keeping his masculine passions in check. When his timid bride finally covered the remaining distance separating them, Michel could see her erect nipples pressing against the thin gown she wore. He clamped his jaw shut over the frustrated groan that wanted to erupt through his tightly clenched lips and reached out to lift her chin so she would be forced to look at him.

"Elena, tell me what's wrong. Surely you know me well enough by now to know I won't force myself on you."

A bitter, self-mocking laugh erupted from between her lips. "Don't be silly. If anyone was forced into this marriage it was you, not me."

"Could have fooled me," he remarked in an attempt to lessen the tension holding sway over the room.

"This isn't funny," she protested his weak attempt at humor, but Michel counted it a minor victory when she didn't step away from him.

He resisted the urge to draw her closer,

thinking it would likely do little to lessen her maidenly fears if she suddenly found her soft yielding flesh pressed against his rock-hard erection. So he gritted his teeth against the alluring temptation standing so close every breath was a test of his prized self-discipline as he was forced to do battle with her floral scent that still clung to her skin from the bath she enjoyed in anticipation of their wedding night.

"Trust me, I'm not laughing." Elena's glance locked with his and then quickly dipped again. "Tell me what's wrong," he urged her, and chanced taking her hand to keep his bride from attempting to put any more distance between them.

Elena felt her cheeks fill with color, but she forced the embarrassing confession through her reluctant lips, "I don't know what to do. Everyone kept trying to tell me how I am to please you, but I can't remember their instructions."

Elena's gaze was directed at her feet, so Michel thought it safe to smile at her ridiculous, but innocently charming confession. "The good ladies of Calei actually thought to instruct you?" This time he couldn't suppress an unholy grin at the picture brought to mind of the matronly ladies cornering his innocent bride with their well-meaning advice.

When her only response to his amused query was a dejected nod, he took pity on her, and tugged on her hand to draw her closer. He noticed it was with obvious reluctance, a reluctance he'd never before sensed in her to be comforted in his embrace, that his bride allowed herself to be pulled closer to him. He reached out to cup her chin and lifted her white face for his perusal, wondering with an inward sigh just how much damage the good ladies of Calei had inflicted upon his plans for the remainder of the evening.

"Elena, contrary to the ladies' erroneous assumptions, it is every man's very great pleasure and privilege to instruct his bride on their wedding night in regards to her intimate duties as his wife."

"Truly?"

Elena's hesitant uncertainty brought a gentle smile to his lips. "Truly," he confirmed in all honesty then released her hand and slid his fingers up her arm to cup her chin. He held her still while he bent his head and claimed a groom's rightful kiss from his very reluctant bride. He felt her sigh in response and let his free hand grip her hip and pull her against him. When her flesh brushed against the noticeable bulge in his breeches, she instinctively attempted to retreat away from him, but he tightened his hold on her and kept her close against him. In the meantime, he deepened the kiss, forcing her to focus her scattered attention when he pulled her mouth open by tugging on her chin with his thumb. As soon as her lips parted in response, his tongue swept inside her mouth to taste, to test, to possess. When she moaned softly in response and her hands clutched at his shirt,

Michel deepened the kiss, and let his hand drop away from her face to capture her straining breast in his seeking hand. She whimpered in response and pressed herself closer against him.

Elena was overwhelmed by the riot of chaotic emotions swamping her. She was afraid of the intensity of her feelings, but she no longer wanted to run from them. This was what she wanted. This was what she'd been dreaming of since the first kiss they exchanged and Michel awakened her to the glorious wonder she could find in the right man's arms. She was here in those arms now, exactly where she longed to be all of those lonely nights in her bed. She tried to draw back from the strength of his arms, but they only closed more firmly around her. At the same time, his hot mouth moved from hers to slide along the column of her throat to close over one straining breast through the thin fabric of her gown. Her knees buckled and she would have fallen if his strong arms weren't holding her so close against his strong, masculine chest.

Her hands were still pressed between them, and she let them explore his hard flesh through his crisp white shirt. Then growing impatient at even the thin barrier the fabric of his shirt presented, she slid her hands down and under his shirt to trail across his hot skin, marveling in the differences between their bodies.

He was hard all over, from where his flesh stretched taut across his broad, muscular shoulders to his flat stomach where his manhood strained against the opening of his breeches. Curious, she let her fingers brush across the manly bulge and thrilled at Michel's groan in response to her soft touch.

"Show me, teach me to please you," she whispered, as his mouth drifted across her skin and he used one hand to impatiently loosen the ties to her gown.

"Touch me, Elena. Let me touch you. Let me love you."

Elena felt her heart melt at the sound of his deep seductive voice, trailing across her skin in mindless pleading. "Yes, anything, everything," Elena let the words of her surrender whisper through her lips.

Hearing them, Michel lifted his head. His eyes blazed blue fire into hers. "Are you certain? Because if we proceed and then you change your mind, I'm afraid I won't be able to stop."

Elena stepped back away from his encircling arm and watched his face fall. Then she reached up to push the clinging gown away from her shoulders and let it fall in a gauzy heap at her feet. She made no attempt to hide her naked flesh from his suddenly avid gaze as it roamed almost violently over her.

"Come to me, wife. Let there be no misunderstanding between us and no misgivings in the light of dawn."

Elena wasn't certain her legs retained enough

strength to carry her even the slight distance separating them, but her will instinctively surrendered to her husband's greater strength, the feminine in her responding in some deeply buried place within her to the will of her mate. When she reached him, and there was only the barest breath of a space between them, she boldly reached up to slide his shirt away from his broad shoulders, all the while, his glance held hers a willing captive beneath his seductive spell. The unusual stone around his neck burned in blue communion with the eyes that willed her to him. Her hands gripped his shoulders as her new husband reached out and cupped her soft breast, his thumb teasing the painfully erect nipple.

"Please…" she moaned, leaning into his strength when he bent his head and let his mouth replace his hand to suckle at her straining breast. Elena's head fell back and she would have fallen to her knees if Michel hadn't reached out and swept her off her feet and into his arms.

"Thank God," she whispered against his seeking mouth, prompting a chuckle from the lips covering hers.

When he laid her on the bed, Elena lay staring up at her husband, admiring his male beauty as he undid the ties of his breeches with hands that shook slightly. He turned his back towards her when he stepped out of his breeches. If he thought to ease her maidenly fears at the sight of his engorged male member, he was only minimally successful, because as soon as he turned to face her, Elena drew in a sharp breath.

Michel saw the fear return to his bride's eyes, but he was losing the battle with his failing patience. It had taken him almost all of his carefully honed discipline just to get his young bride into his bed. Now as he gave into the urge to cover her soft, silky flesh with his hard frame, he didn't bother to disguise his need or his groan of longing when she squirmed beneath his weight. When she tried to push against his chest with her puny strength, he nearly laughed, wondering if she truly believed he would deny himself now, after his epic struggle with his self-control. He bent his head and let himself feast on her soft skin.

"Michel?" At the sound of the worry in her voice, he slipped one hand between their joined bodies and found the damp flesh between her legs. She gasped at his boldness, and tried to push his hand away from her heat. When he ignored her paltry attempt to dislodge him, he pushed one finger inside her heat to stroke, to temp, to tantalize until his bride cried out and lifted her hips against his stroking hand. Soon, it had to be soon, he promised himself as he continued to awaken Elena to the depths of her feminine passion, hoping to drown out her fear with the same overwhelming need for completion that was driving him. When she began to tighten around him, clench his finger deep inside her and rock her hips against his stroking rhythm, something inside of him snapped.

He ignored her cry of protest when he removed his hand and he poised his straining manhood at her moist opening. "Elena, you asked me to teach you to please me."

"Yes." Her soft eyes locked with his, drawing him deeper beneath the spell of her feminine appeal.

"Don't fight me, love. Open your legs for me." He waited for her to obey his command, and then added huskily, "That's it, love. Now put them around me and draw me close to you."

He waited for her soft legs to wrap around him, then he used his hand to ease himself into her. Elena closed her legs tighter around him in instinctive protest. Michel let himself sink deeper into her damp heat and bent his head to capture her lips as he came up against the barrier of his bride's virginity. He coaxed her response to his kiss by sinking his tongue deep into her welcoming heat in an insistent rhythm she was no longer able to resist. She surrendered her weakening will to his stronger one, at the same time he buried himself deep into her virgin's body, in a single stroke breaking through the barrier blocking his entrance.

Their cries echoed in unison, his one of intense male satisfaction, hers in painful, tearful protest. Michel kissed her tears away, but he could no more stop his instinctive male response to her tender, pulsing femininity than he could prevent the pain he knew he was inflicting on her untried flesh. He let his instinct take over, and released his body's natural urging. When Elena attempted again to push him off of her, he reached down one seeking hand to stroke the damp opening straining to accommodate his thrusting passion. Another cry echoed through his bride's soft lips, this one not prompted by pain, but a never before experienced, intense, awed pleasure. Her hips lifted against his hand, then began moving in rhythm with his. His strong thrusts rocked the bed, until Elena, her young body responding to his demands with a will of its own separate from her mind's direction, suddenly tightened around him and she screamed in awe of her first release.

Michel finally let go of his discipline, of his control, of all the months of longing and denying himself, and let his own release roll through him, as with a loud groan of satisfaction, he poured himself into his young bride and then collapsed on top of her.

The space of a breath later, Elena poked him in the shoulder protesting his weight and Michel summoned the last of his strength and rolled off of her and collapsed onto his back. His lips curved in a smile when his bride, bereft of his warmth, scooted close against his side. He reached out one arm to draw her close against his side where she rested her cheek against his bare flesh. Michel bent to kiss the top of her head.

"Michel?"

He thought it was a little late for the anxiety he could hear in her hushed whisper. "Yes?"

"Did I please you?"

His shoulders shook with laughter at the worry in her voice. She hid her face against his side and he rolled over to face her and lift her chin so he could peer down into her face. "How can you doubt my pleasure in you, Elena?"

She blushed at his intense gaze trailing over her naked flesh and sighed happily, scooting closer against his side and resting her head back against his chest. "Is it all right if we go to sleep now?" She asked sleepily and he reached down to draw the quilt over them.

"Yes."

"I love you, Michel," she whispered on a drowsy sigh, leaving Michel to wonder if she was even aware of her innocent confession. He tightened his hold around her and let her vow settle around his heart and lull him into sleep.

CHAPTER TWENTY ONE

Elena woke exactly where she dreamed of being, cuddled close on her husband's broad chest, with his arms wrapped tight around her and the sound of his heart beating steadily beneath her ear. She raised her head for a moment, just to ascertain she was really in his chambers and she hadn't dreamed the events of the previous night. Assured by her quick inspection, she dropped her head back to his chest, settled herself to fit more closely against his muscular frame, and then sighing contentedly, closed her eyes and drifted back to sleep, her fingers tracing little idle designs on his naked flesh.

Beneath her, Michel gritted his teeth against the temptation of his wife's stroking fingers, and when he was convinced she had fallen back asleep, he gripped her hand to cease her restless stroking. She shifted again in her sleep, curling her silken flesh more closely against him, her soft middle cradling his morning erection. His still surprisingly innocent bride had no apparent apprehension of the danger she was in. Her absolute trust in him and his control where she was concerned disturbed him somewhat.

He knew when she woke fully she would be painfully sore from their activities of the previous evening. He'd been less than gentle when he initiated her into her more intimate duties of being his wife. Yet her virgin's flesh had served his pleasure well and now he fought the same fierce battle with his discipline that he engaged in last night. He would have thought the satisfaction he found in her arms and between her soft thighs would have eased his lust somewhat, but contrarily, the memories of their wedding night appeared to be having the opposite effect.

A more considerate husband would leave his young bride to sleep the morning away and allow her to begin to regain her strength from the damaging fears that had pressed in upon her from all sides over the past uncertain months since the inception of her uncle's illness. Michel accepted without being too heavily burdened by the guilt such an admission should cause his conscience that he was obviously not the considerate husband he conjured in his musings to compare himself with, because he had no intention of wasting the opportunity presented him to be alone with his lovely bride and satisfy his body's urgent promptings. And if his young bride squirmed in his arms just one more time in an attempt to settle herself more comfortably against his naked, burning flesh, he wasn't even going to be considerate enough to wake her up before he spread her legs and thrust his burning member into her tight, damp heat.

Michel drew in a shuttering breath in an attempt to gather the quickly shredding tatters of what was once his unassailable self-discipline, amazed that it was his innocent little bride who was making such a mockery of all of his previous, preciously held assumptions about the strength of his control over his natural male lusts. Elena's pure trust in him, rather than serving to strengthen his discipline where she was concerned had the opposite effect of stripping him bare, so he was forced to scramble to summon even the paltriest defense to ward off succumbing completely to her captivating bewitchment.

He always believed he would choose a wife who possessed his twin's bold spirit. It came as a complete surprise to him to discover he preferred for his life's mate Elena's gentle nature and more subdued beauty. Everything about Melissa was larger than life, her stunning beauty, her outrageous opinions, the way she loved, her refusal to back down in the face of even the most reasonable challenge. He loved his twin, but surprisingly he discovered he did not wish to engage in the same daily battle with his wife that he contested with the other half of himself for the majority of his life. His lips curved upward in astonished relief that he was not to be faced with the prospect of doing so.

Thinking of Melissa's new husband, he nodded in silent admiration of his brother-in-law's bolder spirit. Luke appeared quite content with the expectation that he would spend his life attempting to bring Melissa's bold spirit to heel, as if he looked forward with great anticipation to the daily wrangling he would be forced to endure. A battle Michel compared to the one he had often contested with one of the wild Salusian stallions he discovered early in life he had a natural skill in training. Hardly surprising he possessed such a talent. Hadn't he been forced to acquire a soft hand with a wild spirit from the moment of his birth every time he attempted to squelch one of his twin's hare-brained schemes?

His gentle bride stirred again and all thoughts of his wild twin fled his mind, as his body's insistent prodding took on fresh urgency. His arms tightened their hold around her clinging softness as he plotted his strategy to break down her shy defenses against his masculine passion. He did not think he was up to a repeat of the test of his control required of him on his wedding night. His lips lifted into a happy smile when he realized he was well ahead of his first night as a married man. His wife was already naked in his bed and in his arms, and seemed very content to remain there for the rest of the day. Michel decided he could work with that.

Grinning at the foolish thought, he smoothed his bride's waist-length hair in long even strokes down her back, pausing now and again to untangle the silken strands from his rough treatment of the previous evening. His sleeping bride's only response to his initial foray was to sigh contentedly beneath his hands and snuggle closer against his chest. Michel gripped his wife's hips and shifted her position slightly so he was poised at the entrance to her woman's heat. Elena moaned softly in response to his tentative probing. His hands cupped her fleshy backside and squeezed gently. She moaned again and this time when she pressed herself closer against his him, his erect manhood was surrounded by her soft skin. He felt his bride's breathing quicken in drowsy anticipation and felt his own ramp up in response.

He slid his hand up along her finely curved back and brushed the sides of her full breasts pressed against his chest, before sliding one hand between their bodies to tease her nipple erect. A soft cry escaped through his bride's parted lips and she turned her face against his chest to nuzzle his naked flesh. Michel swallowed his own groan of longing as Elena's lips closed around his own male nipple and teased it erect with her tongue. Just when he thought he couldn't wait another moment, Elena lifted her head from his naked flesh and stared up at him with a longing she made no attempt to disguise.

"Michel, do you think we could…is it too soon for us to…"

In response to her hesitant question, he gripped her hips and urged her over his pulsing manhood. She threw her head back in abandon and rose over him to straddle his hips, her head bent close so her long hair enclosed them behind a silken curtain. He grasped the back of her head and pulled her down to him before capturing her lips in searing kiss at the same moment he thrust into her.

If his bride felt the pain of his entry she gave no indication of it. Instead, she sat up and rocked over him, thrusting her hips forward and her head back. Michel cupped her tantalizing breasts above him and lifted his head to close his mouth around one tempting offering. Elena moaned urgently at his attention and Michel quickened his powerful thrusts, driving her closer and closer to the edge, until on a stunned cry she tightened around him and then spent, collapsed against his chest.

Michel rolled her over until his very satisfied, but still drowsy wife lay on her back staring dreamily up into his face. Entranced, he bent and reclaimed the lips she opened eagerly for him, responding to his desire with a wild abandon he would never have dreamt lay hidden within her. Unleashing the full force of his passion at her eager response, he sought his own satisfaction in her welcoming heat, rocking the bed with the power of the rhythm he set and capturing Elena's hands and holding them over her head so she lay completely defenseless beneath him and at the mercy of his masculine desire.

She offered no protest to being held captive beneath him. Instead she linked her fingers with his and clung to him while he took his fill of her.

"Michel..." she whispered his name on an awed cry and he paused for a moment in his pursuit of his own release from the driving, relentless urging of his body's passion to watch her deep brown eyes glaze over and she surrendered to him all she guarded within her to give. She cried out again as he drove into her a final time, clinging desperately to his restraining hands. Helpless to contest his effect on her, Elena arched beneath him and gave herself completely over into his care. Michel watched awed by the depths of her trust in him, by her complete surrender to his thrusting passion. To a man whose faith was so recently tested by the false pledge of loyalty by one who knelt before him and then drove his betrayer's blade into his king's back, Michel was not certain how to reconcile the darkness that dwelt in the hearts of men with the purity of Elena's innocent faith in him. Abandoning his struggle to resolve in his mind the evidence of the disparate natures of men and women he released the desperate hold he maintained over his own passion and poured himself into his wife's welcoming young body.

Silence broken only by the sound of their harsh breathing settled over the bed where they lay spent. Elena grew increasing nervous at her husband's continued silence. They hadn't spoken more than a few words since she and her reluctant groom first consummated their marriage the previous night. She blushed at the memories of the intimacies they shared and couldn't help but wonder if she had pleased him in the performance of her wifely duties. Even though he had in a back-handed way assured her she had done so last night, now she wondered if perhaps she had done enough. Maybe a woman who was closer to his own age, with a mother to instruct her in her wifely duties would have done something different, been more aggressive in her attempts to please her new husband.

She was well aware Michel could have married any of the available daughters of the nobles in Calei, or even returned to his previous home to choose a woman who was more familiar with his past. Elena worried that if she was unsatisfactory in the performance of her intimate duties as his wife, Michel might seek the services of another. She was not so very young not to know that some men kept mistresses to please them in ways that their wives apparently did not, or could not. Tears stung her eyes at the thought of Michel sharing with another the precious bond they just shared. Unknowing and unwilling to ask for the reassurance she needed from her new husband, she let the silent tears spill from her eyes until they landed softly on his naked flesh.

"Elena, did I hurt you?" With the evidence of his wife's silent tears on his chest damning him, guilt rose up within Michel at the memory of his less than gentle treatment of his innocent bride. When she merely shook her head against his chest in response to his question, he braced his weight on his elbows so he could see her face. "If I didn't hurt you, then why are you crying?"

"Are you going to seek out a mistress?" She asked in a devastated whisper.

"What?!! What?!!" How can you ask me such a ridiculous question? Why would I seek out a mistress? Is that what you want? Elena, I'm sorry if I was rough with you. The pain you feel now will fade. It is only because you were a virgin…" Michel let his voice trail off as the enormity of what his new bride was suggesting hit home. Did she believe in her innocence he would be satisfied with a single night with her? Did she intend to return to her previous celibate state? Even if that obscene plan was floating around in her silly head he had no intention of allowing it.

"You weren't rough with me," she denied, blushing profusely and unable to hold his stunned glance for long.

"Then why do you wish me to seek out another woman to satisfy my manly passion?"

"I don't wish it. I wasn't sure…you didn't say if you were pleased with me. No one explained. I don't have a mother to instruct me in such matters. I know you said it was your duty to teach me, but well, you didn't really give me any instruction last night…" Her voice trailed off at the slow grin spreading over his face.

"I see. Forgive me, bride, if I have been remiss in my husbandly duties."

Elena could feel her face getting redder at Michel's gentle teasing, but she summoned the courage to protest tearfully, "No, that's not what I meant."

Michel rolled them both over so his fiercely blushing bride now lay beneath him. He bent down and brushed his lips across hers and then slid his lips along the long, slender column of her throat, to where her soft breasts beckoned for his attention.

"Michel?"

"Yes, Elena. Pay attention, sweetheart. I'm going to instruct you now."

"All right," she answered breathlessly, her hands gripping the sheets, as his mouth slid lower, over her soft middle, to where the damp curls shielding her heat tugged at his will. When his mouth moved lower still to close over her slick opening, and he tasted the evidence of his own release on her, she arched up urgently against him. "God! God! Are we supposed to be doing this?"

He paused long enough to lift his head to stare down into her flushed face. Her glazed, smoky eyes clung to his, her innocent uncertainty over the rightness of the intimacies they shared casting a shadow over the pleasure he gave her. "I'm your husband, Elena. Your body belongs to me now. Everything you have inside of you is mine.

Do not deny me the pleasure of instructing you and enjoying your pleasure in these precious moments between us."

"No, I can't. Don't you know? Don't you understand? It isn't in me to deny you anything. I want to belong to you…to give you everything. I can't be here without you anymore. I can't bear the thought of you sharing such intimacies with another."

Michel's lips curved in a gentle smile as his eyes roamed over her flushed skin, the way her chest rose and fell rapidly in response to her rising passion she was unable to hide from him and then finally met her tearful glance. "Elena, love, why would I seek out another when my wife so generously shares herself with me?"

He bent his head to capture her lips in a deep kiss, sealing his vow of fidelity much as he had sealed their marriage vows to each other the previous evening. Then just as she was beginning to relax in his arms, his lips slid from hers and began their purposeful descent along her soft skin. Now understanding the object of his search, his bride tensed in anticipation and her breaths dissolved into breathless pants. She spread her legs eagerly for his attention and when his mouth closed over the most secret part of her femininity she trembled beneath him and begged him in a soft, breathless voice for more of his lovemaking. When long moments later her breathless pleas turned into an awed cry of feminine release, Michel slid along her damp flesh and buried himself deep within his wife's welcoming body.

When he had gathered himself to the point he was able to speak again, Michel braced his weight on his arms and asked, his lips brushing against her sensitive skin, "Are you pleased with your husband's instructions, wife? Give me your truth, for I have no intention of allowing you to seek similar instruction in another's arms. Is there is some further lesson you would like me to focus on this morning? You have only to tell me what area of the subject matter I have been remiss in covering. I assure you, I am very eager to continue your training in this gravely important area."

"There's more?" His no longer quite so innocent little bride was staring up at him with a curious speculation he found incredibly arousing. Knowing after his long fast, he was far more willing to continue pursuing the subject than his young wife could possibly comprehend, he sighed reluctantly and answered her truthfully.

"There is indeed far more for you to learn of your intimate duties, Elena, and I am anxious to continue your tutoring this evening. But for now, I think it best if I rise and see what fresh crisis awaits me this morning. I would prefer you rest and gather your strength for further lessons this evening."

Elena blushed and giggled at the absurdity of

his suggestion. “Really, Michel, I cannot possibly remain in bed all day. What would people think?”

Michel grinned at her embarrassment and answered her concern with brutal honesty. “Likely they would conclude I was less than gentle with your innocence and you are unable to rise from our marriage bed.”

Her blush flamed even brighter over her fair complexion, and laughing, Michel reluctantly removed himself from between her legs and rose from the bed. He crossed the room to glance out the window on his domain. Elena wasn’t aware until Michel pushed the window covering aside and the bright sunlight streamed through the opening that the day was already well-advanced. Although she understood it was expected for a newlywed couple to linger in their chambers the morning following their wedding, until this morning she had not completely comprehended the true nature of the activities that kept a couple so intently engaged and willing to tarry away from their usual duties. The thought that everyone she encountered today when and if she finally summoned the nerve to leave her husband’s chambers would no doubt comprehend exactly what is what that delayed her, made the prospect of Michel’s suggestion she rest in his bed all day a not unappealing one. Then regrettably acknowledging that would only give rise to worse gossip as to the activities they engaged in over the course of their wedding night, and would no doubt force the servants to speculate that Michel had indeed been overly brutal in his treatment of her, she knew she was just going to have to brazen through her embarrassment and resume her duties as the mistress of her husband's home.

She glanced back at the window to see Michel grinning at the evidence of her embarrassment, as if he was privy to her thoughts. She marveled at the way he stood naked in front of the window as if unconcerned at the prospect of someone seeing him. Elena grinned at the thought of an innocent young maid wandering by and catching a glimpse of her new king in all of his true glory.

"What has you grinning, wife? Am I too bold in hoping your smile is in anticipation of your further instruction this evening in the matter of your wifely duties?"

Elena laughed at Michel's teasing and then quickly pulled the sheets up around her naked flesh when he crossed the distance between them with a purposeful look in his eyes she was already beginning to recognize. It required little more than a swift, effective tug on his part to rid her of the barrier between them, and then he came down on top of her and with a devilish glint in his eyes told her, "Perhaps we'd better go over some additional remedial material now so you are not completely overwhelmed this evening when we return to your lessons."

CHAPTER TWENTY TWO

Elena sighed blissfully as the door closed behind her now fully clothed husband and she collapsed back against the sheets, willing to revel in her laziness for a few moments longer before summoning Lissel to attend her. She considered herself the luckiest of women. Surely no other woman had ever had so magnificent and attentive a teacher to instruct her in her wifely duties. She sighed dreamily at the thought of the cherished moments she had shared with Michel, and knew no matter how long she remained on this earth; no other day and night would ever compare to the one she just spent. At the promise of further such instruction this evening, a trembling longing and intense anticipation filled her, causing her cheeks to heat up in fresh embarrassment. Chiding herself that the keep was not going to run itself, she forced herself to put her daydreams aside and begin her first day as a married woman.

Elena was tempted to look behind her when Lissel, responding to her summons as if she'd been waiting anxiously for it, addressed her nervously, “Yes, Your Highness, you sent for me?”

Elena supposed she was going to have to get used to the ‘Your Highnesses’ from now on as upon her marriage to the king she had not only become Michel’s wife, but his queen.

The initial weeks of her marriage flew by in the same idyllic as her wedding night. She eagerly sought the chambers she shared with her husband each evening and Michel seemed just as eager to continue her instruction in her wifely duties as he had on their wedding night. She was not so naïve she didn’t comprehend that Michel did not feel about her the way she felt about him. She wasn’t even certain it was possible for a man to feel the depth of love and the longing to be in his presence she felt for Michel, but at least he seemed to harbor no regrets about being nudged into marriage with her. She could only hope that in time his feelings for her would grow beyond the rather amused affection he seemed to regard her with presently.

Now that she was his wife, it was a relief to her to be able to offer him something of value in return for all the happiness he gave her. She knew he was grateful to her for taking on the day to day running of the keep and seeing to the numerous social niceties among the ladies of the nobility and his other subjects that seemed completely inexplicable to the male of the species. She didn’t have to guess at whether or not her efforts pleased him because he made a point to express his appreciation to her regularly. His approval only made her more diligent in her efforts to at least remove such small burdens from the grave weight of the responsibility he bore as king.

As time passed, and they settled back into the closer, more unstructured relationship they had enjoyed before Michel became king, she no longer worried over whether or not he was pleased with her in the matter of the more intimate nature of her wifely responsibilities. Michel remained a most attentive husband and appeared quite eager to broaden her knowledge of the subject at every opportunity that presented itself. Elena, eager to be a dutiful wife, was ever his avid student.

So it came as no surprise to her when barely two full months into her marriage, she suspected she was already carrying her husband's child. She kept her suspicions to herself until she was certain. She planned to tell him in the quiet of their chambers one evening so she could share her joyous news with him privately. It was no easy task as the babe she carried within her seemed overly fond of early nights. Elena struggled valiantly to keep her eyes open after her bath, and the fresh, scented oil she worked into her skin, while she waited up for her husband to join her.

Since her marriage Elena had adopted her husband's habit of sleeping nude, as it seemed a silly waste of time to don a gown only to have

Michel remove it as soon as he joined her in the large bed. In the early weeks of their marriage there had been a few occasions when in his impatience to instruct her more completely on the contents of a particular lesson, he'd torn the gown off of her, causing her to hide the tattered remnants in the bottom of her chest the following morning, rather than risk having Lissel come across the shredded garment when she came to straighten their chambers.

Despite her intention to remain awake, Elena fell asleep soon after she slid between the fresh sheets of the bed. That was how Michel found her when he retired to his chambers later that evening. His glance roamed appreciatively over the enticing picture she presented, with one hand flung over her head drawing attention to the fullness of her breasts and the delicacy of her skin. He had already been in a semi-aroused state as he strode down the hallway leading to his chambers. His body had grown accustomed to its nightly feast and was eagerly anticipating its evening repast. Michel was sometimes astonished with the ease in which he'd fallen into the routine of married life, though he supposed he should give credit where it was due.

His new bride was so eager to please him he would have to be an ogre indeed to find fault with her. His eyes roamed over Elena's lovely face, thinking no other had ever appealed to him as much, nor aroused his manly passions so completely. He stripped out of his clothes and in his haste left them on the floor at his feet, before sliding into bed and turning to where his wife slept on undisturbed by his arrival. He gently pushed the sheet aside and drew her naked flesh against his, closing his eyes and drawing in a deep breathe of her appealing, feminine fragrance, while letting his hands roam where they would over her soft flesh. By their eagerness to do so one might reasonably conclude it had been months rather than mere hours since they'd traversed the familiar territory.

"Michel?" His name passed her lips in a faraway whisper in a manner that suggested she was loath to wake from her own fantasies and would prefer it if he joined her in the misty dreams he disturbed. He was more than willing to do so, since he suspected by the rhythm her slender hips now set against his straining flesh; their purposes were one and the same. He drew her closer and bent to whisper his response against her ear tantalizing his drowsy wife with dark, seductive promises of the pleasure they would bring to each other.

She reached for him then, and slithered over him, covering him, all her natural shyness forgotten in sleep as her body's urgent needs pushed aside the shy feminine defenses she was wont to raise against his driving lust. He watched with rising desire the dazed confusion in her glance as she stared down at him from her place perched above him, straddling him, as she drifted in and out of her dreams, seemingly drugged by the passion that rose between them. When his hands reached up to cup her breasts, she cried out softly and urged him to take more of her tender offerings. His lips closed over her and then he used his teeth to bring her to a fresh peak. She moaned and reached up to cup her breasts as she rose above him and took him inside her already damp heat.

Seeing her womanly hands caressing her own softness set his raging passions aflame. Unable to wait any longer for the promise of satisfaction he read in her glazed eyes, Michel drove urgently into her again and again until long moments later he surrendered to the force of his body's insistent need with a loud satisfied shout. In the silent warm moments following their coming together, Michel lay replete with his wife sprawled across his chest, unsure if she was awake or still dreaming until he heard his name on her lips in a hesitant whisper.

"Michel?"

"Yes, love. So you're awake? I wasn't certain."

Elena hid her blush against his chest at his teasing then lifted her head so she could see his face. "I tried to wait up for you, but I guess I fell asleep."

"I assure you, I am not the least bit disappointed with how things worked out."

She smiled at his jesting but immediately her expression turned serious. "I waited up for you to tell you something important."

"What is it?" he asked, letting his fingers trace a trail along her soft skin. He didn't think he would ever grow tired of the feel of her against him, beneath him, above him… When he realized the direction of his thoughts, and the fresh tightening in his loins, he reluctantly drew his attention away from the consideration of what new lesson he would introduce to his eager bride tonight and forced himself to concentrate on her serious expression, curious as to its cause. "Elena?"

"I'm pregnant."

Her soft confession shook him to the core and he sought to escape his sudden discomfort in denial. "Elena, it's too soon. You cannot possibly be certain."

"You're not pleased about the baby?"

Her wide-eyed dismay forced him to gain control over a feeling previously unknown to him, but which he recognized as swiftly escalating panic. "Yes, of course I'm pleased, but it's so soon."

"Not so very soon," his young wife contradicted him gently and he was compelled to concede her point.

"No, I suppose not," he agreed distractedly, but his thoughts were already far from his wife and the comfort of the chambers they shared. He cursed himself for his carelessness in not taking precautions to see to it that Elena did not find herself with child so soon, at least not until after he'd solved the riddle of the curse on his heirs. As things stood he was no nearer to unravelling the mystery that beset his blood than he was on the day he first learned of its existence.

"Michel, if you're not displeased with this news than what troubles you?"

Michel considered lying in answer to his wife's direct question, realized immediately Elena knew his moods well enough to recognize a lie on his lips when she heard it, and then decided she deserved the truth. Better even for her to understand he was truly concerned about the effects of an ancient curse on the child she carried, than to have her believe he was not happy about the blessed news she just gave him. He reached up to brush a gentle hand through her hair. "Elena, you have lived in Calei long enough to know the details of the plague on the royal blood."

Michel was amazed by the look of relief that crossed his wife's face at his words. He couldn't come up with a single explanation for her odd reaction and concluded she did not truly accept that the curse was more than just an old legend without any real ability to hurt them or the child she carried. He only wished he could share her certainty.

"Oh, that's why you reacted the way you did. I thought perhaps you had decided, like Uncle

Barnabas, that you did not wish to become a father."

Michel exhaled a deep sigh and protested, "I imagine your Uncle Barnabas would have been pleased to become a father if he did not already have a child."

"What do you mean?' Elena's brows furrowed in confusion.

Michel replied gently, "Your uncle told me himself that no child of his body could be more precious to him than his beloved niece."

Michel watched tears fill her eyes. "He was the only father I have any memory of."

"I know, and I will do my best to be as worthy a father to our children as he was to you."

"Of that I have no doubt."

At the serene certainty in her face, Michel could not let the matter of the curse rest unacknowledged between them. When her terror for their unborn child threatened to overwhelm her, he did not want Elena to feel she must conceal her fears from him.

"Elena, it is all right to be afraid. We will not long be able to hide your condition, and then you can be very certain the topic of the curse will be on everyone's minds even if they restrain their lips in our presence."

Her serene expression remained unchallenged by his dark truth. At the puzzled expression on his face, Elena leaned towards him to smooth away the fierce frown line between his eyes.

"Michel, I will not waste whatever time we have together with worries of when it will be taken away from us. Haven't I known loss in my life? The one thing I have learned from my grief is to live in each moment, to be grateful for every blessing we are given, and to clutch to my heart every moment of each day and each hour we have together, and rejoice in these precious moments between us."

Awed by her peaceful acceptance of the invisible threat hanging over them and the life of their unborn child, Michel thought to hide his own unreconciled rage at the burden he had inherited from some nameless, unknown ancestor. He would gladly risk life and limb to protect his wife and the child she carried within her. If he thought abdicating his throne and fleeing with them away from the place where the curse began would save them, he would not hesitate to do so. But he feared even if he was willing to take such an unprecedented step, and he was successful in carving out a new life for his family far away from Calei, he would then only be passing along the bane of the curse to the very child he was desperate to protect. No, he would not run away. He would contest his destiny here where it began and God willing remove the stain of the threat from his blood.

CHAPTER TWENTY THREE

Michel divided his time over the next months between the demands of his kingdom and resolving the curse that was an ever present shadow to his joy in his young bride and the growing evidence of the child she carried within her. Every spare moment, which were few…too few, he spent researching the mystery that had descended on his unsuspecting shoulders as surely as had the burden of reclaiming his grandfather's throne from those who had followed the murderous traitor that stole it from him in his sleep. He spent much of that time in the cathedral library where the lamps burned long into the night, until he finally took to his bed for a few hours rest before rising to meet the needs of his kingdom. He would not deny himself the pleasure of the scarce private hours he had with Elena. So each evening he waited to take up the search for the answers he sought until after he'd spent precious hours with Elena, finding both pleasure and peace in equal measure in her loving, tender arms. Then replete, he held her while she fell asleep against his chest and he stroked her long, silky hair in a rhythmic, soothing motion.

He treasured the intimate moments they shared, and held close to his heart the memories of his child's tiny limbs pressing against his mother's swollen middle as if his babe was in a hurry to escape her tender womb. Michel would watch awed as his wife's soft flesh yielded to accommodate their child's sometimes languorous stretching against its confinement, which at times was followed by a rapid flurry of fists, foot and head, as though his babe danced to a music only he or she could hear.

When his unborn child finally settled down and followed his mother into sleep, Michel would slip from his bed and dress before pausing at the door to his chambers to stare back at his slumbering wife, her face peaceful in repose, as if she remained completely untroubled by the demons that tormented him about the threat that hung over their child's life. Some nights Michel would stand there long moments memorizing her features. It was as though some part of him knew these rare, priceless moments they enjoyed were destined to be taken from him, and he sought to clutch them close to his heart so he could carry them, and the memory of his wife's beauty, into the darkness that awaited him in the shadows hovering just beyond his line of sight.

Then he would make his way down the darkened hall and exit the keep, accepting Arden's reins from the stable master's hands, recognizing the man waited up each evening to perform this task for him. Michel thought perhaps the older man wanted him to know he understood what drove his king, and offered this small service to show his support by offering to share, in the only way he could, the lonely vigil Michel labored under. Michel would ride to the cathedral, accompanied by Amele and his guard, where most nights they were greeted by Bishop Maren. The three men would exchange familiar, trifling greetings and the quickly settle down to work among the ancient books and journals in the church's stewardship.

In the swift passage of time since Elena shared the news of her pregnancy with him, the three men spent most nights surrounded by books, journals, maps and family bibles trying to decipher each hand-written document, often struggling against old ink fading on the parchment pages while they searched for any mention of the curse to assist them in finding its resolution.

"Listen to this; I think it's written in King Nathaniel's hand. I don't know how I missed this before," Bishop Maren proclaimed in an excited voice, breaking into the heavy silence that had fallen between the three men, '*My heart tells me I am close to understanding the curse that besets my blood. Alyssa has brought new hope to my house. The people respond in some inexplicable way to her gentle, assured faith. I remember the moment we passed through the gates of Calei, the people lined the streets to catch a glimpse of her and waited hours in the cold so they could cheer her arrival with an enthusiasm even I had not anticipated. It was as if they too sensed the light within her that I was aware of from the moment of our first introduction. In some way I have yet to comprehend, Alyssa's coming to Calei has brought new hope to my home and my subjects.'*

"Didn't the elder say something about King Nathaniel not realizing what he held in his grasp?" Amele reminded them.

"Apparently my grandfather concluded that my grandmother was part of the resolution of the curse," Michel mused, nodding in response to Amele's comment.

"Was it Queen Alyssa or the unusual stone she wore? Though I have only heard rumors of the queen's amulet, I cannot help but wonder if it is the same stone you now wear, Your Highness," Bishop Maren asked.

"Yes, the stone is the same one my grandmother brought with her to Calei, but the clue refers to the daughter of the moon. If my grandmother is part of the resolution of the mystery it seems far more likely she would be connected to the first part of the clue," Michel replied.

"Could the stone be the heart of the sun?" Amele interjected.

Michel shook his head. "If my grandmother

was somehow the daughter of the moon and the Salusian stone the heart of the sun, the curse would have been resolved in my grandfather's time as my grandmother entered Calei with the stone in her possession. In essence, she had already captured it. No, we must be missing something. Is there anything more to the passage you were reading from?"

The bishop shook his head. "No, but we'll keep looking. Like King Nathaniel when he wrote this entry, I think we're close...closer perhaps than anyone has been since the hour he penned it."

All three of the searchers were aware of the new aura of hope that hung suspended over the dim room where they sat huddled around a small work table piled high with old records. It was Amele who finally broke the silence that fell between them, as if the three men feared disturbing it would dispel their burgeoning optimism as easily as a man's voice dispelled the silence. "May I suggest we continue our search tomorrow? The night is already well advanced and you will soon be rising, my king, and greeting the demands of a new day."

Michel nodded his assent. Gaining his feet he addressed the others, "Perhaps I was too quick to dismiss the stone's part in this. Has it not always passed from mother to daughter in an unbroken line for a thousand years? It's very possible the stone is as old as the curse. Perhaps it is in some way connected to its origin."

"If what you say is true, Your Highness, I find it interesting that the stone has returned to Calei in the hands of its new guardian. I believe I recall correctly the elder stating your presence here brought him hope for the curse's resolution…hope that he has not known since the reign of King Nathaniel."

Amele added softly, "That would be the last time the stone and its keeper were both in Calei."

"But I am not the stone's proper keeper, Melissa is."

"Melissa?" Bishop Maren echoed.

"My twin sister. My grandmother passed the stone to her daughter, my mother, who passed it as she lay dying to my younger sister, Rhiann. When Melissa was found alive, Rhiann gave the stone to her, as Melissa, being the elder daughter, was the rightful steward of the stone."

The bishop nodded and added curiously, "How did the stone come to you?"

"Melissa insisted I wear it when I returned to Calei," Michel replied.

"So the rightful steward, as you refer to your twin, insisted the stone return to Calei with you? That's interesting."

"And the elder said I was not to be concerned about its loss because it was in trustworthy hands," Michel added. For the first time feeling true optimism that they were close to the solution they sought begin to take hold in his heart.

"Didn't Queen Elena tell you the stone appeared anxious to escape her stewardship until she made the decision to return it to you when you were injured?"

"Yes," Michel admitted, then added with growing certainty. "The stone is at the center of this. And so is my grandmother. She knows something. She knew she would never return to Calei…and so did the stone," Michel tacked on in an awed whisper. "The stone has been trying to return to Calei ever since it left."

"But it was necessary for it to do so in the hands of the rightful steward," Amele concluded, following Michel's reasoning.

"But I am not the rightful steward," Michel protested.

"Twins have always been the exception, my king. You have every right to wear the stone."

"Perhaps, but I am not the stone's true steward. I need to speak with my grandmother. She is the key," Michel announced.

"You cannot think to make this journey personally, my king. Your wife will give birth soon. Your place is here with your wife, and mine is at your side," Amele quickly inserted when Michel would have interrupted him. "With your permission, I will send Melos with a company of men to seek Queen Alyssa. I believe your conclusion is correct and that your grandmother was somehow able to deflect the power of the curse."

"What do you mean?" Michel wondered.

"Has it escaped your notice, my king that Queen Alyssa managed to elude the effects of the curse for herself and the child she carried?"

"But she was forced to flee Calei for her life," Michel protested.

"I did not say she ended the curse, only that she was able to escape its impact on her and her child. That should give you hope for your family's safety as you now have the stone in your possession."

"You believe the stone will protect my wife and child?" Michel asked awed by the thought.

"I have never known the stone to react to another outside your family, yet it reacted most forcibly to Lady Elena's possession."

"Reacted to it by attempting to escape her grasp and burning her hand," Michel reminded him.

"The stone burned Queen Elena's hand?" Amele echoed.

"Yes, her palm bears the imprint of the stone."

"Before or after you were wed?"

"Before."

"I find that astonishing. In all of the legends I have heard of the stone, there is none where it reacts in any way except to turn cold and dark when it leaves the keeper's hand. Yet it appeared to have the opposite reaction when held in the hand of your wife."

"What do you think it means?" Michel

wondered.

"I do not know, but I think you are right to discover if Queen Alyssa can shed any additional light on this mystery. What do you know of Queen Elena's family?"

Michel considered Amele's question, wondering why he'd never pursued this line of reasoning in his search for answers. "Very little, only that she was Barnabas' niece and that she was sent to live with him as a young girl when her parents were killed in an accident in the mountains."

"Is there anything more in Barnabas' personal journals about Elena's parents?" Michel asked.

"I never thought to research your wife's family. It never seemed significant before, but I will do so immediately, though I think, Your Highness, King Barnabas' personal journals are likely still at the keep," Bishop Maren replied.

"Yes, I will go through them in the morning. For now, let us take to our beds. Amele is right; the sun will soon be rising on a new day."

"Yes well, perhaps it will drop its heart at our feet on its way over Calei, thus clarifying the other half of the clue we haven't yet begun to unravel."

His companions laughed at Amele's wry comment, and then exiting the imposing library, paused to extinguish the lamps on their way out.

CHAPTER TWENTY FOUR

Michel nodded his greeting to the guards stationed outside his door and entered his chambers. As he stripped out of his clothes he went over in his thoughts the results of his research that evening and concluded he had genuine reason to hope the resolution of the ancient curse was within his grasp. Melos would leave in the morning to bring his grandmother to Calei. Though he did not doubt Amele's claim that his grandmother intended never to return to her dead husband's kingdom, Michel did not doubt she would respond to his summons and he felt confident when she did so, another piece of the mystery would fall into place.

Satisfied with his reasoning, he threw a few additional logs on the dying fire, then stripped out of his clothes and crossed to the bed. He stood gazing down at his sleeping wife, heavy with the burden of his babe and thought they would not have long to wait now to meet their child. For the first time since Elena informed him he was going to be a father, Michel felt true joy at the prospect, unburdened by the dread of the curse. He sank down on the bed and gathered his sleeping wife in his arms just as the deepest hours of night before dawn fell over the heart Calei. His unborn child gave him a gentle nudge in greeting, and smiling, Michel gave into his exhaustion and allowed sleep to claim him.

His rest was deep and dreamless, so it came as a surprise to him when a heavy pounding disturbed him in the depth of his slumber. His wife's drowsy voice calling his name, finally roused him,

"Michel, there is someone at the door."

Their eyes met for the briefest of moments, both of them well aware only ill news would cause such an interruption in the darkest hours of night. Michel bent and kissed his wife, "Go back to sleep. I am certain it is nothing for you to be concerned about. The city is not under attack. There is no sound of the bells ringing, alerting the city's defenders."

Elena nodded at his reassurance, but Michel felt her eyes following him anxiously around the room as he dressed then crossed to the door and pulled it open. Amele stood in the doorway, and Michel released a deep sigh at the concern etched into his friend's face. The city might not be under attack, but he could tell the news Amele bore was ill indeed.

"There's been a rock slide at one of the mines. A dozen or more men are trapped beneath the rubble," Amele informed him gravely.

Michel nodded. "I'll come with you directly. Let me share the news with Elena and try to persuade her to remain behind at the keep."

Amele nodded and Michel returned to his chambers only to find his wife already rising from their bed and searching through her chest for fresh undergarments. Releasing a soft curse beneath his breath, Michel swiftly crossed the room. He slid his arms around his wife's rounded middle from behind and drew her back against him.

"Elena, love, I would prefer it if you remain here. There's been a collapse at one of the mines. I'm certain everything that can be done is being done. I must go, but you need your rest."

Elena spun in his arms and raised concerned eyes to meet his equally concerned ones, "Michel, my place is with you and with the families whose husbands and fathers are trapped beneath the rock. How uncaring would it be for me to return to the comfort of our bed while other wives fear for their husband's lives."

Michel reluctantly nodded his approval. "You may come, but you will eat first. I must go with Amele. One of the guards will escort you after you've fed our babe."

He waited for Elena to agree to his dictate, then bent and brushed his lips across her lips before turning back to where Amele waited for him in the hall outside his chambers.

Upon reaching the site of the accident, Michel learned the news was grim. More than twenty miners were trapped beneath the rock slide. All attempts at a rescue had been thwarted by the unstable condition of the mountain. Even as he stood listening to a report by the man in charge of the rescue attempts, a fresh rumble of rock slid down the side of the mountain, burying the trapped men even deeper beneath an additional layer of stone. Amid the crash of stone, Michel could hear the agonized cries of the men's families where they waited a safe distance away.

"Every time we attempt to create an opening wide enough to get a team of men underground, there's a new slide. At this point we don't even know where to focus our efforts, or if anyone is left alive under there."

Michel nodded. "We need to get a man down there to try to make contact with the trapped men. A single man alone has a better chance of making it through the debris without creating enough of a disturbance to bring about a fresh slide."

"That may be true, Your Highness," the head of the rescue team began.

Michel interjected, "But you are reluctant to order a man to his death."

"Frankly, yes."

"Then I will go," Michel stated.

"Your Highness!? You cannot be serious."

Michel met the other man's astonished look. "I am very serious. I too am loath to order a man to his death, but I am even less willing to stand here and do nothing while the trapped men's families look to me to save the lives of their husbands and fathers."

"Your Highness, you cannot take this risk. Allow me to go in your stead," the older man pleaded with him.

Michel's met the other's resolved glance in understanding even as he shook his head, denying his request. "What is your name, my friend?"

"Allon, Your Highness."

"Well Allon, I cannot allow you attempt to enter the mine when I can see the blood seeping through the wound on your leg. I am guessing you have already made such an attempt and it proved unsuccessful."

The other man sighed and admitted, "Yes, Your Highness. I was not able to make it far before the last slide. The others were barely able to pull me out in time."

"Then let us go and retrieve a rope and tools," Michel commanded and the older man reluctantly nodded.

When the two men joined the others, Allon announced, "King Michel will attempt to reach the trapped men. Mason he'll need rope, fresh water, and tools."

From where he stood with his brother, Amele became aware of Michel's intent, and swiftly approached his side. "My king, you surely do not think to carry out this rescue attempt personally.

You are unfamiliar with the mines. There are men here who've spent their entire lives in them and are far more familiar with what to do in the event of another slide."

"I am aware of that my friend. Most of these men, like my good Allon here, have been injured in their attempts to rescue the trapped men." Michel accepted the rope and tools he would need from Mason's outstretched hand. He could see his tunic and breeches were liberally splattered with blood and noted there was a bandage binding the arm he held stiff at his side, while he offered Michel the necessary supplies with his uninjured hand.

"Then allow me to make this attempt in your place, my king," Amele pleaded with him as Michel tied the rope around his waist and stowed the water and tools in the leather pack Allon offered him.

"No, my friend. We both know you do not do well in confined spaces and if I assented to your request I would soon be forced to come in after you anyway," Michel rejoined with a lighthearted smile to ease the pain of his rejection. Amele nodded his acceptance of Michel's reasoning, but Michel could see his agreement cost him.

Michel listened attentively to Allon's instructions as to how to signal the surface if he discovered news of the trapped miners, what to do in order to protect himself in the event of another collapse and how to let them know he was in trouble and himself in need of rescuing. As news spread across the city of the accident in the mines more and more men gathered at the site to offer what assistance they could to the team of rescuers. A stunned whisper rustled through the crowd when it became obvious to the onlookers that the king himself intended to make the next attempt to reach the trapped miners.

"Please, my king, you must allow me to render you this service."

The pleading voice reached him from below and Michel turned in the direction of the source to see young Colin on his knees before him.

"Rise, my friend," Michel commanded and reached down to assist his young guardsman to his feet.

When the younger man stood before him, Michel looked over his shoulder to see his mother fighting tears. He could see Baron James' widow stood a little apart from the crowd of onlookers, as if her neighbors still judged her for the treacherous act of her husband. He met the older woman's worried glance and shook his head.

He reached out to grip Colin's shoulders and gently denied his request, "Colin, your mother has already given two sons in the service of Calei. I cannot ask her to sacrifice another."

The younger man turn to where his mother stood regarding him with anxious tears in her eyes, then he excused himself from his king and swiftly crossed the distance between them and his mother.

He gripped her hands in his and whispered fiercely to her, “Mother, you must not take this opportunity from me to render this service to our king and to our home. If I am to die, let me do so in replacement of the life my father thought to steal, and restore our family’s honor. I understand your fear, Mother, but I am a man full-grown and you must not deny me this chance to serve my king.”

His mother closed her eyes over her tears and nodded once. Colin took her slender frame in his arms and kissed her brow. “All will be well, Mother. King Michel will see to it that you and my sisters are taken care of.”

Colin disengaged from her clinging arms, and returned to kneel before his king. “Your Highness, my mother understands my need to render you this service. I beg of you to allow me to do so and restore my family’s honor in your sight.”

Michel once again reached down to assist his determined, fiercely loyal guard to his feet. “Each man is responsible for his own honor, Colin. You have never defiled yours so there is nothing you need to do in order to restore it in my sight.” Michel could see that the young man’s resolve remained firm. He glanced over his proud shoulders and met the anxious eyes of his mother. She nodded her assent to his silent question and Michel released a heavy sigh. It did not sit well with him to send this young man in his place, but he could see Colin was resolved to go and would likely follow him underground at the first sign of trouble. He nodded his assent reluctantly in answer to the anxious question in Colin's eyes. "You know what you are to do?"

A relieved smile curved the younger man's lips, as if Michel had just bestowed a great favor upon him, rather than having just consigned him a task that more likely than not would lead to his death beneath a mountain of rock. "Yes, Your Highness. I am to seek out the lost miners and when I find them, I am to tap on the stones above our heads to signal the men where they are to dig in order to free us."

Michel nodded and instructed, "If you become trapped, or lost, send a signal to the surface and we will do our best to free you."

An understanding smile curved the young man's lips. "My king, I see that your heart is full of misgivings, but do not grieve my passing, if such is the will of the Almighty. You bestowed upon me a great gift. I render this service freely to Calei, my home, and to my king, both of whom I love. My homeland needs you, my king, far more than it needs a single soldier in its service. You are destined to restore Calei to its previous heights, and I think, to exceed them. I would rather die in its service, than see my beloved Calei deprived of its true king."

Michel blinked back the bitter tears of regret

that stung his eyes. "Go then with my blessing, my friend, and the blessing and gratitude of all true Caleinians."

Colin nodded, his eyes free of the doubts Michel knew were reflected in his own. The younger man, smiling now that Michel had granted his urgent request, bent down to kiss Michel's hand and then rose and turned to the men who waited with the ropes and equipment he would need to find his way below ground.

Minutes later, Michel observed his young guardsman squeeze his way through the narrow crevice that was all that was left of the previous wide entrance into the mine. He noticed Colin lift the lit lantern in his hand as he passed from his sight. Though dawn was already beginning to lift the darkness over the city, beneath the earth it was always dark. Michel felt a hand slip into his and squeeze gently. He turned to look down into Elena's concerned expression. Her clear brown eyes were filled with understanding of his decision and compassion over what she knew it cost him to send another to his almost certain death, rather than take on the task himself. Mingled with her compassion Michel detected barely concealed relief that it was Colin's mother and not her that might lose a loved one this day.

He bent and kissed the top of his wife's heard as his arm came around her no longer slender form. As if aware he must return his attention to the task at hand, and she was a source of distraction away from it, Elena slipped from his encircling arm and made her way over to where Colin's mother still remained standing anxiously apart from the wives and daughters of the missing miners. He watched his wife place a gentle arm around the widow's stiff posture and speak softly in the older woman's ear. Michel nodded his silent approval of his wife's caring, gentle nature and then turned his attention back to where the rescuers huddled in hushed silence waiting anxiously to hear the faint sound of rock tapping against rock.

For an hour or more the same heavy silence reined, but no signal came from either Colin or the other men trapped underground. Michel wasn't certain whether he should be worried or relieved. He had no idea how long it would take Colin to reach the location of the collapsed mine where he assumed the majority of the miners were trapped behind a wall of rock, but at least there had been no additional rock slides, so maybe the ground was stabilizing and they would be able to dig through the slide without fear of another one.

As if to dispel even the uncertain glimpse of hope in his heart, another rumble shook the mountains and more rock crashed down from the steep slope burying deeper beneath another layer of granite, the trapped miners and covering the onlookers in a fine layer of dust. Hushed gasps and tearful, agonized cries echoed from the families of the trapped men before a more ominous silence fell over the lips and faces of the men who waited for even the smallest sign to give them an excuse to mount a fresh rescue operation to free their trapped friends and comrades.

Michel was done waiting. If the curse meant to have him anyway, he could at least offer his life in exchange for its bloodlust. Maybe it would be satisfied with his willing offering and leave his family alone. He approached the waiting men with a determined stride and reached for a rope from the pile of supplies near them.

"What you are planning, my king?" Amele gave voice to the misgiving Michel could see in the grime covered faces of the waiting men.

"I'm going in after them. I shouldn't have allowed Colin to persuade me to take the task upon himself. I likely sent him to his death."

"The boy knew what he was doing, my king, and gladly made this sacrifice on your behalf. Will you in your grief, make his sacrifice meaningless and at the same time deprive Calei of its king?"

"I know you offer me sound advice, my friend, and a better king would heed it. But I am not a man who can stand aside and send another to die in his place, to risk all he holds dear in my service when I am unwilling to risk the same sacrifice for myself and my family. You may blame yourself, my friend, for doing your job too well. I learned most the measure of a man's honor from you."

Too moved to respond, Amele nodded briskly

and reached out to help Michel with his equipment. When Michel was ready to go underground, Amele nodded to where Elena waited with a fixed expression on her face, belied by the terror in her stunned expression. "Your wife and the babe she carries?"

Michel understood what his friend was asking and he raised his gaze to lock with Elena's. He'd avoided doing so before, afraid her fear and her desperate love for him would turn him aside from his intent. He recalled their earlier conversation about the curse on his blood, and her soft words of surest conviction echoed in his ears, "I am not afraid of the price I may one day pay for the great treasure the Almighty has bestowed upon me. If all I have with you and our babe is a few short years, or weeks or even a single day, I will count myself blessed and settle my debt honorably, understanding and accepting that all great treasures are not bestowed without price."

Through her tears, she nodded her assent of his plan and his lips curved in a grateful smile. In that moment he knew he loved her as he could never love another. If he did not pay the highest price for the risk he was about to take at the urging of his honor, he would spend the rest of the time allotted him on this earth, proving to her how much he valued her. With an effort Michel pulled his gaze from his wife's clinging one and turned his focus back to his friend who waited an answer to his question. "Tell my wife and my son or daughter, that I love them and that I'm sorry I could not be around to see what they would become and to share our lives with each other."

Amele nodded and pressed him, "You know I would take your place, if you would but allow it."

"Yes, but we both know this is an undertaking I must pursue alone and if this is to be a final farewell between us, there is something I would have you know. I mean no disrespect to the father God bestowed upon me, but you, my friend, have always been the father of my heart. Watch over my family as you have watched over me."

Amele nodded through his tears and the two men exchanged a brief, but fierce embrace before Michel slid from his friend's restraining hold and picked his way onto the fresh layer of rock, seeking a crevice large enough for him to fit through.

Across the distance separating them Elena watched her husband, her beloved, her king and the father of her child pass through the narrow opening that he hoped would lead him to where the miners were trapped below a mountain of rock. Her heart clenched in agony in her chest but no protest sounded from her lips. As much as she longed to, she knew she could not run after him and throw herself on her knees at his feet and beg him not to leave her. Not when just moments earlier she had kept her silence, offering no protest, when the woman by her side sent her only remaining son in place of his king, knowing as

Elena knew now, that she would likely never see him alive again.

Elena felt the bitter tears of incalculable loss sting her eyes, but she blinked them back. She was aware of the surreptitious, pitying glances cast in her direction, but she refused to allow the tears to stain her cheeks. Nor would she acknowledge the others who willed her with their stares to turn to them for release and comfort. It was not her intent to rudely dismiss such offers, but the futility of them kept her from availing herself of them.

There was no comfort for her to be found except in the arms of her beloved husband. There were no words, no sympathetic gestures, and no offers of assistance that could compensate for the magnitude of her loss. To pretend otherwise would be to distract the attention of those waiting and listening for an improbable, impossible echo of a faint tapping to sound from the depths of the fallen earth and she would not risk such a distraction with her husband's life hanging by a thread.

To think her greatest fear these past weeks was that an ancient curse would somehow find a way to steal her happiness and would someday claim her child's life. But if she was honest with herself she could admit now that she never really believed it would come to that. Michel promised he would keep her and their unborn child safe. She believed him. It was only now she realized he hadn't included himself in his promise. Maybe she was paying the price for their arrogance in assuming they could cheat the fate so many others suffered. But those other losses seemed far away and were suffered by names only, barely familiar names at that. She didn't believe the curse was responsible for her uncle's death. It was an evil man behind the deed and that man was dead. Justice had been served.

The rumors, the old legends, even the death of Michel's grandfather and his sons barely touched her, and to her mind, lent little credence to the threat of the curse. Were there not evil men in every generation? Were they not happy to attribute their evil to a misty bane beyond the reach of men's minds or their ability to defend against it?

How condescending she had been when the news first reached her of the mine's collapse and that there were men trapped beneath the ground. Though she mourned their misfortune it had not really touched her where she lay warm and safe in her husband's passionate embrace. She hadn't fully comprehended what lay behind the vacant stares of the wives and children of those trapped men as they waited anxiously for word, clinging to improbable, foolish hope until even that last tiny straw of comfort was snatched from their clenched fists.

It was only now that she shared their fate she could truly enter into their stunned shock that their whole world was on the brink of crumbling beneath their feet just as the mountain of rock had crumbled and buried their loved ones.

It already seemed as though an hour had passed since Michel wriggled his way through the narrow crevice, but she knew it had only been bare minutes since their glances had locked and held and she'd seen the regret in his, as if he already knew he was leaving her a young widow with a child to raise on her own. She was grateful no one attempted to approach her with hopeful tidings. If she heard the words, 'Elena, dear' accompanied by one more helpful hint as to how she should go on, as to what was the proper way for a queen to behave in such a circumstance, she wasn't certain she would be able to restrain herself from screaming her denial, her rage, her bitter resentment that it was her husband whose life was hanging by a thread, so unless it was one of the trapped miner's wives, or young Colin's mother, who wished to offer their suggestions on her behavior, no one else had better dare attempt to do so. Or they would soon discover their dear Elena was not such a dear after all.

As word spread of their king's heroic deed, and dawn wore away into mid-morning, more and more concerned citizens made their way beyond the city gates to where the others already waited, adding their presence and prayers for the safety of the men trapped underground. If an enemy sought to attack the wealthy kingdom, now would be the time, when even its bold defenders were sick with grief at the loss of their young and courageous new king.

Through it all, Elena stood, neither shifting her weight nor drawing her eyes away from the opening her husband passed through hours earlier. Time lost all meaning for her. She ignored the offers of food and drink offered in quiet, concerned voices. To Elena, they were like so much background noise as were the quiet conversations going on around her and the bracing stories being regaled of prior collapses where all the miners had been found alive and rescued. She neither focused on them nor gave any indication that she had heard them at all. She only stood, still as the statues that graced the keep's courtyard, as she waited for news of her husband.

Beneath his wife's feet Michel picked his way through the mountain of tumbled rock. It was a dirty, laborious, exhausting passage but Michel finally found an opening large enough to sit up in and draw a deep breath. He took a pull from the water in his leather pouch to cleanse his mouth and lungs of the dust that filled his mouth despite the cloth he wore covering the lower half of his face to prevent him from doing so. He'd lost all sense of time since he left the cool morning air of early dawn and passed through the unwelcoming crevice to the dank, dusty world of buried stone and earth.

Depressed at the hopelessness of the task confronting him, Michel sighed heavily and coughed up the dirt that was trapped in his throat. He leaned against the rock wall at his back and called out as he had been doing every few moments since he entered the failing mine.

"Hello! Can anyone hear me?" He paused and waited, his expectation of hearing an answering call still not completely doused by his repeated failures to do so. After a few moments spent waiting for the echoes of his own voice to die down, he cried out again, risking raising his voice to a more forceful level. "Hello! Can you hear me?"

He let his voice trail off again, but this time, within the silence broken by the echo of his own cries, he thought he detected the muffled cries of other voices. Hearing them, Michel sat up straighter away from the wall he rested against and crawled across to the other side where he thought the other voices emanated from. Using one of the iron tools in the heavy leather pouch he wore, he tapped gently on the side of the wall and yelled again. "If you can hear me, tap twice on the wall where the sound of my voice is the strongest."

Michel paused and waited. There it was. On the wall to his right, the distinct, impossibly clear sound: '*tap, tap*'.

In joyous disbelief, Michel scooted over to the wall and tapped three times. Moments later three taps echoed back at him. They were close, closer than he would have believed possible. "Can you hear me? It is King Michel. We have men waiting to dig you out."

"Yes, Your Highness, we hear you."

Michel bent his head to the earth in grateful prayer, and then he lifted his head and asked urgently, "Is young Colin with you? Baron James' son?"

A moment of silence was followed by an unwelcome response. "No, Your Highness, we haven't seen any sign of him. We've been trapped here since the second collapse. We were able to dig ourselves out of the initial rock slide and took shelter beneath a ledge when the ground shook and we knew another slide was imminent."

Michel took a moment to offer a prayer for the safety of his young guardsman, and then replied, "We're going to get you out. All is in readiness. It shouldn't be long now. Is anyone injured?"

"Not enough to allow himself to be buried down here," a relieved voice replied and Michel found his first smile since the news of the mine's collapse reached him, and he dug in his pouch and removed a heavier tool. He looked around for the strongest, most stable rock above him in an effort to avoid setting off another rock slide and began tapping. When no response could be heard from above he tapped harder, and then finally, swung the tool against the rock above him with all of his might, only to be rewarded for his efforts with a layer of dust and gravel breaking free from the bottom of the stone and showering him with its spray.

Disgusted, Michel wiped the grit and tiny stones from his eyes and prepared to change his location and begin again the painstaking process of signaling the surface. Before he could swing his arm and connect with the rock above his head, he heard it. An answering signal from above. They knew where they were. They were coming for them.

"They heard us. They're coming," Michel shouted into the silence and heard the echoes of joyful relieved cries from the trapped men.

Michel scooted back to where the trapped miners waited on the other side and leaned his weary back against it in silent communion with their anxious vigil. He took another swallow of water then used some of it to dampen the cloth secured across his mouth and nose. Removing it, he attempted to wipe the irritating grit and stones from where they embedded themselves in his eyes and took up residence behind his eyelids. He abandoned the effort when he realized his crude efforts were doing more harm than good.

Instead, using the damp cloth to wipe the layer of fresh dust from his face, he closed his eyes, leaned his head back against the side of the small opening, and settled back to wait, offering another silent prayer Colin would be found alive, and a second prayer of gratitude he would live long enough to spend another night in his wife's warm and loving embrace. Perhaps even long enough to see his son or daughter birthed. A contented smile curved his lips at the thought and shifting his weight on the ground to tuck one tired leg beneath the other; he drew himself up into a tight ball, wrapped his arms around his bent knee and dipped his head to rest wearily on his raised knees.

His last unthinking action probably saved his life. For an instant later, the roof caved in around him, the wall he leaned against disappeared and he fell backwards into the cavern that provided shelter for the trapped men. Hearing their alarmed shouts, and remembering the protective ledge they took shelter under, Michel instinctively scooted himself on his back to the sound of their voices and just barely escaped having his head and chest crushed by a large boulder that landed where he had huddled only moments before.

Unfortunately his right side was not so fortunate. The boulder brushed passed him close enough to carved jagged pieces of flesh from his shoulder, arm and leg before continuing on its deadly course to bounce across the far wall and settle there, completely oblivious to the agonized cry that erupted from the lips of the man it very politely refrained from obliterating as it had done everything else in its path. Another shower of smaller rocks and grit followed. These were less agile, or seemingly not as courteous of their larger companion, because one of them, in its carelessness, struck a glancing blow across Michel's temple, rendering him senseless, and then proceeded to spring against the far wall near its larger companion, but it did not settle there. Instead it ricocheted off the wall and came back to carve out another huge gash from Michel's arm that they lay limply at his side.

CHAPTER TWENTY FIVE

On the surface, Elena's relieved tears at the news Michel had reached the trapped miners and the men awaiting just such a signal were already preparing to rescue him, turned to fresh horror when the earth beneath her feet shook anew. She watched terrified as the men who moments earlier eagerly prepared to descend into the depths to restore her husband to her jumped in panicked fear off the pile of shifting stone. She wanted to scream at them to go back, go back, but the words wouldn't form in her throat. She couldn't help herself. Her courage failed her at this, the final test of her resolve. She collapsed to her knees and gave in to the heart-rending sobs she'd held at bay, wrapping her arms around her stomach and cradling her unborn child protectively in their embrace.

Beneath the unsteady surface, Michel lay unmoving under the careful hands of those tending his injuries.

"Well, my young king, I must admit you give

me cause to doubt your claim that you do not pursue your own death with the same reckless abandon of your twin."

Coming to his senses, Michel cringed at the sound of the familiar voice echoing through his dazed thoughts and replied with an effort at levity, "Yes, well, I don't blame you. I seem to have had a run of bad luck lately." As if appreciating his efforts, Michel heard the amused laughter of his companion, and added in a resigned voice. "I imagine your presence here does not bode well for the success of our efforts to return to the surface."

The echo of his companion's deep sigh sounded between them, accompanied by the reluctant confirmation of Michel's dark assumption. *"Regrettably not."*

Michel nodded. His misty companion had already cheated fate once for Melissa's benefit, and admittedly when he'd warned Michel of Baron James' treachery. Michel imagined his companion was not in the habit of handing out second chances, or even third chances as in his case, as a matter of course.

"You imagine correctly, my young king."

Michel opened his eyes to meet death's direct gaze and made a final request of his twin's unusual friend. "Well, perhaps before we go, you will satisfy my curiosity in regards to the mystery of the curse."

His companion's eyes lit with ready amusement, and then considering the matter, eventually nodded his assent to Michel's request. *"I do not see how it could do any harm to grant your request at this point, but at least allow me to render you a small service. Though my labors are unassailable there is no reason for your passage from this life to be accompanied by the pain you bear now."* Before he even finished speaking, Michel felt an instant relief from the agonizing, mind-numbing pain in his limbs and in his head.

"Thank you. Let me assure you the service you rendered me was by no means a small one."

Death nodded and then sat on the floor near where Michel lay and leaned his back against the wall. *"I cannot tell you the number of times I tried to convince your sister it was not necessary for her death to be accompanied by the violent end she seemed intent on inflicting upon herself."*

"Let me guess," Michel interjected. "She didn't listen to your sound advice."

Amused laughter erupted from his companion. The arbiter of death laughed until the glimmer of tears appeared in his eyes. Finally gaining control over his amusement, he reached up to wipe them away and sat grinning at Michel's amused expression. *"I must admit, I find the two of you highly entertaining. I cannot remember when I have laughed like that, or enjoyed the company of two humans more."*

"Regrettably I cannot return the compliment as I have no real basis for comparison, but I am glad you will be by my side to accompany me into the next phase of my existence."

"Graciously spoken, my young king. I hope that you may one day consider me the friend your sister does."

"I already consider you a friend. You have bestowed on Melissa and me a priceless gift. Did we not enjoy years together we would not have had without your act of mercy? Did you not give me time to come to love my wife and create with her the child she carries? How could I consider you anything less than a friend? Do not think I blame you now for doing what you must."

His companion's expression turned to one of wonder and then coalesced into one of mutual respect. "Thank you, Michel, if I may?" At Michel's assenting nod, he continued, "Before we leave this depressing place, let me at least satisfy your curiosity in regards to the ancient curse that was laid upon your blood."

Michel sighed deeply, foolishly perhaps given the circumstances but he was aware of a feeling of intense satisfaction that he was to learn the source of the mystery behind his months of searching before he left this world.

"The stone you wear around your neck," his companion began.

Reaching for it, Michel asked, "The Salusian stone?"

"Yes, though it was not always known by that name and if it is eventually recovered," he worded delicately the implication behind his

words and added, *"it will no doubt come to be known by other names by future generations."*

"So the stone does have some bearing on the curse's resolution just as my grandfather suspected."

"Not the stone itself, but what it represents, and who it represents," Death corrected. *"The stone is merely a remnant of what was once a great jewel worn by the gods who walked the earth before the days of men. The original gem held captured moonlight, but when the stone was shattered into hundreds of pieces similar to the one you wear, the moonlight was lost and the stone's power greatly diminished."*

"The daughter of the moon," Michel echoed softly.

"Exactly."

Michel pondered the details of the story he'd just begun to hear and sought clarification of a particular point. "When gods once walked the earth before the days of men? Are you telling me this stone has been in existence longer than men?"

His companion shrugged and admitted, *"It is difficult to say. Only men concern themselves with the passage of time. The Almighty's other children exist beyond time's limitations."*

Michel was quite certain he'd lost whatever fragile grasp he retained on reality after the blow responsible for his previously throbbing temple, but he was enjoying his perhaps imaginary companion's account too much to concern himself greatly over its loss. "The Almighty's other children?" he repeated.

"Of course. Did you think man was the creator's only offspring?"

Michel sighed and admitted, "To be honest, I never gave the issue a great deal of thought."

"Understandable, given the limitations of your current existence. However, mankind is not totally without experience of the gods I refer to."

"Really?"

"Yes, they are the Almighty's firstborn. They walked this world when it was still young and before men covered its virgin surface. Some remained beyond the advent of man's dominion. They found the daughters of Eve worthy of their attention and took them as mates for their sojourn here on earth." At Michel's disbelieving look, he added, *"I believe men refer to them as angels."*

"Angels?" Michel repeated stunned, no longer certain he was hallucinating.

"Do you wish me continue with the tale?"

"Yes, please, forgive me. I find it difficult to comprehend how the stone around my neck, the one whose importance I have always dismissed could have once been part of a vessel of moonlight worn by an angel."

Death's lips split into a wide grin. *"You find such a happenstance more difficult to accept than the chance that you are sitting beneath a fallen mountain having a conversation with death?"*

Michel sighed ruefully, "Admittedly I have not

yet had the opportunity to rank the two events in the order of which I believe to be the more fantastic, but despite the omission, I am fascinated by your account and anxious to learn its conclusion."

Nodding, his companion took up his tale where he left off. *"As I was saying, the firstborn who lingered after the spread of man's influence sometimes dwelt among them and took the daughters of Eve as mates."*

"Men believed them gods," Michel remarked.

"Yes. Their conclusion was understandable and not so very far from the truth. The firstborns' power and magnificence far exceeds the grasp of men." At Michel's attentive nod, he continued, *"When the firstborn mated with the daughters of Eve the children they produced were of a noble lineage no longer seen on earth."*

"They were half angel and half man," Michel concluded.

"Yes and no. The firstborn are not physical beings, but spiritual ones. In order to interact with men and take up residence in the physical world they had to create physical bodies for themselves which they patterned after the existing higher inhabitants of earth."

"Man."

"Yes. In this form they were not in their purely angelic state, so the children they produced with their earthly wives were not considered true descendants of the firstborn. They were however,

a considerably higher life form than those of the primitive men inhabiting the earth at the time. In order to foster the evolution and advancement of the race of men, they attempted to keep their bloodlines free of the stain of lesser men."

"I think I see where this is going. The daughters of the angel who wore the moonstone came to be known as the daughters of the moon."

"Yes, very good, my young king," Death announced, seemingly both surprised and delighted by Michel's grasp of the intricacies of his story. *"The moniker lingered long after the last of the firstborn grew weary of the limitations of their physical existence and returned to their natural form. The offspring they left behind however remained a powerful force on earth and became great and wealthy kings in their own right."*

"How did the stone become fragmented?" Michel asked.

"Its power, and the power of those like it, was deemed too dangerous to leave behind in the hands of men. Before they left, each of the firstborn broke the stone he wore, the symbol of his true nature, and distributed the pieces to his children, or to others who rendered him faithful service for his sojourn here."

"The legends imply even pieces of the stone, or at least the piece that has passed down through my grandmother's blood, retained some its original power."

"Yes, well, men seem to prefer to instill objects with mysterious powers rather than accept the truth that all power rests in the will of its bearer."

Michel nodded. "So because its creator was possessed of great power, men came to believe the source of that power was from the stone, rather than the other way around."

"Yes, exactly."

"So the stone has no power of its own," Michel concluded surprised to find himself a little disappointed at the confirmation of his suspicions about the stone's nature all along.

"Not necessarily. The stone is reflective of the power of its bearer. Alone, or in the hands of an ordinary man, your conclusion would be accurate. In the hands of one of the descendants of its creator, that is something else altogether."

"How did the stone become wrapped up in the history of Calei?"

"That should not be too difficult for you to reason out. As I told you, the offspring the firstborn left behind became powerful kings. Their daughters were coveted for their great beauty. As the offspring of the great ones mingled their blood with that of lesser men, their power was slowly diluted until generation by generation they became as other men and subject to the violence and envy of those who would conquer their kingdoms and capture their wealth for themselves...the wealth often most coveted by their enemies was the beauty of their daughters."

"One of the Caleinian kings attacked the kingdom where there remained a daughter of the moon."

"Not only attacked, young Michel, but destroyed. Your ancestor was an arrogant and proud man. He ascended to the kingship as a young man not much older than yourself, and thought to enlarge his kingdom and thereby his influence across a wide swath of the lands surrounding Calei's current boundaries. He looked favorably upon one of the neighboring kingdom's daughters, but her father considered the young king beneath his daughter's lineage and rightfully so, I'm afraid. I regret to inform you your ancestor was a boar of a man and nothing at all like the gentle, learned man who fathered him. Incensed by the neighboring king's refusal to bestow his daughter upon him, the young king thought to teach the man a lesson."

"His plan was to not only capture the king's daughter he desired, but he planned to keep her as his mistress and deny her, the admittedly in this case, questionable respect of making her his wife. The defending king's soldiers fought bravely in defense of their king and his young daughter, but in the end they were overwhelmed. The girl's father, the king, died defender his daughter from your ancestor's ugly reach. Just as your ancestor advanced to claim his prize, the young princess leapt to her death from the parapets of the castle wall, cursing your ancestor and all of the

descendants of his blood, until such day one of them laid his heart at the feet of a daughter of the moon."

"The heart of the sun does not refer to the sun in the sky," Michel concluded.

"No."

Michel released a deep sigh of both regret and resigned acceptance. "It's ironic, is it not? That just when I have within my grasp the power to resolve the curse besetting me and my descendants, I will be denied the opportunity to do so."

"Young Colin was right, my young monarch. Your life was far more valuable to your people than that of an ordinary soldier. Sometimes arrogance reveals itself in surprising forms."

Michel nodded, then challenged, "But if it were not for my arrogance, I would not have learned the truth behind the origin of the curse."

"True. As you pointed out, the circumstances are filled with irony."

Resigned to his fate, Michel asked, "So what happens now?"

"I was wondering the same thing myself."

"What do you mean?"

"Do you not intend to negotiate with me for your life? You are aware I have the power to defer your departure from this world because I granted a similar deferral to your sister."

"What is the price of such a deferral?"

"Your sister paid no price for the boon I

granted her," his companion informed him.

Michel met his direct gaze and believed him, and then comprehension dawned. "You paid the price for her."

"Very astute of you, my young king. Yes, there is no escape from the natural order of things. There is a price to be paid for such a deferral. In your sister's case I elected to bear the burden myself, rather to trouble your sister's bold spirit with such an unpleasant consequence."

"Thank you. I will gladly bear the burden of my sister's debt to you my friend, but I will not seek to add my own to it. No, if it is the will of the Almighty I depart this life, so be it. I am but his humble servant for him to order as he sees fit."

"As you wish."

CHAPTER TWENTY SIX

"Your Highness, Your Highness…"

Voices reached Michel from a great distance. He wasn't certain where he was and assumed the voices were calling to someone else. He was not a king here…wherever here turned out to be. He tried to open his eyes and look around him, but the weight was more than his current weakened strength was up to.

"Where are you?" He whispered to his companion, and then realized his friend had left him. Perhaps that was the nature of his work, to escort the dead to their new life and then return to earth to continue with his labors.

"I am here, my friend."

The familiar voice assured him, but that wasn't right, Michel thought dazedly because it wasn't death's seductive voice he thought he heard above him, but another one deeply familiar to the life he'd once led. He struggled for a moment to recall the name of the man it belonged to.

"Amele?"

"Yes, my king, lie still and let us tend to you.

You have lost a great deal of blood and we must get you back to the surface before the entire mountain falls down around us."

Michel leaned back against the cushion someone eased beneath his aching head. His right side felt like it was on fire. "Colin?"

"I am here, my king," Colin's fervent voice reached him and at the sound, Michel released a deep sigh of relief and leaning back, surrendered to his resurrected pain. It would appear that he too had been resurrected.

He wondered about the penalty that would be exacted from him for his awakening into his previous life and suspected it would be an evil one. Hadn't death confirmed as much when he told Michel he had taken upon himself the punishment of Melissa's debt so as not to burden her with it?

Michel wondered if his unusual friend thought to accept the same burden on his behalf, but if that was the case, Michel was unwilling to leave matters as they stood. A man did not burden his friends with his own rightful debts. How he was going to balance the scales between death and himself, he had no notion, but he was determined to do so. He fell asleep as his mind sought a way to repay his obligation.

The next time Michel woke it was to the sound of wild shouts and cheering. Dazed and confused he tried to free himself from the shadows dragging him back under the darkness stalking him. Then his attention was captured by a soft voice calling his name.

"Elena," his lips framed his wife's name, then curved in a contented smile at the sensation of her soft touch stroking his matted hair away from his filthy, dust-covered face. Struggling with greater determination against the shadows clouding his thoughts, he finally managed to find his way free and pry his eyes open to feast upon the sight of his wife's lovely face.

"Michel." Tears shimmered in her dusky eyes and she pressed a clenched fist against her lips to force back the relieved sob that he could see was trying to break through the faltering control she held over her emotions.

"Elena, love, I have so much to tell you," he began excitedly, remembering despite his confusion he had important news to relay to her. In anticipation of doing so, he tried to rise from the pallet he rested on.

"No, no, you mustn't try to get up. Lay back and rest," she accompanied her demand with a gentle push against his shoulders.

He was in the mood to be accommodating because he allowed himself to be settled back against the pallet, reaching for the hand that continued stroking his flesh as if its owner feared he might disappear. Capturing her hand in his uninjured one he raised it to his lips and kissed his wife's fingertips. "I love you, Elena."

He saw the stunned joy enter her eyes at his declaration and cursed himself for his own stubbornness, reminded of what it almost cost him…cost them all. “I have so much to tell you,” he added, his voice fading as his pain demanded his attention.

She bent close to him and asked, “What is it? What could you possibly have to tell me that was more important than what you just confessed to me?”

His brows drew together as he struggled to remember his crazy dreams when he was buried under ground. He grew increasingly agitated when they eluded him. Then another remembered promise intruded upon his focus, distracting him away from the recollection he sought. “I should probably have told you this before now.”

“Told me what?” Elena asked concerned.

“I made a promise to my sister, Melissa.”

“Your twin sister?” His wife confirmed.

“Yes.”

“What is this promise?”

Michel’s thoughts continued to drift from the object of their discussion in search of the missing hours he spent underground. “What is this promise?” Elena repeated and he turned his attention back to his wife’s anxious eyes.

“If we have a daughter…” He closed his eyes against the deepening shadows tugging at his will.

“Yes, if we have a daughter…” Elena prodded.

Michel forced his eyes back open. “If we have

a daughter, I promised my sister we would name her Melissa."

He watched the relief wash over his wife's expression at his confession. "I assumed, my love, you would want to name our daughter, Melissa."

"You don't mind?"

"No, of course not."

"That is good, because I made another promise to my sister," he broached the other half of his promise to his twin with a little more caution.

"What is this other promise to your sister?"

"If we have a son…"

"Yes, if we have a son…." Michel could see the laughter lurking behind his wife's attentive gaze.

"I also promised we would name him Melissa."

Elena's eyes widened at his guilty admission and her lips curved in an amused grin. Michel could see by the speculative glance she gave him that she suspected he was teasing her. When he held her glance while he waited for her to realize he was serious, she gasped and confirmed, eyeing him incredulously, "You are serious?"

Michel nodded.

Finally accepting he was completely serious; Elena leaned back on her heels and giggled. She raised her fingers to her lips to smother her burgeoning laughter while her shoulders shook with the force of her amusement. Finally, unable to retain her precious control, she laughed uproariously until tears slid from her shining eyes and down her cheeks. Finally she regained her control and bent and brushed her lips across her husband's. "Then, my love, I hope you do not mind if I pray to our heavenly father that this child within me now is born a daughter, else our son shall be burdened with a woman's name in addition to an ancient curse besetting his father's house."

"No," Michel whispered through his pain at the reminder of the curse. "That was what I wanted to tell you." He struggled into a seated position to gain better clarity over his thoughts so he could convey his important news to his wife. Immediately, stronger hands than Elena's gentle ones restrained his attempts to rise. Both defeated and irritated by his own weakness, Michel allowed himself to be settled back against the pallet beneath his wife's watchful gaze.

Even the small exertion on his part gave rise to enough pain in his injured side to distract him away from his urgent need to confide his discovery to his wife. He grimaced against the sharp discomfort even as part of him was grateful for it. His throbbing limbs kept him beyond the reach of the shadows that lingered on the edge of his consciousness waiting for him to drop his defenses long enough to drag him back down to the abyss of nothingness.

"What was it you wanted to tell me?" Elena

asked softly, smoothing his hair away from his face in a soothing caress.

Michel heard the whisper of his wife's voice from a great distance. He stared back up at her beautiful countenance and felt his lips curve in a smile of contentment that he didn't die in that dark pit, buried beneath a ton of rock and granite. Now he would have the chance to tell her his news, to take away the anxiety about their unborn child's future she attempted to hide from him beneath a placid smile. It was to have been his fate to die beneath the mountain and become one more victim of its ire at man's intrusion on its domain and his theft of its precious treasure.

Yet, for some reason he had been spared. Why? He felt the answer dancing along the edge of his confused thoughts. He attempted to raise his injured arm to reach for it, fighting against the will of the one who gently restrained his reach. It was vital he clasp the misty light circling above his head, certain the answers he sought resided within, but no matter how mightily he strained, the shimmering light receded further and further from his reach. They were winning…the shadows, strengthened by his distraction with the light. Gleefully, it seemed to Michel, their clinging tentacles closed around him and dragged him back to where death and darkness ruled.

Just before he surrendered to an enemy beyond his waning strength, he thought he remembered the news he was so anxious to relay to his wife.

There was a price to be paid for cheating death the way he had and he was only just beginning to pay it.

CHAPTER TWENTY SEVEN

Michel woke to the muffled echo of his wife's agonized screams. He threw off the quilt and was halfway out of his bed and reaching for his sword before Amele turned from his stance at the window and hurried to his side.

"No, my king. Your wife is in no danger," he explained, reaching for the sword, and then pulling back at the expression on Michel's face. "Queen Elena is in labor."

Michel sank back down on the bed, his sword slipping from his grasp. "Labor? It's too soon. How long have I been asleep?"

Amele bent to retrieve the sword and place it a safe distance from Michel's grasp. "Not long enough for the amount of blood you lost, my king. The queen began her laboring early this morning. She is settled in the next chamber." When Michel jumped up off the bed to hurry to his wife's side, Amele pushed him back down. "The midwives are attending your wife. I am certain you are aware, my king, your presence in the room will only remind your wife of your grave injury and cause her to worry about you rather than preserving all of her focus for bringing your babe into the world."

Michel allowed himself to be persuaded by Amele's logic. "You said she started her laboring early this morning. Is something wrong? Why is it taking so long?"

Amele lifted his shoulder in a resigned shrug. "I am certain nothing is wrong with your wife's laboring. We would know. Babes enter the world on their own schedule, my king. There is nothing a man can do to hurry things along."

Michel nodded, and then jumped up off the bed. Ignoring his pain at his sudden movement, he gave in to his restlessness. He strode across the room towards the door. When he heard Elena scream again, he closed his eyes against the torment, knowing there was nothing he could do to ease her anguish. He pulled open the heavy wooden door with enough force to have it banging against the wall. To the astonishment of the men guarding his door he strode passed them down the long hall and exited through the tunnel leading to the stairs to the keep's stone wall.

He drew a deep breath as he exited into the early evening air and raising his eyes to the full moon overhead, he prayed fervently for his wife and babe. At the sight of the glowing moon something tugged at his memory. Something to do with the daughter of the moon. He struggled with the tantalizing hint of a memory for long moments before abandoning the effort in frustration. He turned long minutes later at the sound of the door opening behind him. Amele stood there, a wide grin on his face. In each of his bent arms he cradled a tiny bundle.

Michel lifted astonished eyes to Amele's. "Elena?"

"Your wife is fine and resting comfortably. The midwife gave her a sleeping draught, so the honor falls to me to introduce you to your son…and daughter."

Michel accepted the little burdens into each of his arms and awkwardly lifted them to brush his lips against each tiny forehead. Amele nodded in satisfaction and then retreated from the wall, leaving Michel alone so he could become acquainted with his new his son and daughter.

As if aware of the significance of the moment, his babes opened their eyes, the same identical blue as his and Melissa's. Smiling down into the curious faces of his son and daughter, the veil concealing his memories of the hours he spent underground fluttered away, revealing the answer to the mystery of the curse.

The daughter of the moon and the heart of the son. He looked back up at the moon and smiled. Around his neck, he felt the Salusian stone heat against his flesh. Elena was a daughter of the moon. That was why the stone reacted to her possession of it. His wife had captured the heart of the son. His heart. The curse was lifted. His family was safe.

"My felicitations, my young king."

Michel swung around at the sound of the familiar voice. He grinned in death's direction. "I am glad you are here. There is something I wish to discuss with you."

Imperious brows arched over black eyes. *"I admit you continue to surprise me my young friend. My presence is rarely greeted with such enthusiasm."*

Amusement danced in Michel's eyes in response to his friend's self-mockery. "I would introduce you to my son and daughter, but I have a bit of a dilemma in regards to their names."

"Is it not a human tradition to name their offspring after a worthy ancestor?"

"Yes, generally, but that is only when one has not made a rash promise to his twin sister in regards to his babe's names."

Death's laughter sounded around them. *"I should have known your twin had a part to play yet in this drama."*

"Yes, well," Michel responded grinning, "I promised Melissa I would name my firstborn after her, whether the babe be a son or a daughter."

"And you have been blest with one of each."

"Yes, but I can hardly name both my son and daughter Melissa. Think of the confusion that would give rise to. So to keep peace with my wife, I have decided to name our son Amele Nathaniel Barnabas and to keep my promise to my sister, our daughter will be Melissa. I would like to honor my grandmother as well, but I can hardly name her Melissa Alyssa."

"You could name her Melissa Rhiann after your younger sister."

"Yes, I considered that, but there is someone else I would prefer to honor. So my friend if you would tell me your given name, I would like to name my daughter after you. If you would prefer my son bear your name rather than my daughter, I can honor my grandfather if I am given a second son, but I thought you would not mind having your name linked to my twin's."

"My name?" His companion echoed in soft astonishment.

"Yes. I am assuming Death is not your given name. I have noticed that a man's reputation sometimes becomes so entwined with his occupation; his name becomes synonymous with his work. I wondered if that was not the case with you."

"You wish to name your daughter after death?"

Michel felt the force of his friend's piercing gaze. "I wish to name my daughter after my friend, and a close friend of my family. Not in repayment of my debt to you, because that it is a separate matter and one I wish to raise with you at another, more appropriate occasion."

"I thought you had forgotten our discussion."

"I did, at least the details of it. I knew there was something important that kept tugging at my memory, but I couldn't bring it to light. Then Amele placed my daughter in my arms and I knew in that instant the curse was lifted, because even if my heart had not already been captured by my wife, it would have leapt from my chest and dropped to my daughter's feet when our eyes met for the first time."

"Yes, the terms of the curse have been fulfilled. Your family is safe from its long reach."

"And your name, my friend. With your permission, of course."

Death's lips formed into a slow grin. *"My name? Yes, I believe I will enjoy having a daughter of the moon bear my name. You may name her...."*

CHAPTER TWENTY EIGHT

Michel sought out his wife after passing his sleeping twins into the care of a waiting servant. He entered the bedroom where Elena still slept and stripped out of his clothes as he crossed to the bed. He slid naked beneath the sheets and pulled his wife's softness against him. Sighing with contentment, he closed his eyes, falling quickly into a deep, dreamless sleep. For the first time since he was rescued from his intended tomb, the shadows left him alone.

Long hours later, when the light of dawn pierced the opening of the window covering, Elena stirred against him and her voice drowsily called his name.

"Michel?"

Michel squeezed her close in response. "”Yes, love?"

"Have you seen them? Aren't they beautiful?" She asked, then anxiety clouded her gaze and she repeated, "Love?"

Michel smiled. "Yes, Elena, I have seen our son and daughter and they are indeed beautiful.

And, yes, Elena, my love, did you doubt my pledge to you?"

"I thought maybe you had forgotten, or that I had dreamt it." She confessed warily.

Michel grinned, "No, my beloved, I have not forgotten my love for you." He bent to kiss her soft lips at the relieved happiness in her expression at his confirmation. Then he raised his head and said, "And I have finally remembered the important news I was so anxious to convey to you when I was brought back to the surface."

"What is it?" Elena lifted her head from his chest to peer into his face.

Smiling, Michel settled her back against his chest and began, "I wish to tell you a story about the daughter of the moon and the heart of the son…" When she quickly raised her head and opened her lips to question him, Michel shook his head and pushed her head back against his heart and continued with his tale. "A long, long time ago when gods walked the earth…"

CHAPTER TWENTY NINE

A few weeks into his new life, Michel was once again awakened in the dead of night by a soft knock on his door. He slid from his bed and dressed quickly, retrieving his sword out of force of habit, though he had no real expectation of needing it for the meeting he was heading to.

He turned at the door to look back on his sleeping wife and their babes who slept nearby so they would be close at hand when they woke hungry and seeking nourishment from his wife's fuller breasts. Smiling with contentment, Michel pulled open the door and passed into the hall, hoping his babes would not wake before he returned. He enjoyed the intimate moments spent with his wife and babe's when they woke in the night and Elena put their tiny mouths to her breasts to nurse.

Amele waited for him in the hall. "Melos has returned. They're waiting for us where we camped in the mountains."

"She will not enter the city?" Michel asked softly, as the two men strode quickly down the hall.

"No, my king. Forgive me for saying so, but your grandmother is an incredibly stubborn woman."

Michel laughed. "You would know that better than anyone, my friend."

"Indeed," Amele's agreement was heartfelt and long-suffering.

The Salusian party waited for them in the same clearing where Michel first looked down upon the capital city of the land he now ruled. His grandmother separated herself from her escort and the former queen of Calei met the current king at the edge of the line of trees near the stream where Michel misplaced her precious inheritance. Before any words were spoken between them, the two exchanged a fierce embrace. Then pulling apart they regarded each other with direct, discerning glances.

"You are well?" Michel felt compelled to ask, though he could see his question was unnecessary. The long years since she escaped the grasp of her husband's murderers rested lightly on her beautiful face.

"Yes, my Michel, I am well, as always."

"My sisters?"

"Very well. You are an uncle twice over. Melissa gave her husband a beautiful daughter they named Michel, and Rhiann was delivered of the healthy son and heir Nathan so desperately longed for. They named him Ruark after your older brother. And you, I think, have important news to share with your grandmother?"

Michel's lips curved in a contented smile. He harbored little doubt his grandmother did not need him to deliver his important news for her to be aware of its contents, but he played along. "Yes, I am a father to twins, a boy and a girl. My son is Amele Nathaniel and my daughter, Melissa."

"Twins? If there is justice in this world they will lead you a merry chase. I trust I may presume their mother is now your wife?"

Michel laughed. "Yes, Elena was my predecessor's niece and I believe another daughter of the moon."

"So you lifted the curse. I suspected you would."

"You knew?"

"Yes."

"But you didn't tell me?"

"I considered doing so, but in the end I decided it would likely do more harm than good. The heart does not bow to the will of the mind and often resents its interference in matters beyond the will's understanding."

Michel considered her explanation. "You didn't love him."

Alyssa shrugged delicately. "I didn't not love him. Nathaniel was a good man. In time it's very possible I would have grown to love him, but no, I didn't love your grandfather when we were married, and he was taken from me before I could learn to do so."

Michel removed the Salusian stone from around his neck and placed it around hers. The stone glowed with the soft white light of a full moon. "The daughter of the moon."

"Yes."

CHAPTER THIRTY

"Well, my queen, in what direction do we head now?" Amele asked the woman he had loved since he was a young man. They stood alone looking over the gleaming city from a clearing in the old forest. The spot was not far from the one where they separated from his brother, Gabriel, decades earlier, when they were fleeing a traitorous assassin.

"I am no longer a queen, Amele," Alyssa corrected him with a smile.

"Ah, there you are wrong. You will always be my queen. I ask again in what direction do we go when we leave Calei."

Alyssa raised her head to meet his serious glance. "You would leave your home?"

"You have been my home for forty years, my queen. I have fulfilled my promise to you to watch over your grandson and to restore your husband's blood to the throne that was taken from him by a traitor's blade. Michel no longer needs my guidance. He is destined to restore Calei to its ancient glory."

Alyssa smiled and replied, “And his son, King Amele, will follow in his stead.” Her smile deepened at Amele’s reaction to her teasing. Then she sighed and asked, “You would truly leave Calei again so soon after you’ve just returned home? What of your brother, Gabriel? You have just been reunited with your family.”

Amele shook his head. “Gabriel knows where my heart lies, my queen. Tell me, where is yoursleading you now?”

Alyssa leaned forward into the strength of his arms. They closed securely around her. “My heart longs for my home, Amele. I am weary of this wanderer’s life. I wish to close my eyes at night beneath the light of the moon shining on the home of my childhood. Will you accompany me, my friend and my one love?”

“Always, my queen.”

CHAPTER THIRTY ONE

A month after the birth of his twins, Michel stood looking out on his kingdom from his high perch on the tower peak where the mountains shimmered softly beneath the light of a full moon.

"Thank you, my son."

He was stunned by the form of address he thought he heard, especially considering his own mother was dead and his grandmother had left the mountains surrounding Calei not long after her arrival. The former queen lingered long enough to be introduced to his wife and her great-grandchildren before slipping away as quietly as she had arrived. Michel swung around but discovered no one had disturbed his sanctuary. Smiling, he decided Barnabas had good reason for his amusement when Michel accused him of succumbing to the mystical nature of his kingdom.

Recognizing the encounter he was about to embark on would prove yet again his own arrogance in his swift and mocking judgment of his predecessor's susceptibility, Michel sighed deeply and nodded his head in silent acknowledgment of his departed friend. Then he replied in answer to his unseen guest, "You are not my mother."

"No, I left this world too soon to be blest with the gift of children," the feminine voice replied.

The truth struck him with brutal intensity. "You're the king's daughter…the one who cursed my ancestor's blood."

"Yes."

"Then, why do you thank me? I have rendered you no service worthy of your gratitude."

"Ah, but you have, my young king. You have freed me from the consequences of my own foolishness."

The confession was accompanied by a wistful sigh and confused, Michel confessed, "I don't understand."

"I used the power bestowed on me to curse your ancestor, thus binding me in death more securely to him than a lifetime spent subject to his foul will. I am now free to begin living again…to try to find my way back to the light I once knew."

"I am sorry for what my ancestor cost you. Is there any way I can repay my blood's debt to you?"

"You already have, Michel. Remember it is not only your grandfather's blood that runs through you, but your grandmother's as well. You are one of us, you and blood of your blood. May you and yours be blest and not repeat the same mistake I made and suffer the consequences of falling away

from all I was in a moment of grief and anger."

Michel was reminded of the shadows he contested against and his driving urge for vengeance against his grandfather's murderer. For some reason he also recalled his debt to his friend, Death. "Is it a long way back?" He wondered in a soft voice.

"Yes, my son, but love is ever the companion of the light. Cling to it as you would your last breath, for it will be your salvation."

"And the salvation of those who are condemned to wander in the shadows?"

"Some wander because they are lost. For others it is their penance before the Almighty. I know of whom you speak, and he is not lost."

...EPILOGUE

Death followed the little girl up the steep steps leading to the keep's wall. His namesake was proving more mischievous then the aunt whose name she also bore. Young Melissa, with her striking blue eyes and long dark curls, was always up to some mischief. Keeping her safe and out of trouble usually fell on her less rebellious twin, but today Amele was off with his father and the other warriors training in the art of war. Melissa had not been happy at being left behind, so she'd slipped away from the watchful eye of her long-suffering nurse and was intent on at least keeping an eye on her twin brother from her view on the wall.

Even now she was using all of her young strength to push open the door to the stairwell leading to the wall and squeezing swiftly through the narrow opening before her strength failed her and the heavy wooden door slammed shut in her face. He could hear the muffled echo of his young charge's nurse calling her name from somewhere below in the keep, likely near the king's personal chambers, where Melissa was no doubt ordered to wait for her father and brother to return and not to get into her usual mischief.

A wide smile split the young girl's face at her escape and emboldened by her achievement, she hurried over to the side of the wall and began climbing the side, finding hand and footholds in the crevices in the stone to assist her in her climb. Shaking his head, Death leaned back against the wall and released an amused sigh at the disaster that was no doubt about to strike.

As if becoming aware of his presence, the young princess swung her head around, clinging precariously to her hold on the side of the wall. When she didn't see anyone, she muttered beneath her breath, chided herself for her foolish fear, and then continued her climb to the top of the wall.

She was so excited when she managed to reach the very top and stand on its narrow ledge; she performed a triumphant little dance in celebration. Running feet and horrified shouts sounded from the direction of the watch tower, when the guard posted there spotted his king's young daughter in deadly peril of the precipitous drop from the top of the wall.

Distracted, Melissa turned in surprise in the direction of the shouts. Her fear of being caught by one of her father's guards and the resulting punishment she would receive from her parents at this latest venture made her turn too swiftly along the wall to escape the consequences of her impetuous triumph and her small feet slipped from their sure stance. Waving her arms in a desperate attempt to regain her balance, terror filled her eyes when she realized she was about to plunge to her death. Papa would definitely not be happy about that. Her mama would probably cry.

Tears slid down the young girl's cheeks as she reached out desperately for the hands of the guard running just as desperately in her direction, but they both knew he wouldn't reach her in time.

Shaking his head and recognizing in resignation that this would be an oft repeated rescue, Death stepped forward and tugged the girl forward and into his arms. For a moment, startled blue eyes met amused black ones as the girl's small hands latched onto his shoulders and then her slender arms wrapped frantically around his neck. A moment later she toppled to the stone floor between the wall and the keep.

Dazed, and overcome with impossible relief to see his king's young daughter escape from certain death, the guard from the watch tower reached the princess where she sat on the floor, dusting off her bruised knees. He reached for the mischievous princess and drew her against his heaving chest with hands that shook.

"Princess, are you all right? Are you hurt, child?"

Melissa wriggled against his strong arms, and raised confused blue eyes to those of the man who held her in his shaking grasp. "No, I'm not hurt,

Miller, but where did the other man go?"

Confused her would-be rescuer replied, "Other man?"

"Yes, the one who saved me. He pulled me back from the edge when I was about to fall."

The guard shook his head, thinking terror must have addled the young princess' wits. "There was no one else here, Princess. Perhaps it was an angel who pulled you back. The good lord knows I would never have reached you in time."

"An angel?" Melissa echoed curiously. "Do angels have black eyes?"

Stumped, the guard shook his head. "I couldn't say, Princess. I've never seen an angel before."

Melissa grinned and a knowing light entered her young eyes. "I have." Then she added as another thought struck her, "We don't have to tell Papa about this, do we Miller?"

The End

Keep reading for a preview of Lynn Wood's new book, "*Mary Elle*", a story of romantic suspense coming Spring, 2015.

MARY ELLE

...PROLOGUE

The little girl waited in line for her turn with Father Byrnes. His line was the longest. She felt a little guilty that Father John's line was empty. Was he sad that no one wanted to give their confession to him? Though the thought disturbed her somewhat, the guilt she felt was not enough for the seven year old Mary Elle to give up her place in line. She exchanged a nervous but silent glance with her friend, Mary Jean, and noted her friend's hands shook when the red light changed to white above the door to the confessional announcing it was her turn with the priest.

Mary Elle gave her friend an encouraging nod as she opened the door wide enough for her to slip through and then pulled it shut behind her. Mary Elle knew what the little room looked like inside. Sister Connie showed them. The space looked like a closet with a kneeler and a small screen, so the priest could hear her. Some of the kids chose face to face confession, but Mary Elle preferred the privacy of the secret little room. If she was going to lie to a priest, she thought it would be easier if she didn't have to look him in the eye when she committed her sin…

18259697R00277

Made in the USA
Middletown, DE
28 February 2015